To Sue
with best wishes
Mike Thexton

FIRE AND WATER

Xessus IV

Fire and Water

Mike Thexton
Illustrations: Johanna Gousset

First published in Great Britain in 2021 by
Lanista Partners Ltd

45, Leyborne Park
Richmond - TW9 3HB
United Kingdom
www.xessus.com
ISBN 978-0-9553185-4-2

A catalogue record for this book is available from
the British Library.

Designed by Luisa Hiromi Yatsu Simon.
Printed and bound in Great Britain by Clays Ltd, St Ives plc.

for Kathy and Izi,
the best lockdown company

Characters from
XESSUS I - III

Lebasi, just turned 16,
the magistrate's son

From Trengam, Lebasi's home town:

* Xela, his father, magistrate of the Westwall District, part of the province of Xessus

* Marrak, the magistrate's agent, who reports to the king and comes from the country's capital city, Egator

* Perra, 25-year old leader of a rebellion against the laws that Xela enforces

* Faya, a 16-year old girl, Perra's cousin, who helped Perra plan the rebellion

* Ruffur and Sammas, two boys who roughed up Lebasi in The Magistrate's Son

In history:

* Dennara, the leader of a rebellion by Xessans against the king, 140 years ago

* Rednaxela Third King, who ordered that Xessus should be destroyed as punishment for Dennara's rebellion

* Riadsala, Rednaxela's son, who banished Dennara to the wilderness beyond the Westwall and implemented The Mercy: Xessus would not be destroyed as long as Xessans lived under severe restrictions

* Xela, Dennara's youngest son, who decided not to go into exile with his father, and was forced to mark the foreheads of his father and brothers with a brand in the shape of the five-pointed star of Xessus

At the farm below the Westwall:

* Gortan, the patriarch, who nicknamed Lebasi's father 'Xela' because he regards him as a traitor, before sending him away from the farm to Trengam when he turned 16

* Nareb, Gortan's eldest son

* Nareb's brothers Dareff, Yacul and Terrol

* Tharkon, a powerful man from Egator who helped plot the invasion

* **Tik, Lebasi's 12-year old cousin, Terrol's daughter**

* Sinder, Tik's cousin – one of Yacul's sons

* Tik's aunts Beronnie, Zanda and Mella, and her grandmother Adilla

* Mallam, the hermit who lived on the cliffs of the Eagle's Nest, Tik's friend, mortally wounded by Nareb and Dareff at the end of The Warning

The Westwall Guard:

* Riadsala, the captain, the youngest son of Rednaxela Fourth King

* Narus, the senior sergeant, and the other sergeants Bordan, Drogan and Tarran

* Verb, an ordinary soldier who befriended Lebasi and Tik

* Tassie, one of the cooks, who Tik believed might be her sister

In Egator, twenty-four days' walk to the south:

* Rednaxela Fourth King, descendant of his namesake and of the first Riadsala

* Shelba, Lebasi's mother, who he thought had died when he was a baby but is held hostage to ensure Xela's compliance with the king's laws

From the wilderness:

* Rodera, a branded man, who brought a sickness to pass to the magistrate, and died in the gateway at the end of The Warning

* the Xessan exiles, descended from the rebels who went into the wilderness with Dennara – they brand their sons to keep alive the memory of their banishment

* the Thrarn, a warlike race who have taken control of Dennara's people

* El-Kazzak, the prince and general of the Thrarn, killed by Lebasi at the end of The Westwall Guard

* Niram, an officer of the exiles, and Muscot, a soldier who identified Lebasi as an intruder when he was spying in the enemy camp

Xessans are not allowed to speak their ancient language, but some in the countryside still do so. Lebasi learned it from his father when he was young, and so he can understand the exiles. He and Tik can speak either in old Xessan or in the king's language.

1
FADING

'Don't die, Lebasi.'

Tik found Lebasi's hand, hanging down the horse's flank, and squeezed it. His fingers were cold. She stood on tiptoe to hear if he was still breathing, but she couldn't get her ear close enough to his mouth. Each time she tried, the horse took another step. She struggled to reach up and keep pace at the same time. At the fourth attempt, she lost her footing and nearly fell backwards off the narrow track.

She shook his shoulder, but he didn't react. She closed her eyes and pressed her palms against her temples.

'Don't you dare. I can't do this without you.' She whispered the words without thinking, and they surprised her. She had never needed anyone before, not even Mallam. She had used her own wits to survive on the farm all her life until everything went crazy at Midsummer, and among the Westwall Guard since then. Now she had to find the way to Egator. The furthest she had been from her home was a day's walk, and she admitted to herself that every step of that journey had frightened her. But Riadsala had asked her to carry a message to his father, to warn him of the terrible weapons of the invaders, of their brutality. *We must fight them until they are beaten.* If she could tell the king that, in time for him to prepare, the sacrifice of Riadsala's soldiers would have achieved something.

If the enemy reached Egator before she did, her friends would have died forgotten in the furthest corner of the kingdom, for nothing.

The capital city was impossibly far away, and she didn't know how to get there. The road would be full of strangers; she didn't trust strangers. She didn't trust most of the people she knew. Only Lebasi, now that the others had… now that the others were… no, she refused to think about Tassie and Verb and Narus and Riadsala. She had saved Lebasi from the battlefield, Lebasi alone. She couldn't lose him as well.

The last thing he had said was that it was hard to breathe lying across the saddle. Every step the horse took brought them nearer to Marstor, where she was sure she could find a doctor, but if he stopped breathing on the way, there was no point. So, make it easier for him to breathe. But how? Getting him down would be difficult, and getting him back up again if he didn't wake would be impossible.

She made up her mind. She called out 'Stop!' startling herself with her own voice, tiny in the emptiness of the night.

The horse walked slowly on, planting his great hoofs neatly in the middle of the path. She tried again, but realised that if he understood words at all, he probably only recognised commands in the language of the Thrarn. She felt in the darkness for the leather cord she knew was attached to his bridle and pulled on it gently, tapping his shoulder with her other hand. She wondered if he would feel anything through the armour that covered his neck and upper body, but at least he turned his head to glance at her. He carried on walking at the same pace.

She was distracted by the reflection in the deep black pool of the horse's eye. It was nothing more than a flickering red dot, there and gone as the animal blinked, but she knew it was the glow of embers in the distance behind her, the aftermath of the fire that had destroyed her home. She had focused on the path ever since they had emerged from the woods onto the open hillside, not wanting to see below her what she was sure the invaders had done. If she didn't see it, maybe she could pretend it hadn't happened.

Her home. Gortan had given her that token; her father said it proved she owned the farm. She pictured herself hiding it inside the well when the Westwall Guard came. The well might have survived the fire: it was made of brick, it was in the open away from the wooden buildings. She wiped her sleeve across her eyes. One day, she would go back to look for that token, and claim what remained.

The path widened and the horse stopped. He nodded to her, then bent his head to eat some grass.

Tik stroked his neck. 'Thank you,' she whispered, wondering if she could teach him to understand her. Or if he would respond to the tone of her voice. She didn't suppose the Thrarn general had shown him much kindness.

She had been worried that Lebasi would slide off the saddle, so she had bound his wrists to a strap that ran under the horse's chest. The three-quarter moon gave enough light for walking, but the knot was a different matter. She had tied it in a hurry and the movement on the journey had tightened it. She clenched her teeth and tried not to tear her fingernails as she fumbled and tugged at it. The horse took no notice of her scrabbling.

At last she felt one of the cords move. Now she could tell which piece to pull, she worked it loose and the knot fell apart. She hurried round the horse's head and took hold of Lebasi's legs, then tensed herself and pulled. He didn't move. She tugged harder and felt him begin to slide over the saddle. A moment later, she was lying on the floor with his dead weight on top of her. He made no sound. She struggled out from under him and listened in close to his mouth.

'Come on, Basi. You made it back from the other side of the wall. Don't leave me now.'

She couldn't hear anything – she wished the horse's champing was quieter – but she was sure she could feel the faintest movement in the air. What would help his breathing? Gortan had taught the farm children what to do if someone was unconscious. She pulled one of his knees up, leaving the foot on the ground, and then leaned on the bent leg to roll him over onto his side. She arranged his arms straight out in front of him. She put her fingers against his neck, sure she could feel a pulse. But was it just her own?

The horse took a pace forward to find a different patch of grass, removing its shadow. In the moonlight Lebasi's face was the colour of old bones, and as empty of life. Tik turned away, searching in her mind for something she could do to wake him.

Water. She knew there was a spring along here that bubbled out of the rock. They hadn't passed it, so it must be a short distance ahead. But how could she carry water even a little way? It would run out of her hands.

Even generals have to drink. Tik stood and reached up to run her palms over the saddle. She could feel two leather bags strapped to it, but she couldn't see how to take them off or to open them. She hurried to the moonlit side and knelt down to speak softly in the horse's ear as he grazed.

'I'm going to try to climb up on you. Please don't go anywhere.'

The horse paused for a moment, then carried on eating.

The foot-ring was a long way off the ground, easy for a Thrarn to reach but impossible for her. She held on to some straps with one hand and helped her foot into the ring with the other. The horse chose that moment to take another slow pace forward.

Hop – hop – *hup.* She lifted her leg over the back of the animal and found herself sitting as the general had sat. Her right foot slipped out of the ring, which was hanging much too far down for someone of her height. It wasn't comfortable with her legs pressed out sideways by the width of the horse, but at least it was easy to stay on such a broad seat.

She found that there were two more canvas saddlebags on the other side. The buckles that secured them were easier to undo than her own knots. She tossed the bags on the ground one by one, behind the horse so he wouldn't tread on them.

How to get down? She couldn't use the ring. She shuffled around so both her legs were facing the same way, then slid, fell and sprawled, laughing with relief that she was no more than winded by the drop. The horse took no notice.

She examined the bags. The first one was a disappointment. It contained only a scroll, three feathers and a small glass bottle that Tik guessed must contain ink. She had seen Gortan teach writing to her cousins, and Sinder had passed on the knowledge by making the signs with a stick in the sand. She shook away the memory. Where was Sinder now?

The second bag gave her what she wanted – a wooden cup and, even better, a water-skin. She told the horse to stay where he was and hurried along the path to find the spring. It was only fifty paces away, a small pool at the foot of the cliffs. She scooped water into her mouth – *cold!* – then held the skin under until it was full. She rubbed life into her hands and ran back.

Tik knelt beside Lebasi and used the skin to squirt some water onto his face. He didn't react. She listened for his breathing again and tried to find his pulse, but her own heart was beating so fast she wasn't sure that she would be able to detect it even if it was there. She held the water-skin by his mouth and wet his lips, but he made no movement. She sat back and covered her face with her hands. She couldn't do this without him.

How had he become so important to her? What did she know about him, really? He had turned up at the farm on Midsummer – she tried to work out how many days had passed, but couldn't be

sure whether it was nine or ten or eleven. Not many, but her life before seemed a long time ago. He was her kin, that she knew – maybe the only one left. That was important.

He was brave and loyal, he had proved that much. He had risked everything to rescue his father Xela from Gortan – he was clever, too – and he had done the same to keep her safe when the bad soldiers had come to the farm. He had pleaded with Riadsala not to keep her tied up, offering to take any punishment if she broke her promise. And he'd refused to pass the blame onto her when Riadsala was accusing him of protecting Gortan and Nareb because they were his own family – he could have told the captain that she had signalled to the enemy army. He would never let her down.

Except now, by dying.

She was so tired. She tried to keep her eyes open. When they closed, faces appeared – the last time she saw each of them. Verb, tears in his eyes, holding up his hands in apology for binding her and dumping her in the cart that was supposed to take her to Anessam and safety. Tassie, standing in the corn, her mouth open, not wanting to let Tik go but knowing she had to. Riadsala –

Riadsala. Had she made a promise to a dying man? Mallam had told her not to do that. *He cannot release you.* She didn't know whether Mallam meant Riadsala's ghost would haunt her, or something else, but she was sure that she had no choice: she must go to Egator to do what the prince had asked her, with Lebasi or without him.

As she rolled over to get up, the buckle on the third bag dug into her shoulder. She picked it up and weighed it in her hand. It was light enough to be empty, but when she put her arm right inside there was a leather pouch at the bottom. She ran her fingers over it, feeling the shape of something inside, small round balls like dried peas.

She snatched the pouch out and stared at it in the moonlight.

She pictured Rodera, seemingly on the point of death, fumbling with one like it. Her fingers were trembling so much that she had to put it on the ground to untie the cord that fastened it. She had never seen Rodera's charro close to – he had always taken a pellet from the bag furtively and looked away as he ate it, as if he was ashamed – but this must be the same thing. It shone white in the moonlight.

She knelt beside Lebasi again. How could she make him swallow it? He might choke. But it had worked so quickly on Rodera, maybe she just had to get it into his mouth. She pulled his lips apart, then his teeth, poked a pellet inside and quickly pushed his mouth closed.

Nothing happened.

She banged her hands together. Surely it was charro. She closed her eyes and made herself see the branded man. By the stream on the way back from Marstor, on the way across the fields, he had washed the drug down with water. But up on the Westwall Field, where she saw him for the last time – he was on the open hillside, he had nothing with him that he could drink. She remembered him gulping. Maybe he had bitten on it to make it easier to swallow.

One way or the other.

She didn't think she could dig around in Lebasi's mouth for the bead she had already given him, so she took out another and held it carefully between her fingers. She laid Lebasi's head in her lap and tried to work out how to make him bite the charro and not her. She held his jaw with one hand and opened and closed his mouth. She carefully pushed the fingers of the other hand inside his cheek to wedge the drug between his back teeth, trying to hold his head still so it wouldn't fall down his throat.

'Come on, Basi,' she whispered. She took her fingers out of his mouth, put her hand on top of his head and pushed. There was a faint crunching sound as his teeth crushed the pellet.

She held her breath.

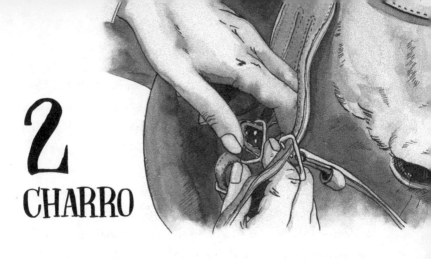

2
CHARRO

To begin with, Lebasi was painfully conscious. The sting of the brand was sharp and the bruise on the side of his head added a dull ache. Even though the horse walked slowly, every step jolted him. His arms were stretched down one side of the animal, tied to something, and the weight of his legs on the other tugged at his shoulders. Worst of all, he found it hard to breathe. But he couldn't trouble Tik by asking her to change anything. She had already saved him – again.

By the time they entered the wood, dusk had fallen, and it was darker still under the canopy of the trees. Lebasi wasn't sure if he was dreaming, lulled into sleep by the rhythm of the horse's tread. He opened his eyes when leaves and branches started brushing against his back – *no light at all* – the sound of the horse forcing its way through foliage. The smell of the animal mixed with the scent of sap from broken twigs. He tried to suck it in, but his lungs were crushed against the saddle.

He was in a dark place. Maybe it was the tunnels under Trengam. He was trying to escape – was he breaking Perra out of the cells again? The rocks were closing in. He felt the weight of earth above and below, squeezing the life out of him. Blackness, silence – no, there was a whispering voice – Tik? What was she doing here underground? He could hear her talking, but the words were obscure. He wanted to answer, but it was impossible.

He felt himself falling. It must be a dream. *Wake up before you hit the ground*, that was what they said. *Or you die*. How would anyone know that?

He could see a point of light in the distance. It was coming closer. He was aware of his heartbeat, fluttering lightly, running out. The pain was leaving him. He was cold.

Suddenly he felt a brutal punch, right over his heart. No, not a punch – a giant hand had dug into his ribcage and was gripping – squeezing –

'AAAAAAAAAAAAAAAAH'

He sat up. He jumped to his feet. He spun round, his fists raised, sure that something terrible was attacking him. The moonlight dazzled him, the sound of the horse chewing was deafening.

'Lebasi!'

He turned to face the voice, holding the sides of his head to try to focus. There was someone standing –

'Tik?' His voice sounded slow and blurred in his own ears.

'I thought you were dead.' She hugged him and pressed her head against his chest, then leaned back to stare up at him. 'Are you all right? Your heart –'

'Not all right. Spinning.' He sat down, then stood up again.

'Here, drink something.' She handed him a water-skin. His hands were shaking and he spilled half the contents as he tried to aim at his mouth, so she led him past the horse to a pool by the side of the path. He lay down and scooped up cold water until he couldn't drink any more, then held his breath and dunked his head. When he pulled it out and wiped his sleeve across his eyes, he could see Tik properly.

'Sorry. I don't know…'

She put her arms around his waist and turned her head to the side. 'I thought you were dying. I found something on the horse that looked like charro. I knew it kept Rodera alive, so I put some in your mouth.' She paused. 'Two pellets.'

A vivid picture came into Lebasi's mind – so vivid it was almost as real and immediate as the moonlit track and the girl – of Rodera, lying on the threshold of the Westgate with the vultures waiting behind him, restored in an instant to overpowering strength.

'Two?'

She held him tighter. 'I couldn't see how to get you to swallow the first one. So I put one between your teeth and got you to bite it. I think you must have swallowed the other one at the same time.'

Rodera disappeared. Lebasi was back inside El-Kazzak's tent, watching the captains discussing the attack on the wall, the general ordering a triple dose of charro for all the men. He heard Niram protesting that taking that much might kill them. And if it didn't, coming down again as the drug wore off might finish them instead.

Lebasi put his hands on Tik's shoulders and gently pushed her away. 'We need to go somewhere.'

'Not rest?'

'You remember Rodera. I'll be the same or worse than I was before when the charro stops working. Where are we? Where are we going?'

She pointed along the track. 'This leads to Marstor. I've never been all the way along it, but it keeps high and we won't meet the Thrarn.'

'All right. Let's go.'

Tik turned back. 'There's the horse. What are we going to do with him?'

Lebasi hesitated. Memories were jumbling through his brain. He laughed out loud at the image of Marrak saying *a boy with a pack is going somewhere, but a boy with nothing is just a boy.* A boy and a girl with a massive armoured animal that only existed in legends

– they wouldn't be able to slip unnoticed through the countryside. On the other hand –

'We'll bring it. If I start to fade, I can get back on it before the charro runs out completely.'

They returned to pick up the saddlebags. The fourth held some biscuits and dried meat, which they shared out. They discarded the writing materials and brought only the pouch of charro, the water-skin and the cup. They fitted it all into one of the bags which Lebasi slung over his shoulder. He hardly felt its weight.

Tik picked up the rein and stroked the horse's neck. 'Come on, you. We're going to Marstor.' The horse nodded and started to walk, pausing only for a moment to drink at the spring.

Lebasi couldn't stop talking. His thoughts kept coming in no particular order, and he was compelled to tell them to Tik as soon as they occurred to him. Being tied to the dragon – hiding in the rocks outside the enemy camp, so thirsty – crossing the line back in the spring – Xela saving the life of Faya's sister – the brand – Perra taking his punishment for him – Ruffur and Sammas and the old woman Nomara – Barten and his family – nearly drowning and being saved by Verb – running away in the woods – Verb saving him again – shooting the crossbow that killed the Thrarn general. He wanted to dash ahead, but the horse chose a steady walk and Tik stayed beside it. He had to dance forward a few paces, turn and walk backwards, hop from side to side, turn again.

Tik tried several times to interrupt him. At last he paused for breath, and she managed to ask, 'How are girls treated in your town?'

Concentrating on the question took an effort. *So many other things to say.* But she had saved him, she deserved an answer. 'Treated? I don't know what you mean.'

Tik stared past him. 'Do you have friends that are girls?'

The hand clutched at his heart again. He had a vision of Faya, clearer in the dim light than Tik, walking beside her. 'Yes. Well, just one. But I don't have many friends that are boys either. I'm the magistrate's son. People don't like him so they don't like me. At least, I hope that's why.'

Tik laughed. 'Tell me about her.'

Lebasi managed to start at the beginning. The charro made him say aloud things he had hardly even admitted to himself before. How much he had always liked Faya, from when they started school in the youngest class. How much it hurt when she began to shun him as everyone else did. How pleased he had been to find her apprenticed to the donkeymen on the same day as him, how angry he had been that she ignored him and talked to those idiots Ruffur and Sammas, how easy it had been for her to goad him into crossing the line.

'She did that deliberately?'

'Perra put her up to it. Ruffur and Sammas joined in just because they like causing trouble, but Faya wanted to get back at my da. My da chose her brother to be sent to the king's army. I didn't know he took people's children away until she told me. The best and the bravest. She'll never see him again.'

'But you said she was your friend.'

'After he punished me for crossing the line, I wanted to hurt my da as well. I didn't know that Faya had agreed with Perra to get me to break Riadsala's Mercy. I helped Perra escape from the town jail, then kept him hidden while he planned a revolution. Faya brought food for me to give him, and I took back messages for her to pass to Perra's friends.'

Tik whistled. 'And they were plotting against your da?'

Lebasi's words slowed down. 'I knew that, but I tried not to think about it. It was only when my da had left town to come to the Westwall and the revolution started, and they trapped my da's agent Marrak in the house, that I faced up to what I always knew, that they really meant to hurt him. Maybe kill him. Perra must have been sending messages to your grandfather somehow.' The thought of it made his chest hurt. He blinked away tears. 'I got everything wrong. I had to try to put it right. So I ran away to warn my da.'

'And you caught up with him too late. I found you hiding in the wood just after he'd gone into the farm.'

The charro let Lebasi see the scene as if it was happening again. 'Yes.'

Tik asked slowly, 'So is Faya your friend still?'

At last Lebasi had to think before he spoke. 'I don't know. The last time I saw her was when I was trying to get out of Trengam in a cart. Perra's men were guarding the gate and they were looking for me, but it was Faya who climbed on the wagon to check if I was there. And she saw me, I know she did, but she said there was no one. I don't know why.'

Tik reached out and punched his arm. 'I do,' she said, laughing.

✳ ✳ ✳ ✳ ✳

After the moon set, they had to go slower, but even the starlight was enough to pick out the pale line of the path. Then, as the sky ahead grew light above the mountains, it was easier to see where they were putting their feet. At last bright rays in the high air told them the sun had risen behind the distant rocky peaks.

'Lebasi?'

'Yes?'

'How are you feeling?'

'Why?'

'You've stopped running ahead. And you've stopped talking.'

Lebasi nodded. His head had started to hurt again. His legs felt heavy. He shaded his eyes. 'How far do you think it is to Marstor?'

'It's still a long way. Twenty thousand paces, maybe more.'

Lebasi scanned the landscape below them. The high track cut across the hillside, rising and falling a little. There were woods on the lower slopes, then open country. A ground mist covered the fields, but not far ahead he could see a building poking above it. Smoke rose straight up from a chimney.

He pointed. 'See there, a farm. Do you think we can get down to it? I don't think I can make it to Marstor without resting.'

Tik reached under her tunic and produced a leather pouch. She opened it and took out –

'The farsight! What are you doing with that?'

She pulled it open and put it to her eye. 'I'll tell you later. Riadsala gave it to me to show to the king.'

Lebasi opened his mouth and closed it. He had talked and talked and not thought for a moment that he ought to listen. 'I'm sorry.'

Tik lowered the farsight to look at him. 'For what?'

'I haven't asked you anything.'

Tik grinned. 'I gave you a double dose of charro. It's not surprising. There'll be time for that later.' She closed the instrument and put it away. 'I can see a break in the trees – maybe a track going down to that farm. Do you want to get back on the horse?'

Lebasi remembered how lying across the saddle had crushed the breath out of him. He shaded his eyes and estimated the distance. 'No. I think I can make it that far. Let's go.'

His legs grew heavier as they went, but the line of smoke in the air came closer. The side-track was well-trodden, zig-zagging where the hillside was steep. The trees showed the marks of someone having cut back branches to keep the way clear. When they came out onto open fields sloping gently downhill, the farm was only three hundred paces away, a square stone building with fruit trees on the left and a low hill on the right. There were sheep grazing on grass that shone a brilliant green in the early sunlight. Something about the peaceful scene made him shudder with fear: it reminded him of the Westwall Field in the middle of the battle the previous day. It was the charro, he told himself – it made his mind's eye see terrible things that weren't there. But the Thrarn were coming – they could bring that terror here.

The horse stopped and shook its great head. It tapped the ground with its hoofs and took small steps from side to side. Tik dodged away, dropping the rein. It stood still, and stared at them.

Lebasi held out his hand towards its face. 'I think it wants something.' The horse nodded, snorted, and wriggled its shoulders.

Lebasi reached up and put his hand on the plates of armour that covered the horse's neck. 'We should take this off.'

Tik protested. 'If you're about to fall over, we should go to the farm.'

Lebasi took no notice. This was important. He slipped the saddlebag off his shoulder and started fumbling with the straps that held the metal on. 'It's brought me here. I think it's tired of wearing this stuff. Maybe it's uncomfortable, and all that metal must be horribly heavy. It's no distance to the farm.'

The horse lowered its head so Tik could unfasten the mask that covered its nose. Lebasi freed the buckles but couldn't reach high enough to lift off the armour. The horse dropped to its knees. Both of them had to work together to move the metal. When they had put it aside, the horse stood up again and bent its neck to flick its head towards –

'The saddle too?' Lebasi asked.

Nee-hee-hee-hee.

Lebasi unbuckled the strap running under the horse's chest. He had hardly undone it when the horse lowered itself to the ground, twisted one way to dislodge the saddle, picked itself up again, took a couple of paces forward to be clear of the humans, then fell to its knees and rolled over on its back.

The horse was so huge, and the sight of it wriggling and kicking was so surprising, that Tik and Lebasi were helpless with laughter.

They didn't notice someone approaching. A woman's voice called out, 'What in the name of Xessus is that?'

3
DOCTOR NEEDED

Tik turned round sharply, stared for a moment, then started laughing again. She had grown so used to the sight of soldiers and their weapons that a young woman pointing a broom at them, as if it was a sword, was ridiculous. Beside her, Lebasi bent double, his hands on his knees. Then he pitched forwards on his face, without even putting his arms out to break his fall. Tik stopped laughing.

The woman shouted, 'What's so funny? Who are you? What's that monster?'

Tik knelt beside Lebasi and rolled him onto his back. His eyes were closed. She could see his chest moving, at least.

'Please help us. My friend's sick. I need to fetch a doctor.'

The woman lowered the broom. 'There's no doctor nearer than Marstor.'

'Have you got any medicine? Something for fever?'

The woman put a knuckle to her lips and glanced over her shoulder. 'How sick? Is it catching? I've a baby.'

Tik rested her hand on Lebasi's neck. It was certainly hot. She thought about it – brand, charro, blow to the head. Surely that was enough to make him this ill. 'I don't think he's got an illness he can pass on. He's been through a lot. Please.' She sat on the grass so she could cradle Lebasi's head in her lap. His breathing was shallow and quick.

The woman came closer, lowering the broom, concern wrinkling her forehead. She hesitated, formed silent words with her mouth, then nodded. 'I'll get help.' She set off back towards the farm.

Prrrrrp.

Tik realised the horse was looking over her shoulder. He leaned forward and nudged Lebasi's arm with his nose. No reaction. He made snuffling noises in Lebasi's ear. Lebasi stirred. Tik put her hand on his cheek. 'Basi, wake up! We're nearly there.'

He opened his eyes and whispered something. She leaned close to catch it. 'Please,' he murmured, 'no more charro.' He closed his eyes again.

The sound of running footsteps announced the woman's return. She panted, 'Trefal is coming to bring him to the house. I'll go and boil some water.' She set off again.

A tall, heavy-set young man was walking up the slope, pulling something behind him. He kept his eyes fixed on the horse as he manoeuvred the something around to lie next to Lebasi – a sheet of canvas between two poles. He pointed to it and explained to Tik in a slow, deep voice, 'It's a drag-barrow for moving hay and corn. Hope it'll do for him.'

He knelt down and lifted Lebasi onto the sheet, surprisingly gentle for someone so large. Tik offered to help, but he said, 'Best I do it that's used to it,' and picked up the handles. The ends of the poles made two lines in the dew. Tik followed behind, watching Lebasi being jogged about but not waking up.

They passed through a gate into a yard that was much smaller than the one Tik was used to at her home, containing only a single house rather than five. In other ways it was similar – there were ducks and geese around a small pond, chickens pecking at the dirt, and pens on the far side with goats and pigs peeking out at her. She could tell immediately that this was a well-run farm: it was tidy, the animals looked healthy, the buildings were solid.

Trefal stopped outside the door and lowered Lebasi to the ground. The woman opened up, rubbing her hands on an apron she hadn't been wearing before. 'Can you lift him, brother?'

'Reckon.' He knelt and slid his arms under Lebasi's shoulders and knees, and carried him through into the house. He stopped just inside, shuffling his feet, until the woman said, 'Don't worry about your boots, dear, I'll clean up later. Put him on the bed in there.'

Tik followed him into a darkened room. She ran to the window and pushed open the shutters. The sunlight showed her woven rugs on the floor and the walls, a fireplace, chairs, a small table, a bed. Trefal laid Lebasi on it and backed away, wiping his hands on his shirt. He glanced at Tik. 'He'll be all right?'

Tik knelt and put her ear against Lebasi's chest. His heart was beating very fast. She shook her head. 'I don't know.'

No more charro, he had said. But what if he needed it?

She jumped to her feet and ran out of the room, across the yard and back up the slope to where the armour and saddle were lying on the grass. She checked that the pouch of charro was still in the saddlebag, took a drink from the water-skin to lighten it, and carried it back.

The woman had taken Lebasi's shirt off and was laying hot, wet cloths on his skin. The scent of the herbs in the water made Tik drowsy. She realised that it was a long time since she had slept at all, and much longer since she slept a full night. She sat and watched, noticing for the first time that the woman had a swollen belly. She was the youngest child on the farm, but she had seen pregnant farm animals, and she guessed that this was how a human must look when she had a baby on the way.

The woman wiped her hands on her apron and turned to Tik. She said, 'I'm Feleda.' She nodded at the mark on Lebasi's forehead. 'Where has he come from? A boy with that mark, and a – is that really a horse, like in the stories?'

Tik started to undo Lebasi's boots. 'I'm Tik, and he's Lebasi. He's from here, from Xessus. He's the son of Xela the magistrate. He was captured by the army of the exiles and they branded him. And they have horses. This one found him on the battlefield. Carried Lebasi when he couldn't walk. The horse looks frightening, but he's really gentle.'

Feleda stopped what she was doing and stared at Tik. 'What are you saying? Battlefield – an army?' She put one hand to her mouth and rested the other on her belly. 'What do they want? Where are they?'

Tik didn't want to upset her – she knew that was bad for animals when they were about to give birth – but a comfortable lie would be worse. 'They want Xessus. Or maybe the whole kingdom. They were outside the Westwall' – Tik had to pause and think – 'yesterday evening.' She pulled off the left boot and turned her face away. She reckoned Lebasi's feet must have been inside for a long time. She started on the other one, holding her breath.

'But why did they brand him?'

'Because that's what they do. That's the kind of people they are. We have to fight them until they are beaten.' She pulled off the boot and sat on the floor, suddenly unable to go on. She had done what she could for Lebasi, and the relief of getting him to someone who might help had left her exhausted.

Feleda left Lebasi and rested her hand on Tik's shoulder. 'Poor girl, you look all in. There's another bed upstairs. Trefal will show you.'

'No, I'll stay here.' She curled up on the floor. 'Please wake me if he gets worse or gets better. And anyway by midday. I'll go on to Marstor to get the doctor.' She closed her eyes.

❄ ❄ ❄ ❄ ❄

'Tik! Wake up!'

The room was dark. Tik panicked – it must be night-time, she should have set off ages ago. She jumped to her feet. Feleda caught hold of her arms. 'Where are you going in such a rush?'

'I've slept too long. It's late, I have to go.'

'You needed to rest. It's early afternoon.'

Realising that the shutters were closed, Tik relaxed. Then she hurried to Lebasi's bedside. 'Has he woken up at all?'

'Not really. He's been muttering in his sleep. I don't know what he's talking about. Something about people being able to open the gate. He's said it several times. He must be worried about it.'

Tik felt in her pocket and produced a small wooden peg. She put it in Feleda's hand. 'If he wakes up properly, and if he says something about the gate, tell him I shut it, and show him that. He'll know what it means – the lock won't work without it. Now, I need to fetch the doctor.'

Feleda protested, 'You need something to eat before you go.'

Tik realised that she was right, but she didn't have time. She asked, 'Have you got something I can take with me?'

Feleda packed a small bag with bread, fruit and dried meat. While she gathered the food, she told Tik that her husband was in Marstor working as one of the mayor's guards. 'The place was all abuzz with talk of rebellion just before Midsummer. I don't know what they'll do when they hear about this army.'

Tik thought, *they already know – or at least, the mayor does. I told him days ago*, with the mirror-machine. Maybe he didn't want the people to panic. Maybe he was worried that hotheads might join the uprising, thinking that the invaders would help them fight the king, when really they meant to take the Xessans' land.

She tried to concentrate on what Feleda was saying. 'My Rennik is someone the mayor trusts. He sent for him on Midsummer's Day and he's been there ever since. Normally he goes for two days and comes home for two days.'

Midsummer was the day Xela arrived at the farm. Even if the mayor trusted Rennik enough to tell him about the army, Feleda wouldn't know. She hadn't seen her husband since before Tik had sent that signal. Tik asked, 'Will he help me find the doctor, if I ask for him?'

'I'm sure he will. But mind how you go. The town's full of all sorts of people, if you know what I mean.'

Tik guessed she meant men like Denga, the soldier who had tried to grab her in the woods below the Westwall. As long as she only met ones like Verb – she gulped. The memories kept catching her unawares. Verb was dead, along with all those decent men who had sung round the campfire as they made ready for battle. Could it have really been only the night before last?

She handed Feleda the bag of charro. 'This is very strong medicine. Maybe too strong for him. He asked me not to give it to him again. But if you believe he's about to die, and I'm not back, put one between his teeth and make him bite on it.' Feleda stared at the pouch as if it was magic.

As Tik crossed the hillside back towards the high track, she wondered if the horse would try to follow her. She knew it was silly, but she was disappointed that he didn't appear. She had spent years exploring the countryside on her own, with only the hermit Mallam for a friend. But since Midsummer, she had grown used to company, to spoken conversations instead of sign language – with Lebasi, Tassie, Riadsala, the soldiers of the Guard, even Rodera, the day she had spent walking with him. It was strange to be alone again. In a very short time she had come to love the horse's smell, his noises, the expressions on his face, the way that he seemed to understand what was happening at least as well as any human. She stood at the edge of the trees and scanned the view, but she couldn't see him. Maybe he had decided to leave them and look for his own kind. The only ones he would find in Xessus would be with the Thrarn. The thought that he might go back to the enemy was even more disappointing.

Once she was on the level path, she held the pack in one hand and ate with the other as she walked. She had had nothing but half the general's rations since yesterday morning – no, since the evening before that. The whole day of the battle, she had eaten nothing at all. She finished everything Feleda had given her and stopped briefly to drink from a stream. She felt much better for having slept, even briefly, but Marstor on its hill seemed a long way in the distance.

She had a good view of the countryside, all the way to Nampetch on its own hill away to the south. Beyond that, a heat-haze blurred everything into pale nothingness. She could see no sign of the Thrarn horsemen – cavalry, Lebasi had called them when he was telling her about the battle. He must have learned the word from the enemy. She smiled. She had asked herself in the night-time how much she knew about him; after he had taken the charro, she knew a great deal. All of it made her even more sure that he would never let her down.

She thought about the girl Faya, wondering if she ought to be jealous. She laughed the thought away. She had heard stories of girls and boys falling in love, but she had never seen that at home. Her da had told her he had loved her ma, but her ma had died when she was born. She thought that Lebasi must be in love with Faya, but Tik didn't feel that way about him at all. He was her cousin, more like a brother that she had only just met. She made up her mind to find Faya and tell her all the good things that Lebasi had done. She didn't think Lebasi would do himself justice. Not like her other cousins, who were forever bragging to each other about the smallest thing. It had taken the charro to loosen Lebasi's tongue, and then he had told her everything, good and bad, without showing off. If anything, the opposite – he had said more about the things he was sorry for.

Another thought struck her. She hadn't said anything to Lebasi about his sister in Egator, Riadsala's playmate until the queen declared that a prince should stay apart from the servants' children. She told herself she hadn't had time, what with trying to make sense of everything he was telling her and worrying about getting him to a safe place, but that wasn't the whole truth. She realised that she did feel something like jealousy of the nameless girl, even if not of Faya. She had never had a brother or a sister. She had wanted Tassie to be her sister, and now she wanted Lebasi to be her brother. As far as he knew, Tik was his only kin, his cousin. They belonged to each other and to no one else. What if he knew he had a real sister of his own? She shook her head. She ought to tell him. Maybe when he was better.

When she judged she was halfway to the town, she stopped for a rest and took out the farsight. There were people working in the fields as if everything was normal. Yet the enemy riders must be out there, somewhere. They had burned her farm. What would they do next?

She put the instrument away, trying not to think about the possibility that they had gone to Anessam. Tassie would be there, and the rest of her family. There was nothing she could do for them but hope.

It was early evening before she was close to the town. The high track continued to the north-east, but she could see the line of a side-path running down to the fields and all the way to the walls. She had seen Marstor many times from far away, just a shape in the distance with a flashing light on the top when she sent and received signals from the ridge above the hermit's home. Now the sinking sun picked out every detail of the roofs, the avenues running around the hill, the streets climbing to the top, the bell-tower over all. Everything about it made her want to run away. Woods and fields were what she was used to, with no buildings beyond the little group of houses and barns that was her home.

She sighed. *Used to be her home.* Not any more.

As she came nearer, she found workers joining her from the fields, some carrying tools, some with sacks of produce on their backs, a few driving sheep. They could be her own family coming in from a day's work, but they were all strangers. Until Tharkon the southerner arrived on Midsummer's Day she had never met anyone who wasn't family. She hoped that no one would speak to her or ask her what she was doing. She wondered how to find Rennik, and how to avoid the bad people.

She slowed down as the town loomed over her. The road was crowded in front of the gate. It made her think of a mouth, swallowing up the people and animals passing through it. Her pulse and her breathing quickened.

There were men at the gate checking the people passing in. Everyone held up their knuckles to show their tattoos. Tik stopped to scan the crowd – there were no children. No one young enough to have plain hands like hers. Would they just let her in? Would they help her, if she asked? Feleda had said the town was stirred up by the rebellion. Tik's thoughts ran round in circles.

The line stopped. Tik was close enough to hear one of the

guards challenge a grey-haired man. 'Hey! I don't know you.'

The man mumbled something in reply. The other guard pushed him in the chest. 'No out-of-towners. Mayor's orders. Too many troublemakers out there.'

The man spoke louder: 'I don't want trouble. I need the doctor.'

The guard shook his head. 'Orders is orders. Clear off.'

Tik expected the man to argue, but he turned back and shuffled away along a path that ran around the wall, muttering under his breath. She wondered if he would try again at a different gate.

'What are you doing outside?' The same harsh voice snapped her attention back to the guards. The people in front of her had passed through, and now she was at the head of the line.

She decided not to admit that she came from the countryside. She tried not to look nervous as she said, 'I've got to find Rennik.'

The two men stepped towards each other to block the road. They weren't armed, but they were big. She was standing five paces away from them, ready to run if necessary. But run where? She had to get inside.

'Who's Rennik?' asked the one on the left.

'He's working for the mayor. I've come –' Tik thought of something that might work '– with a message from his wife.'

The one on the right beckoned her to come nearer. He leaned forward to study her face. 'So you're not from the town? I don't recognise you.'

She looked from one face to the other. They were too like Denga. She couldn't kick both of them at the same time –

The one on the left reached out an arm. She was ready. She dodged to the side and sprinted round him. She was inside the gateway – a tunnel through the wall – before the other one realised, slipping in between the people, some of them calling out, no one stopping her – onto a paved road between buildings – sheep,

sheep everywhere – she was swimming through sheep – she heard bleating and swearing behind her.

She reached a crossroads – uphill straight ahead, too hard to run that way – and turned left. She was surrounded by stone, no living plants or trees. If she was in her own forest, she would know how to hide from someone chasing her. She was lost here: the smells were all wrong, the buildings cut out the sun, sound echoed from all sides.

A stitch slowed her down. She touched her toes and glanced around. No one was taking any notice of her. She felt conspicuous, but she realised that she was shorter than everyone else. As long as she mixed in with the crowd, the guards wouldn't see her. She skipped and weaved, a girl in a hurry, but not someone trying to escape pursuit.

She tried to guess how to find the mayor. She reckoned he would be at the centre of the town, at the top of the hill. That's where he had sent his signals from – the mirror machine would be in the tower at the summit.

Now there were more people coming the other way – she was approaching another gate. She hesitated, but realised that the guards here wouldn't be looking for her. She kept to the side of the road and found another main upstreet opposite the gateway. She turned onto it and started climbing, fixing her eyes on the gap between the buildings at the very top. The mayor would be there. He had promised to help her when she signalled to him for the last time. He would send the doctor to Lebasi.

Halfway up the light changed. She turned and saw that the sun had just set behind the mountains – her own Eagle's Nest, a long day's walk to the west. There were fewer people now, but she had surely lost the pursuers. Some of the passers-by studied her face more closely than she liked, but no one spoke to her.

The slope eased. She reckoned this must be the last crossroads before the top, one more level road running around the hill. There were four men deep in conversation on the uphill corner to the right, so she jogged silently across on the other side. She was nearly there.

'That's her!' One of the men pointed. The guards from the gate, with two more. She pushed off to run, but her foot slipped on a smooth cobblestone. She sprawled on the ground, feeling the breath knocked out of her, hands grabbing her arms.

4
MISTAKES

He'd got everything wrong. All the way back to the spring, when he'd fallen for Faya's teasing and walked over the boundary line – that was the start of it all. If only he hadn't done that, everything would have been all right. How had he been so stupid?

Sometimes Lebasi was awake and remembering and sometimes asleep and dreaming. He drifted from one to the other without being able to tell the difference. His heart thumped painfully as he pictured himself opening the Westgate, watching from somewhere else – as Nareb and the southerner had been doing, when he'd given away the secret code so they could open up for the invaders. He saw vultures circling as Rodera led him across the Westwall Field. But the ground was full of dead soldiers – that wasn't right – they came later – because of what he'd done.

The scene shifted: Rodera was lying in wait by the side of a road. That was wrong, as well – surely he hadn't been there – but he could see it now. Xela was walking towards the ambush – Lebasi tried to shout a warning, but he couldn't make a sound. *The warning*, that was what Rodera had called the disease he carried. They were fighting, Tik was joining in, pulling Rodera off his father. It was all his fault that Rodera was in Xessus at all. Tik had tried to stop him passing his sickness to Xela.

Now he was back in the courtroom in Trengam. Sendra, the

fierce elder, was listing his crimes. Surely she only knew about him crossing the line? No, she was telling Xela how he had freed Perra from jail and helped him plan his revolution, bringing the Westwall Guard to carry out Rednaxela's order to burn Xessus. Lebasi tried to turn away from the shock and disappointment in his father's face, but he could not.

He was desperate to find his voice, so that he could explain himself. He'd rescued Xela from imprisonment too at the farm, and he'd prevented Perra's doomed ambush of the Westwall Guard, and saved Perra from the execution that would have led to the end of the Mercy for sure. He'd closed the gate on the invaders, stopped them making their sneak attack over the wall. But Sendra ordered Bennek to gag him, and she carried on. She accused him of failing to warn Riadsala about Gortan and his treacherous family at the farm, leaving the Guard open to attack from behind. Lebasi wanted to say that Xela himself should have done that, but Xela had disappeared into the background and all he could see was Sendra's face.

He realised this must be a dream. The image of Sendra faded away, but she was replaced by more pictures that didn't need her voice to describe them. He tried to open his eyes to stop them coming, but his eyelids wouldn't work. Old Bamal giving him that soup – he should have realised that there was something funny about the way the cook was acting. Moz and Bamal telling him after he'd drunk it that there was a dose of charro dissolved in the broth. Even allowing for that, he should have known that jumping over the wall was a stupid idea. He had dreamed of saving everyone by spying on the enemy, of being the hero. But he'd only made everything worse. He'd let himself be caught. He'd told El-Kazzak that there were three thousand men on the wall. He'd thought that was what Riadsala wanted the enemy general to think, but he had given El-Kazzak the reason to attack with all his troops, thousands and thousands of them. Three hundred defenders didn't stand a chance.

His pitiless memory showed him the worst image of all. He was standing in the gateway, saved by Riadsala from the enemy's dragon, amazed to be safe behind the closed door. Riadsala told him to lock the gate, trusted him to do the right thing. He saw himself putting the pegs back in the bottom row of the lockbox. Stupid, unforgiveable. He should have taken them with him. Why leave them there to let Nareb open the gate when he got free?

He saw the enemy soldiers swarming up onto the Westwall Field, the Thrarn horsemen pushing them aside to ride over the ridge and gallop on into Xessus. That was his doing. Until then, the Guard were holding the wall. If he had only taken away the pegs, picked up a rock and smashed the lockbox.

'There now, it's only a nightmare.' A calm voice, a real one. Something cool and damp pressed against his cheek. He opened his eyes and tried to sit up. He was in a dimly-lit room. Bright lines showed around the edges of closed shutters: the sun must be blazing outside, but inside dusk had fallen.

A young woman put a hand on his chest and easily pushed him back down. He was so weak. He stared without recognising her.

'Who are you? Where's Tik?'

She wrung out a cloth into a basin and mopped his chest with it. He realised he had no shirt on. He tried to sit up again, but she kept her hand on him and shook her head.

'Lie still. You're not well. I'm Feleda, and this is my house. Your young friend's gone to Marstor to fetch you a doctor. Until they get back, I'm looking after you.'

Lebasi moved his legs and realised he wasn't wearing anything at all under a thin sheet. His eyes opened wider. Feleda tutted. 'Don't fret. I've a husband and a little brother and a baby boy and I've bathed all of them when they've had a fever. Your clothes are clean and hanging out to dry and you're cooling off.'

Lebasi stared at the ceiling and tried to think of nothing. Feleda was talking, but he couldn't concentrate on her voice. The pictures were coming back. He was lying on the Westwall Field, pinned under a broken wagon. El-Kazzak was searching for him, shouting his name. Mocking him, calling him little man, taunting him that he could never do anything to hurt his master.

'Lebasi!'

He opened his eyes. Feleda was frowning down at him, her eyes reflecting candlelight now. The shutters were dark. He was cold – very cold – shivering. His hands closed on blankets. He could feel the weight of them pressing on him – but he was so cold –

'Is he dying?' Another voice, a man.

'Hush, brother. Lebasi, you need to drink something. Trefal's going to help you sit up.'

Lebasi felt powerful hands lifting him, holding him steady to stop the shaking. He had no strength to resist. He could only see Feleda's eyes. There was a spoon at his lips – something warm – he gulped it down.

'Good boy.' She fed him some more. He couldn't taste it, but it seemed to be thicker than water. 'Chicken soup,' she explained. 'Good for fever.'

He could only manage a few mouthfuls. He shook his head, sure that he would be sick if he tried to swallow another spoonful. The hands laid him back down. He closed his eyes.

He snapped them open. 'Is it night? Where's Tik?'

Feleda rested a hand on his shoulder. 'Don't worry. She'll be staying over in Marstor. She couldn't get there and back in an afternoon. Rennik will be seeing she's all right. She'll be here tomorrow.'

'But it's not safe. The enemy –'

'She said the enemy were outside the wall.'

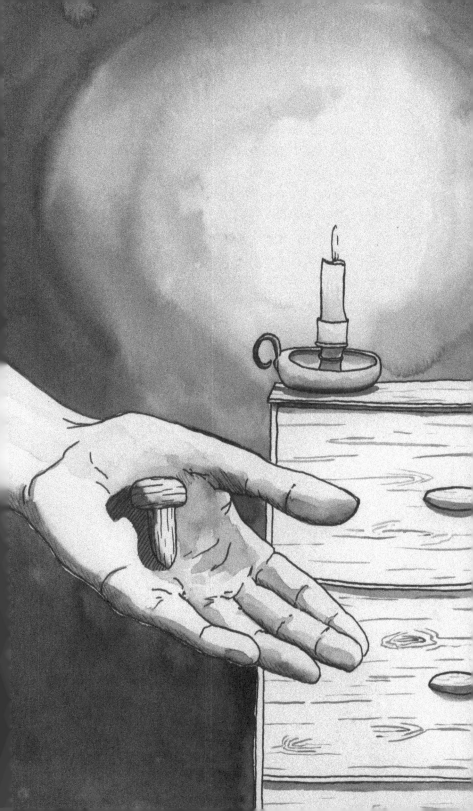

'But the gate was open.'

'Oh.' Feleda's face disappeared from the candlelight. He saw her hand holding something – a wooden peg. 'She said she shut the gate, and if you were worried about it, I should show you this. She said you would know what it means. I don't.'

Lebasi closed his eyes. He knew. It meant Tik didn't make the same mistakes that he did. If it had been Tik in the gateway instead of him, Nareb wouldn't have been able to unlock the gate, the Guard would still be holding the wall. Riadsala would be alive. Verb would be alive. Narus would be alive.

Riadsala had been right to give Tik the farsight, to trust her, not him.

Feleda's voice faded away. The dark dreams returned.

5
ALFAS

'Let me go!' Tik struggled, but the men were too strong. One of them wrapped his arms round her shoulders and the other grabbed her legs.

'No outsiders in the town,' the one behind said in her ear.

'Mayor's orders,' said the other. 'Too much trouble out there.' They turned and started carrying her sideways down the hill.

At least they only seemed to want to put her outside the gate again, nothing worse. But that was no good for Lebasi. They hadn't gagged her, but maybe they would. She tried to breathe normally, not to give away what was coming – she might only have one chance to shout. Then, as loud as she could, 'I need to speak to the mayor. I've come from the Westwall. I'm Gortan's granddaughter.' Would anyone hear?

The men stopped. The leg-man looked down at her. 'You've been at the Westwall? I thought you said you were from some farm, bringing a message from someone's wife.'

'That was on the way here. I live by the Westwall. I can tell the mayor what's happening.'

Shoulder-man didn't loosen his grip. 'He's busy. We've got our orders.'

Tik could sense leg-man's hesitation. She fixed her eyes on his. 'Look, if he doesn't want to talk to me, I promise I'll walk back to the gate so you won't have to carry me. And I won't try to run away.'

The guard lowered her feet to the ground and took hold of one of her elbows. 'All right. Might be important.'

The other man muttered something about wasting time, but he let go of her shoulders and gripped her other arm. Together they started back up the street towards the gap in the skyline that she had been making for.

The buildings on either side ended. The ground flattened and opened out into a broad square criss-crossed by two avenues of trees. Tik craned her neck to look up at the top of the tower. She was sure that was where the mayor signalled from. Leg-man stopped and leaned down to face her.

'I'll go and ask. No tricks, all right?'

Tik watched him walk across to a group of people near the centre of the space. They were all facing away, listening to someone Tik couldn't see. Shoulder-man's grip was hurting her, but she didn't have the energy to complain. Surely the mayor would agree to see her.

The man was whispering to a woman on the edge of the group. He pointed towards Tik. The woman spoke to someone else, then ran across towards her. Tik was surprised at how fast she moved – she looked as old as Grandma Adilla.

She smiled at the guard and held out her hand to Tik. Her voice was as strong as her legs. 'Thank you, Raggan. I will take her to see the mayor.'

Raggan was reluctant to let her go. 'I thought –'

'Yes, thank you, I understand. You are off duty now? Go and get some supper.' They passed the other guard, who nodded to Tik but didn't speak. The woman leaned close to her ear and whispered, 'Thinking is not their strong point. I hope they have not hurt you.'

Tik smiled back. 'I'm fine.'

The woman led her by the hand. The crowd was stepping aside, making a passage for her, revealing the centre of their attention: a man with a long white beard sitting on a high-backed chair. He was surely older than Gortan. Everyone had turned to look at Tik, but she was spellbound by the sight of the man she had signalled to from so far away. His smile was as kind as the words he had sent to her: *We will care for you, for Mallam's sake.* As Tik drew nearer, she saw a cloudy whiteness in his eyes. He held out a hand to her, apparently aware of where she was standing, even though she was sure he was blind.

'Good evening, young Tik. I am sorry that you have found it difficult to reach me. To be honest, after the last message you sent with the mirrors, I did not expect you to come. If I had known you were on the way, I would have told the guards to watch for you.'

She glanced behind her at the tower – how could he signal?

The mayor seemed to guess what she was thinking from her silence. 'My agent makes the signals and reads the replies so he can repeat them to me, as I think you learned to do with Mallam.'

He offered his hand and she took it in her own. It reminded her of the hermit's hands, and how he used them to speak to her. Mallam had pretended to be deaf and without speech, but the mayor was truly blind.

She said, 'The Westwall Guard were defeated. Some of the invaders are in Xessus, riding on horseback, very dangerous. But most of the enemy army ran away outside the wall after the battle, and I locked the gate. It will take them time to get it open again. When they do, you will not be safe. There are thousands of them, and they have no mercy.'

Tik was aware of murmurs of alarm from the crowd around them, but the mayor's expression did not change. He closed his other hand over hers. 'They do not plan to share the land with us?'

'No. Lebasi said they want to drive out all the people who stayed. They call us traitors and slaves. Even the ones who wanted them to come back. Even those of us like my grandda who have waited all their lives to welcome them.'

The old man sighed, and sat up straighter in his chair. 'So be it. We have made different plans for different possibilities, for what we hoped and for what we feared.' He raised his hand and swept it across the gathering. 'You all know what to do.'

The murmuring stopped. The ones closest to the mayor stepped forward, touched their hearts in respect, and marched away. They were followed by those further out. The mayor nodded to each one, somehow sensing where and who they were.

When all that were left were four strong-looking young men, Tik guessed that they would carry the chair. The mayor turned to her again. 'Now, my child, I said we would care for you, for the sake of my old friend. We cannot guarantee your safety, I fear. Tonight you will be my guest.'

'Sir –'

'My name is Alfas, child.'

'I need the doctor to come with me. I left Lebasi – Xela's son – at Feleda and Rennik's farm below the high track. He's very ill.'

The old man considered. 'The doctor is likely to be needed in many places.'

Tik insisted, 'He has to come to Lebasi. Captain Riadsala told me to warn the king, to tell him what these invaders are like. I have to go to Egator, and I can't do that without Lebasi.' Since the first time she said it, when it surprised her, the idea had grown strong in her mind. Now it made perfect sense. Surely Alfas would see it.

He stroked his beard. 'I am sorry, child. I have to think of so many different people. You cannot leave until morning, when we will discuss it again. For now, I will ask the doctor to talk to you, at least. For now, it is time to eat and to rest. Come.'

Alfas turned to one of his attendants. 'Tell the first person we pass to find Aynar and have him come to my house. Send for Rennik, as well.'

The man leaned forward and murmured something in the mayor's ear. He nodded. 'Very well. Tik, you will meet Rennik in the morning. Tonight you can explain to the doctor what is wrong with Lebasi, and he can advise you what to do for him.'

The men fitted wooden poles to the sides of Alfas's chair and lifted it, two in front and two behind. Tik followed down the cobbled street, sure that Lebasi needed the doctor in person, and wondering how she could persuade Alfas to let him go.

✣ ✣ ✣ ✣ ✣

'Wake up!'

Tik felt a hand shaking her shoulder. For a moment she couldn't remember where she was. It was still dark, at least in the room where she was sleeping. She was in a bed – when had she last spent the night on a mattress, with solid walls about her?

'Come quickly. Follow me.' A man she didn't recognise was pulling her up by the hand.

'What's happening? Who are you? Where's Alfas?'

The man half-turned as he led her out of the door. 'He's ahead of us. Being carried.'

The mayor's house was the largest building she had ever seen. There was an open courtyard in the middle with a fountain playing, and she had spent the night in one of many rooms leading off it. There had been servants to bring a delicious dinner and lanterns to eat it by and freshly squeezed juice to drink and warm water for washing, but the courtyard was empty now. She glanced up as she followed the man across it – the stars were mostly gone, and the glow in the sky told her dawn was coming soon. Even so early, there were plenty of people moving in the street outside, uphill and downhill, hurrying. Tik took in the expressions on faces, the murmured discussions. This was not a normal morning. Something was happening.

The man held her arm, walking in front to clear a path through the crowd. He glanced back to say, 'I'm Rennik. How is my wife?'

There was something in the way he asked that told Tik he was worried about her. She realised that she had hardly paid attention to Feleda the previous day. She tried to picture her now. 'All right, I think. She was worried that Lebasi being ill might be bad for the baby.'

Rennik nodded. 'I hear you want the doctor for your friend.'

'But Alfas says he's needed here.'

Rennik gave her arm a gentle squeeze and leaned in to whisper, 'I'll see what I can do.'

They crossed the lowest avenue and approached one of the gates. From the patterns of dawn in the sky, Tik guessed it must be the south-eastern entrance to the town. The tunnel through the wall was in darkness – the gate was shut.

'Up here, quick.' Rennik pointed to a flight of steps leading to the top of the wall. She ran up them two at a time and took in the scene. It was not as impressive as the Westwall, but there was a path and a parapet, and people leaning on the brickwork, looking out, reminding her of Verb and his friends on guard with their spears, peering down at the invaders' camp in the wilderness. She recognised Alfas, one hand on the stones and one on a stick, staring down at something with his sightless eyes. Everyone was silent.

Rennik tapped a man on the shoulder and whispered in his ear. He moved aside so Tik could stand on a step beside the mayor and look over. She bit her lip. Lined up across the road below were four Thrarn horsemen. If they were aware of hundreds of people watching them, they showed no sign of it. Their animals flicked their tails and twitched their heads, but otherwise they could have been made of stone.

Alfas asked softly, 'These are the Thrarn you told us of?'

'Yes. Some of their horsemen rode into Xessus before the army ran away after the battle. They nearly caught me, and they burned my farm.' She scanned the horizon. 'There were more than this. Thirty or forty, probably.'

'People of Messtor!' One of the horses stepped forward. The rider took off his helmet and ran his hand through his thick yellow hair. He spoke Xessan with a harsh, throaty accent.

'Who is in charge?'

'I am.' In spite of his age, Alfas's voice carried clearly in the still air.

'Then know this. Your town and your land are forfeit to the Thrarn. We will return with our army in six days. You will leave the gates open. Any who have left by then may escape with their lives and with what they can carry. Anyone remaining in the town will be held to be an enemy of the Thrarn.'

If Alfas was surprised or dismayed, his voice showed no sign of it. 'Where would you have us go?'

The man pointed behind him. 'South. That is the only place that is safe for you. Go to the king you serve. Xessus is ours.'

The light was growing stronger. Tik realised that each of the other three riders had someone sitting behind them on their saddles. Someone small – children? The leader was putting his helmet back on. As he turned his horse round, each of the others pushed their passenger off. They sprawled on the ground and did not move.

'Six days for you to leave. Or join these farmers.'

The horses broke into a trot, leaving the bodies behind.

* * * * *

Tik followed the mayor's attendants back to his house. As his chair proceeded through the streets, he gave a succession of orders to people who set off running in different directions. By the time the men set the chair down outside Alfas's front door, there were only Rennik and a handful of followers left. They followed him through into the meeting room that took up most of the ground floor. He leaned on his walking stick and raised a hand for silence.

'So, now we have seen these Thrarn. Where is Tik? Tell us again what you know of them.'

Tik stepped forward and tried to organise her thoughts. 'Lebasi says they always lie. They'll probably come sooner than six days.'

Alfas nodded. 'I suppose it depends on whether they want us to have left, or whether they want to catch us leaving. I will take it into account.'

'Riadsala said they have no mercy, no law, no honour. They have terrible weapons – poisonous smoke that kills you if you breathe it, and a machine that shoots fire like a dragon.'

Someone ran into the room from the street. He bowed to Alfas, struggling to get his breath back. 'Sir, we opened the gate when we were sure they were gone, and we recovered the bodies. The state they're in makes it hard to be sure, but we believe they're Incor and his wife and son from the farm near the Nampetch border.'

'I see.'

'Beg your pardon, sir, but you don't. Everyone on the wall thought they were children, because they were so small in the arms of the men who had killed them. But Incor was a big man, and his son taller than him. These Thrarn are giants, and they are riding on monsters.'

Alfas leaned on his stick and fixed his blind eyes on something in the distance. 'What are the people saying?'

'There's panic, sir, that's not too strong a word for it. We're trying to keep order, but those that saw them are terrified, and the tale of them is getting taller as it travels among the ones that didn't see them.'

Alfas called his remaining attendants one by one and gave them instructions. Tik wondered at his calmness, and his apparent control of everything he could not see. At last the only people left were Rennik and Tik.

'Rennik, I need you here to help with what I plan to do.'

Rennik put his hand on his heart and lowered his head in respect; but he spoke firmly, as one who expected Alfas to agree with him. 'Sir, my wife is pregnant, and she is caring for the boy Lebasi who may pass on a sickness to her and to our baby boy who is half a year old. If we have six days – or five, or four – I would like to make sure that she is safe. I can get there and back by nightfall, and I can make sure Tik rejoins her friend.'

Alfas rested his chin on his fingertips. 'There are a great many things to be organised.'

Rennik stood up straighter and stuck out his chin, even though Alfas couldn't see it. 'A great deal has already been done. There are good men and women who know what to do without me looking over their shoulder. For one day, at least.'

Alfas slowly nodded. 'Very well. There and back. I understand that Feleda is important to you, Rennik, but I – we – have so many people depending on us. We have to think of them all.'

Tik asked, 'And the doctor, for Lebasi?'

The mayor closed his eyes. Tik held her breath. Rennik cleared his throat.

'Yes, Rennik?'

'I hear that the magistrate's son has seen these Thrarn closer than anyone else. There may be need of his knowledge. For the sake of all the people who depend on us, not just for him.'

Alfas held up his hand. 'Very well. There are reasons enough. Maybe we can do without the doctor for a day, if you can ensure his safe return by tonight. Go quickly, and go well.'

6
HEALING

'Lebasi.' A man's voice intruded into his dreams. 'I've come to see what's wrong with you. I'm a doctor.'

'Da? Is that you?' He opened his eyes. A stranger was leaning over him, a man with short white hair, a trim beard and blue eyes. Not Xela. Of course not Xela. He was far away, probably dying of the disease that Lebasi had brought into the kingdom.

The man laid his hand gently on Lebasi's forehead. It felt pleasantly cool. 'No. My name is Aynar. I know your da, though. He and I are old friends.'

Lebasi tried to sit up. He only had the strength to raise his head and scan the room before falling back. His voice was a dry croak. 'Where's Tik?'

The doctor was holding a small glass bottle with sand in it. He took Lebasi's wrist lightly in his fingers and turned the bottle upside down. Lebasi could see sand trickling through a narrow point in the middle.

'Where's Tik?' he repeated.

The man concentrated on the bottle for a moment longer, then put it in his pocket and laid Lebasi's hand back on his chest. He smiled. 'She is having a well-deserved meal in the next room. Don't worry about her. Tell me how you got into this state.'

Lebasi tried to organise his thoughts. Where to begin? Maybe with the charro the cooks had given him. After that he had had a day with no food and drink in the hot sun, then El-Kazzak had forced him to breathe something that made him obedient, then – he flinched at the memory – they had branded him. That was after the exile's commander Niram had given him charro again so he would feel the hot iron less. He had hung from his wrists while the dragon carried him up to the Westgate; had been overpowered by Nareb in the battle, hit on the side of the head by a falling machine, carried across the back of a horse, and fed another double dose of charro by Tik.

Aynar examined him while he spoke. He stared closely into his eyes, ears and nose. He sniffed Lebasi's mouth. He ran his fingers along the line of his jaw, examined his fingernails, tapped on his chest in different places. When he had finished, he took out the bottle of sand again and held Lebasi's wrist.

'What is that?' Lebasi asked.

Once again, the doctor waited for the last of the sand to fall before answering. 'It measures time.' He placed Lebasi's left fingertips on his right wrist. 'Have you done this in school? That is your blood being pumped round your body by your heart. You probably feel it yourself from the inside, but I can sense it here. I know how many beats a heart normally makes in the time it takes the sand to fall, and comparing the numbers tells me a great deal about how you are.'

Lebasi wasn't sure he wanted to know, but he needed to ask. 'How am I?'

Aynar tapped his fingers together. 'Your heart tells me that you are running a race, not that you are lying in bed. You have been through a great deal. But you are strong, and you will get well again.' He turned towards the door. 'Feleda! Tik! Can you come in here please?'

Lebasi felt the pulse under his own fingers quicken. He tried to lift himself up, but he was so heavy. There they were, the woman who had come in and out of his dreams – she had been real – and Tik, grinning at him, wiping something from her eye with her sleeve.

He let go of his wrist and turned his face away. Tik, who would have saved the Westwall Guard, if only she had been there instead of him.

'Basi? What's wrong?'

Lebasi couldn't think of a way to explain it. He let the doctor talk instead.

'He has had a number of shocks to his health, but I do not think he is any risk to anyone else's. He does not have a disease he can pass on. He needs rest more than anything. I can give you some herbs to make up medicine for him, and some ointment to soothe the burn on his forehead. He will get better, but I think he should stay in bed another day and then only start to exercise very gently. I recommend you do not try to travel anywhere for at least three clear days from now.'

'But the enemy may be at Marstor –'

'I know. All the more reason for this young man to be fully recovered before he tries a perilous journey.' The doctor turned to Feleda. 'I think you can try to keep him awake for a little, now. Open the shutters.'

Sunlight blazed on the wall beside the bed. A gentle breeze brought in a fresh scent of grass and the buzz of insects. In spite of himself, Lebasi turned over and tried to smile at Tik. 'Thanks,' he whispered.

The doctor was studying her face, tapping his chin. 'Speaking of perilous journeys, there is something I would like to do for you, young woman.'

'But I'm not ill.'

Aynar laughed. 'No, you are remarkably healthy. But I fear for the women and girls when there is an invading army at hand. Not that I have any experience, you understand. It is just the stories that are told. Unpleasant stories.'

Tik folded her arms. 'I can look after myself.'

The doctor nodded and bent to rummage for something in his bag. He sat up again holding a pair of scissors. 'From what Alfas has told me, I don't doubt it. I just want to make it easier for you. A little trick, something the hero Xessus would approve of.' He sighed. 'The stories tell us that boys aren't much better off than girls, but maybe a little.' He pointed the scissors at Tik's hair. 'It's got to go.'

✳ ✳ ✳ ✳ ✳

When Lebasi next woke, the sunlight had been replaced by a single candle. Tik was dozing in a chair beside the bed. He tried not to wake her, but his throat tickled and he coughed. She opened her eyes and smiled at him. As she leaned closer to the light, he saw that her head was almost completely bare.

'What do you think?' she asked, running her hand over her scalp. 'The doctor cut my hair really short, then he shaved off what was left. It's cold.'

'Does he think you look like a boy now? I can't tell, because I know you're a girl. But the first time I met you I wasn't sure straight away, even when you had hair.'

She held up a small bottle. 'He's given me something else. It's an ointment for bad skin. It won't make any difference to me, but it's purple. He says if I put some of that on my face people will think I'm ill and they might leave me alone.'

'They might think your hair fell out because you're ill.'

She stuck out her tongue and laughed. 'You must be feeling better.'

Feleda appeared in the doorway, holding another candle. 'Just when the little one has stopped needing night-time feeds, here you come along. I'll make up some of the doctor's medicine.'

The hot drink made Lebasi drowsy. He slept, and woke, and took more medicine, and slept, and woke. Sometimes Tik was sitting by the bed, sometimes she was curled up on a mattress on the floor. Lebasi was dimly aware of daylight passing and night returning.

'What day is it?'

Tik counted on her fingers. 'It'll be Moonsday in the morning.'

Lebasi stared at the ceiling. 'It's ten days since I saw my da. Did they have any news of him at Marstor?'

She shook her head. 'They don't know what's happening in your town. The mirror messages haven't been working for days. Alfas doesn't know why – whether it's the rebellion or the invaders. But he has no news even from Nampetch.'

'What's happening in Marstor?'

She told him about the riders, the order to leave.

'Are they going to go?'

'I think so. The mayor said they had made different plans for things that might happen. He didn't seem to be surprised by what the Thrarn said. He wanted the doctor back as soon as possible. Rennik had to go with him to make sure he arrived safely.'

Feleda brought medicine and soup. He tried to listen to what Tik was saying, but he drifted in and out of sleep. There were things he remembered but wondered if he had dreamed them.

It was still dark when he next woke, but he could see Tik's open eyes glittering in the candlelight. He whispered, 'Did you tell me that Mallam was Xela's father, or did I imagine it?'

'Yes. It was why he went to live on the mountain – he fell in love with his brother's wife. He was sure that Gortan would kill her, and probably him too, if he ever found out.'

Lebasi turned the thought over and over. 'Xela might be dying. He ought to know who his father was.'

Tik said, 'I know. I wish there was time. But there isn't. We have to get to Egator before the invaders, and they're already south of us, and we can't move until you're better. We have to hope they spend some time here in Xessus so we can get a start on them.'

Lebasi started at the ceiling. In his dreams, he had wanted so much to explain to Xela, to ask his forgiveness for all his mistakes. He knew that Tik was right – warning the king was the most important thing – but he wished there was a way to see his father before they left.

She paused. 'There's more. Things Riadsala told me. Your ma, she was his nurse. She's still alive in Egator, looked after in the king's house.'

Tik stopped. She looked away, then at her hands. She took a deep breath before meeting Lebasi's eyes again. He could see that hers were watering, but he didn't know why.

Lebasi felt a pain in his chest as if he had taken more charro. 'How long have you known that?' he breathed.

'There's been no time,' Tik snapped. She turned her head and twined her fingers together.

'I have to tell my da. If he's got the branded man's illness – he can't die not knowing.'

Tik shook her head. 'What if that means the enemy gets ahead of us and we can't find a way past them? Then a lot more people die.' She turned and stared out of the open window into the darkness. 'I made a promise to a dying man. Mallam told me you have no choice if you do that. I have to do my best for Riadsala.'

Lebasi felt a different pain. He recognised it as jealousy. He had been the one who saved the Westwall Guard, who closed the gate, who stopped the sneak attack on the wall. Riadsala should have given the farsight to him, told him to take the message to the king. Tik had made that promise, but he hadn't, because the prince had chosen her.

He shook himself. It was ridiculous. He had been unconscious. But the feeling stayed.

7
LONE PINE FARM

Tik placed her fingertips on Lebasi's wrist as the doctor had shown her. She didn't have the bottle of sand, but she was sure that his pulse was slower and steadier than before.

'How are you feeling this morning?'

He pushed himself up on his elbows. 'A lot better. I'm going to get up.'

'Take it slowly. The doctor said that the fever would leave you a bit wobbly.'

She helped Lebasi to sit and swing his legs round onto the floor. He leaned forward and put his head between his knees. She was relieved to see him move, at least. There had been times in the last two nights and the day in between when he had been so hot, tossing and turning and sweating, and then so cold, sometimes shivering, sometimes frighteningly still, that she wondered if the doctor had been too confident about his recovery. She wondered if Lebasi had heard everything she had said to him, or if he would remember. Some of them were things she wouldn't have said if he had been awake. They were things she had never thought she would say to anyone.

She rested her hand on his shoulder. 'Are you going to be sick?'

He breathed deeply. 'I don't think so. I'll just stay here for a moment.'

She went to the kitchen and fetched some of the herbal tea that Feleda had made from the doctor's ingredients. He was still bent double when she came back, so she held the cup under his nose. She reckoned that the clean smell would help.

'He said this one won't make you sleepy. This is for when you're ready to get up.'

Lebasi lifted his head slowly and took a sip, then a longer draught. He drained the cup. 'It's good.' He smiled. 'Not as strong as charro.'

'The doctor wanted to know all about that. He even tried some.'

Lebasi stared at her. 'What happened?'

'He wanted to be safe, so he cut one of the pellets in half and swallowed it. Then he felt his own wrist with that sand bottle and he said his heart was going twice as fast as normal. He told me that you shouldn't have any more, unless it was an emergency. It might kill you.' She wondered if it was right to tell him what else the doctor had said. Of course it was. *Too many secrets.* 'Or you might start to need it. To depend on it. Like Rodera.'

Lebasi studied the dregs in his mug. He sighed, then nodded. 'He's right. I know it won't do me any good, but there's part of me that wants it. The men on the other side of the wall – they were all happy there was going to be a battle. The fighting, the danger, having to kill people – they weren't thinking about any of that, just that they'd be given charro.' He shivered. 'Their faces in the firelight – they didn't look human.'

Tik remembered Verb and his friends making ready round their campfire. They hadn't been looking forward to the fight at all.

Feleda came through the doorway, carrying her baby in a sling on her hip. 'Good morning, Lebasi. I'm glad to see you sitting up.

I'll make you some proper food. The best that Lone Pine Farm can offer you.' She went back into the kitchen.

Tik noticed Lebasi shiver again. 'What's wrong, Basi? Are you sure you're not going to be sick?'

Lebasi slowly stood and started to walk unsteadily across the room. 'What she called the place. Reminded me of something. But it's gone.'

Tik was used to good farm food, but she had to admit that the breakfast Feleda put in front of them was better than anything she had ever had at her home – fresh bread, creamy cheese, berries, a thick slice of bacon. She was relieved to see Lebasi eat it all and ask for more. Maybe they would be able to start soon.

Feleda cleared away the plates and refused Tik's offer of help. 'Go on outside, you two. Lebasi could do with some sun, I reckon.' She held up a finger. 'You, my girl, need something to cover your head. Hot day and no hair, you'd get sunstroke.' She went out of the kitchen and came back with a broad-brimmed straw hat.

Tik was happy to be in the open air. She had watched by Lebasi's bed ever since the doctor left, following his instructions about medicine and water. She had been curious to see how this farm compared to her own home, but she had made herself wait. She stood in the farmyard and took in the view. It was smaller, but then it only had to support one family. But it was a pretty place, set in a shallow valley that ran from west to east, with pastures rising gently towards the steeper slopes where the high track must lie somewhere in the forest. There was an orchard of fruit trees that must be hiding the view of Marstor, and nearer at hand neat pens for pigs, goats and chickens. She spotted Trefal out in the fields minding some sheep. She scanned around for the horse, but there was no sign of him.

She asked, 'How far do you think you can walk?'

Lebasi stretched his arms out wide and took a deep breath. 'Let's see if we can get a view towards the Westwall.' He pointed to a rounded hill behind the farmhouse. 'We might be able to see something from up there. I think I can make it.'

He did, but it took much longer than Tik had expected, even allowing for how ill Lebasi had been. She realised her plans would have to wait. He surely wouldn't be ready to start the walk to Egator for several days. This was one small hill, and who could say what difficulties and dangers lay on the road south? When she thought about the journey her stomach had butterflies in it, and when she thought about the time passing it was worse, but it was plain that he was doing his best. It would do no good to nag him. At last they were at the top, skirting a group of pines with one tall, ancient tree in the centre.

Tik pointed the farsight along the line of the high track. She shook her head. 'The Westwall's round the corner where the ridge bends. We can't see much from here.'

She handed the instrument to Lebasi and looked about her. 'It's funny that she called it Lone Pine Farm. There are lots of pine trees up here, and even more on the hillside above the fields. But I suppose that big one in the middle might have been there on its own before all the others grew up around it.'

Lebasi lowered the farsight. He turned round slowly and stared down at the farm below them, the track leading east towards the Marstor road, the town itself which they could now see clearly beyond the orchards. He sat down on the grass.

Tik crouched beside him. 'What is it?'

'I've remembered. When I was in the enemy camp, one of the exiles was talking about the farm his family had, back in Dennara's time. It has to be this one. He said there was a cart track from the main road, a little rounded hill behind the farm with a single pine tree on it. That's here, isn't it? All these other trees have grown up in a hundred and forty years. Muscot, his name was.'

'How did he know so much about it?'

'He'd heard about it from his father, who'd heard about it from his father, who'd heard about it from his father, who maybe remembered growing up here. They've passed things down all these years, to remind themselves that they were exiled – the brand, and stories of their home on the other side of the wilderness. He thought that's what the invasion was about, he was coming home. One of the others told him that wouldn't happen – the Thrarn were going to lead the army to Egator. That was just before someone noticed that I hadn't got a star on my forehead.'

Tik shook her head. 'There's probably an exile like that for every farm in Xessus. You said it yourself, this Muscot's not in charge of what the army does. And he might not have made it through the battle.' She used the farsight to scan the track all the way to the main road, then left and right to where the pines obscured the view. 'There's no one coming or going.'

Lebasi picked up a pine cone and threw it half-heartedly. 'I've just got a bad feeling about it.'

Tik sat beside him and put her arm round his shoulders. She leaned her head against his. 'That's the charro, remember? You'll have a bad feeling about everything for a while.' She pulled him up. 'Come on, let's take a look from the other side of the trees.'

They walked through the copse of pines, pausing to run their hands over the wrinkled bark of the tall one in the centre. Tik was distracted by a woodpecker flying past, so Lebasi was ahead of her. She heard him groan.

As she stepped out of the trees she asked, 'Are you all right?'

Then she saw what he was looking at, and gasped, 'Oh.'

He crouched down, and she joined him. She took out the farsight and scanned to the south, south east, south west. Columns of smoke were rising, six or seven that they could count, spread across the countryside in different directions, in the middle and far distance. Not the homely wisps of chimneys. Ugly, thick, coiling snakes, with leaping flames at their foot. She handed the instrument to Lebasi without speaking. He turned towards the west and spent some time sweeping the horizon.

He collapsed the farsight and handed it back. 'I don't understand. First, why they're burning farms, and second, who's doing it. If there's an army out there, they're hiding. You remember what the enemy looked like out in the wilderness. If they were here, they would stand out, surely.'

Tik put the farsight away in its pouch and tucked it under her tunic. She pointed back towards the Westwall. 'It's the horsemen. There aren't so many that we'd be able to see them, but they can cover a lot of ground quickly, and no one's going to fight them. They started with my home. I wonder if they're making sure the exiles don't have a reason to stay, even before they arrive. All the people who think they're coming home. Home won't be here.'

Lebasi rubbed his hand over his eyes. 'What are we going to do? They're already between us and Egator. And I don't think I'm going to be able to run away from anyone.'

Tik tried to sound more confident than she felt. 'We'll find a way. Don't let the charro tell you otherwise. You said it yourself, there isn't an army out there – there are some horsemen, riding around burning farms. We can find a way in between them. And you can hear the horses coming from a long way off, believe me. Tassie and I had to hide from them.'

Lebasi stood up. 'All right. But we'd better get Feleda and Trefal and the baby to go to Marstor. If the horsemen come here –' He didn't finish the thought.

8
VISITOR

They found Feleda hanging washing out to dry. Her little boy was lying on a blanket in the sun, happily gripping a wooden spoon and gurgling to himself. Lebasi sat down beside him and gave him a finger to hold. He hoped Tik didn't mind explaining what they had seen. He needed more energy before he could face bringing bad news. The baby smiled at him and waved his arms and legs in the air. Lebasi tried not to think of what must have happened on those other farms they had seen from the hilltop.

Feleda carried on as if she wasn't hearing Tik's words. When she had pegged the last of the baby's clothes to flutter in the gentle breeze, she turned to face them and rested her hands on her tummy.

'This is my home. I'm not leaving.'

Lebasi stood up, fighting against dizziness. 'But what if the enemy come?' He pointed to the south, where the trees hid what they had seen from the hill. 'They're burning buildings. Tik saw what they did to those people they brought to the gates of Marstor.'

Feleda folded her arms across her chest. 'My mother and father are buried in the orchard, and my mother's mother and father, and my grandfather's mother and father. Someone says he lived here in the days before the prince came, and he's coming back to take it from me?' She snapped her fingers. 'Never!'

Lebasi opened and closed his mouth, trying to form words. 'You can't stop them. It's not him, it's the Thrarn. You and your family are more important than the farm.'

She shook her head. 'You come from a town, Lebasi. Rennik is the same. I love him, and he loves this place, but it is not the same for someone whose family have not worked the land for generations. This is more than just my land. The land is me.' She nodded at Tik. 'Ask your friend. She understands.'

She tucked the empty basket under one arm, scooped up the baby under the other, and went back inside. Lebasi stared after her. He turned to Tik and whispered, 'We've got to make her see sense. She can't stay here.'

Tik sat down, wrapped her arms round her shins and rested her chin on her knees. She took off her hat and fanned herself with it. Her head looked too small without hair. As if she had the same thought, she rubbed her scalp, then sighed. 'There's not much we can do about it. We have to go south. We're going to have our own problems.'

'But she's –'

'She's like my grandda would have been, if he had known the invaders were going to take our farm. He wouldn't have left, either. Your land and your kin, that's what matters out here in the country.'

Lebasi flopped down on the grass beside her. 'Saving your kin is better than dying on your land, surely.'

Tik shook her head. 'What can we do, if she won't listen? She's helped us, and we're grateful, and we want her to be all right. But there's a whole town full of people over at Marstor, and we want them to be all right too, and what about the other towns, and all the people between here and Egator in the enemy's way? We can't worry about them all. We can't worry about any of them. The only good we can do is warn the king about what's coming.'

Lebasi stared at Tik. Her mouth was set in a tight line. He didn't feel strong enough to argue with her, and the conflicting thoughts running round his head made him tired. Surely it was wrong to abandon someone who had shown you hospitality. Was there a Xessus story he could remind her of to make the point?

Tik picked up his wrist again. 'How are you feeling after walking up the hill? When do you think we can start?'

He let her take his pulse. He could feel his heart thumping. It was the argument with Feleda rather than the exercise, but both showed his weakness. He didn't want to disappoint her, but he had to be realistic. 'Sorry, Tik. I'm not ready yet. Probably not tomorrow, either.'

Tik nodded, then stood up, brushing the dust off her tunic. 'One step at a time. That's how we're going to get there. Do some more walking later today, then again tomorrow. Go and lie down for now. I'll bring you some medicine.'

She marched off to the kitchen. Lebasi stared at her retreating back, then couldn't help smiling. 'Yes, doctor,' he murmured under his breath.

✳ ✳ ✳ ✳ ✳

That afternoon Lebasi and Tik explored the pastures and the orchard. They still saw no sign of the horse, but they found some droppings that didn't look like cow-pats and definitely came from a large animal.

Lebasi prodded the lump with the toe of his boot. 'This hasn't dried out yet. It must still be somewhere near.'

Tik burst out laughing.

'What?'

'Feleda said it. You really are from a town, aren't you? He must still be somewhere near. That is definitely a boy horse.'

Lebasi thought of objecting that the only time he had seen the animal in daylight was after she had given him a double dose of charro and he wasn't able to concentrate on anything, but he decided to let it go.

On the far side of the orchard from the farm, they lurked behind the last trees to scout out the view. Tik took out the farsight and trained it on the road. She handed it to Lebasi. They took it in turns to watch, finding no words.

It seemed that the whole town was on the move. From the gate in the distance on their left, all the way to where the road disappeared behind a fold in the landscape on their right, there was an unbroken line of people heading south. There were sheep and donkeys among them, laden with panniers and luggage. Some people were wheeling handcarts. There were a few ox-wagons with passengers, those too old or too young to walk. The shadows of the fruit-trees lengthened in front of them, and still the column of citizens streamed out of the gate.

Tik put the farsight away. 'Do you think the Thrarn will let them go?'

Lebasi had been wondering the same thing, not wanting to put the thought into words. 'They're burning farms, and they killed some of the farmers, we know that. They lie, they play tricks. They might just want the people outside the town walls to make it easier to –' He tried to close his mind to what could happen. 'To make it easier.'

Tik stood up. 'But if they are letting them through, maybe we should go and join in. We'll just be two people in a big crowd. They might take more notice of us if we're trying to travel on our own.'

Lebasi shook his head. 'Unless there's room for me on one of those wagons, I don't think I can do it. Give me another day. We can catch up with them.'

✱ ✱ ✱ ✱ ✱

The next morning they were under the trees again, this time staring at an empty landscape. Apart from flocks of birds, nothing moved. The roofs of Marstor shone in the sunlight. They took it in turns to use the farsight, but they couldn't see anyone.

Tik stood up and looked around. She whispered, 'Did you hear that?'

'What?'

'I thought I heard the horse.'

Lebasi strained his ears. He shrugged. 'I think it's – I think he's not here any more. Maybe he missed the other horses, and he's gone back to join the army.'

Tik peered between the trunks as they walked back towards the farm. 'I hope not. I want to believe he's on our side.'

Lebasi laughed. 'Do you think an animal chooses sides?'

Tik wagged a finger at him. 'You didn't see him on the battlefield. He saved your life. He wouldn't let me leave without you. That horse is a lot cleverer than most animals.' She sniffed. 'Than most humans, for that matter.'

Lebasi held up his hands. 'All right. I'm sure we've been kinder to him than El-Kazzak was. Easier to carry, for sure.'

Tik studied him as they walked. 'How are you feeling today?'

'Much better. I'll be ready tomorrow.'

'All right. Let's leave first thing in the morning.'

✶ ✶ ✶ ✶ ✶

After they had eaten dinner, Lebasi and Tik sat in the bedroom discussing their plans. Lebasi had crossed some of the country to the south before, on his way to stop Perra ambushing the Westwall Guard. But his knowledge ran out not far south of Nampetch, and their words ran out too. They sat for a while lost in their own thoughts.

Feleda came in with a backpack she had found to fit Lebasi and another that could be adjusted for Tik, and said she had laid out food on the kitchen table: apples, nuts, dried meat, cheese. 'Take as much as you can carry,' she told them.

They didn't have much else. Lebasi held the bag of charro in one hand, the empty backpack in the other. He had a sudden urge to open it, to check how many pellets there were. He was still feeling weak – maybe he should put one in his pocket for the next day, to help him keep up with Tik. Perhaps he could take the other half of the one the doctor had cut up. He stood still, aware of his own pulse, beating slow and steady.

Tik interrupted his thoughts. 'What are you waiting for?'

He shook himself and thrust the charro into the bottom of the backpack. 'Nothing.'

✳ ✳ ✳ ✳ ✳

That night, Lebasi lay awake for a long time, remembering his journey from Trengam to the Westwall, imagining doing it again with Tik and an army to avoid: cut across country, keeping to the woods and hedges for cover. Get onto high ground where they could, or climb trees, and use the farsight to stay as far away as possible from any soldiers they might come across. Catch up with the townspeople in two or three days, carry on with them until they were out of Xessus. Then try to move faster than the masses, to reach Egator first and pass on their warning to the king. It was only a vague plan, but it would have to do.

He woke up. One of the farm dogs was barking. The window showed the grey gloom before dawn. He swung his legs to the floor and bent down to feel for his boots.

'Basi?' Tik's whisper from her bed was wide awake.

'I'm getting up. The dog sounds like he's seen something.'

They hurried through to the kitchen and peered out into the yard. The dog was standing very still, staring down the track. In the half-light they could see his ears pricked forward, his teeth bared. He let out another sharp bark.

Trefal appeared, struggling into a shirt. He walked straight out into the yard, whistling softly. The dog backed towards him, but kept its eyes fixed on the same spot. Trefal knelt beside it and rubbed its back, asking softly, 'What's up, boy?'

Tik pointed. 'There!' Lebasi followed her arm and saw a man, standing beside a tree on the edge of the orchard.

He muttered, 'Muscot.' He pictured the man who had handed him over to the Thrarn – the man who had ranted about traitors and slaves, not worthy of the land, the man who cringed pathetically in front of the Thrarn officer. The memory was like a dose of charro. He bounded out of the door and marched towards the intruder. Tik was saying something, but the roaring in his ears drowned it out. Trefal hurried after him. The dog trotted at their heels, growling.

The man stepped away from the tree. He was dressed in the light tunic of the exiles' army, with no armour or helmet. There was a sheath on his belt – Lebasi could see the handle of the sword in it – but he made no move to draw his weapon. He put his hands above his head and called out, 'Friend! Friend!'

Lebasi kept his eyes on the hands and the sword. When they were ten paces apart he stopped and jabbed a finger. 'No further, Muscot. I remember you.'

The man shook his head. 'That's not my name. I don't know who you are.' The light was stronger now. His eyes drifted to Lebasi's forehead. 'I'm a runaway, like you. Please help me.'

Lebasi tried to remember Muscot's face. It was impossible. He had seen him briefly by firelight, and he had been trying to avoid meeting anyone's eyes. But the man's voice sounded different – deeper. He was bigger than Muscot had been.

'Running away from where?'

'From the Thrarn, of course. They're ordering us to do terrible things. I can't bear it. I slipped away in the night.'

Lebasi held up a finger for quiet. He listened hard. There was nothing but the sound of the birds greeting the morning. 'You don't think anyone's following you?'

The man shook his head.

'And you're not Muscot? Whose family once owned this farm?'

'This farm? No. my great-great grandda was from way south of here, near Awato. My name's Caldar.'

Lebasi pointed to the sword. 'If you don't mean to fight, take your belt off and drop it on the ground.' Caldar did so.

Trefal walked forward and held out a hand to the man, who flinched backwards before he realised that Trefal was simply greeting him. 'You better come in. My sister'll give you breakfast, I reckon.'

Tik appeared at Lebasi's shoulder. 'What do we do now?'

'Let's scout down through the orchard to see if there's a sign of anyone else. I think he's probably telling the truth. The Thrarn play tricks, but they don't need to do that here – if they want to attack a farm, all they have to do is ride in.'

The sun was just coming up over the eastern horizon. They had to shade their eyes to see the same empty scene that they had observed the previous day. The town, silent and still. The fields and the road, devoid of people. Flocks of birds, more numerous today, as if they had realised that the growing crops were now all for them. They ran back. Lebasi picked up the sword-belt. He pulled the blade half out of its sheath, feeling its weight. It was lighter than the one Rovert had given him to try on the Westwall Field – he could hardly lift that – but it was heavier than the spare the soldiers of the Guard had given him to keep. That must still be hanging in the tree where he had left it on the night he had the crazy idea to go and spy on the enemy.

They found Caldar sitting at the kitchen table. He started

when they came in, and he couldn't sit still. He kept twitching, blinking, rubbing the backs of his hands. Feleda gave him a mug of tea, and his hands were shaking so much that he slopped some of it on the floor.

Too much charro, Lebasi thought. *Or too much fear of the Thrarn. Or both.*

He sat down opposite the man and leaned towards him. He asked, 'How far away are the enemy?'

Caldar stared at his forehead again. 'What do you mean, enemy? You're one of us.'

Lebasi shook his head. 'Where were you on the morning of the attack on the wall? Who was your commander?'

'In the centre. Niram's division.'

'Then maybe you saw me. I was tied to the front of the dragon.'

Caldar's mouth dropped open. He spilled some more tea. 'You're the spy? You can't be. There's no way the spy could have lived.'

Lebasi pointed at his forehead. 'Does this look more than a few days old to you? I survived. Where are the enemy now? Where have you run away from?'

Feleda put a plate in front of Caldar. His eyes dropped from Lebasi to the food, up to Feleda, back to Lebasi. Lebasi saw a tear form and run down his cheek. He whispered, 'This is for me?'

Feleda clicked her tongue. 'Eat it quick or the dog'll have it.'

She came back with breakfast for them all. Caldar ate hungrily and spoke in between mouthfuls. Slowly his tics and twitches calmed down. He told them that another army had arrived outside the Westwall on the second day after the battle, commanded by El-Kazzak's even more brutal older brother. He had picked out men at random, ordinary soldiers and commanders, and beheaded them himself for their failure to take the wall. It had taken them another day to open the gate.

Tik interrupted. 'How did they do that?'

Caldar shook his head. 'I don't know. But we all marched up through it. El-Kazzak's army first, and we were driven like sheep at double-speed to the town on the coast. Annassam.'

Tik's knuckles whitened as she gripped the edge of the table, leaning forward as if to see into Caldar's thoughts.

'Nearly everyone had left. Some on foot, but most by boat, I reckon. There was nothing in the harbour, and we were told they've a big fishing fleet.' Tik sat back.

Caldar had finished eating. He pushed his plate aside and took a long drink of his tea. Then he covered his face with his hands. Tik whispered, 'What happened?'

The man shook his head. 'The people who were still in the town, we had to - no, I can't describe it. But I couldn't go through it again. I snuck out of the camp that night. Nearly got caught. Spent yesterday in the woods hiding. I could see soldiers marching on the road, some going south, some coming east. I reckon they're going to the town on the hill there. Messtor, we call it. They'll probably get there this evening.' He shivered. 'I hope everyone's gone.'

Lebasi started to say that they had, but a noise made him stop.

Heavy hoofbeats, getting nearer. A horse coming up the track. *It could be their friend...*

Too many footfalls. *Two horses.*

Caldar stood up. 'I'm sorry,' he said. 'You'd better give me my sword.'

9
THRARN

Tik asked, 'What are you going to do?'

Caldar took the sheath from Lebasi and drew the blade. He sighed. 'I'm not going back, that's flat. They kill deserters. So I'll try to go down fighting. And give you time to get away. You need to go. All of you, now.'

The hoofbeats stopped in the yard. They could hear the snuffling and breathing of the horses. Tik looked from face to face. Feleda, eyes shut, holding the baby close to her mouth, whispering in his ear. Trefal, a puzzled expression, watching his sister. Lebasi, his fingers pressed on his temples, staring at the table. No one looking towards the window. Caldar stood up quietly and padded across the room.

'Is there anyone here?' The words were Xessan, but the thick accent made them hard to understand.

Feleda opened her eyes. 'What sort of voice is that?' she whispered.

'Thrarn,' Tik mouthed.

The baby let out a cry. Feleda rocked him in her arms and stood up.

Caldar muttered 'Go' and walked out of the door, holding the sword behind his back.

Feleda led the way into the bedroom Tik and Lebasi had used. Tik pulled Lebasi after her. She was acutely aware of the sounds from the yard, as if there was no wall in the way – the Thrarn shouting insults, Caldar replying. Feleda put her hands on Lebasi's shoulders and fixed her eyes on his. Her voice was low but firm. 'Do something for me, Lebasi son of Xela. Take my child Aminna to Rennik. He is at Marstor. You can get to the high track without them seeing you.'

Lebasi stepped back. 'We can't leave you –'

Feleda laid the baby on the bed and started untying the carrying-sling she wore. 'There is no time to argue. You must go, and you must go now. You will do this kindness for me, as I have cared for you. Tik, get your packs.'

She slipped her arms through the loops and shrugged it on. She grabbed her hat from a hook on the wall. Feleda was tying the sling round Lebasi's shoulders – nestling the baby inside – helping him arrange his backpack so the straps didn't pinch the child. She handed Lebasi another bag that Tik hadn't seen before and said, 'I packed some things for him, knowing this might happen.' She stroked her son's head, then took hold of Lebasi's arm to get him moving.

There was more shouting from outside – the clang of metal against metal – a thump. A harsh laugh.

Feleda put her finger to her lips and hustled them out of the back door. 'Trefal and I will give you time. Go well, Tik and Lebasi.' She stretched out a hand as if to drive them away, saying firmly, 'You did not bring them here. Never think that you did.' She stepped back into the house and closed the door behind her.

Tik took in the horror on Lebasi's face. She felt the same, but there was no alternative. He hesitated, still facing the wrong way, staring after Feleda. She pulled his arm. 'She's right, Basi. There's no use us all getting killed. We can't fight them, and she can't run, not with a baby inside her.'

Lebasi made a strangled groaning noise, but he turned and

started moving. Tik's legs felt weak, just when she needed them to be strong. The open hillside stretched out above them to the cover of the trees, sheep grazing quietly, taking no notice of what the people were doing.

'Don't look round, don't look round,' Tik muttered as she half-ran, half-walked. There was a shout – Trefal's voice – then a scream – Feleda. Tik blinked away tears and kept going. She could hear Lebasi gasping for breath beside her.

Another shout – not Trefal – Thrarn. *Don't look round.* Maybe they would search the farmhouse first. Maybe they were too heavy, wearing too much armour, to run uphill. Maybe they wouldn't bother to chase two children and a baby.

Hoofbeats.

Lebasi came to a halt, panting. Tik knew it wasn't worth saying anything. They were no more than two-thirds of the way to the trees. They had never stood a chance of getting there. Together they turned slowly to face downhill. The two horsemen were trotting towards them, not hurrying. Tik hadn't been so close to Thrarn before. She knew they were big, but their sheer size, their bulk, seemed to stop her heart. Tall helmets added to their height, hiding their faces. Heavy gloves held the reins. Swords drawn in the other hand, held upright, a glint of sunlight flashing up and down the blades as if they were on fire. Beside the armoured horses the sheep looked like newborn lambs.

Tik reached out and took Lebasi's hand. There was no point in running. They would have to face the end together. He squeezed her fingers.

The riders stopped ten paces away and dismounted, each swinging a leg over the back of his horse with surprising grace for such big men. They took off their helmets and hung them over the post on their saddles. Tik glanced down – if she could find a good stone – if she could throw hard enough, straight enough, maybe – there were no stones. Just bright green grass that the sheep had clipped short. Behind the swordsmen, their horses started to graze.

The one on the right pointed his sword at them. 'Where are you going?'

Lebasi didn't say anything, so Tik didn't either.

The other soldier took a step forward. He jabbed his gauntleted finger towards Lebasi's forehead. 'Another deserter. You disgusting rabble. We will take your body back to show the others what we do to those who run away.'

Tik gripped Lebasi's hand. Her heart had started again – she could hear it pounding in her ears. It was getting louder. She tried to calm her breathing. She fixed her eyes on the face of the man on the right. If he was going to kill her, she was going to look at him while he did it. She was afraid, of course she was, but she wasn't going to show it. She had plenty of practice with her uncles' bullying. This would be just a little more than that, and then it would be over.

The thumping was very loud. It seemed the Thrarn could hear it too. The man she was staring at turned – she turned –

The horse, *their* horse, was crossing the pasture at speed. The man held up his hand as if to welcome him, then frowned, took a step back. The horse stopped just short of the two men, reared up on his back legs, and straightened his right foreleg as if he was throwing a punch.

Tik closed her eyes. She heard a crunching noise, a shout from the other man, the thump of the horse's forelegs landing again. She dared to look. The first man was lying on his back, his arms spread out, not moving. The other was running downhill, but the horse was chasing him. He butted the man with his huge head and he fell, rolled over, scrabbled backwards, his sword lost in the grass. The horse reared up again – she turned away.

When she found the courage to look again, he was trotting back towards them in a wide circle. He stopped in front of the other two horses and shook his head at them, making noises that sounded like orders in animal-language. They lowered their eyes, like a pair of her cousins being told off by Gortan, and turned to walk away. They took no notice of their fallen riders. Their horse nodded to Tik, as if to say 'That's all right', and bent down to bite a clump of grass.

Lebasi sat down heavily, his arms wrapped round Feleda's baby. Tik knelt beside him and held onto him, waiting for her pulse to slow down, surprised to be still breathing.

A crackling noise made her turn her head. She jumped to her feet. Smoke was pouring from the windows of the farm.

'If they are –' Lebasi started, struggling to stand up.

Tik pushed him back. 'Save your energy. You've got the baby to carry. I'll go and look.'

She ran downhill, bounding and leaping, knowing that it was hopeless but knowing equally that they had to be sure. It had been bad enough leaving Feleda and Trefal to face the Thrarn, but if they were merely injured and could be saved... they would not be able to live with themselves if there was any doubt. By the time she reached the back door the roof was alight. She dropped to her hands and knees and tried to see under the smoke. Something creaked, and she jumped away just before part of the roof collapsed in a shower of fire and sparks. She ran around the house and into the farmyard. There was Caldar, lying – she looked away. She took a deep breath and turned again. To be sure. Yes, he was clearly dead. There was a terrible wound in his neck and his tunic was drenched in blood.

More of the house caved in. She kept going to the other side, past the animal pens. She heard squeals of panic from the pigs and bleating from the goats, but she had no time to help them. There was no safe way into the building, but she was sure that Feleda and Trefal were not outside. There was a window – she covered her mouth with her sleeve and glanced through it – a blast of heat drove her back. But in that instant, she had seen enough. One of the roof timbers lying on the ground, burning fiercely. Two bodies underneath it, quite still. She walked back slowly to open the gates and let the livestock out.

Lebasi didn't look up until she was standing right in front of him. He had untied the sling and was cuddling the baby in his arms. Tik could see that Lebasi had been crying, but the baby was asleep. She simply shook her head.

She crouched down and stared at the child. Crowding in among all her other thoughts was a feeling of relief that Feleda had asked Lebasi to take him, not her. She had handled lambs and chicks and other baby animals, but she had never had to deal with a little human. She had no idea. Her second thought was that Lebasi was still recovering. She had put more food in her own pack to allow for that. How far could he carry that much weight? She asked, 'What are we going to do with a baby? We don't know how to look after it.'

Lebasi stroked the child's hair. '*Him*,' he murmured. 'Look after *him*.'

10
AMINNA

Lebasi was grateful that Tik had the energy to take charge. She took out the farsight and scanned the horizon. 'I can see a lot of people on the move on the road from the coast towards Nampetch. That must be the army that Caldar ran away from.' She counted on her fingers. 'If the horsemen at the gate really meant six days, that would be the day after tomorrow. But those soldiers could be at Marstor this evening, if they want to. That's what Caldar said.'

She took hold of Lebasi's hand and pulled him upright. He wiped his sleeve across his eyes and refastened the sling. The baby stayed asleep. Part of Lebasi wanted to wake him up, to tell him the awful news. How could he be so peaceful? But he guessed that was the voice of the charro in his head, as he had come to think of it. After the wild positivity, a long dark valley of wretched thoughts. Better for the baby not to know. Nothing would change what had happened. He would find out, one day. From his da, if Lebasi and Tik could find him. That was the important thing.

Tik's voice sounded determined, but Lebasi guessed she was forcing herself for his benefit. 'Come on, Basi, we can be there before them. I know the way, it's not too far. Feleda said Rennik will be there. We'll go and find him.'

She led the way to the high track and set a steady pace. Marstor grew slowly nearer. From time to time the child cried, but Lebasi sang to him and he slept again. Tik said nothing. Every few hundred paces she took out the farsight and scanned the view, but she didn't offer it to Lebasi or tell him what she saw. Each time she put it away, she seemed in more of a hurry. After a while, he couldn't keep up with her. The sun blazed down on the hillside. He held the bag Feleda had given him over the baby's head to protect it, and wished he had a hat like Tik's.

At last she stopped by a tall stone and let him catch up. She pointed down the hill. 'This is where the path breaks off and goes down to Marstor. I think we can rest here for a moment. Have something to eat.' Lebasi sat on a flat rock while she rummaged in her pack. He undid the sling and realised that the baby's cloth was wet. He sighed. He guessed that Tik didn't know what to do. She was the youngest on the farm, so she had never had to look after a baby.

The bag contained some dry biscuits, a bowl, a spoon, and a stoppered flask that turned out to contain sheep's milk. Two spare clean cloths that were neatly folded, not packed in a hurry. Lebasi eyes watered as he held them up. 'She was expecting this. And still she didn't leave.'

Tik shook her head. 'Maybe she hoped it wouldn't happen, but made sure she was ready if it did.'

Lebasi used the water from a nearby spring to wash Aminna, then laid him on one of the dry cloths to wriggle in the sunshine. He rinsed out the other and spread it on a rock to dry. By this time the baby was grizzling, so he cradled him in his arms and fed him some of the biscuit mixed with the milk. He found that concentrating on putting food in the hungry infant's mouth took his mind off what had happened. But when Aminna smiled at him and made a sound like a chuckle, he had to blink back tears.

As he put a fresh cloth on, he noticed Tik staring at him.

'What?' he asked.

'How do you know what to do? You've never had a younger brother or sister to look after, have you? Or cousins?'

He shook his head. 'I don't know much. But we learn in school. Mothers bring in their babies and everyone has to have a go, from the very start. I think it's something from old Xessus – everyone's supposed to know how to look after people.'

He finished the job and started arranging the sling. Tik was still watching him with a strange expression on her face. She was blushing. Even her bare scalp was pink under the pale fuzz of new hair, and he was sure it wasn't sunburn. He sat back on his heels and frowned at her. 'What is it?'

She twisted her fingers together. He wasn't used to seeing her being nervous. It worried him. 'There's something I haven't told you,' she began.

He waited.

She took a deep breath. 'I'm sorry. I don't know why I didn't say before. Something else Riadsala told me.'

She paused again. He fastened the last strap and stood up. Aminna yawned and closed his eyes.

'Your mother. She had a baby soon after she arrived in Egator. A girl. She was Riadsala's playmate until the queen decided her son shouldn't mix with the servants' children.'

Lebasi swallowed. His mouth started to form a question, 'Is she…' He found he could not finish it.

Tik nodded. 'Xela's. She's your sister.'

Sister. The thought ran round his head. He had a sister. Xela had a daughter.

He had to tell Xela.

Tik stepped towards him and gave him an awkward hug with Aminna in the way. She didn't seem to want to meet his eyes. She murmured, 'Are you cross?'

He shook his head. 'Cross? Why would I be cross?'

She gave him a wobbly smile and wiped her sleeve over her eyes. 'Because –' She stopped, her face breaking into a broad grin, and pointed over his shoulder, He turned his head to see the horse ambling towards them.

'See,' she said, 'I knew he was on our side. He's coming with us.'

Something else caught her eye and the smile faded. She took out the farsight again and focused on the valley below.

'What is it?'

She put the instrument away and pulled on her pack. 'Soldiers. Much nearer than I thought. Not the whole army, but definitely invaders. They're on the road from Nampetch. We need to get to the gate.'

Lebasi thought that the rest and food and Tik's news would have given him energy, but if anything he felt more tired. Aminna was heavier. The sun was on his back now, but it seemed hotter. It was awkward walking downhill without being able to see his feet. In moments Tik was running ahead of him, turning and beckoning. He tried to hurry, but stumbled. He slowed down again. He mustn't trip over and fall on the child.

He had to tell Xela. The thought ran around his head. Tik wanted to go south straight away, and she was right, that was important. But Xela might be dying. It was one thing to wrongly believe he was Cirtap's son rather than Mallam's, but this mattered far more. His eyes prickled as he remembered Xela saying how Shelba had left him. She had agreed that their baby Lebasi would be taken to Egator as the king's hostage, and they would have other children; but she had put all the doctor's sleeping medicine in his dinner and had gone herself. She could not have known that she would have another child – Xela had only come back from the capital city the day before.

Lebasi felt the warmth of Aminna pressed against his chest, and wondered if this was how Xela had carried him when he was small and he didn't have a ma to look after him. What had he said? *I cannot look at you without thinking of her, and I cannot think of her without pain.* Is that how it would be for Rennik?

He had to tell Xela.

The ground levelled out as they entered cultivated land. Even though walking was easier, his legs felt so heavy. He wondered if he could somehow ride on the horse, but he dismissed the idea.

They had left the saddle behind, lying in the field above Feleda's farm. He didn't think he could climb up without it, let alone stay on. He started counting steps to focus his mind, as he had done before, on other long journeys. He lost count and started again.

He had reached a thousand twice, or was it three times? He had to stop. He was sweaty and thirsty, his head ached, he would do anything to be able to cool himself down. He stared down at the channel by the side of the road, wondering –

'Basi!'

He looked up. Tik was running towards him. The town rose up behind her, walls on the outside, coloured roofs, the line of a downstreet visible in places between the buildings, up to the bell tower at the top. It looked just like Trengam.

'Basi, come on. You've stopped.' She put a hand on his shoulder. 'It's not far now. But we need to hurry.'

He remembered what had caught his attention. He pointed at the trench beside the road. 'There's something wrong. These water-channels – they're dry.'

Tik pulled at his arm. 'There's no time to worry about that. The people have all gone. Maybe they need people to make the water flow.'

Lebasi shook his head. 'I don't think the water would run out this quickly. I was apprenticed to the waterworkers for a while at home. They must have stopped the flow before they left.'

The horse padded up, surprisingly quiet for something so large. Tik pointed along the roadway. 'Please, Basi. Let's get to the gate.' He nodded and moved his feet. She put her hand on his arm and walked beside him, glancing constantly across the fields to the right.

Lebasi squinted in the same direction. The pain in his head had settled behind his eyes, and he found it difficult to make out the distant view. 'What is it?'

'Soldiers coming round the side of the town. I think they've noticed us.' She pointed ahead. 'And I think the gate is shut.'

As they approached the wall, he could see that she was right. He hoped that meant someone had stayed behind. What was the point of closing the gates if the town was abandoned? But would they open up? Tik let go of Lebasi and ran ahead. He glanced to the right and kept walking. He could see figures in the distance now.

Tik was banging on the gate. Lebasi hadn't the breath to shout to her that it would be too thick. They wouldn't hear her fists through it. Her voice sounded thin and small in the silence. 'Please open up! I need to see Alfas, and we've got Rennik's baby boy with us.'

Lebasi caught up and stood beside her. He was breathing hard, and his shoulders were drooping. Tik's hopeful smile was clearly forced. There was a doubtful note in her voice as she said, 'We can rest in a moment.' Then she shouted again for the gatekeeper.

The gate stayed shut.

She cupped her hands round her mouth and bellowed, 'Open up! We need to get in quickly!'

The baby woke up and started to cry.

The gate stayed shut.

The horse arrived and stood on Tik's right, staring south. It pawed the ground with one of its forelegs, then walked a little way in that direction.

Good, Lebasi thought. *That'll slow them down.* Or stop them altogether. But there would be more of them. He covered Aminna's ears with his hands and joined in the shouting.

A window snapped open just above their heads. Tik stumbled backwards into Lebasi, who nearly overbalanced. A face appeared in the gap.

Tik gabbled, 'Let us in, quick. There are enemy soldiers coming.'

The man's eyes flicked up and down again. 'You've got one of them monsters with you. Who's to say you're not the enemy?'

Tik banged her hands together. 'Don't be –'

Lebasi put a hand on her shoulder. If she was rude to him, he might just close the window.

She lowered her voice. 'You can see we're not. We're escaping from them. I'm Tik and this is Lebasi. Alfas sent the doctor to treat Lebasi a few days ago. Raggan was guarding this gate when I was here before, he knows who I am.'

The face disappeared. The window slammed shut. Lebasi held his breath. There was the sound of something heavy being moved, then half of the gate started to swing back. A hand appeared, beckoning them in. 'Quick now,' the man urged.

Tik stepped aside and waved Lebasi through the opening. He turned to see why she wasn't following. She was calling to the horse, but he turned his great head and shook it, then trotted a few paces further away from them. Lebasi spotted four men like Caldar, fifty paces off, swords drawn. They weren't coming any closer – not while the animal was in the way.

Tik called to him again. 'Come on, we need you.' She hesitated in the gateway.

'You're in or you're out,' the man said. He grabbed her arm and pulled, catching her off-balance. She stumbled inside, and two men pushed the door shut behind her. They lifted a wooden beam into place to lock it.

'No!' she shouted. 'We can't leave him out there with the enemy.'

The man shook his head. 'And we can't leave the gate open. You're safe in here for now, but Xessus only knows what'll happen tomorrow.'

Lebasi leaned against the wall of the gateway while Tik argued with the guard. The cool stones were soothing against his back. The words echoed about him. Suddenly he imagined himself back in the threshold of the Westgate, Riadsala telling him to lock the gate. Trusting him. The pain in his head was overpowering. He let himself slide down to the ground.

11
MARSTOR

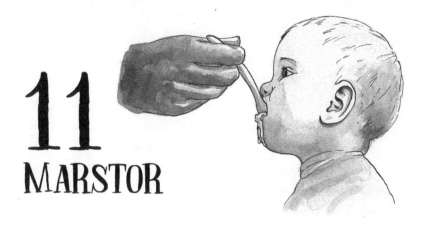

Tik guessed that there would be steps up to the top of the wall as there had been by the other gate on that other morning. She found them just outside the gateway and ran up them two at a time, startling a man who was leaning on the stonework. She took no notice of his 'Who in the wide world are you?' as she stuck her head out through one of the slots in the parapet.

Fifty paces to the left, the horse was standing, facing away from her. Beyond him, as far again, four scouts were arguing with each other. Two were half-turned, their comrades gripping their arms, trying to persuade them to stay. One of the keener ones had drawn his sword and seemed ready to keep going north. One was holding a crossbow – she shivered. She didn't fancy a swordsman's chances of getting close enough to the horse to hurt him, but a bowman could keep clear...

The horse made a noise like a scream. Her eyes snapped back to him – walking towards the group, shaking his head, rearing up and pounding his forelegs down. She laughed as all four men set off running. A bowman would still have to hold his weapon steady enough to aim it, and that would take some nerve with something the size of the horse coming towards you. The horse trotted round in a tight circle. Tik called to him, but was disappointed when he didn't look up. She tried again.

'You can come in now, I'll get them to open the gate!'

But the horse carried on along the track that ran beside the town walls. She followed him with her eyes, then realised that someone was prodding her shoulder. She slid back and dropped her feet down to the path along the top of the wall.

The man she had ignored earlier was standing behind her. His face was very red. He bellowed, 'What are you doing, shouting about opening the gate?'

She opened her mouth to say something, then suddenly felt very tired. She shook her head. 'I was talking to the horse, not the men.' He stared at her as if she was mad. She realised that what she had just said probably made no sense to him at all. She walked slowly past him and down the staircase. He made no attempt to stop her.

Down in the gateway, one of the guards came out of a doorway carrying two mugs of water. He handed one to Tik and one to Lebasi, who was still sitting on the ground with the baby cradled in his lap. Tik sat beside him and felt the coldness of the water spreading out from her throat across her chest.

The man crouched down in front of them. He wasn't one of the men who had chased her when she was here before. He looked from one to the other. 'Now then, you two, time for answers. Who are you? Whose baby is that? And what'd you bring it here for? Everyone with children has gone south.'

Tik glanced at Lebasi, who was taking a long drink. She guessed that she was in charge for the moment. 'He's Rennik's son. We were staying at his farm. The Thrarn came.' She heard Lebasi sigh beside her. 'His wife couldn't get away. She asked us to bring the baby to his father. There was nowhere else for us to go.'

The man ran his hand through his hair. His tone softened. 'I'm sorry. You're all in, I can see that.' He called out behind him, 'Anyone know if Rennik is still in town?'

Someone called back, 'He'll be with the mayor round by the south gate.'

Lebasi asked, 'Can you warm up something for the baby to eat?'

The guard stretched out a hand to stroke the child's head. 'Sure we can, if we've got anything. Is he weaned?'

Lebasi held up the bag. 'We've got a little milk left over and some bits of bisuit. I just want to give him something hot.'

The man led them into a room set in the middle of the wall. Three other guards were sitting round a table. The first one added some sticks to the fireplace, poured the flask of milk into a pan and started heating it. One of the others went through a doorway and came back with some dry cloths. He handed them to Lebasi. 'No point in washing the other ones, lad. We can leave them as a present for tomorrow's visitors, eh?' He bared his teeth in a mirthless grin.

While Lebasi cleaned and changed the baby again, Tik told him what she had seen from the wall. She couldn't keep her voice steady when she described the horse trotting away. 'At least he hasn't gone to join the invaders. But I can't see how we'll find him again.'

Lebasi put a hand on her arm. 'He may be better off outside. He's got plenty to eat and drink out there. And he probably wouldn't like being closed in.'

Tik nodded. 'I don't like it either.'

The men went to join the lookout on top of the wall. Lebasi held Aminna in the crook of his arm, tested the temperature of the food on the tip of his tongue, and started to spoon it into the boy's mouth. He had been grizzling for some time, but now he contentedly chomped and swallowed.

Tik stared at the innocent little face. She whispered, 'How is he not missing his ma?'

Lebasi grunted. 'I suppose nothing bad has ever happened to

him. Feleda would have made sure of that. He doesn't know how to be unhappy yet.'

Tik's throat tightened at the thought of telling Rennik, but she knew they had to. When Lebasi had cleaned the baby's face, she gathered up her pack again. As Lebasi tied the sling round his shoulders, she put her hand on his arm. 'Do you want me to carry him? I'm not as tired as you.'

Lebasi wouldn't meet her eyes. 'I'll manage.' He hesitated. 'Tik, I'm sorry – you had to work hard to get me here. I wouldn't have made it without you.'

She helped him put the baby in the carrier, then stood back to check that he was comfortable. 'That's all right,' she said. 'I reckon we've got a long way to go. One day soon it'll be you keeping me going.' She realised that it was true, even now: concentrating on Lebasi had helped her put what happened at the farm out of her mind. She might have given up already if she had been alone. *I can't do this without you*, she thought. But she wouldn't tell him that.

She shouted thanks up to the men on the wall and led the way to the avenue. It was strange to be in the same place where she had pushed her way through the crowds to escape from the gatekeepers, now with no people and no noise. They turned right and followed the cobbled road with storerooms and animal yards on either side. There were no defenders, but they saw signs that the people of Marstor had made preparations for the invaders. Where the south-western downstreet met the avenue, they had to climb over a barricade of overturned carts, bedframes and wooden planks. Lebasi tried not to jolt the baby, who was turning his head from side to side like a curious little bird. He stopped on level ground and looked back at the barrier.

'What do you think that's for? Surely they aren't going to fight. Nearly everyone's left, and they haven't got any weapons.'

Tik shrugged her shoulders. 'Maybe they just don't want to make things too easy.' She glanced behind her. 'I don't know why anyone's still here, though. The Thrarn said that anyone who stayed, they would treat as an enemy. They can't fight, but if they're not going to fight, they should have gone with everyone else.'

As they approached the southern downstreet, at last they saw movement. A group of men were building another roadblock. There were more men on the wall, lit up in the evening sunshine, all looking out. They caught some words being shouted to the outsiders.

'That's Alfas, the mayor,' Tik said. They stood in the street, straining their ears to hear.

'You have come a day and a half earlier than you told us,' he was saying. 'Give us tonight, at least. You can camp in the fields outside the wall. We will open the gate at first light tomorrow.'

They could not catch the reply. Alfas was helped by two of his attendants down the stairs to ground level. Tik gripped Lebasi's arm. 'There's Rennik,' she whispered.

Rennik was in the middle of lifting Alfas into his chair when he noticed them. He turned and stared at Lebasi, Tik, the baby in Lebasi's arms. His face twitched. Tik could see his lips moving as if he was trying to hold in a scream.

Alfas raised his hand. 'Rennik, what is the matter? What have you seen?'

The man's words came in a strangled croak. 'It is the girl Tik, sir, and the boy Lebasi. And my son.'

Alfas sighed. 'Ah.' He beckoned Lebasi and Tik forward. As before, he seemed to know where they must be standing. He spoke quietly, his voice full of sadness. 'The fact that you are here tells us a story that you will not want to tell. You have done well to save the boy. Rennik, you must take him now and go.'

Rennik protested, 'Sir, I cannot –'

Alfas waved his hand. 'No, you owe it to your wife and your child, and to these two who have striven to bring him here. You have done the work of three men these past days. Go to the refuge and wait there for any others who will join you.'

Rennik bowed and touched his forehead. Lebasi untied the sling and gently handed the baby to his father, mumbling 'I'm sorry.' The child stayed asleep.

Rennik started to ask, 'How –' He could not finish the question. He wiped his arm across his face.

Tik shook her head sadly. 'Two Thrarn horsemen. They burned the farm. Feleda couldn't run. She gave us the baby and told us to bring him here.' She wanted to explain how it was that they had escaped, how they had survived when those he loved had died, but she could see from his face that he was not really listening.

He asked in a small voice, 'Trefal as well?'

Tik nodded. Rennik lowered his head and closed his eyes, hugging his child tightly. He whispered, 'I begged her to leave, when I came with you and Aynar. But she wouldn't.'

Lebasi put a hand on his arm. 'We tried too. I think she knew what might happen. She packed a bag for Aminna last night, before the Thrarn came this morning.'

He opened his eyes again, stood up straighter, made the sign of respect to Alfas, and nodded to Tik and Lebasi in turn. 'Thank you,' he said, 'for saving my son.' Then he set off back the way they had come.

Alfas rested his chin in his hands, his elbows on his knees. He waited until Rennik's footsteps had faded before speaking. 'Tik, Lebasi, you have done a fine thing by bringing the child, but you cannot stay here. You must leave tonight, by the north gate under cover of darkness, and be well clear of the town by morning. You cannot risk being part of what will happen here tomorrow.'

Lebasi's shoulders drooped. Tik could see that he was trying to gather his strength to agree, or maybe to disagree. She had said it earlier: this was her day to be in charge. She touched her forehead in respect, sure that the mayor would somehow know that she had done so.

'I don't think we can, sir. Lebasi is only just getting better from being ill, and he's carried the baby all day.' She glanced sideways at him. 'I'm tired myself, and I might not be able to do it either. If we met anyone and had to run, I don't think we could get away. We need to rest.'

For a moment, Lebasi seemed about to deny it, but his face showed nothing but relief that Tik had taken the decision for him. She put her hand on his arm. He nodded. 'She's right, sir. I don't think I could make it to the north gate, let alone anywhere else.'

Alfas stroked his beard. 'Very well then. You will stay at my house tonight. You will have to join us in our endeavours in the morning, because it will not be safe to leave. Tomorrow, anyone in the town will be held to be enemies of the Thrarn.' He smiled, baring his teeth. 'But we will find a way, an opportunity for you to escape.' He signalled to his attendants to lift the chair. 'Perhaps it is for the best. What is a story without someone to tell it?'

* * * * *

They ate a dinner as good as the breakfast that Feleda had cooked them that morning, a long time ago. Tik was surprised at the number of people coming and going during the meal. Food kept appearing from the kitchen, and men kept entering from the street, taking a plate and sitting down. They ate hurriedly, spoke little, and left again. She was too tired to count them properly, but he reckoned that there must be fifty or sixty.

Lebasi leaned across and whispered, 'They can't be planning to fight, surely? At least the Westwall Guard were soldiers.'

Tik tried not to dwell on her memory of the night before the battle. She considered telling Alfas that the enemy would overwhelm them, but decided that he must know already. As soon as she had told him about the Thrarn, four days ago, he had made a plan. No, he had made plans before that – he had chosen the one that he would put into effect, once he knew what the Thrarn were like. She stared across the room at the blind man, wondering what he was telling his people to do.

When they had finished eating, one of Alfas's attendants led Tik and Lebasi to a room with a row of beds. 'I'm afraid there's only one free,' he said, pointing to a mattress at the end of the row. 'This is where Rennik was sleeping. You can have that.'

There was just enough space for both of them. Tik was tired, but she expected her thoughts would keep her awake: what had happened today, and what might happen tomorrow. Lebasi's steady breathing told her that he, at least, had been able to let the day go.

12
FIRE

Tik was shaking his shoulder. 'Time to get up, Basi. Alfas wants us to go to the top of the hill.'

Lebasi struggled to sit up. 'Now? We've only just…' He realised that Tik was holding a candle, which she didn't have a moment ago, and there were men lying in the other beds, who hadn't been there. Some of them were getting up, stretching, pulling on tunics.

She smiled at him. 'It's nearly dawn. I left you as long as I could. Here.' She pressed a warm mug into his hand.

Lebasi suppressed a groan. He felt no stronger now than he had the previous evening. But there was no choice: he drank his tea, accepted a hunk of bread and jam that Tik brought, pulled on his backpack and followed her out into the street. The crescent moon hung overhead in a black sky, but the stars were fading.

They climbed the hill in silence as the light grew stronger. Lebasi noticed that the smells of the town were still there, even if the people had gone. He recognised a refreshment-house and a butcher's shop by the scent of stale beer and meat.

Above the third avenue, Lebasi spotted something out of place, among everything else that reminded him of home – all the way up the street there were the usual animal drinking-troughs, regularly filled from the town cistern under the Space, but here someone had arranged planks round one of them, reaching out across the road.

Lebasi hesitated as he stepped over them, trying to work out what they were for. Tik pulled on his hand to hurry him up.

They found Alfas sitting in his chair at the top of the street, from where, if he could see, he would have a view all the way down past his own house to the walls and the enemy camp outside. They hung back while men ran up with reports and departed with instructions. One of them glanced at them and whispered something in the mayor's ear.

He beckoned them across. 'Good morning. Let us hope that the spirit of Xessus is with us today, my children.'

Lebasi felt a chill run through him. The old man was smiling, but his blind eyes made the expression into something sinister. His voice was quiet and his audience was close by, but it reminded Lebasi of El-Kazzak addressing his troops before the attack on the wall. He asked, 'What's going to happen? Surely you can't fight them?'

Alfas shook his head. 'We have no swords or bows, and we have few men. But we have some tricks that we can play.'

At that moment the sun cleared the eastern horizon and the bell sounded above their heads, a single pure note ringing across the town.

Lebasi shaded his eyes and stared down the street. 'Are we just going to wait for them to come and capture us?'

Alfas waved a hand. 'I do not think they are interested in us. They have an army of thousands that has recently crossed a wilderness. What they want and need most urgently is food. They will know that the towns of this district all have stores of grain and flour, cured meat and dried fruit, and Marstor has the most fertile land, therefore here are the richest stores of all. There are provisions to be had in Nampetch and in Trengam, but in Marstor there is enough to carry twenty thousand men to the gates of Egator.' He lifted up his stick and pounded the ground to emphasise his words.

'They shall not have it, while I am the mayor of this town.'

There was a flash of reflected sunlight from somewhere at the foot of the hill. One of the attendants said, 'They have opened the gate, sir.'

Alfas steepled his hands and tapped his lips. 'The main warehouses are right there near the south gate. I am sure that they have asked people in the countryside to describe to them the layout of this town, and those people will have told them, willingly or not. So they will start by loading up grain and meat onto their wagons. I do not think they will worry about us until later. Why waste time and effort climbing this hill?'

'But you said you would stop them.'

'We have other provisions that are less interesting to them. Each town in Xessus has its own special industries. We make and keep a great deal of pitch, for waterproofing, and oil for lamps. Look about you.'

Lebasi and Tik took in the scene on the Space. At the top of each downstreet there were stacks of barrels: small ones, large ones, the sort that held beer or fruit or pickled vegetables.

Tik asked, 'Have you brought all the food up here? Won't they see that the storerooms are empty and come looking?'

'Food is not what the barrels contain.'

The attendant interrupted again. 'The signaller says it's as you predicted, sir. They're starting with a meal. They've set up cooking stations all along the road.'

Alfas gave a thin smile. 'Good. Let them be well fed. It may make it harder for them to run up the hill when they realise they need to.' He beckoned to another man and started to give orders in a low voice.

Tik pulled at Lebasi's sleeve. She hissed, 'What do you think's going on?'

They walked slowly across to the nearest pile of barrels, not sure if they were supposed to look or not. Lebasi took in the acrid smell, the ooze of pitch on the ground at the bottom of the pile, the oil-soaked rags poked into holes in lids. At a safe distance, men tending a fire in a metal drum, hardly for warmth or for cooking.

They turned to each other at the same moment and said, 'Xessus and the burning mountain!' Lebasi led the way back to the top of the downstreet. The legend was a little different – the hero besieged on top of a hill that spewed out hot molten rock, as usual one man against a multitude, using his shield to shovel fire down on his attackers, round and around until they were all burned.

Tik was shaking her head. 'He's crazy. I thought he was a kind old man, but he's as bad as Gortan.'

'Why? You don't think it'll work?'

Tik made a sound like a growl. 'What about the people on the road? They're just three days ahead. Old people. Children.' She waved her hand around the Space. 'If he attacks the enemy here, it's not just these men that are going to get killed.'

Lebasi scratched his head. He kicked at the dust. 'You heard what he said. He wants to make it harder for them to get to Egator.'

Tik snorted, 'Boys!' She stomped away and sat in the shade of a building at the top of the street, studying the distant view with the farsight. Lebasi decided to wait until she calmed down. He could see her point of view, but he also understood what Alfas was doing. There wasn't a good answer, and it wasn't the mayor's fault – the invaders had put him in an impossible position. Lebasi thought of his father, made to enforce Riadsala's Mercy in order to keep Shelba alive in Egator, not knowing whether the king's hostage was already dead.

The thought reminded him – *sister*. They needed to set off south as soon as possible, but bringing Aminna to Marstor had put them the wrong side of the invading army. Maybe he could persuade Tik that it would be safer to go by way of Trengam.

He found himself wondering why she had kept that back. She had told him about Mallam being Xela's father, and Shelba being Riadsala's nurse. He remembered how she had looked away and hesitated that day at Feleda's house, and how she had been embarrassed when she finally let on by the high track on the previous day. She had deliberately chosen not to say. Maybe she had decided that it would make him more determined to see Xela before they left Xessus.

He stared at her for some time while she continued to ignore him. If that was what she thought, she was right.

The morning passed slowly. Lebasi waited close by Alfas's chair, keeping out of the way while listening for clues about what was happening as occasional mirror-flashes brought news of the enemy's activities from spies hidden on top of the wall. Shortly before noon, Alfas called his men together. Lebasi sensed Tik shuffling up beside him, but he didn't look round. If she was still angry, he didn't want to know. He was angry too.

'They have finished eating. They are coming now to load the provisions they hope will take them deep into the kingdom.' He turned his blind eyes up to the sky, feeling the sun on his face. 'We will let them bring their wagons in. Then we will give the signal. Wait until the gates are closed and the fire is set in the fields, and then we will begin.'

The men divided into groups of three and took up positions beside each pile of barrels. Alfas was left with only his four chair-bearers. Lebasi asked, 'What do you want us to do, sir?'

Alfas jabbed a finger at Lebasi, then at Tik. 'I want you to live,' he said. 'To escape. To take your message to the king. So be ready. The northern gate will not be closed, and we hope the enemy will not penetrate into that sector of the town, so you should be able to get out that way, even in daylight.' He turned towards Tik. 'My child, my eyes are poor but my hearing is very good. I understand that you do not approve of my plan. I do not do this lightly. The people on the road know what we intend. They are hurrying south, hoping for enough confusion to reign here that they will be beyond Enola before the enemy fully realise what we have done. But in any case, I judge that more people will die if these brutes get what they want; more than will die if we deny them their supplies.' He tapped one palm against the other fist. 'It is the work of a mayor or a magistrate, to weigh difficult choices against each other. I have never before had such heavy weights in either hand.'

Tik said nothing. Lebasi glanced at her. She was studying her feet, scraping the dirt backwards and forwards with her shoe. He turned back to Alfas.

'How are you going to shut the gates? And set fire to the fields?'

They were interrupted by a shout from someone up in the bell tower. 'Soldiers crossing the seventh avenue.'

Alfas held up his hand. 'There is no more time, children.' He called out, 'Give the signal. Start the fires.'

Tik and Lebasi left Alfas calling out orders to his bearers and ran to the top of the downstreet. They pressed themselves against the wall of a refreshment house and peered round the corner. As Tik trained the farsight on what was happening below, the bell rang out above them – the usual long peal that signalled rising, noon, curfew, day after day, but then again and again, CLANG CLANG CLANG. The sound seemed to be inside Lebasi's head.

Tik handed him the farsight. 'They're not coming very fast – yet.'

He lined it up badly. He was looking much too close – cobblestones – water. He lowered the instrument, then raised it again. 'They're running water down the street. Why –'

A shout came from a few paces away: 'Fire alight!'

They stared at three men pulling and pushing a large barrel onto its side. Black smoke was pouring out of a hole in the top.

CLANG. The bell rang one last time and stopped.

'Away!' the men shouted as they rolled the barrel over the edge. They didn't stop to watch it, but ran to the pile for another.

For a moment the barrel hardly seemed to be moving at all. Then it was gone, faster and faster, spilling smoke behind it, following the central gutter in the middle of the street. It reached the second avenue which was level like a step on a staircase. On the far side there was another lip where the slope started again – the barrel flew for a few paces, then kept rolling, spewing out a black fog behind it. Lebasi tried to follow it with the farsight. It was hard to see what was happening further down. He wondered if the men coming up were aware of what was about to hit them.

'Fire alight! Away!'

The first barrel leapt again at the third and fourth avenues, and at the fifth it landed too heavily for its frame. Lebasi saw it burst, a shower of fire spraying in all directions. A wooden veranda on one of the shops started to burn.

'Fire alight! Away!'

Lebasi raised the farsight, training it higher, looking out into the fields. He whistled. 'It's like Alfas said. The corn is burning.'

To the right of the road, a thin line of fire stretched across the town fields. A *straight* line. Suddenly the flames were spreading to the left, breathtakingly fast, again in a straight line. The fire reached the road and appeared on the other side of it. He remembered the dry channels – they must have stopped the water to make the corn burn more easily. And maybe they had filled some of them with oil.

'Fire alight! Away!'

Tik grabbed the farsight from Lebasi and pulled him back from the downstreet. They stared together across the Space. The tallest piles of barrels had been by the three nearest streets, and the men were working their way through them. Smaller groups were taking more time on the other streets. The smell of burning pitch hung in the air and caught in Lebasi's throat.

Tik marched across to where Alfas was still sitting on his chair, the only man stationary in the middle of the action. He had one elbow propped on his knee, his hand in his chin, stroking his beard, turning his head slowly from side to side to catch the sounds around him. He turned to face them, his blind eyes staring into the space between Lebasi and Tik.

She cleared her throat. 'Alfas, sir…'

He nodded and smiled. 'You must leave. I know.' He raised his right arm and pointed behind him. 'There should be no fire on the northern downstreet. The barricades we put up in the last few days were to keep the enemy in the south of the town. Their soldiers will be busy now with the fires. You should have a clear passage.'

Lebasi started to say goodbye, but Alfas held up a hand. 'Wait.' He plucked at a chain round his neck and pulled it over his head. A small gold disc hung from it. He held it out. 'Son of the magistrate, this is my badge of office. From today, I am no longer the mayor of Marstor. From today, there is no Marstor. Take this to your father and tell him what we did here. Tell him that we did not do it lightly, but we decided that we had no choice, myself and the elders of the town.'

There was another shout from the watchman in the tower. 'Second avenue, southern downstreet.'

Alfas pressed the badge into Lebasi's hand. 'Go now, and go well, Tik and Lebasi. Take my badge to the magistrate, and take your message to the king.'

They ran, dodging between men sprinting to reinforce the

group at the head of the next street. As they passed by, they saw one of the barrel-rollers fall sideways, clutching at his neck. Lebasi shouted, 'Crossbow! They must be close.' They passed another pile and another group, then another, and came to the top of the northern street. Lebasi had a stitch in his side and had to stop. Tik pulled at his arm.

He gasped, 'Just a moment. Downhill from here. I'll go faster.'

She nodded and took out the farsight. He turned to look back across the Space. The remaining barrels at the southern street-head must have caught fire, whether that was part of Alfas's plan or not. The column of flame rose taller than the buildings, with men appearing and disappearing in the smoke at its foot, fighting hand to hand. At least they were exiles, not Thrarn, but Alfas had said that the townsfolk had no swords. It wouldn't be a long battle.

Lebasi was surprised to see Tik grinning as she put the farsight away. 'What?'

'I swear that horse can see the future. He's out there waiting for us.'

13

THE HIDDEN HOUSE

The sounds of fighting faded as they hurried down the cobbles. If it had not been for a swirl of smoke above them, and the absence of people, Tik could have imagined it was a normal day. The gate stood open and unattended, and outside she felt she could breathe again. The horse, waiting patiently a hundred paces along the road, nuzzled her hand in greeting. She tried to think about what to do next, not what must be happening behind her.

It was only the middle of the afternoon, and she was keen to get far from the town as quickly as possible, but she knew they were heading in the wrong direction. They couldn't go south – not while there was a fire in the fields and an angry army in the way – but they shouldn't keep walking north. She also realised that Lebasi needed more rest. They reached a low wall that must mark a boundary between the town's neat fields and the open pasture, and followed it a short distance east to a hut that was half-full of hay bales.

'Let's stay here and see how things stand in the morning,' she suggested.

The hay made a comfortable bed, but neither of them slept much. They took it in turns to keep watch, alert for any sign that the enemy army might be advancing to this side of the town. The human invaders did not trouble them, but they could not avoid staring at the fire as it spread from building to building, licking around windows, bursting through roofs. Even when they took a turn inside, they could not escape the smell and the sound of destruction. Tik wished she could close her ears. She didn't want to talk about it, and there was nothing else worth saying, so they passed the night hardly speaking.

They set out at first light, as soon as they could see well enough to avoid the irrigation ditches as they cut across the fields. Even the horse, strolling at times in front, at times behind, seemed subdued by what had happened. None of them looked round. They could taste the smoke on the light breeze, catching in their throats. Patches of it drifted past them, darker than the morning mist.

Lebasi seemed to have recovered some of his strength, at least. He led the way without pausing or explaining, and Tik didn't ask questions. She resigned herself to going in the wrong direction for now. They had come from the west, the enemy were south, and the mountains were north, so they could only go east. The question nagged at her: how could she make it to Egator before the Thrarn, when their army was in the way?

They reached the edge of a forest that covered the lower slopes and found a path that stayed under cover of the first trees, rising and falling a little as it traversed the hillside. The countryside below them was deserted – no people, no animals. Fields of crops that no one would harvest. Farm buildings with no smoke from their chimneys. Here and there, the ruins of houses that had been burned by the horsemen.

They had been aiming for a skyline and slowly gaining height. Now, with the sun high overhead, they found themselves on a ridge that gave them a view of the land ahead. They stopped on a rocky outcrop to eat. Tik took out the farsight and scanned in all directions. For the first time she could see three towns. The one to the east must be Trengam, Lebasi's home, still a long way off.

Nampetch was almost due south, and Marstor was far behind them. She dared to look back for the first time, but turned away quickly as the scene of devastation jumped too close to her in the lens. She turned instead to Nampetch, which was the opposite of Marstor: serenely peaceful in the bright sunlight, with no sign of movement. Perhaps its mayor had given up his food stores without a fight.

On the flat ground in the distance, west of Nampetch, the exiles' army had made a camp. She wondered if the men who had attacked Marstor had retreated there, or if they had all perished in the fire. How angry the Thrarn must be. Surely they would take revenge on the townsfolk, defenceless on the road. She lay down on her stomach, telling herself it was to hold the farsight steadier; she did not like to admit, even to herself, that what she really wanted was to make herself smaller in case anyone was looking the other way. Did the Thrarn have farsights? They had poison smoke and black powder and a dragon. But surely they could not see her at this distance.

Lebasi interrupted her thoughts. 'Can I have a look?'

Tik handed the farsight over. Lebasi trained it on some woods ahead and downhill. 'I think that's where Barten's house – oh, no.' He stood up.

Tik stayed low, wondering if he had seen enemy soldiers. 'What is it?'

His words came in a rush. 'I have to go down there. There's a body in the fields. It's near the farm where they helped me. I have to know what happened. If there's anyone there needing help, I have to do something.'

Tik checked with the farsight. 'All right. If the soldiers have been there, it looks as if they've gone now. But let's be careful.'

Lebasi led the way downhill, keeping low to the ground. Tik did the same until the noise of hoofbeats reminded her that there was no point in trying to be inconspicuous. They crossed a low stone wall and entered a close-cropped pasture. In the centre, lying on his back, was the body of a man – no, when they reached him, Tik could see it was a big boy, with an unlined face and hairless chin. His eyes and mouth were open. He looked surprised. There was a crossbow bolt sticking out of his chest.

Lebasi knelt beside him and reached forward to close his eyes. He covered his own face. His shoulders were shaking.

Tik put her arm round him. 'Do you know him? Who is it?'

Lebasi took a deep breath and wiped his sleeve across his face. 'His name was Preddo. He never had any luck, and he never did anyone any harm, and he didn't deserve this.'

He sat back heavily and turned his head towards the woods. 'I have to look. I can't bear it, but I have to know. Barten and Harka, Dewen and Folla – they were all so kind.'

They approached the wood cautiously. Lebasi cast about, then shook his head.

'I thought the house was in a clearing just inside the trees here. But I can't find the path. Maybe I've got it wrong – maybe this isn't the place.'

Tik glanced behind her. 'It must be somewhere here. He wouldn't be far from home, would he?' She dropped to her knees to check whether a mark on the ground was really a footprint, leading straight into a mass of creepers and branches that looked at first sight as if they were part of the surrounding undergrowth. She pushed it aside. 'Here,' she said. 'I think this is a path. They've covered it up.' It reminded her of the secret den she had made with Sinder in the copse at home.

Lebasi struggled through the foliage and ran ahead. Tik followed, turning a corner to see a solid house built of logs, undamaged by fire. Lebasi was in the doorway, calling names softly,

then louder. He disappeared inside. Tik stood in the farmyard, taking in the silence and the beauty of the wood.

'They're gone.' Lebasi came out carrying a spade. 'No bodies. No damage. I don't think the soldiers found the place – there's even food in the cupboards.'

Tik pointed at the spade. 'What's that for?'

Lebasi planted it in the ground and fixed his eyes on hers. 'I'm going to bury Preddo.'

She understood. She had taken care of Mallam's body, one of his last requests. She asked, 'Is there another one? I'll help.' Lebasi smiled and turned to go back into the house. Tik realised that she hadn't seen him smile since before Marstor.

Preddo was too heavy to move, so they dug a hole beside where he lay in the field. They watched and listened, ready to drop their tools and run if there was any sign of his attackers returning. As they worked, Lebasi talked. He had to pause regularly to mop his forehead with his sleeve and catch his breath, but it was a big hole, and he had time to tell Tik what he knew of the boy. He started with himself crawling in the dark through the wood, where Barten, the farmer, found him. He had bandaged Lebasi's ankle and guided him across Marstor land, even though he knew Lebasi was Xela's son, and Xela had taken Barten's eldest boy as one of the best and bravest for the king's army. He recounted Preddo's story – born brain-sick, abandoned by a father who committed suicide when he was a baby, brought up by a mother the townspeople believed was under a curse, given up to be transferred from Nampetch to Marstor land when he was seventeen. He'd been taken in by Barten and Harka and treated as their own kin, even though he was a different kind of boy from their own Nerek. Tik had heard some of it before, jumbled up by the charro. This telling was more like a Xessus legend, sad and happy and angry all at once. And true.

'I think that's deep enough,' said Lebasi, scrambling out of the hole. 'A manheight or so, that's what I've heard. Safe from animals digging you up.'

Tik pointed at the arrow. 'Do you think we can pull that out? I don't think he should be buried with it.'

Lebasi had to put a foot on Preddo's chest and twist as he tugged. Tik determined not to look away. She had never met this boy, but she felt that she had something in common with him – growing up among people in the town who didn't accept him. She would show him respect.

They couldn't lift his body, so they had to slide him over the edge of the hole. Preddo rolled all the way over and ended up facing the sky. Lebasi climbed back in and tried to arrange his arms across his chest, but they wouldn't bend, so he had to leave him as they had found him in the field, with his hands by his side. Neither of them spoke as they shovelled the earth on top of him.

Lebasi patted the ground flat with the back of the spade. He stood for a moment with his hand to his forehead in the sign of respect, and Tik copied him. No one had died on the farm since she had been born; she wondered if Lebasi had seen burials in the town and knew what to do. Maybe telling the dead person's story was part of it.

He picked up the arrow and thrust it into the ground at the head of the patch of freshly-turned earth. He said, 'If Barten and Harka come back, they'll know he's buried here.'

✳ ✳ ✳ ✳ ✳

'What do you think happened?' Tik asked, as they sorted through the food in the larder.

Lebasi stared out of the window to where the trees hid the view of Preddo's grave. 'I remember my da talking once about what happens to bodies after you die. That stiffness, it comes on soon and goes away after a couple of days. So Preddo probably died yesterday or maybe the day before. Perhaps he was out in the fields when the enemy came and couldn't hide in time. Or maybe he was drawing them away from the house, to protect the family.'

He pointed to gaps on the shelves. 'The rest of them didn't leave in a panic. They've taken supplies. Chosen things, not just grabbed stuff in a hurry. Barten will have made a plan, and it'll be a good one.' He peered into a storage jar, as if it might contain an answer. 'But I don't know whether he will have gone to hide in the mountains, like Rennik, or will have gone south with the rest of the people.'

Tik held up a basket of apples. 'Do you think it's all right to take their food?'

Lebasi nodded. 'They took me in once, and I think they'd do the same again. The laws of old Xessus say to help a stranger.'

She put some fruit on the table. 'I think we should have a cold meal. I don't think they'd thank us for lighting a fire and telling everyone there's a house here, after they've done so much to hide it.'

Lebasi shifted from one foot to the other. He clenched and unclenched his fists, staring up at the ceiling, then turned to face her, leaning forward on the back of a chair. His words came quickly. 'We're almost at Trengam. There's a road south from there, and if we go that way maybe we'll have gone around the enemy instead of through them.'

She folded her arms across her chest. 'You want to see Xela.'
He nodded.

She studied his expression. He wanted her permission. How had it come to this? It was an eightnight since she promised Riadsala that she would take his message to the king. If anything, she was further from Egator now than when she had knelt beside the dying prince on the Westwall Field.

What would Lebasi do if she said no?

But – *I can't do this without you.* The thought came back into her head, even stronger than before. She needed him, and he would not let her down.

He was speaking again, but she was hardly listening. 'It's a fair way to the town, but we can go in a straighter line than when I came here before. As long as the countryside is as deserted as it was today. It won't take long.'

'All right,' she said at last. 'As long as we can get on the road straight afterwards.'

He beamed at her. 'Of course. Promise.'

14
HOME

'I can't see anyone.' Tik lowered the farsight and handed it to Lebasi. He took his turn scanning the roofs of Trengam, glowing in the early morning sunlight.

'It's difficult to tell,' he said. 'The buildings get in the way. All we can see is the northern downstreet running down to the gate. There could be an army hidden everywhere else.'

Tik shook her head. 'No smoke. I think the people have gone. And Xela didn't set fire to the place like Alfas did.'

Lebasi studied the gateway. 'I think this one's shut. I hope one of them is open.'

They followed paths through the fields to the north-eastern road, then on to the eastern approach. The horse strolled behind them, stopping to eat, trotting to catch up. When they had a clear view of the eastern gate, Lebasi shook his head. 'That would have been the best one. My house is near the bottom of that downstreet. I could run in, see if my da's there, run out again. But it's closed too.'

The sun was halfway to the zenith by now, and the light picked out every detail of the buildings above the wall. The bell glinted in its tower. The silence pressed down on Lebasi. He led the way on south, keeping away from the wall, feeling a crawling sensation in his scalp.

They passed through a copse, grateful for a moment to see only trees and bushes. Even the insects and birds were unusually quiet. At the far edge, their path met another road. Lebasi peered round the last tree trunk, then grinned. The gateway was a dark shadowy hole in the wall, but through it he could see sunlight on stone. The gate was open.

A sudden shiver ran down Lebasi's back. He pulled Tik back into the shelter of the trees and crouched down, staring all around to try to see anything that had caused it. His heart was thumping and his legs were wobbly.

'What is it?'

'I don't know. I think it must be seeing the town like this. Not knowing what it's going to be like in there.' She nodded.

He took a deep breath. 'Tik, I think you should stay out here.' He held up a hand as she protested. 'Hear me out. I know the place. I've spent half my life hiding in the alleys and buildings. If I run into trouble I can get away. It's like you in the woods at the Westwall – that's your place, and this is mine.' She folded her arms and scowled at him. 'Tik, we can't risk both of us. We need to take the message to Egator. If there's a trap in there, only one of us should get caught.'

She turned her face away. 'If there might be a trap, why are you going in at all?'

Lebasi put his hands on her shoulders and waited for her to meet his eyes. 'If we'd been able to go straight south from Feleda's, I would have gone with you, you know I would. But everything that's happened has pushed us this way, and now we're here, I can't just walk past without knowing if he's there.'

She closed her eyes, let out a long sigh, opened them again. She looked up at the sky, down at the ground, at last at his face. 'I suppose you're right,' she muttered. Then, louder, 'Just don't get caught.'

He smiled, trying to cover up his own nerves. 'Don't worry. I told you about the bullies who used to chase me. They grabbed me once when I wasn't paying attention, but they never got close after that. You've got the horse for company.' He looked into his backpack and took out most of the food he was carrying. 'I won't need this. I'll be here again before the middle of the afternoon – probably a lot sooner. But if I'm not back, and I haven't signalled to you somehow, you'll have to get going.' He pointed the way ahead. 'There's a road from the south gate that heads towards Awato. At least, that's what I've been told. That's the direction Marrak sent the signal to call for the Guard.' He lowered his hand and put his head close to hers. 'But I'll be back, all right? We'll be on that road together, this evening.'

She nodded. 'I'll be in the woods here. Make the pigeon call if you don't see me.'

Lebasi put his hands to his mouth. *Croo croo, croo croo.*

She chuckled. 'Or something like a pigeon. At least I'll be able to tell it's you.'

He laughed with her, then turned and jogged towards the open gate, having to concentrate in order not to stumble as he ran. He wondered if his mind was playing tricks on his body, or if he wasn't fully better yet. He had slept well in a bed at the house in the woods, but Tik had woken him early again. There was no time to rest now – he would have to keep going.

He approached the opening on tiptoe, listening hard to the silence. He knew that there were doorways where people could hide, but if anyone was lying in wait, they were being very patient. He sidled into the tunnel through the wall with his back against the stones, opening his eyes wide in the sudden gloom. He passed the entrance to the gatekeeper's room. To be able to come and go without having to explain yourself – it was almost as uncanny as the silent town. He remembered Perra telling the townspeople it was what the revolution would give them.

The lowest avenue was empty, the air heavy and still. He jogged north, focusing his mind on getting to his house, not thinking about what he might find there.

As he turned the corner into the eastern downstreet, something up ahead moved. He dodged into a doorway and clamped his mouth shut to stop a shout of surprise. Fifty paces away, a small dog stood in the middle of the street, staring at him, its ears pricked, its tail straight up. Someone's pet, left behind. He stepped out and started towards it, holding out his hand. 'Here, boy.' His voice was croaky. The dog sprang round and scampered away.

He paused on the threshold of his home and rested his fingers on the handle. At the start of Perra's revolution, two days before Midsummer, he and Marrak had stood here and stared at the Xessan flag flying from the bell tower. It wasn't there today. Marrak had barred the door against Perra's men, but now it opened silently with a gentle push. He stepped inside and let his eyes adjust. He slipped his backpack off and set it quietly on the floor.

He sniffed. He recognised the sour smell that had hung about Rodera. Did the disease he carried have its own scent?

'Da?' He found he was whispering. That was no use. *Louder*. 'Da? Are you here?'

If Xela was ill, he would surely be in bed. Lebasi padded up the stairs. The house seemed to suck the sound out of the air. He had a sudden memory of the way it had been when the snatchers came for him – being carried down these stairs in the middle of the night, gagged and bound, by men who made no noise.

He stepped through the open doorway into his father's bedroom. He only realised he had been holding his breath when at last he let it out. The bed was neatly arranged with blanket and pillow, as if Marrak had just finished his morning chores. A gentle breeze drifted through the window, bringing the fragrance of flowers in from the garden. Xela was not there; there was no sign that anyone had been in the room for days. Lebasi leaned on the doorframe. Maybe it was good news. Maybe it meant he was well, that he had gone south with the townspeople. But he realised how much he had wanted to speak to him –

The scent. There had been that smell downstairs. He ran back down and turned into the eating room. For a moment, he thought it was empty, but his nose told him otherwise, so he took another pace. He saw a pair of bare feet on the floor behind the table.

'Da!' He ran, he pulled the table aside, he knelt down. Xela was lying on his back, his eyes closed, covered with his travelling cloak. His face was thin and his beard was whiter than Lebasi remembered it. He looked older than Gortan. Lebasi wiped his sleeve across his eyes and lifted the cloak to find his father's wrist. He couldn't feel anything moving under his fingers. He put his ear close to Xela's mouth and shook his shoulder. Nothing.

He rocked back on his heels and stared at the ceiling, digging his fingernails into his palms. This was his fault, this was what he had done – he had opened the gate and let in the man who gave the sickness to his father.

The man – the man who had lain dying in the gateway –

He jumped up and ran to the hall. He tipped the backpack out – it must be here – he grabbed the leather pouch and ran back into the eating room. He emptied the pellets onto the table. He crouched beside his father again. What had Tik told him? She had put one in his mouth, and one between his teeth. It had saved him, but it had nearly killed him. Maybe a smaller dose – he searched through the little beads and picked out the half-sized one left by the doctor's experiment. He pulled Xela's mouth open with one hand, trying to part his teeth just enough to put the drug between them. He pressed up on his father's chin and heard a faint crunch.

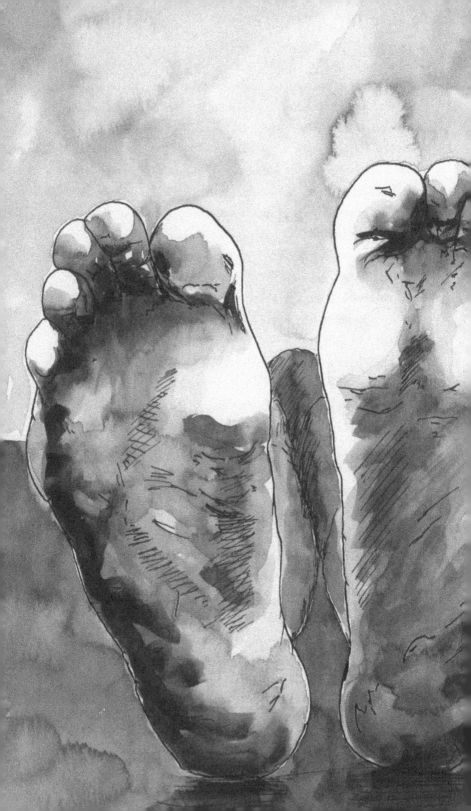

Nothing happened.

'No, no, no!' he shouted. Maybe Xela's mouth was too dry, he wasn't swallowing it. *Water*. He hurried into the kitchen, wondering if the pump would be working, with no waterworkers in town, but found there was no need. There were pans and jugs of water standing on the table with cloths laid across them. Marrak must have left them. The agent's name in his head produced a surge of anger. How could Marrak have abandoned his father?

He came back with a wooden beaker and lifted Xela's head. For a moment, he worried about pouring it down his windpipe, then realised he could hardly make things worse. He tipped a little into his father's mouth.

Xela's eyes snapped open.

Lebasi fell backwards and banged his head on the table. Xela levered himself into a sitting position, his back against the wall. He stared at Lebasi.

His voice was different – weaker, croaky. 'Is this one of those dreams that comes at the end, or are you really here?'

Lebasi winced as he touched his hair and felt the stickiness of blood. Spots swam in front of his eyes. He tried to focus. 'I'm here.'

Xela's voice grew stronger. 'You must stay back. You must not catch this.' His eyes were unnaturally wide, showing the whites all round.

Lebasi nodded. He glanced at his hands. Rodera had made sure Xela was bleeding when he passed the sickness to him. Maybe it could only be caught through blood. But Lebasi's fingers now had his own blood on them. He'd had his fingers in Xela's mouth. Which hand had he used to put the charro between his teeth? He shook his head. No time to worry about that.

He found he was still holding the beaker in the other hand. Most of the contents had slopped out on the floor, but he reached out and set it within Xela's reach. He whispered, 'I thought you were dead.'

Xela stretched out a shaky arm and took the cup. Even though it was nearly empty, he spilled half of what was left on the way to his mouth. He put a hand on his chest, taking deep breaths. His eyes kept staring. He said, 'I thought so too. I'm not sure I was wrong. Death might be a dream, and the dream might be like this. But I thought it would be more peaceful.'

Lebasi held up the bag of charro. 'I gave you the medicine the branded man had. Only half a pellet. I've had it too, and I know it hurts.'

Xela asked, 'What day is it?'

'Firesday.' Lebasi was surprised that he had an answer without having to think.

'Firesday,' Xela repeated. 'I think Marrak left three days ago, with the last of the townsfolk. He said he would set out some food in the kitchen, but I haven't been strong enough to get up.'

Lebasi clenched his fist. 'Marrak just left you like this?'

Xela sighed. 'I sent him away. I pretended that I was not as weak as I was. There was nothing he could do here except catch the same disease. The people needed someone to lead them south.'

Lebasi carried on talking as he searched the cupboards for food. 'When I left to come looking for you, the townspeople were about to lock Marrak up.' He found cheese, nuts, some bread that wasn't too stale, butter to make it edible, a fresh cup of water. When he returned with the plate he was surprised to see Xela sitting at the table. He was staring at the beads of charro. He picked one up and held it up to his eye.

'This brings back the dead, does it?'

'The doctor at Marstor said it speeds up the heart. If you keep taking it, it will work less and less, and you'll need it more and more. And when it wears off, you feel a bit worse each time.'

While Xela ate, Lebasi told him as much as he could of what had happened at the Westwall and at Marstor. He knew there were other things he had to say, but he wasn't ready yet.

Xela pushed away his empty plate and took a drink. He stared out of the window, his eyes still hardly seeming to blink. 'They came here, the same as Marstor. Riders outside the wall, the order to leave, the dead country folk left to make sure people obeyed. I was already ill. It was Marrak who organised it all. I think everyone's gone. I haven't heard anyone at all. But I've just been lying here.'

Lebasi lowered his head. He would have to go back to Tik soon, they would have to find the way to Egator. He could not leave his da behind, but he was too weak to travel. He might give them the illness. He would certainly slow them down. Lebasi knew that if he even suggested taking him with them, Xela would tell them to leave him behind and go, just as he had told Marrak. Lebasi might never see him again. He had always hated the way Xela kept secrets. He could not hate himself for the same thing.

He stared at his hands. 'Da, I've made so many mistakes. Everything I've done…' He tried to think of where to start.

Xela's voice was gentle. 'Of course you have. We all –'

Lebasi looked up, tears filling his eyes. 'You don't understand. I've done terrible things. I –' His voice failed him again as he stared into his father's sunken face.

'You opened the gate and let the branded man in. You blame yourself for what's happened to me.'

Lebasi gasped. 'How did you know?'

Xela's face twisted into something that might have been a smile, if he hadn't been so emaciated. 'I have been ill for an eightnight with nothing to do but think. I remembered you standing there in the gateway that morning, after I showed you the lock box on the weapons store the night before. The only way a man in Rodera's condition could have come into the kingdom was through the gate. It is the magistrate's job to work out the truth. I am surprised it took me so long.'

'Aren't you angry?'

Xela slowly shook his head. 'I would probably have done the same. You are my son, like it or not. We are made of the same stuff. I understand you better than you might expect.'

'But there's worse. At the end of the battle, when Riadsala rescued me and we closed the gate, he left me to lock it. I should have smashed the box, thrown away the pegs. Tik thought of that later when she shut the gate again, but I didn't. She took away one of the pegs so it couldn't be unlocked. If I'd done that, Nareb wouldn't have been able to let the invaders in, they wouldn't have won. Everyone died because of me.'

Xela reached a hand forward, then drew it back. 'You can't know that. There were thousands on the outside. They would have got over the wall in the end. They would have found a way to open the gate. And you were in no state to know what you were doing. You mustn't blame yourself.'

'I can't help it. It's all my fault.' Lebasi stared at his hands again.

'Look at me.' Lebasi raised his eyes. Xela leaned forward and tapped the table for emphasis. 'The mistakes you have made are honest ones. You thought they were the right thing at the time. You learn from them. A mistake is only wrong if you know it's a mistake and you do it anyway.'

'But I can't forget...'

'Of course you can't. And you shouldn't. I said, you learn from what you did.' Xela leaned back again. 'Believe me, I know what you feel. You probably don't realise how other people are. You and I, we remember everything, every little detail. It's useful, sometimes. It can be torture, sometimes. If you let it. Most people won't remember what they had for dinner last night.' He tapped his fingers together, narrowing his eyes. 'For instance, I'll bet you can tell me what we ate the night you let Perra out of the jail.'

'Chicken and rice,' Lebasi said without thinking. His mouth fell open. 'You know?'

Xela nodded. 'It's my job, remember. I think you were getting around to telling me. I've saved you the agony.'

'But how?'

'I told you, I've had a lot of time to think. Besides which, I have had a talk with Bennek, and another with Anibor, since I've been back. Bennek was a little more honest than before, when it no longer mattered. I worked out when Perra escaped – the third Mindsday before Midsummer – and where he must have gone, and Anibor confirmed that he had shown you the tunnels a few days before. And that Perra had been hiding ten paces from my garden, and he fooled Marrak that there was no one there. No one else but you could have warned Perra that Marrak was coming. By the time Anibor told me, it didn't seem likely that there'd be a waterworkers' guild for me to sack him from.'

Lebasi could think of nothing to say. He felt sick. It was worse than the dead feeling that charro left behind when it wore off.

Xela banged his fist against his palm, a reminder of his old self. 'You're not listening. I understand why you did what you did. What matters is what you do now. There is no mistake so bad that you can't redeem it, while you still have breath and strength. What did Xessus say to the soldiers who wanted to surrender?'

Lebasi nodded. 'A cradle holds no courage. We choose what lies in our graves.'

'Meaning?'

Lebasi pictured Ivar explaining the legend in school. 'Your

character is up to you. Nothing is fixed, while you are still alive to change it.'

'And in that particular story?'

'You will be remembered more for the last thing you do than for what went before. You can be brave all your life, but if you run away at the finish, then you die a coward. And you may start as a coward, but if you turn and fight in the end, you will be honoured as a hero.'

Xela smiled. 'You know your legends. So. I am still the Warden of the Westwall. I know a way to get rid of the invaders. I cannot do it myself, so I am going to send you.'

15
FAMILY IN FLIGHT

Tik watched Lebasi disappear into the shadows of the gateway. She waited a moment to see if he would wave, or come back out, or signal to her, but he was gone. She carried on staring after him, resisting an urge to follow. *Ridiculous.* He had been right to go without her. Annoying, but right. She told herself she didn't want to be closed in by buildings again. She was used to being alone in the woods. But those were her own woods, and these were not. The ground was flat, not sloping. The trunks were different, not the tall brown-barked beeches she was used to, but thinner and shorter with white flaky skin. Grass grew between them. There were no boulders, no fallen trees to provide cover. It wasn't a proper wood at all.

The horse had wandered out of sight. Tik was sure he would find them again when they were ready to leave. She caught a movement in the corner of her eye – a squirrel was nosing at her backpack. She chased it off, then crammed Lebasi's food in with her own and looked for a way to keep it safe. She settled on wrapping her blanket round the pack and hanging it from a broken branch – the squirrels would have to get through the blanket, and it was clear of any animal that kept to the ground. She balanced the hat on top of it – she wouldn't need it under the shade of the leaves.

There was a dry patch of ground to sit on with her back against the tree and the food just above her head. She settled down to wait for Lebasi to return.

She closed her eyes and pictured Preddo lying in the field. Lebasi had been so upset about him. She felt a prickling in her eyes. Feleda, Trefal, Marstor, Preddo – they were going to have to get used to bad things happening. Xela – she had been so busy, thinking about where they were going and what they were doing, that the fact that Lebasi might find his father dead had hardly crossed her mind. She bit her knuckle, and stared across towards the walls of the town, wishing she could see through them. Lebasi's body had taken a battering, but maybe it wasn't the only part of him that was suffering.

※ ※ ※ ※ ※

There was nothing to do but keep small animals away from the food. There was nothing to see apart from the empty fields and the roofs of the town shimmering in the sunlight. There was no sound beside the buzzing of insects and the call of birds – no, there was something. Tik stood up and turned to face in each direction, trying to pin it down. Voices, very faint. Getting louder. From the north – the way she and Lebasi had come. She pulled out the farsight and risked leaving the backpack, dodging from tree to tree to keep hidden.

From the shelter of the last tree, she realised that she didn't need the farsight, and she wouldn't need to hide. Only a hundred paces away, coming slowly towards her, an ox was pulling a cart. A tall, white-haired woman held the leading-rope, her back very straight in spite of her age; two younger men, two young women and a line of children walked behind, the tallest about the same height as Tik, the smallest maybe only four or five years old. Six healthy-looking sheep followed in a line. The cart was piled high, ropes criss-crossing the load to secure more baggage than it was designed to carry.

They're like us, Tik thought. A farming family, three generations. She searched for the grandfather, but couldn't see him. As they came closer, she started to be able to make out what they were saying. The children were complaining, loudly.

'When can we stop?'

'I'm hungry.'

'Why do we have to –'

One of the younger men shouted, 'Shut up, all of you! You're driving me crazy.' *Just like Nareb would.*

The older woman pointed ahead. 'They've a right to be tired, Nattras. We'll stop in the shade of these trees, have a bite to eat.'

Tik didn't want to talk to the strangers, but she was curious to watch them. She scanned the walls, the roofs and the gateway with the farsight. There was no sign of Lebasi – no sign of anything. She turned it to the road, and gasped – a face jumped right in front of her. She lowered the instrument, and realised that of course the child was still fifty paces away, unaware she was being watched. But it was a *girl*. She had never seen one before – Tassie was the youngest woman she had ever met.

They're not like us. She wondered if any other family had a secret history as terrible as hers, the determination of her great-great-grandfather and her great-grandfather to make sure that no girls grew up on the farm.

She stared at each of the children in turn. She had never seen people smaller than her, apart from Feleda's baby. All her boy cousins were older and bigger, and she had only met grown-ups in Marstor. She edged around the tree as they steered the cart off the track, trying to get a better view. The thin trunk wasn't wide enough to hide her properly, but they weren't paying attention. The ox lay down in the shade a little distance away, flicking its tail. The sheep settled down to graze. The children stretched out on the ground, men checked over the load, and the three women set to work by the cart, finding food and plates.

'Hey! Who's that?' One of the children jumped up and pointed at Tik. She didn't want them to chase her: there was nothing for it but to raise her hand in greeting and step out into the open. The young men grabbed tools from the cart – a spade and a pitchfork – while the women herded their children behind it.

She took another pace forward, letting them see that she wasn't a threat. She realised that each of them stared at her head before looking at her face. She had grown used to having so little hair – now she had a thin fuzz that felt funny when she ran her hand over it – but it must still look strange to these people.

She called out, 'Hello. I'm Tik. I didn't mean to startle you.'

The men didn't lower their makeshift weapons. They were moving slowly sideways, left and right, taking quick glances all around before fixing their eyes back on her.

One of the women stepped out from behind the cart and walked towards her. She was the same height, had the same brown hair and swollen belly as Feleda. For a moment Tik wondered if it could be her, but of course it wasn't. Even so, the image of the burning farm flashed in her mind. It made her gasp and put her hand over her eyes.

She heard the woman calling out to the others, 'It's just a child.' She felt the woman's hand on her arm. 'There now, don't be upset. We'll not hurt you. Are you all alone?'

Tik wiped her sleeve across her eyes and stood up straighter, angry with herself. She shook her head. 'No. I'm waiting for my cousin. Who are you, and where are you going?'

'Here, come and join us.' The woman pulled gently on her arm and Tik let herself be led. The young men circled, checking in all directions. The children sidled out from behind the cart, eyeing her curiously. Tik returned their gaze, taking in their round faces, plump arms and legs. She tried to disguise a grin. No wonder they were complaining. They didn't look used to walking long distances.

The woman was listing their names, but Tik paid no attention. She didn't expect to spend any more than this short time with them. Two of the children shuffled apart to leave a gap for her, and she sat between them.

'Where is this cousin? Boy or girl?' the pregnant woman wanted to know.

Tik pointed towards the walls, now in shadow as the sun had passed over the zenith. 'He's a boy. He went into the town for something.'

The white-haired woman asked, 'How old is he?'

'He's sixteen.'

She blew out her cheeks. 'And where are your parents, the both of you?'

Tik opened her mouth, then closed it again. It would take far too long to explain. She shrugged her shoulders. 'Gone. We're travelling south together.'

The grandmother leaned forward and smiled at her. 'Best you come along with us. We'll look after you.'

Tik shook her head. 'That's very kind. But we're fine. We –'

They started talking to each other as if she wasn't there, discussing whether 'this maybe cousin' would be coming back, whether it was safe going into the town, whether he was irresponsible for leaving Tik alone outside. Tik tried to make herself heard.

'I'm – we're – all right. We don't need any help. He'll be back later. There's no one in the town. But what happened to you? Why are you going south?'

The talking stopped. The smallest child rolled over and pressed her face against her folded arms. One of the men tapped his fist into his palm. The other stared at the floor.

Tik said, 'I can guess. You were visited by –'

The pregnant woman interrupted her. 'Hush now, there's no call to talk of it in front of the children.'

Tik shrugged. 'Why? They must know what happened.'

'We were told to go,' said the grandmother evenly. 'By huge

men on monstrous great beasts. They burned our neighbours' farm. Killed the family. No reason.' She stopped for a moment, sadly shaking her head. 'Told us we could live, but we must leave. Abandon the land our family has worked for generations.' One of the younger women was quietly weeping into her apron. 'We had no choice. They gave us a day to pack up.'

Tik nodded. 'They did the same thing to a whole town. I saw them. Where have you come from?'

The woman pointed to the north-east. 'That way. This is our third day on the road.' She leaned forward. 'A town? They drove out a whole town? And you were there?'

'Yes. Marstor. This is Trengam, and it looks empty too. My cousin's gone to check.' Tik worked out in her head: three days on the move, one day to pack up – they had been visited by the Thrarn the same day that Caldar had come to the farm, and set off on the day that Marstor had burned. The horsemen must have split up and travelled across the whole of the countryside.

'Why?' The question sprang into her mind and out through her mouth.

'What d'you mean, why?'

'Why are they burning some farms, killing some people, but driving other people out, letting them live?'

That started them all talking again. The younger children were crying, the mothers shushing them, the fathers arguing about whether they should have tried to resist. The grandmother held up her hands for quiet. 'Hush now. My sons, you know you could not have fought them. Maybe that is what our neighbours did, and at what cost. We have our lives, and we have what we can carry, and we have each other. Let that be blessing enough for the time being.' She turned to Tik. 'And how old are you, that speaks so easily of such horrors?'

'I'm twelve,' she replied.

She reached out to those sitting next to him. The children on either side of Tik held up their hands to her, and in a moment they were all joined in a chain. The old woman closed her eyes, and Tik saw that everyone else did the same. She kept hers open. Her family had never done this.

They were all silent for a moment. Tik was aware of the buzzing of insects, the breath of the breeze on her face, the sun hot on her nearly-bare scalp. A squeeze from the little fingers clasping hers. The old woman broke the silence, her head lifted. 'Let us all remember the story of Xessus and the apple tree. There will be a future. Right now we do not know where it will be, but our children and our children's children will see it.'

Tik watched as everyone nodded, murmuring words of agreement. Then they all opened their eyes. One of the young men smiled at her. 'Will you share our meal with us?'

Tik said that she had enough of her own, but they insisted. The women passed out food – bread, cheese, fruit, cured meat. She wondered if they had any idea of how far they would have to travel, and how hungry they might be before they could find new stores. She had already come further than most Xessans journeyed in a lifetime, and she wasn't any nearer Egator than when she started.

The children asked her about her home, and she noticed the women nodding approvingly as she described the farm and her family. Half of her wanted to tell them the truth – her bullying uncles, her insane ancestors who had decreed that there would be no girl children, the wickedness that had got rid of any that came along – but her anger was mixed with embarrassment. Her kin were something to be ashamed of, but they were hers. She was one of them. Telling these people would be like sneaking on one of her cousins to Gortan. That would have got them the punishment they deserved, but it wasn't the right thing to do. Besides, these people seemed so different. They would think she came from a family of monsters, and must be a monster herself.

After the children had stopped asking for more food, the women packed everything back onto the cart while the younger men roused the ox. When they had manoeuvred it between the cart's shafts and hitched it up, the old woman flicked its side with a stick and it started its slow progress south again. The sheep followed. The children walked with Tik, asking her more questions, while the grown-ups were whispering urgently among themselves. Tik stopped at the other end of the wood where the track they were on crossed the road to the town gate.

The old woman stopped too. She handed the stick to one of her sons, who kept the ox moving forward, and bent down to talk to Tik. 'Will you not come with us? I don't like to leave you here all alone.'

Tik pointed towards the town. 'I've told you, I'm not alone, and that's why I can't leave. My cousin will come back and he won't know where I've gone.' The woman paused, and in the quiet between them, Tik became aware of other noises.

The town was no longer silent. It was hard to say what the sounds were, or where exactly they came from, but she could hear what must be shouts in the distance, thumps and crashes carrying faintly on the air. She pulled out the farsight and put it to her eye, ignoring the old woman's questions.

Men. On the section of the downstreet that was lined up with the gate, she could see men. A group of them, walking uphill, going into one building after another. Tik groaned.

'What is it?'

'The invaders. They're here.'

The woman put her hand on Tik's shoulder. 'You'd best not

wait, then. Too dangerous. I can't leave you, a young child –'

She shrugged her off and stepped back. 'No,' she said. 'You've been very kind, but Lebasi will come back, and I need to be here when he does.'

The woman spread her hands as if giving up, then nodded over Tik's shoulder. She half turned, but one of the sons had already wrapped his arms around her. The old woman moved surprisingly quickly, slipping a length of rope over Tik's wrists as the young man held her, then grabbing her ankles as she tried to kick out and tying them together.

For a moment the shock took Tik's breath away. This had happened before. Verb and Tassie had tricked her in order to remove her from the Westwall Field before the battle began. But she had known and trusted them. What were these people going to do with her?

And what would happen when Lebasi came back and didn't find her? What about their packs, their food?

Tik struggled against the ropes as they laid her in the back of the cart, shouting at them to let her go. The children jabbered questions until the son yelled at them to be quiet.

She wasn't sure whether the old woman was talking to his grandchildren or to her. 'We can't leave a girl on her own waiting for someone who's probably already been taken by these brutes and won't be coming back.'

She stared up at the sky, blocking out the possibility that she could be right. She mustn't be right. Her mind filled with a single thought. Lebasi, where are you?

16
SURPRISE MEETING

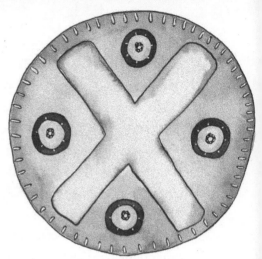

'You have to turn off the water,' Xela said. 'That will make them leave.'

'What?' Lebasi shook his head. 'What good will that do?'

'There's a dam in the far north-east of Xessus. It's where the water comes from to fill the channels and keep us all alive through the dry season. There's a man there, Dralor – you'll need my badge. It's in the drawer over there.'

Lebasi found the gold disc he had seen for the first time when Xela met Riadsala outside the walls of Nampetch after Perra's failed ambush. He turned it over in his hands, remembering. He reached into his pocket. 'Da, Alfas gave me –'

Xela showed no sign of noticing that Lebasi was speaking. 'You tell Dralor the keeper to free Artay, goddess of drought. That's the code. Show him my badge, give him that order from me. It should come from all the mayors of the district, but you can make him understand.'

Lebasi shook his head. 'The invaders aren't staying. They want Egator, not Xessus.'

Xela jabbed his finger at Lebasi. 'You said you want to put things right. This is what you need to do. Without water, they cannot stay.'

'You're not listening to me. They're going to leave anyway.'

'You cannot know that. They have driven us out of the towns. That shows they want to take our place. You must do as I say.'

'I have to go with Tik to warn the king. We have to get ahead of the enemy. I don't have time to go looking for this dam.'

Xela slapped his hand on the table. 'And I don't have time to waste arguing with you. I'm the magistrate. I know –'

Lebasi stood up. 'You don't know,' he shouted. Xela was still talking. He told himself his father was sick, he had taken charro, he wasn't thinking straight. But another voice said that this was how he always was, charro or not. He didn't listen. He always knew *everything*.

'If you don't do this, then you will be –'

Lebasi swept away his words with his arm. He raged at his father. 'All right, you know about Perra, you know about the gate, you know all the answers. But you know *nothing*. Let me tell you what you don't know. Who was your father? Gortan? Wrong. It was Mallam. He told Tik before he died.'

That, at least, silenced Xela. He sat with his mouth open, his eyes still staring with the whites showing.

'There's more. Shelba is alive in Egator. She was Riadsala's nurse, like a second mother to him. She refused to be married to anyone else. You've got a daughter, my sister, born just after she was taken there. They're in Egator, which is where the Thrarn are going, and turning off the water in Xessus won't do anything for them. They need Tik and me to warn the king about what's coming. To have any chance of surviving.'

Xela held up his hands as if he was warding off blows. His lips were moving, but Lebasi couldn't tell if he was saying anything. There was a roaring in his ears as if he had taken charro himself. He pointed at his own forehead. 'Have you even looked at me? Do you care? I've been branded with the star of Xessus, and I'm going to Egator, and the king might have me put to death, for the mark on my face if for nothing else, but it's what I have to do. Wasting time turning off the water would be another mistake, worse than any of the others. Coming here, that was a mistake. Tik said we should be going south. I've cost her a day at least, for nothing. I knew that was wrong, too.'

A muscle was twitching in Xela's cheek. That was usually a sign of his temper. What would the drug make him do? Lebasi grabbed his rucksack and ran, slamming the front door behind him. In the street he wiped away hot tears. He regretted what he had said, but it was all true. He didn't want Xela to open the door and call him back. He didn't want to know if Xela would try. He didn't want to find out that Xela didn't care enough to try. He ran to the alley uphill from the house to get out of sight, and scrambled over the wall into the garden, reckoning Xela would never look for him there. If his father did come to the door, Lebasi didn't hear him. The throbbing in his ears was too loud.

He sat with his back against the wall under the eating-room window where, an age ago, he had eavesdropped on Xela and Marrak arguing about sending for the Westwall Guard. He stared at the gold disc in his hand, his mind running in circles.

Xela was sick. If he went to Egator, he would probably never see him again. He couldn't leave without making his peace.

Tik was waiting. She was depending on him. They had to go to Egator. He couldn't delay.

He could hear movement inside. At least the charro had worked its magic: Xela was on his feet.

The charro – he felt a tightness grip his heart. He had left it behind on the table. He clenched his fists and closed his eyes. He had to go back for it.

No. He was better off without it. Xela needed it more than he did.

Yes. It was his. He had been generous to share it with his father.

That thought shocked him. Had he become like the exile soldiers, looking forward to a battle because fighting meant they would be given the drug?

He couldn't leave.

He couldn't go back.

He couldn't stay. He made the decision.

He crept away from the window, ran to the wall and climbed back into the alleyway. He could cut across to the south-eastern downstreet, without going past his front door again. Beyond the rowan tree, where the alley turned up the hill, he took a narrow passageway between walled gardens. He slipped the badge in his pocket as he jogged, feeling it click against the one that Alfas had given him. He had tried to give Xela the mayor's message and his badge, but he wouldn't listen.

Footsteps. The sound broke through his thoughts only at the last moment, as he realised someone was about to appear round the next bend. He glanced behind him. There was a doorway –

Oooof. Someone ran straight into him and knocked him backwards. He felt arms enfolding him as he was lifted off his feet. Gasping for breath, he turned his head.

'Ruffur?'

The big boy carried him through the doorway. Sammas followed, as Lebasi knew he would. They crossed an empty backyard and went into the storeroom of a house. Ruffur stepped to the side of the doorway and slammed him against the wall. Lebasi drew in breath to shout – who to? – but Ruffur clapped a meaty hand over his mouth.

'Shut up, you stupid menker. You'll get us killed,' he hissed.

Lebasi's brain started working again. The last time he had been held against a wall by Ruffur and Sammas, they had been angry. Now they looked different – scared. They weren't hurting him.

There were more footsteps. In the passageway. In the yard. Harsh voices.

Not speaking the king's language. Not speaking Xessan. Thrarn.

The noises grew suddenly louder. The men were right outside the doorway. Ruffur held his breath. The sound faded. They waited.

Lebasi opened his eyes wide, trying to signal to Ruffur that he was suffocating. Ruffur removed his hand and Lebasi filled his lungs with air.

'Sorry,' the big boy muttered.

'What are you doing here?' Lebasi whispered back.

Sammas put his finger to his lips and pointed towards the door on the far side of the room. Glancing behind them, they tiptoed to it and closed it behind them. There was a table with four chairs round it. Sammas flopped onto one and blew his cheeks out. 'You're welcome,' he said.

'For what?'

'Saving your skin.'

'All right. Thank you. But what *are* you doing here? I thought everyone had left.'

Sammas sniffed. 'Nearly everyone. Some big blaggers come and tell us to run away, and the whole town packs up and goes? Not us.'

'What about your parents? Do they know where you are?'

Ruffur's low voice sounded like a growl, but he didn't seem angry. 'My da said we should look for people who stayed. Make sure they were all right. Tell them to go.'

Sammas grunted. 'Well, we can't stay here on our own for

ever. But we're going when we're ready. When we choose, not when someone orders us to.'

'Who was chasing you?'

Ruffur turned as if to check that the door was still closed. 'First outsiders we've seen. We've been here three days, just us, no sign of strangers, just a few others who decided to stay. This morning we heard people in the street.'

Sammas interrupted. 'We spied on them. Some normal size, some huge. The normal ones with –' He stopped and stared at Lebasi, slowly raising a finger towards the mark on his forehead.

'I'll explain later,' said Lebasi quickly. 'What about the invaders?'

Sammas lowered his arm. He paused a moment, as if trying to recall what he had been talking about. 'We went to warn some of the people we knew had stayed. We came up to Nomara's –'

'You remember her, Basi, don't you?' Ruffur's voice lowered even further. He ground his teeth.

'Of course I do. She chased you two off.' Lebasi was about to remind them that they were picking on him for something that he hadn't done, but Ruffur surprised him by wiping his sleeve across his eyes and sniffing.

'She was all right, was Nomara. She came to see my ma and da, that evening. Sat and talked with them about how the young people today have no respect. I was in the next room, waiting for her to tell on me, and then I'd get the end of my da's belt, no question, but she never did. Finished by saying, "Your boy Ruffur, I'm sure he wouldn't do anything like that," and then she left.'

'Me too, the same evening,' said Sammas. 'She wanted to make a point, but she gave us a chance.'

Lebasi snorted. 'You didn't take it, though. You kept after me until Faya called you off.'

Sammas waved the objection away. 'That's not important.

They killed her.'

Lebasi put his hand over his mouth. 'Why?'

Sammas gave a rueful laugh. 'You know how she was. We got there a bit too late to warn her. Heard her shouting at them, telling them she wasn't scared, if it needed four of them to deal with an old woman they weren't much of an army. That sort of thing. Then she wasn't shouting. Didn't make a sound. We thought they must be taking her away, so we waited for them to go, but when we checked in her garden she was lying there.'

'You're sure she was –'

'Course we're sure,' Ruffur growled. 'We checked, like he said.' He sniffed and wiped his arm across his eyes. 'So then we decide to come and look for your da.'

Lebasi's mouth dropped open. 'My da? What for?'

Sammas said, 'Because he'd know what to do. We knew he stayed behind. The elders went with the first lot, then Marrak got together everyone else who was going. He said Xela was ill so he couldn't travel.'

Lebasi shook his head. 'But you –'

'Just 'coz we make a bit of trouble, doesn't mean we don't know Xela's a clever man,' Sammas said. 'And maybe he's recovered. We wanted to make sure before we leave.'

Lebasi shook his head. 'He's hasn't. I saw him. He's still too ill to go anywhere. I had to leave him.' He tried to keep his voice neutral. *I had to run out because he made me so angry.*

Ruffur nodded. 'Well, we're crossing the avenue back there and some of them come out of a house and we have to leg it, and then we bump into you.'

Sammas put a finger to his lips. They sat in silence, listening to voices outside. Sammas flicked his eyes towards the stairs in the corner. They crept across the room, barely breathing, and tiptoed to the upper floor. There were more voices now, and marching feet. He padded across to an open window to listen, taking care to keep his head down.

The feet stopped tramping. An order rang out – Lebasi could tell it was a Thrarn speaking Xessan: 'Split up. Check for any sign of occupation and bring out any food you find.'

Lebasi turned to find Ruffur and Sammas staring blankly at him. 'The big ones are sending the normal size soldiers into the houses. They're looking for food and people. This place looks empty. If we get out of sight and keep quiet we should be all right.'

Sammas glanced again at Lebasi's brand. 'You understand their language? When did that happen?'

'Long story,' he whispered. 'Later.'

There was a crashing sound below as someone kicked the front door open. Sammas pushed Ruffur towards a clothes-cupboard that was big enough for him to get inside. Lebasi lay on the floor between the bed and the window. He could see Sammas's feet moving across to stand behind the open door.

'Some food in the larder here, sarge.' someone called out.

'Bag it up.' The voice was close – on the landing. Lebasi saw boots stop in the doorway and turn towards him. They stepped into the room. Lebasi held his breath. He could hear something, a creaking noise, it must be Ruffur moving in the cupboard. The boots took a pace towards it –

'Sarge!' A shout from the street outside. The boots changed direction. Lebasi silently rolled under the bed as the man made for the window.

'What is it now?'

'We've found an old man in the house over here.'

'Why are you bothering me? You know what to do.' Lebasi bit his lip. What if they broke into his own house? What would they do with Xela? 'If he doesn't give you any grief, tell him to follow the rest of them south.' Lebasi tried not to let out the breath he had taken in.

There was another shout from downstairs. The sergeant muttered something about 'useless menkers', paused for just a moment by the cupboard as he crossed the room, then strode out of the door. The sound of his boots crashing down the stairs was followed by the slamming of a door. Lebasi listened for some time to the searchers working their way along the avenue outside. At last it was silent. Lebasi picked himself up and peeked out of the window. There was no one in sight.

He opened the cupboard. Ruffur seemed reluctant to come out until he saw Sammas walk across to sit on the bed.

Sammas's voice was loud in the silence. 'What are we going to do now?'

Lebasi stared at him. *We?*

17
PIGEON CALLS

To start with, Tik tried shouting. She didn't expect anyone to come to rescue her, but she might annoy them enough to let her go.

The one who had grabbed her leaned over the back of the wagon. He had a length of rope in his hand, and his expression reminded her of her uncle Nareb, but what he said could not have been more different. 'Look, I'm not going to hurt you. These are my kids, I'd never lay a finger on them, and no more I'd do anything to you. But if you don't shut up I'm going to have to gag you.' He looked over his shoulder towards the town. 'We don't want to draw attention to ourselves, do we? We don't know if this lot are letting people go.'

Tik stopped shouting. She used the rope between her wrists to hook onto the frame of the cart and pull herself up to a sitting position. The man wedged a blanket underneath her to make her more comfortable.

'That's the way,' he said. 'It's for the best. You'll see.'

Tik shook her head, scowling at him. 'You can't keep me tied up forever. Soon as you untie me, I'll go looking for my cousin.'

The man shrugged. 'Oh well, we'll just have to keep you tied up until you realise that's not going to help. See it our way, will you? What would you do if you found someone all on their own, surrounded by danger? It's the law of Xessus, we have to take you in.'

Tik protested that she wasn't on her own, but the man ignored her. She gazed back down the road at the wood in the distance where her backpack was still hanging from a branch. There was no sign of Lebasi in the open ground between the gate and the trees. At least the cart moved very slowly, but if the man did as he said, she might never find Lebasi again.

She closed her eyes and tried to think of a plan. The rope was tight round her wrists and ankles, and the knots were good ones. Her head felt hot in the sunshine. She wriggled her bottom to get more comfortable. Long days and short nights, hard journeys and trouble overcame her. She dozed.

One of the women screamed. Tik opened her eyes, expecting to see soldiers approaching. The men were swearing, the children jabbering. The cart came to a stop. She twisted round to see what was happening.

Nee hee hee hee

The horse trotted into her field of vision and looked down at her. He shook his head and made a blowing noise. She laughed out loud and held up her bound hands to greet him.

The younger men were edging forward on the left and the right, armed again with the pitchfork and the spade. 'Steady now,' one said to the other.

Tik shouted, 'Don't try to fight him. He's stronger than you are.'

They took no notice. The one with the pitchfork held it out in front of him. The end wobbled up and down unsteadily. *Brave,* thought Tik, *but not that brave.*

Tik grabbed the post on the corner of the cart and hauled herself upright. She jumped down onto the road, just managing not to fall, and hopped towards the horse. She turned round to face them, feeling his breath on the back of her neck.

She shook her bound hands at them. 'Don't you dare hurt him.'

Both men stepped back, their mouths open. The man who had spoken to her earlier beckoned to her with the spade, holding the other hand up as if to block out the horse from his sight. 'Come away, missee, quick. He's one of them monsters the invaders ride on.'

Tik grunted in frustration. 'I know what he is, and he's my friend. He won't hurt you if you don't try to attack him.' She hoped that was true.

The horse put his great head over her shoulder and rubbed his cheek on hers. It was all she could do not to fall over.

'See?' she said. 'He's gentle.'

The man on her left lowered his pitchfork. He stood up straighter and ran his hand through his hair. He didn't take his eyes off the horse, but he asked, 'What're we going to do, brother?'

The other one kept the spade raised in front of him. 'If it's not going to attack us, I guess we just keep going.'

Tik held her wrists out. 'Untie me. Let me go.'

Spade-man said, 'You know we can't do that. We can't leave you here.'

Tik hopped back so she was right next to the horse's shoulder. 'You'll have to,' she said. 'I'm not leaving him, and he won't let you take me. So you can leave me here tied up or not tied up.'

They gave in, as they had to, in the end. She made soothing noises to the horse, hoping he wouldn't tread on the man who needed all his courage to crawl forward and undo the knots. He still pleaded for her to give in and go with them, but the horse pawed the ground as if to show his disapproval, and she watched them put their tools back in the cart and carry on. She hugged the horse's head and stroked his cheek, then set off back up the road, rubbing life into her wrists.

By the time she found her backpack again – still safe from squirrels – the sun was setting behind the town. The buildings were shadowy now, and she could detect no movement anywhere. No one on the walls. No one signalling from a rooftop. No one at the gate.

Middle of the afternoon, he had said. If I don't come back, you'll have to get moving.

Tik lay on the grass under the trees, scanning the town with the farsight until the light was too poor to use it, scouring the view for any clue about where Lebasi might be. She was as sure as she could be that he hadn't crossed the open ground while she was making her way back to the wood. She wondered if he would have worked out what was happening without the farsight if he had come out of the gate while she was arguing with the farmers. He should have been able to see the horse at least, and he might have guessed that she was with him.

Come on, Lebasi. I can't do this without you.

A thin sliver of moon rose in the evening sky. It wouldn't give a great deal of light for travelling by night. Better to wait here, perhaps, whatever he said. Maybe the invaders would have moved away by the morning. She could keep off the roads and stay out of sight. If she had to do it alone.

Croo CROO croo, croo CROO croo

Tik sat up, grinning, and made the call back. She searched the open ground all the way to the walls – where was he?

Croo CROO croo, croo CROO croo

She groaned. She should have realised that it was too good. She was talking to a real pigeon.

The shadows deepened. The evening was cool under the trees. She wrapped herself in her blanket, but dared not go to sleep in case she missed Lebasi returning. She sat with her back against a trunk, trying to detect anyone coming through the gloom.

Croo croo

Tik snapped her eyes open. It was darker than a moment ago – she must have slept. Was that a pigeon, or did she dream it? She held herself very still, straining her ears. She thought she could hear footsteps out in the field, but she could make out no movement.

Croo croo

Her mouth spread into a smile. Surely that was Lebasi. She cupped her hands over her mouth and answered.

Voices. She became very still again. One voice could be Lebasi calling to her, but two? People whispering to each other? She had given away her position. She moved silently into a crouch, then stood up, listening. She was sure now that there were at least three people out there – people who didn't want to be heard. Would enemy soldiers be hiding in the dark? Only if they were trying to catch her, and they would only know she was there if Lebasi had told them. She was sure he wouldn't have done that. She edged backwards into the trees, feeling behind her with an outstretched hand.

'Tik!' Lebasi's voice, a hoarse croak from somewhere to her left.

'I'm here,' she whispered back. 'Is someone following you?'

'Ow!' A different voice, lower and louder.

'Quiet!' Lebasi again.

'A branch poked me –'

'Shhhh' came from two directions.

Tik crept towards the noises. In the dim moonlight, she made out three shapes that weren't trees.

'Basi, who's with you?'

One of the shapes moved towards her. 'I thought you might have gone,' he said, and wrapped his arms around her. 'You were supposed to go,' he whispered in her ear. 'But I'm glad you didn't.'

She hugged him back, still trying to make out any features in the other two shadowy figures.

'Hello,' the low voice rumbled.

'I'm Sammas, and this is Ruffur,' said the other voice.

Tik pulled away from Lebasi. 'Ruffur and Sammas? But –' She felt a finger pressed against her lips.

'I met them in the town,' Lebasi said. 'They saved me from running into some Thrarn.'

'But why are they here?'

Sammas's voice came from a little nearer. 'There's nothing for us in the town any more. We're coming with you.'

'But –'

Ruffur interrupted, 'Reckon you could use some help. More eyes to watch for trouble. One to stay awake while the others sleep. And we've got food, too.'

Tik wanted to object that they had plenty, and they could look after themselves, and they had travelled all the way from Marstor without needing extra eyes, but Lebasi touched her lips again. He whispered, 'I'll explain in the morning. It'll be all right.'

Sammas said, 'We should go south a bit before the moon sets. We'll have to stay on the road in this light, and then find some cover until daybreak. Then we can see what's what.'

More protests boiled up in Tik's chest. Who were these boys to decide what they would do? They were the ones who had given Lebasi so much trouble, she was sure of it. And now he was going to forget all that and travel with them? Without asking her? How did he know they wouldn't do something stupid or treacherous?

'Is the stuff I took out of my pack here, Tik?' Lebasi asked. 'I've got some more food as well. Ruffur's da's the butcher, and he left some dried meat behind. We've got enough to keep us going for an eightnight at least.'

It took a little time to even out their packs in the dark. Tik

handed things to Lebasi without speaking. He tried to put a hand on her shoulder, but she twitched it away.

'In the morning,' he muttered.

✢ ✢ ✢ ✢ ✢

Tik was woken by a shout of alarm. She rolled over out of her blanket and jumped up, remembering who she was with and where they were, in a clump of trees around a side-track they had found just before the moon set and it became too dark to do anything. It was morning, but not by much. To the west, the sky was still dark.

Who had shouted?

'What in the world is it?' Sammas's voice.

She followed the noise to the edge of the trees, where the two boys were crouching behind a fallen trunk, peering over.

Tik grinned. She stepped between them and used her hands on their shoulders to help her jump up onto the tree trunk, then skipped down the other side and ran out into the open field.

'Hello, you,' she said, reaching up to stroke the horse's nose.

Nee hee hee, he replied, nodding to her. He twitched his shoulder, flicked his tail, and went back to eating grass.

She walked briskly back, trying not to laugh out loud at the boys' goggling eyes. She nodded over her shoulder. 'He's coming south too. He keeps watch, sorts out trouble. Doesn't even need to bring any food.'

✳ ✳ ✳ ✳ ✳

When Sammas had recovered, he said that they ought to press on while the enemy army would probably not yet be on the move. 'They'll be having breakfast and all that. We can eat later. We should find somewhere high up where we can see anyone coming.'

Tik had to agree it was a good idea. She just wanted it to have come from herself or Lebasi. It was what they were going to do anyway. She didn't want Sammas to believe that he was giving them orders. Ruffur scrambled up a tree to check for danger ahead. Tik decided she didn't want them to know about the farsight, even if it could be useful. She would keep it out of sight.

In the night, they had walked in silence. Now Tik's curiosity overcame her anger. She let Ruffur and Sammas take the lead while she fell into step beside Lebasi and asked what had happened in the town. When he explained Xela's instructions to make for the dam in the north-east, she started to protest. Lebasi held his palms up.

'It's all right. I'm not going to do it.'

'You're not?' What did you say to him?'

Lebasi didn't respond straight away and didn't answer her question. 'I've been thinking about it ever since – that, and what he said about making mistakes. Wasting time turning off the water when we should be warning the king – that would be wrong. He couldn't see that and I couldn't make him understand. But I know it, so I won't do it.'

Tik nodded. She asked him to go on, waiting for an explanation for the presence of Lebasi's enemies. He told her how they had hidden from the invaders, then spent the afternoon dodging from street to street first to reach Ruffur's house to collect packs, clothes and food, and then to escape by the gate.

She asked, 'Do you trust them?'

Lebasi opened his mouth, then closed it again. 'No Xessan,' he muttered. 'No secrets. There've been too many secrets.'

Tik glared at him and mouthed the question again, but they were interrupted by Sammas asking, 'What was that she said?'

Lebasi answered, 'She was talking Dennara's language – what everyone spoke in Xessus before Riadsala's Mercy. People aren't supposed to remember it, but they still use it in the countryside.'

Sammas stopped walking and turned to stare at Lebasi. 'You knew what the soldiers were saying, when we were hiding in the house. How do you understand it?'

Lebasi nodded. 'My da taught me. When I was very young.'

Ruffur whistled. 'That's a surprise.'

Sammas hadn't been distracted. 'So what did she say?'

Tik didn't care whether he knew what she thought or not, but Lebasi just shrugged. 'It was nothing.' He pointed to a low stone shelter a little way uphill from the road. 'There's a good place for us to rest and eat. We can see the road ahead and behind, and we'll be well hidden. Come on.'

18
THE ROAD SOUTH

Too many secrets. The thought filled Lebasi's head as they walked. He couldn't bring himself to tell the others, even Tik, that he had left Xela in the middle of an argument. He didn't want to remember it. He had told Tik the important thing, that he wasn't going to follow his father's orders.

Tik's dislike of Ruffur and Sammas could be a problem. He couldn't ask her about it without them hearing, but he guessed they reminded her too much of her cousins, back on the farm. All he could do was to give her time. He grinned at the thought – the previous sixteen years hadn't been enough to make him like Ruffur and Sammas, but his opinion of them had gone up in the last day. He couldn't expect Tik to forget what he had told her about them so quickly.

There wasn't much sign of that happening. They chose to keep off the road in case the Thrarn cavalry appeared, so they marched on field-paths a hundred paces or so to the side of it. Where crops were growing they kept in single file, zig-zagging beside irrigation channels, but even crossing open pastures Tik wouldn't walk next to him. He asked her about her day waiting outside Trengam, but she shook her head and said that nothing much had happened. He guessed she was still resenting being left behind, and decided not to tell her that he was sure he had been right. If she had been with him, they would have been caught.

If she had been with him, she would have known about his argument with Xela.

Sammas and Ruffur filled the silence. They related what had happened in Trengam after Lebasi left – Perra winning over the crowd on the Space, or at least persuading them to settle down to the best ever Midsummer feast. They had celebrated the end of Riadsala's Mercy, the overthrow of Xela and Marrak, the imprisonment of all the informers and snatchers.

'The day after, there were a few sore heads,' Sammas said. 'Some from drinking, some from fighting. But Perra wanted to start running things his way. He called another big meeting where the men who'd been locked up overnight were brought out one by one and offered a deal. If they admitted what they'd done for Xela and promised to join the revolution, they'd be set free.'

Ruffur grunted. 'Some of them thought it was a trick, wouldn't say anything. Must've reckoned Perra would get them to tell everyone about all the bad stuff and then hand them over to the crowd.'

Lebasi asked, 'Was it a trick?'

Sammas laughed. 'No. We thought it might be, too, but Perra's not like that. The last thing he wanted was half the town in the jail and the other half having to guard them. Anyone who said the right thing was let go. People saw that Perra was telling the truth, and then nearly everyone joined in. After all, Marrak was locked away in your house, Xela was gone for good, and the elders were too frightened of what might happen to do anything at all.'

'That must have been Midsummer's Eve. I saw Perra three days later outside Nampetch. What happened in between?'

Sammas explained how Perra had set out his plan for dealing

with the Westwall Guard – to ambush them, as Xessus did in the legend. To start with the crowd had been full of objections, but Perra had talked them round. 'By the time he called for volunteers, it looked like the whole town put their hands up.'

Ruffur nodded. 'Including us. But he wouldn't take anyone younger than eighteen. Or older than thirty.'

Lebasi recalled the scene as Perra ordered his men to attack and the Guard had overpowered them in an instant. 'They never stood a chance,' he said. 'Farmers and tailors and shopkeepers against proper soldiers. And Riadsala knew what they were doing. It's not really a Xessus story, that one – it's something Dennara did when we rebelled against the king before. Riadsala saw Perra standing by a bridge, and he guessed there would be men hiding in trenches by the side of the road.'

'Riadsala?' asked Sammas, and Lebasi had to explain that the captain of the Guard was the king's son, sharing his name with the prince who had put down Dennara's uprising.

'That all happened on Firesday after Midsummer. That night my da set off back from Nampetch. What happened then?'

Sammas laughed bitterly. 'I suppose Perra took all the fighting spirit with him. He walked out of town with his make-believe soldiers on Sunday. Two days later Xela comes back, says it's over. Tells people not to come near him because he might be ill, but no one's going to touch Xela anyway. By the time he gets to your house the people keeping Marrak locked up have quietly disappeared. So things went back to normal.'

'Normal? Didn't Xela punish people?'

Ruffur shook his head. 'We didn't see Xela. Marrak was in charge, with the elders. But he went round telling people to go back to work as if nothing had happened. There were a few fights, people settling arguments that started in the revolution, but by the time those horsemen turned up an eightnight ago, it was all quiet.'

Lebasi turned it over in his head. A hundred and forty years ago, the old king Rednaxela had ordered his son Riadsala to burn Xessus to the ground in punishment for Dennara's rebellion. Riadsala had dared to disobey him, and had established the Mercy to control the Xessans. Marrak must know that the rebellion would end the Mercy. Xela had feared that mere signs of trouble could bring the Westwall Guard into the province to carry out the ancient threat. Maybe Marrak was waiting to see if the new Prince Riadsala would return from the Westwall. Maybe he was waiting to see if Xela would get better.

'So Marrak told everyone to leave?'

Sammas nodded. 'Didn't have to try too hard, after people had seen the riders. Or the bodies they left behind. Easier for Marrak to persuade people to run than it was for Perra to get them to fight, and that's the truth.'

Lebasi hardly heard what he was saying. He was thinking about Marstor: Rednaxela's order had been carried out. A Xessan town had been burned to the ground, destroyed completely – by the Xessans themselves, not because the Mercy had been broken, but with the same result.

He finally saw the chance to ask the question that had been nagging at him for days, more so since he had been in the empty streets of Trengam. 'What was Faya doing all this time? Did she leave with the rest?' He tried to sound as if the answer was unimportant.

Sammas chuckled. 'Wondered when you'd get round to her.' Lebasi knew he was blushing.

Ruffur didn't seem to notice. 'Yup, Faya and her family went the first day.'

'She asked me to give her love to you if you came back,' Sammas added.

'Really?'

Sammas rolled his eyes. 'No. Idiot!'

Lebasi strode ahead and tried to ignore Sammas's laughter. He'd walked into that one.

Lebasi dumped an armful of sticks on the ground beside the fireplace that Sammas was building out of stones. Ruffur appeared from between the trees, his arms cradling a heap of mushrooms.

Tik eyed them suspiciously. 'Are you sure they're safe to eat?'

Ruffur knelt down and laid them carefully on a flat stone. He picked them over with his pudgy fingers, leaning in close in the twilight. 'Reckon so,' he said. 'I'll eat 'em if you won't.' He opened his pack and started rummaging inside. 'Got to make the most of what we can find, so what we've brought will last longer.'

Lebasi was surprised at how quickly Sammas built and lit a fire, and how little smoke it made. Ruffur produced a pan from his pack and started frying the mushrooms. Sammas glanced up at Lebasi. 'What are you staring at?'

'Nothing. Just thinking you're good at this.'

Ruffur chuckled. 'We don't all have someone to do it for us.'

Lebasi was about to protest, but he realised it was true. Marrak had always done all the cooking. He had learned some things in class – he reckoned he could light a fire without flint and tinder, if he had long enough – but he wouldn't be able to make a meal in the open air that smelled as tasty.

Sammas stood up and thrust a water-skin into his hands. 'If you're looking for something to do, how about filling this?'

Tik picked up another skin and followed him to the edge of the trees. 'We'd better be quick,' he said, as they scanned in all directions

for signs of danger. 'It'll be dark soon, and there's hardly any moon.' They hurried across the field until they came to a water channel.

As they crouched down to fill the skins, Tik asked, 'Is it all right to drink?'

Lebasi shrugged. 'It'll have to be. It's flowing, at any rate. It's when the water's standing still that it goes bad.'

Tik stood up and banged the stopper into place. 'How is it still flowing, though? There can't be any waterworkers any more.'

Lebasi recalled Anibor's lectures. 'There are some pumps that are worked by the wind. I suppose they'll break down in the end if there's no one to repair them. But while the water comes out of the dam, it's going to carry on running in the channels.'

'Have you changed your mind about turning it off?'

'No. I don't think the Thrarn want to stay in Xessus anyway. If I go and tell the man to stop the water, it won't make any difference. Except maybe to a few people who've hidden out.'

Halfway back to the trees, Tik whispered again, 'Do you trust them?'

This time, Lebasi decided she deserved an answer. 'Yes.' he said, without hesitating. 'Things change. When it was me and my da and Riadsala's Mercy, they were on the other side. But now the invaders are here, we're on the same side.' He pushed the first branches apart and tried to spot where the fire was in the deeper darkness. 'Even if they're still annoying. Anyway, it's like drinking the water. What choice do we have?'

✷ ✷ ✷ ✷ ✷

Sammas snapped a stick in half and poked the pieces into the flames. 'Best keep it low,' he said. 'I built the stones up round it so it shouldn't show. But a little light goes a long way on a dark night.'

Tik murmured, 'My grandda always says that.'

Ruffur asked, 'In Marstor, same as our town?'

Tik shook her head. 'Marstor land, not the town. I come from a farm.'

Lebasi said, 'Maybe there are sayings that everyone in Xessus uses, that go back before the Mercy. What else does your family say, Tik?'

Tik thought for a moment. 'If life was sweet as an apple, you'd still be grumbling about the pips.'

Lebasi laughed. 'My da says that.' The thought of his da caught him unawares, and he was glad of the darkness. He kept talking and hoped they wouldn't notice. 'What about "If only is a waste of breath"?'

'Waste of air,' said Tik.

'Waste of time,' said Ruffur. 'Same idea.'

'Tell us a story, Basi,' said Sammas.

'What?'

'Come on, you know them all from class. You're better at it than me and Ruffie. You're probably better at it than Ivar. Something to listen to while the fire burns down. Then we can take turns watching.'

Lebasi was surprised and flattered. 'Which story do you want?'

Ruffur suggested, 'Shasho and Artay – that's a good one.'

Lebasi gulped. This time he couldn't hide his reaction. He could almost see the scene the last time he had told that story, sitting in the chair in Barten's farmyard, with Dewen and Folla and Preddo crouching in front of him, hanging on his words. The last time he saw Preddo alive.

'Sorry,' he croaked. 'Not that one. Anything else.'

He could just make out Ruffur's shoulders shrugging in the glow of the embers. 'All right. How about the one about the pigs and sheep?'

Lebasi nodded. 'In a year without a number,' he began,

organising the words to follow, the tale of Xessus the hero cornered inside a farm, making his escape by driving the livestock out –

He stopped and drew in a sharp breath. Ruffur asked, 'Not that one either? What's up?'

Lebasi clapped his hands together. 'Ruffur, you're a genius. That's it, exactly.'

'Now you're being sarky. I only asked –'

'No, I mean it. It's what the Thrarn are doing. Xessus escapes by stampeding the farm animals towards the farmers, and they're so busy trying to catch their livestock that they don't notice Xessus getting away.'

Ruffur's grunt showed that he didn't see how this had anything to do with the Thrarn, but Sammas and Tik both exclaimed.

'Yes!'

Sammas turned to his friend. 'Don't you see, Ruffie, they're driving all the people south in front of them. The rest of the Westwall Guard are in their fortress at Enola, getting ready for an army to attack them, and the first thing to appear is thousands of ordinary people with all the possessions they can carry, frightened half to death.'

'And maybe they open the gates and let them in,' added Tik, 'and the enemy arrive before they can shut them again.'

'Or the soldiers are just so busy dealing with the old and the sick and the hungry that they aren't ready to defend their walls,' said Lebasi.

Ruffur growled, 'And I worked that out all by myself? You're welcome.'

Sammas broke the silence. 'Now we know that, what do we do?'

※ ※ ※ ※ ※

Lebasi was woken by a hand on his shoulder. He opened his eyes to find Tik kneeling beside him in the dim light before dawn, her finger to her lips. She leaned down to whisper in his ear. 'You were supposed to be on watch.'

He glanced round to check that the other boys were still asleep, muttering, 'Sorry' under his breath.

'It doesn't matter. I won't tell.'

He nodded. They quietly arranged sticks in a pyramid before waking Ruffur and Sammas by striking sparks into the dry grass at the base of the fire.

'All peaceful?' asked Sammas, standing up and stretching. Lebasi nodded. Ruffur went to collect water while Tik searched the floor of the wood for anything edible.

'I've been thinking,' Sammas started, as they rolled up their blankets and tied them to their packs. 'If we can get to Enola before the Thrarn, we can tell the Guard what's going on.'

Tik snorted. 'We don't even know where Enola is.'

Sammas scowled at her. Lebasi quickly said, 'I think Enola is on the only road south. If we find the road, we'll find Enola. But we don't know what or who is in the way, or how far it is.'

The low sun picked out the tops of buildings poking above the morning mist ahead of them. They agreed that it would be foolish to walk into a town when they couldn't see if it was occupied by the enemy, so they made for the ridge that bounded the valley on the west. They hurried across open pastures towards a thin strip of woodland that had been left uncleared along the crest of the hill. It was a relief to reach the trees and rest without fear of being spotted. The mist slowly dissolved, revealing an empty landscape. Lebasi shaded his eyes and studied the town, now below and behind them, but he saw nothing moving.

They found an old road that followed the ridge, sheltered from the sun above and from watchers below. It was overgrown in places and didn't seem to be in regular use, but Lebasi could tell from the way the surface was sunken between banks that it had in the past been a main highway for wagons as well as walkers. After a while, they came to some ruined walls that might have been a fortification. He wondered if there was a time when safe travel demanded being up high with a view of anyone approaching.

While they kept to the track they might have been in the middle of a large wood on flat ground, but a few paces to either side brought them to the edge of the trees and opened up a view of pastures sweeping down into broad valleys. In the distance ahead they could see a blue haze that might be the sea. On their left lay the road from Trengam that they had used as a guide for most of the previous day. Up here they were able to move faster without having to worry about where the nearest cover might be, or twist and turn among the irrigation channels, or wonder if anyone was watching them from the farms and villages they passed. Hidden in the trees, they were the watchers, and they could see no one at all in the whole of the landscape.

During one halt to check the view and the position of the sun – nearing the high-point, almost midday – Lebasi strained his eyes against the shimmering heat-haze and tried to guess how far away the sea lay. Something in the distance flashed, sunlight reflected on metal.

He kept his eyes on the spot and reached out a hand. 'Tik, can you lend me the farsight?'

He heard her angry grunt and could almost feel the glare she must be giving him.

'What's a farsight?' asked Sammas.

Lebasi turned to meet Tik's furious eyes, holding up his palms. 'It's something Riadsala gave to Tik to show to the king as proof that she's bringing a message from his son. It's what makes Tik the most important person in Xessus right now, the one person the king is likely to listen to. But it's also very useful for finding out what's happening a long way away.' He held out his hand again. 'Please, Tik.'

She muttered something in Xessan and took her pack off. As Lebasi suspected, she had the farsight tied round her waist under her tunic. She stepped behind a tree and came back with the instrument's leather pouch in her hand. Ruffur and Sammas stared as Lebasi took out the metal tube, twisted and pulled it to its full length, and put it to his eye. He raised the farsight towards the coast, then handed it to Tik. She used it, made to put it away, then offered it to Sammas.

'Here – you look through the narrow end and you point it where you want to see. But don't drop it. It's a surprise, the first time.'

Sammas accepted it as if it was made of eggshells and put it to his eye. A smile slowly spread across his face. 'Wow. That's – oh.' He lowered it again and turned to Tik and Lebasi. 'Soldiers on the road. A lot of them.'

Ruffur coughed. Tik nodded, and Sammas gave him the instrument. He too grinned as he looked through it, then grew serious as he swept it from left to right. 'They're going south, same as us. The ones at the front are way ahead. So much for getting to Enola before them.'

Lebasi beckoned them through to the other side of the ridge. He took the farsight and trained it on the road from Trengam. He handed it to Tik, who passed it on to the boys in turn.

Sammas sat down on a fallen tree-trunk and shook his head. 'More of them coming up behind us, left and right. What are we going to do?'

Lebasi tapped his fingertips together. He realised it was what his father did when he was trying to make a decision. 'I tell you what we're not going to do. We're not going to give up hope. We know they're there and they don't know we're here. We'll keep under cover and keep going south, and we'll see how the land lies. We can move fast, we're well hidden. If the fly stays out of the web, the spider goes hungry.'

Ruffur laughed. 'My da always says that. But he's usually talking about steering clear of Xela.'

Lebasi nodded. 'I suppose my da was a bit like a spider sitting in the middle of a web, what with all his reporters and snatchers. I never knew, because no one ever told me – not him, not any of you.'

Sammas put a hand on his shoulder. 'It's all right. You're not him. And Ruffur's da probably deserved a bit of trouble from yours, anyway.'

�֍ ✾ ✾ ✾ ✾

The ridge and the trees ended at the same point. Lebasi and the others crouched down behind a rock to survey what lay ahead of them. The track carried on down a steep grassy slope and joined the coast road, where a column of soldiers stretched unbroken in either direction. Not much further on, there was a town – unmistakeably a town, but nothing like the ones they knew, Trengam and Marstor and Nampetch. It wasn't built on a hill, and it didn't have a wall round the outside, and it extended for thousands of paces to the east of them, buildings of stone and wood jumbled together without the orderly criss-crossing streets and avenues of their home.

'It must be Awato, where the governor lives,' said Lebasi.

Tik lowered the farsight and shook her head. 'It looks empty, like Trengam. I can't see anyone at all.'

Sammas borrowed the farsight to study the soldiers on the road. 'They're not going into the town. They're carrying on past it.' He swung the instrument towards the coast, then handed it back to

Tik and pointed. 'Do you see there, where the buildings run down to the sea? I suppose that's where ships come in, although there aren't any now. If all the soldiers keep going and none of them stop here, maybe we can find a way along beside the water. The main road to Enola must be over there to the east where they're all marching, but perhaps the four of us can sneak round the side without anyone noticing.'

Lebasi tensed for a moment at the sound of approaching footsteps, then relaxed. 'Five of us. Look who's back.'

Nee hee hee, added the horse, trotting out of the trees behind them.

19
THE SEASHORE

Birdsong woke Tik the next morning. She sat up, still wrapped in her blanket, and took a moment to remember where she was. Then she remembered something else – she had been allocated the last watch of the night. She jumped up, cursing Ruffur for having fallen asleep. But she found him sitting against a tree, wide awake, shielding his eyes against the low light of the rising sun.

He stood up, stretched his hand above his head and muttered 'Morning' in his deep voice.

Tik glared at him. 'Why didn't you wake me?'

Ruffur shrugged. 'Wasn't sure when was the right time. All looks the same in the dark. Anyway, I didn't feel sleepy and I thought –'

'You thought I was just a girl and you'd do it better?'

Ruffur's mouth opened and closed. He shook his head. 'No. Nothing like that. I just –'

Tik turned away, not wanting to hear his explanation. She had been doing fine with Lebasi – and the horse – and these boys were going to make everything go wrong, she was sure of it. Everyone they had met had made things worse. The family outside Trengam had seemed kind, then they had tied her up. She had thought Alfas was a gentle old man, but he was crazy. Even Feleda – she had refused to leave her farm when it was the only sensible thing to do. Ruffur and Sammas were strangers to her, she didn't trust them. Hadn't Lebasi told her that they were his enemies? They were pretending to be friendly, but people didn't change. For some reason Lebasi couldn't see it, or didn't want to see it. Maybe he was still frightened of them. She wondered how she could get him on his own to persuade him that they should somehow get rid of the others and carry on as they had done before.

Breakfast took the last of the water they had been carrying. On top of the ridge there were no water-channels, so they hadn't been able to fill the skins since yesterday morning. Tik scanned the hillside below them with the farsight. Now they had seen it, she might as well use it.

'There,' she said, pointing to a jumble of rocks and lush ferns a few hundred paces down the right-hand slope. 'Those plants won't grow without water. There must be a spring.'

Sammas said, 'As soon as we leave the trees we can be seen. Specially if that horse follows us.'

Tik had been thinking the same, but she snapped at him, 'We have to have water. And we can't hide up here forever. We've got to get moving.'

Lebasi stepped between them. He said, 'It looks like the coast road is clear this morning. Let's keep the farsight out, take it in turns to watch, get ready to take cover.' He grinned at Tik. 'If their soldiers are anything like the Westwall Guard, if they spot us they won't tell anyone. They won't want to have to run up this hill to try to catch us.'

Tik wasn't amused. 'They're not like the Westwall Guard,' she hissed. 'Verb, Narus, Tassie. They were our friends.'

Lebasi's face fell. He picked up his pack without saying anything and started down the hill. Ruffur and Sammas stared at Tik.

'What?' she barked.

'We need to hear what happened,' Sammas said. 'The Westwall Guard were your friends? We've grown up hating the soldiers.'

Tik picked up her pack. She realised that she and Lebasi had talked about what happened in Trengam, and Ruffur and Sammas had told their story, but they hadn't explained anything about what had happened at the Westwall. A whisper in her head told her he was right, they ought to know. She shrugged it away.

'Later,' she said, and jogged after Lebasi.

✻ ✻ ✻ ✻ ✻

As they descended the hill, their view narrowed. The blue of the sea was blotted out by a wall of sand that extended as far as they could see to the north-west, a manheight or two tall. The land on either side of the road was completely flat, dry dirt scattered with low scrubby bushes and weeds. The salt smell and the cries of seagulls reminded Tik of her home.

She stood in the middle of the road and searched for signs of movement in each direction. 'Nothing,' she said at last. 'I think all the invaders have gone east.'

'Let's get out of sight in case anyone comes by,' Lebasi said. He set off towards the nearest buildings, a few hundred paces along a rough path to the south.

The edges of the town consisted of ramshackle huts made of wood and earth. A little further on, the dirt track became a paved road. The sound of the horse's metal shoes click-clacking on the hard surface seemed so loud in the silence of the empty town that it must attract attention, but there was no sign of anyone near enough to hear.

The road curved, and suddenly the buildings on their right stopped to be replaced by water – not the open sea, but a broad area without a ripple closed in on each side by long breakwaters built out from the land. There were wooden towers at intervals along the edge with arms reaching out over the water and ropes hanging down. The harbour was empty – not even a small boat remained.

As they walked on along the quayside, Sammas pointed at the machinery. 'This must be what they use for loading up the ships with all the things we send to the king.'

Ruffur grunted, 'He's going to have to do without it, unless he comes and pushes these Thrarn back into the wilderness.'

Tik shook her head. 'The Thrarn are coming to him. We've got to get there first.'

Sammas stopped. 'You've said that a few times. You've got that farsight to show the king that you've got an important message. But what is it? I think it's time you told us.'

'You're right,' said Lebasi. 'We can tell you everything that happened as we go along. But the big thing is that the Thrarn have terrible weapons that we don't have in the kingdom. So the king's army has to think of a way of defending itself. If they don't know what they're facing, they won't stand a chance.'

'What weapons?' asked Ruffur.

'Poisonous smoke, that kills you if you breathe it. They throw it in canisters among the other side's soldiers. And a machine that makes fire and shoots it out – they call that a dragon. Black powder that explodes – burns up in a flash with a big bang and blows things apart like a lightning strike.'

'And charro,' said Tik.

'What's that?' asked Sammas.

Lebasi ran his hand over his face. Tik saw for a moment the look in his eyes that she remembered from Rodera. 'It's a medicine they give to the ordinary soldiers to make them fight,' he said. 'Very powerful. Makes you think you can do anything – one of the exiles said it makes you strong, though you have no food, and brave, though you have no courage. I've had it three times now, and I'd say that's about right. But it makes you crazy, too.'

Tik took off her hat and fanned her face with it. 'There's

another part of the message. Riadsala was the king's youngest son. He was the captain who led the Guard at the Westwall. He said he thought one of his two older brothers must be plotting with the Thrarn against their father.'

Sammas whistled. 'That's quite a message to have to tell the king. How are you going to break it to him?'

Tik shook her head. 'We have to get there first. I'll think of what to say just as soon as we can see Egator.'

They passed the shoreward end of the second breakwater. Ahead on their right lay open water, stretching out to the horizon. Gentle waves lapped the sandy beach a few paces away. Tik had visited the seashore near her home, but she didn't enjoy it. Some of her cousins swam, but she didn't like the water. The emptiness of it unsettled her.

'Big, isn't it?' said Ruffur. 'D'you think there's another side, or does it go to the edge of the world?'

'Somewhere out there is where the Thrarn come from,' Lebasi said. 'One of the scientists from Egator sailed out there to see what he could find, and what he found was the Thrarn. I don't know if they captured him or he was happy to work for them, but their general told me that they've been using his knowledge to make their weapons ever since. That was a hundred and forty years ago. Meanwhile the old Riadsala, who put Xessus under the Mercy, told the clever people in the kingdom that they mustn't study anything that could be used for war. And they've stuck to farming and medicine and things like that ever since.'

Sammas murmured, 'That's a big head start.'

Ruffur swung his pack off and untied his water-skin. 'Time to fill up, anyway,' he said, walking towards the water.

'Stop!' Tik called. 'You can't drink the sea.'

'Is that a saying on your farm?' asked Lebasi.

'No. It's just the truth. Sea water's salty. You'll get sick if you try drinking it. It doesn't quench your thirst at all.'

Ruffur put the skin back in his pack. He rubbed his hand through his hair and spoke without meeting Tik's eyes. 'Look, I believe you. But I've never seen the sea before, and I might never see it again, so I just want to try it, all right?'

Tik rolled her eyes. 'If you have to. But be quick.'

Ruffur knelt down to scoop a handful of seawater to his mouth. He spat it out straightaway. 'Yuk! Salty.' He wiped his hands on his shirt as he climbed back up to join them.

'Told you,' said Tik, shaking her head.

'It is a saying, though,' said Sammas.

'What is?' asked Tik.

'You can't drink the sea, it's too big –'

Lebasi joined in, 'You can't eat the ground, it's too hard.'

Ruffur, who was rinsing his mouth with some fresh water from his skin, added, 'But if you stand up tall, you can breathe the sky.'

Tik shook her head. 'I've never heard that one. It must be a town thing.'

'I think it's just about hoping for the best,' said Lebasi.

The buildings on their left came to an end, and a view opened up along the southern edge of the city, where it hugged the rim of a steep-sided valley. Straight ahead was a strip of land fifty paces wide, with the sea on the right and a steep, smooth, grassy slope down to the valley on the left.

Tik walked slowly to the edge of the slope, taking out the

farsight. 'This doesn't make sense,' she muttered.

'Why not?' Ruffur asked.

She put the instrument to her eye and scanned the view. 'Because the land over here is a whole lot lower than the sea. I didn't think that was possible.'

She ignored the voices of the others behind her as she tried to understand what she was seeing. The bottom of the valley was a patchwork of fields and irrigation channels stretching from one steep side to the other and far into the distance. Everywhere was covered in the bright green and yellow of growing crops, rows of leafy fruit trees, or brown ploughed earth. Right below her there was a small lake, spreading along the foot of the sea wall. She searched for its source and found a river on the far side – or was it another man-made ditch? It seemed to have very straight sides, raised up above the flat floor of the valley.

'This must be Awato's home fields,' said Sammas.

'Bit bigger than ours,' grunted Ruffur. 'They must grow more food here than they can possibly eat.'

'I suppose they send the rest to the king,' said Sammas.

Tik murmured, 'But how is it dry? The river ought to run out into the sea, and if it did, this would all be full of water.'

Lebasi snapped his fingers. 'This must be where Xessus built his wall to imprison Shasho and Artay. What we're standing on keeps out Shasho– the sea – and there's enough water down there so there's never a drought.'

'Shasho doesn't come from the sea. Shasho comes from the mountains,' Ruffur objected.

Tik asked, 'What do you mean?'

She was surprised to see Ruffur blush. 'Just what my grandma says. Or used to say, to scare me if I was naughty. "Watch out for Shasho, boy, she comes unstoppable from the mountains, fire in her eyes. If you see the lights in the north-east, you know she's a-coming. Make for higher ground." She'd make claws of her hands and chase me like a monster. When I was smaller than her.' He shrugged. 'Maybe she was wrong. But I don't think Shasho is the sea.'

Sammas nodded. 'My grandma said the same.'

Lebasi laughed. 'You're cousins. His grandma is your grandma.'

'All right. But she also said Artay comes on the dry south wind after midsummer, burning the crops. And the story is about a wall in the mountains that imprisons Shasho and Artay behind it. Not a wall by the sea.'

Tik was staring into the distance. She lowered the farsight and pointed. 'People. Lots of them. What are they doing?'

Lebasi stood beside her, shading his eyes. She handed him the farsight. 'On the south side of the valley, near the river, or the big water channel, whatever it is. See?'

Lebasi nodded without lowering the instrument. 'I think there are people working in the fields. I can see wagons – they're harvesting. Don't they know there's an army coming?'

He handed the farsight to Sammas, who scanned the northern rim of the valley. 'They must know,' he said, 'because there they are, beyond the end of the city. I can see horses. I can see smoke, but they're not burning houses, those are cooking fires.'

Tik started walking. 'We can't work it out from here. Let's keep going.'

✳ ✳ ✳ ✳ ✳

Halfway across the sea wall, the track they were following was raised up as it passed by some machinery on the valley side. Lebasi ran across to take a closer look. Out of breath, he reported back. 'Pumps. They look like the ones that bring the water up to the cistern at the top of Trengam. I worked on them when I was apprenticed to the waterworkers. Back home, it takes four oxen to turn the machines, and people to keep everything running. I guess if the Thrarn have driven the waterworkers away, this valley will slowly fill up with water from that river.'

Tik was taking a closer look at the water channel below them. 'Very, very slowly,' she said. 'There's hardly any water in it.' She put the farsight away. 'I suppose it all spreads out into the fields and gets used up growing things.'

Ruffur muttered, 'I think someone's coming.' He pointed back along the sea wall. They all followed his arm, even the horse, and saw six or seven figures marching along the valley rim near the last of the buildings.

'Come on,' said Tik. They hurried south, glancing over their shoulders, confirming that the men were following. A sick feeling grew in the bottom of her stomach. She searched the view ahead for a way out, but she couldn't see one. The sea wall, the beach and the valley all ended in a line of sheer cliffs blocking their path. They came closer and closer, hoping to see the line of a track, but there was none. There were no cracks or gullies that hinted at a way to climb, and the waves washed right up to the foot of the rocks. The slope of the wall down into the valley was steep and covered in low, prickly bushes. They came to a halt fifty paces from the rocks and turned to wait.

'Tik,' said Lebasi, 'maybe it's time to put Aynar's ointment on your face.'

THE VALLEY

← pump

20
CAUGHT

Tik took off her hat and backpack and rummaged for the little glass bottle.

Lebasi whispered, 'Make sure you don't get any on your clothes. That would give it away as a trick.' She grunted something in reply and leaned forward to tip the liquid on her head.

'What's she doing?' asked Sammas.

Lebasi ignored him and turned his attention to the approaching men. They weren't hurrying, but they were marching steadily. *Unstoppable*, he thought, *like Shasho*. He had grown used to the feeling of the burnt skin on his forehead, but now he was acutely aware of it again. If they guessed who he actually was, they would surely kill him: the spy, branded by El-Kazzak before the attack on the wall. He didn't think anyone but Tik knew that he had also released the crossbow bolt that had struck down the Thrarn general after the battle. But if they didn't know who he was, they would kill him for who he appeared to be – a deserter. What happened to Caldar had proved that. At least they were exiles, not Thrarn – the seven men who rounded the pumping machinery and kept coming were a normal size.

The horse stepped forward beside Lebasi, also staring at the approaching soldiers. An idea started to form in his head.

'What do you think of this?' asked Tik.

They all turned to look at her. An irregular purple mark ran down her right cheek and onto her neck. Lebasi knew several people in Trengam who had been born like that. He also knew that there was nothing wrong with them – it was just a mark on the skin. But it was now the most striking thing about Tik's appearance. He hoped the soldiers wouldn't look any closer.

'What've you done that for?' asked Sammas.

Lebasi lowered his voice. 'Listen, all of you. You're going to have to trust me. Let me do the talking. Ruffur, Sammas, you won't understand – they'll only speak Xessan. Tik can explain later.' He paused, glancing over his shoulder. They were almost within shouting distance. 'I hope.'

Tik grabbed his arm. 'What are you going to do?'

'No time to explain. You'll hear what I tell them.' He jabbed a finger at the other boys. 'You stick together, all right? Look after each other. Look after Tik. And remember she's not a girl any more.'

'Come here!' The soldiers had stopped a hundred paces away. The one in front shouted the order.

Lebasi started walking and the others followed. He kept his eyes forward, but he listened for the horse's hoofs. To his relief, he heard their clip-clop just behind him. If his idea had any chance of working, it depended on the horse.

He watched the lead soldier intently as he approached. A junior officer, he guessed. Maybe a sergeant like Narus or Bordan. *Not like Narus. Narus was my friend.* He judged when the man was about to say something – forty, thirty paces away, the man opened his mouth – Lebasi called out first. 'I've found you at last!'

The sergeant pointed his sword at Lebasi. 'What do you mean, deserter? You've run away, we've come to give you what's coming.'

Lebasi stopped and gaped as wide as his mouth would go.

'That's all wrong! I'm not a deserter. Everyone else deserted me.'

The man took a step forward, his sword still raised. 'How can that be?'

Lebasi put his hands on his head, as if the memory hurt. 'There was the big battle at the wall. We were winning. Then I got knocked on the head, and when I woke up, everyone had gone.' He shuddered at the memory. He was hardly acting. 'There were just dead bodies, and crows and vultures, and me.' He turned and pointed. 'And this horse. This was the general's horse. I saw the general, he was dead.' The soldier lowered his blade. Lebasi hoped that was a good sign. 'I didn't know where everyone had gone. The horse started walking, so I followed the horse. That's what I've been doing ever since, what is it, twelve days?'

The man took another pace forward. 'All right, if that's true, how have you managed to live on your own for twelve days?'

Lebasi waved his hand at his companions. 'I met these boys.' He paused for an instant to see if any of the soldiers reacted, but none of them paid special attention to Tik. 'One of them speaks our language. We've found food in abandoned buildings.'

'You must have seen the army out in the countryside. Why didn't you come back?'

Lebasi reached up to stroke the horse's shoulder. 'I thought it was important to keep track of him. He was the general's.'

'So why didn't you bring him to us?'

Lebasi spread his hands. 'On my own? I can't make him go anywhere. I can only follow him. But now you're here, maybe we can bring him back together.'

One of the other soldiers leaned forward and whispered in the sergeant's ear. He listened, keeping his eyes fixed on Lebasi, then said, 'The general's horse, eh?'

Lebasi nodded.

The man's voice took on a cunning tone. 'I reckon anyone bringing back the general's horse would get a reward from the Thrarn.'

Lebasi nodded, smiling, but guessing that this was not going the way he had hoped.

The sergeant waved his hand, and the men spread out behind him, all drawing their swords. He sneered at Lebasi, 'So maybe we bring back a deserter's head and the general's horse, and we get the reward.'

Sammas's voice came from behind. 'What's happening, Basi?'

Lebasi glanced round. 'I shouldn't be able to understand you,' he whispered. 'But it's not good.'

The soldiers formed a semi-circle. Lebasi considered running, but there was nowhere to go. He put his hand on the horse's shoulder again. 'He's not that easy to handle,' he tried.

The horse lowered his head and bared his teeth. The nearest soldiers backed away. He made a deep, throaty noise unlike anything Lebasi had heard from an animal before – he only knew that he was glad it wasn't directed at him. The animal sprang on its front feet, surprisingly quick and agile for something so large, first to the right and then to the left. Two of the soldiers turned and ran. One dropped his sword and lay on the ground, covering his head.

'I've seen him kill someone.' Lebasi called out. 'You have to be very careful around him.'

The sergeant slowly paced backwards away from the horse, keeping his eyes on him. He put his sword back in the scabbard on his belt and held up his empty hands, as if the animal might understand that as a gesture of peace. Lebasi took a deep breath and reached up to pat the horse's neck. He lowered his head and allowed Lebasi to stroke his nose.

'See. I've made friends with him. You won't bring him in without me.'

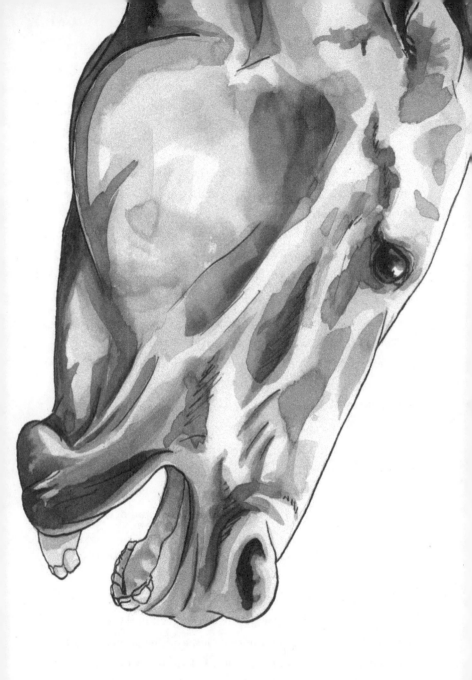

The sergeant glanced round for his men, who were gathering behind him again. The ones who had run away were creeping back, trying not to be noticed. He swore at them using words that Xela had never taught Lebasi, then turned and stood tall, as if he was regaining control of the situation.

'All right. You lead the horse, and keep it away from me and my men. And we'll take you back and you can tell the Thrarn your story and see if they believe it.'

Lebasi asked, 'What about these boys?'

The man looked at them properly for the first time. 'Xessans, eh? Well, I've no quarrel with children. We'll send them down in the valley to join their folk.'

Lebasi heard Tik start to say something in Xessan, so he spoke loudly over her. 'All right then, let's get going.'

21
INTO THE VALLEY

The soldiers formed an escort, two behind, one on each side and three in front, all keeping twenty paces from the horse. As they started back towards Awato, Tik hissed to Lebasi, 'What are we going to do? They can't split us up.'

Sammas whispered, 'Can you let me and Ruffie know what's going on?'

Lebasi glanced round. He nodded. 'I don't think they can hear if I keep my voice down. But if they come any closer, Tik will have to fill in the gaps.'

Tik listened as he explained that he had convinced the soldiers he wasn't a deserter but a survivor of the battle at the Westwall, and that they had agreed to take him back to the army camp because he could control the horse. She heard the words he was saying, but all the time the same thought ran round and round her head: *he's going one way and I'm going another.*

When Lebasi had told the boys that they were being sent down to the valley, Sammas asked the question for Tik: 'How will we get back together again?'

Tik wondered if Lebasi felt as confident as he sounded. 'I'll find a way to escape. I'll look for you on or near the main road south.' He patted Tik on the shoulder. 'Listen out for a pigeon that sounds a bit sick.'

They reached the north end of the sea wall and turned right on a track that followed the edge of the incline. All the way round, the slope was the same steep, even gradient, covered in grass and prickly bushes, possible but difficult to climb down or up. After a hundred paces, the sergeant stopped and turned. As Tik approached, she saw a narrow path descending diagonally into the valley. She wasn't ready. She needed to talk more to Lebasi. He couldn't leave her alone with Ruffur and Sammas. She felt sick.

'Right, you three. This is where you go down. Sito and Brema will take you to make sure you go where you're supposed to.'

The two soldiers beside the sergeant objected. 'Come on, sarge, there's nowhere else they can go.' 'Why us, sarge? It's horrible down there.'

He barked at them, 'Because you ran away, you useless menkers. Now do what you're ordered. You can cope with three children, can't you?'

The men walked reluctantly towards them. One of them spoke very slowly: 'Do you understand what I'm saying?'

Tik took her hat off and held it up. She saw the man take in the mark on her face and look away, which she guessed meant that Aynar's plan was working, for now at least. The man was embarrassed to examine her too closely. 'I understand you. The others don't.'

'All right then, I'll go in front, Brema at the back, no dawdling, no complaining, no funny business. You tell them.'

She repeated the instruction to Ruffur and Sammas, waiting for Lebasi to say something, to do something, to make the horse rescue them again. But all he did was to call out as they started down the track, 'Thanks for all your help, boys, and the company. Go well, and remember to breathe the sky.'

Tik wondered if that was a saying on the other side of the

wilderness, or if Lebasi was taking a risk that the exiles would suspect he wasn't who he claimed to be. He was telling her not to lose hope, but as she took step after step she felt her spirits lowering. Breathe the sky – she could hardly breathe the air. She trusted Lebasi, no one else. Being left with Ruffur and Sammas was worse than being left alone.

They marched down the track in silence. The afternoon sun shone on their backs, and the air seemed thicker and hotter as they descended. First Sito, then Ruffur, Brema, Sammas, and finally Tik started to slap at insects landing on their arms and legs. There were too many: their bites were itchy rather than painful, but soon they were covered in them.

When they reached the valley floor, Sito stopped and turned round, waving his hand in front of his face. He beckoned Tik to the front of the line. 'We're going to leave you here. You walk that way.' He pointed diagonally across the flat fields to the south side. Tik couldn't see what lay over there, only a heat haze shimmering and dancing. 'We'll be watching, to see that you do. And if you make us come and get you, you'll be very sorry. All right?' He smacked his palm against his thigh and swore. There was blood on his hand when he held it up. 'You've got no choice, anyway. Your people are over there.'

Tik nodded and explained to the others. They set off on a track that zig-zagged along the edges of fields, following the intricate network of water channels. The men took another path that climbed the slope again.

When they were out of earshot Sammas said, 'At least they didn't take our packs.'

Ruffur agreed, 'Yeah, we've still got our food.'

Tik snapped, 'How's that going to help us get Lebasi back?'

Sammas turned to face her. 'You heard what he said. You're the important one. You've got the message to take to the king. We have to let him look after himself. If we can keep going south, we take the chance.'

Tik stared at him. 'We – we can't just leave him a prisoner.'

Sammas slapped an insect that was biting his neck. 'I think that's what he wanted us to do. He managed to stop them killing him straight off, but he couldn't make them let him go. You saw how many soldiers went past on the road. If he's in among that lot, there's nothing we can do for him.'

Tik shook her head. All she could think was I can't do this without him.

Ruffur's huge hand on her shoulder was surprisingly gentle. 'He's clever, is Basi. Don't you worry about him. He'll talk his way out of anything.' He blew out his cheeks. 'If it was me, I'd be dead already.'

Sammas tutted at him. 'Not funny, Ruffie. No need to make her think of that.' He turned and started walking. 'Not funny,' he murmured again. 'True, though. No question.'

Ruffur stopped. Tik kept walking. She heard him ask, 'It's going to be all right, isn't it, Sammie?' and Sammas reply, 'Sure thing, Ruffie. You said it right. Basi's clever. He'll have a plan.'

She turned round and glared at them. 'How can you be so stupid? The last time he was in an enemy camp he ended up getting branded and being tied to the front of a dragon-machine. And that time he sneaked in, he didn't get marched in by a bunch of soldiers guarding him. And he had Riadsala and the Westwall Guard to rescue him. We're –' She couldn't think of a word to finish her thought. She saw Ruffur sit down heavily by the side of the track, blurred a little by the water in her eyes. She set off at double speed, not caring if she left them behind.

A hand grabbed her shoulder. She twitched it off, but Sammas took hold of her other arm and spun her round. She tried to kick him, but he was ready with his foot to block her. She snarled at him, 'Leave me alone!'

He spoke quietly, but she could tell he was holding his temper in. 'You know what Basi told us about you, back there in the town?' He jabbed a finger at her face. 'That you were the bravest person he'd ever met, bar none. And the cleverest. That you had never let him down, and you never would. He'd walk through fire for you, would Basi.'

Tik stared. She had been ready for most things that Sammas might say, but not that.

Sammas nodded his head back towards Ruffur, but he kept his eyes fixed on Tik's. 'Ruffie's brave in a fight, no one more than him, but he gets anxious if he has to think. So I do the thinking for him. I'm not as clever as Basi, and that means I'm not as clever as you, but I do my bit to keep Ruffie going. And I don't need you making it more difficult.'

Tik tried to form words but couldn't.

'Ruffie believes what he's told. He likes a story. So he hears what Basi says about you and he thinks if you've given up then we really are finished.' Sammas took in a long breath, then he released Tik's shoulders. She stayed still. His face relaxed, and the anger left his voice. 'Me, I believe what I see. I haven't seen any of what Basi said. I'm waiting for you to show me.'

Tik stood with her mouth open. She felt as if he'd slapped her. She wished he had – at least then he'd have been in the wrong. She tried to think of something to say that wasn't a feeble excuse. There was nothing. Instead, she asked, 'Lebasi said that about me?'

Sammas looked away across the fields, as if he was trying to pick out a group of figures and a horse on the skyline. 'Something like that. He's better with words than me.'

Tik narrowed her eyes. 'You're not just teasing me, like you did him about Faya?'

Sammas turned back and sucked in a breath. 'Oooh,' he said. 'Ouch.'

'What?'

Sammas rubbed the back of his head. He wouldn't meet her eyes. A shadow fell across her as Ruffur joined them.

'You should have put that right, Sammie,' he grunted.

Sammas spread his hands. 'There wasn't a good time. And then there wasn't any time.'

Tik demanded, 'What?'

'It was a joke, a tease, that's all. Faya did say something like that when she was leaving. She went to Xela's house to see if there was any news of Basi. Turned out he was off with the army at the Westwall. She heard we were staying, so she came and asked me to tell Basi she'd see him on the road south. That she'd be looking out for him. Didn't exactly say to give him her love, but something like.'

Tik gasped. She felt hot. She punched Sammas in the chest. He didn't try to stop her, so she did it again, and again. He caught hold of her fists and held them, avoiding her eyes. 'You – you – you *menker!*' she shouted. 'Do you have any idea how much he likes her? He's gone off as a prisoner thinking she doesn't care, when she does.'

Sammas shifted from one foot to the other. 'I'm not proud of it.'

'You wait,' Tik said. 'Ruffur's right – Basi's lucky. He'll come back somehow, and when he does, you're going to tell him the truth, and you're going to – you're going to –' She couldn't think of anything humiliating enough for Sammas to do, so she turned her back on them and strode off. She didn't care whether they followed her or not.

Sammas stopped and mopped his forehead with his sleeve. He shaded his eyes to peer ahead. 'What is that stink?'

Ruffur grunted, 'Smells like the outflow from the sewers back home.'

Tik pointed. On their right now, much nearer the sea wall that hemmed in the view in that direction, there were people who were obviously using the water channels as a latrine trench. Turning the other way, she could now make out more people moving about in the haze, but it was hard to tell what they were doing. A line of ox-wagons was trundling slowly on what must be a road running from south to north. She could make out the line of it cut into the hillside where it climbed up towards Awato. When she tried to work out where the wagons were coming from, she spotted a structure that

must be a bridge over the river. She traced the road as it zig-zagged up the higher ground bounding the valley to the south. But there were no wagons on the bridge or on the other side of it.

'That must be the way to Enola,' she said.

Ruffur asked, 'If the invaders wanted everyone from Xessus to leave, why are these people still here?'

Sammas said, 'We'll find out when we get there. Let's keep a bit to the left, see if it smells any better.'

They reached the road as the last of a line of wagons trundled past. They were loaded with vegetables: piles of cabbages, turnips and beetroots, squashes and gourds of every colour, bundles of green leaves, bright orange carrots.

'They mustn't have got enough food in the towns to last them all the way to Egator,' Tik said. 'They're getting the Xessans to harvest what's ready. That's why they're keeping them here.'

Work had finished for the day, though. That was clear. Thin columns of smoke from cooking-fires added to the haze. To the left of the road, men were walking in from the fields, spades and other tools over their shoulders. They marched silently, slowly, their backs bent. No one paid any attention to Tik, Ruffur and Sammas until they were only a hundred paces from the bridge.

A man was standing in the middle of the road, facing the other way, his hands on his hips. Tik could see a short sword hanging from his belt. One of the invaders, then. She stopped a respectful distance from him and cleared her throat. She didn't want to draw attention to herself, after what Aynar had said, but she had no choice. The boys couldn't speak Xessan.

'Excuse me, sir.'

The man turned sharply and half-drew his blade. He ran his eyes over the three of them and slid it back into its scabbard. 'What d'you want?' he asked. He sounded tired rather than angry.

Tik risked taking her hat off. She wanted to show respect, to keep the man friendly, and hoped he would also be put off by the purple mark. 'My friends and I have just arrived. We met some other soldiers back there who told us to come down to the camp here.'

The man nodded. As she expected, his eyes shifted left and right, not settling on her face. 'All right. You'd better go and see the boss.' He turned and pointed to where two men were talking, fifty paces further on. 'That's the man in charge of the camp, on the left. He'll tell you where to go.'

Tik thanked him and led the boys on. She focused on the men, one tall, with a grey beard, a helmet tucked under his arm. The way he stood, very upright, reminded her of Narus. The other man was shorter, bald, with a neat beard that covered only his chin.

'Marrak,' Ruffur growled.

'What's he doing here?' asked Sammas. 'I thought he'd have been well on the way back to the king, seeing as he's the king's man.'

'Is that Xela's agent? The one who lives with Lebasi?' asked Tik.

Sammas snorted. 'That's one way of putting it. Makes sure we're all following the rules. Runs the reporters and the snatchers for Xela. Or – used to run them.'

They were close enough to catch scraps of the men's conversation. Tik was surprised that they sounded polite, almost friendly. The soldier was an exile, not one of the Thrarn. Rodera had ranted about the Xessans who stayed behind, calling them traitors and slaves, but maybe he had taken too much charro. This man looked more like a Xessan than Marrak did.

They noticed the children waiting and turned. The soldier nodded to them, then touched his forehead to Marrak. 'Good night.' he said. 'I will see you in the morning.'

Marrak returned the respect. 'And a good night to you, Niram. Thank you.'

The soldier marched past them on the road the wagons had taken. Marrak rubbed his hand over his eyes for a moment, took a deep breath, then focused on them. His eyes opened wider in recognition.

'Sammas and Ruffur. You have just arrived from Trengam?'

Sammas nodded.

'You may be surprised that I am glad to see you. I am surprised myself, but it is so. In a moment I hope you can tell me what is happening there, and if you have any news of Xela. But first I must tell you how things stand. You are fit and strong enough to work on the harvest, so you will not be allowed to cross the bridge. You must stay here with us.' He waved his hand to indicate the camp. 'And who is this?'

Tik took off her hat. She had been thinking through everything Lebasi had told her about his father's agent. Good things and bad things. Good meals on the table, washing clothes, looking after the house. Caring for Basi. Marrak had wanted to defend him when the revolutionaries came to the house to collect him – he had thought they wanted to hurt Lebasi and had made it clear he would put his body in the way. But he had also given the order for Lebasi's mother to be sent as a hostage to the king. He had kept control of Xela ever since with the threat that a bad report about Xela's behaviour would harm her. He had never let Xela know if she was alive or dead. He had never told him he had a daughter. Mainly bad, then.

Marrak studied her without looking away. She returned his gaze, setting her mouth in a tight line. The dye and the cropped hair suddenly seemed a pathetic disguise, but she wasn't going to flinch.

He smiled, baring his teeth. 'No, it will serve,' he said, as if he could read her thoughts. 'Most people do not look.' He stroked his beard. 'You are not from Trengam. How have you fallen in with these two ruffians?'

She sensed, rather than saw, the boys folding their arms across their chests and stepping in close behind her. What had Lebasi said about being on the same side? She recalled a Xessus legend, when the hero had to fight in a three-way battle – there was a saying, *my enemy's enemy is...* She shook her head. 'My name is Tik, and I am Xela's niece. Don't you be rude about these boys. They're my friends.'

22
UPPER CAMP

Lebasi watched his three companions descending into the valley as he walked along the rim above them. He hoped they had believed his confidence, but he hadn't convinced himself. He had no idea how he would get away from the enemy camp – if they didn't kill him straight away when he arrived. He hadn't even had time to make peace between Tik and the boys. If she carried on distrusting them when they needed to rely on each other, they wouldn't get anywhere.

At least the guards weren't interested in talking to him. They kept their distance and marched in silence. Lebasi tried to think of a story he could tell. The problem was that he had none – if he was an exile, he would know about the country beyond the wilderness. He ought to have family, he should be able to name names that people would recognise. He would give himself away on the first question. He could try saying as little as possible and pretending to be stupid, but would they believe that anyone could be *that* stupid?

Then again, might someone recognise him? His failure to remember Muscot's face when Caldar came to the farm reassured him that the men who had turned him in to the Thrarn wouldn't know who he was. They had only seen him in the dark. The soldiers who escorted him to be branded – they had walked beside him, looking ahead. The ones who pushed the dragon had been behind him. And El-Kazzak was dead.

Niram – he was the only one who had seen Lebasi close to in daylight, when he put the charro in his mouth to lessen the pain of the branding. Maybe Niram wouldn't have survived the battle. Caldar had said the new general had executed some of the commanders for failing to take the wall properly. That would make him a little safer, but Lebasi wished it might be otherwise. Niram had been kind. Too many good men had died on the Westwall Field.

The houses crowded down to the edge of the valley, leaving only a narrow track. Some of them were grander than any home in Trengam, built of stone with large windows and pretty gardens visible over low walls. Lebasi guessed that important people in the town would want the open space of the valley and the distant view rather than having to look at other buildings. He started as he caught movement in the corner of his eye, thinking for a moment that some of the townspeople might have stayed behind – no, it was a group of Thrarn sitting on the veranda of the largest house of all, a row of bottles on the table between them. One of them stood to get a better look at Lebasi and the horse going by, but his friends shouted at him and he returned to his drink.

When the buildings stopped, Lebasi reached the crest of a short rise and realised that he was looking down on another town – one without houses. On the open pastures to the east of Awato, the army of the exiles had set out a camp with streets to walk down, criss-crossing among neat lines of equipment and bedding. Without buildings to block the view, he could see everything laid out like a living map. Lines of men were marching from one place to another. Ox-wagons were appearing over the edge of the valley.

Smoke rose from cooking-fires.

The narrow path opened out into a broad track leading away from the valley rim. A hundred paces ahead, a group of men had spotted them. They were shading their eyes against the sun, pointing, talking to each other. The sergeant raised his hand for a halt and turned to Lebasi with a cunning expression.

'Right,' he said. 'We're here. Reckon we can get some help and handle the horse now.'

Lebasi edged closer to the animal and glanced behind him. The two men at the back were keeping their distance, but they had their hands on their sword-hilts.

Behind them, a man appeared over the skyline, twice as far away as the exiles but still bigger than them. Lebasi recognised the Thrarn who had been drinking in the garden. He heard the sergeant mutter swear-words. The soldiers heard his heavy footsteps and looked round, then stood sharply to attention. Lebasi did the same.

The man stopped and put his hands on his hips. 'Explain,' he said. 'What are you doing with one of our horses?'

The sergeant stepped forward and saluted. 'Sir, we found this lad over beyond the town, him and the animal. We took him for a deserter, so we're bringing him in.'

Lebasi tried not to flinch as the Thrarn scowled at him. He heard the heavy shuffle of hoofs as the horse turned to face the giant. Would he go back to his old masters?

The horse snorted as if dismissing the idea. He put his head over Lebasi's shoulder. His huge eye seemed to wink. Lebasi imagined Tik saying *he's on our side*. He had killed the Thrarn at Feleda's farm.

Lebasi stood up straighter. It was as if the horse was breathing strength into him. He touched his forehead in the way he had seen the exiles saluting and said, 'I'm no deserter, sir. He's the general's horse, sir, El-Kazzak's. I followed him from the battlefield.'

The Thrarn leaned forward to study the horse more closely. The sergeant started to say something, but the giant held up his hand and cut him off. 'You are sure, little man?'

Lebasi nodded vigorously. 'I saw the general get down from him. Then I got knocked on the head and woke up later when everyone had gone. He was close by the general's body. It was the same horse, no doubt about it.'

The Thrarn turned to the sergeant. He pointed to Lebasi. 'Our new general will want to hear this. It may be that this soldier knows more of what happened to his brother than anyone else. Take him to the corral and give him to the grooms. He can help look after the animals until El-Arnor has questioned him.'

As the Thrarn marched back up the hill, the soldiers all breathed out together. The sergeant gave Lebasi a nasty smile. 'You've stopped us getting that reward. But rather you than me for a chat with the general.'

Lebasi followed the soldiers along the side of the camp leading away from the valley, trying to think of a plan. The streets of Awato on his left might offer places to hide, if he could escape. But it was clear that the Thrarn had chosen that as a more comfortable place to stay than the open field, so he ran the risk of running into them. He guessed that any branded man caught outside the camp would be treated as a deserter.

In any case, what was the use of hiding in Awato? He had to go south, to find Tik again. He had to hope she would make peace with Sammas and Ruffur, but she might wait for him as she had waited outside Trengam. Even if he succeeded in lying low in the town until the army had moved on, that was the opposite of what they were trying to do. He needed to get down into the valley and on the road to Enola before the enemy did.

And when would that be? What were they waiting for?

They passed the last lines of bedding on their right. The end of the camp was marked by a line of wagons stretching out across the fields. For a moment Lebasi wondered whether this was a defensive wall, but as he drew nearer he could see that they were neatly stacked with gear for horses – saddles, bridles, armour, straps and bags of all sorts. The horse made snuffling noises and walked a few paces ahead. Lebasi could guess the reason – the low sunlight picked out a mass of his friends, casting long shadows. The nearer ones turned and trotted across to greet him.

A man wearing a leather apron stepped out from behind the end wagon to see who was coming, wiping his hands on a cloth before hanging it over his shoulder. As he came nearer he dropped a tool he was carrying, broke into a run and called out a greeting.

'You're back! I never thought I'd see you again!'

For a moment Lebasi thought he was talking to the soldiers, but they didn't show any sign of recognition. He ignored them and came straight to the horse, reaching up to stroke his nose. 'There now. Mountain.' He smiled at Lebasi, then turned to the sergeant. 'Where'd you find him?'

The sergeant nodded at Lebasi. 'You'd best ask him. We're just bringing him in. Word of warning to you - El-Arnor's coming tomorrow to have a talk with this lad.'

The man showed no sign of being worried. 'All right.' He walked round the horse, inspecting him. He stopped by Lebasi, leaned against the horse's shoulder and reached down to pick up his foreleg. The horse nuzzled his neck as he checked the hoof. The man lowered the leg to the ground, wiped his hands on his apron and beamed at them all. 'Made my day. you have. You've brought back my best friend.' He reached up and scratched the horse's ear. 'We'd better get you tidied up for the general. But you can go have a natter first.' The horse nodded and trotted off to meet the others.

The sergeant fixed Lebasi with a shrewd gaze. 'I'm not convinced by your story, boy. You're lucky to have made it this far. But you'd better be ready for the morning.' He set off back towards the camp with his men.

The horse-man looked Lebasi up and down. Lebasi did the same, taking in his broad shoulders and strong arms, his face reddened and lined from working in the sun, his hair bleached almost white. 'What's your name, lad? I'm Yanna.'

'Lebasi.'

Yanna put his arm round Lebasi's shoulders and led him towards the wagons. 'Where's your place in the camp?'

Lebasi bit his lip. He had avoided questions all afternoon, but there was no escaping them now. He hoped the plan he had formed would sound more convincing to Yanna than it did in his head.

'I don't know. I just got here. I've been following the horse ever since the end of the battle.' That much at least was broadly true.

'Whose unit were you in, though? We can find your sergeant and get you sorted out.'

Lebasi stopped and ran his hand through his hair. He didn't have to fake a scared expression. He turned his head to left and right as if searching for something.

'What is it, lad?'

Lebasi shook his head. 'I can't remember. I got knocked on the head at the end of the battle. And there was the charro. Triple dose. Everything before that is fuzzy.' He stared at his feet, trying not to blush.

Yanna squeezed his shoulder. 'That's all right. I don't suppose anyone's looking for you. If someone recognises you, you can go back to them. In the meantime, you can stay here.'

Lebasi stammered a thank you.

Yanna smiled back at him. 'Don't thank me yet. If you're eating with us, you'll have to work with us too. I'm always looking for help. And I can see you're not afraid of the horses, like most of this lot are.' He waved his arm to take in the whole of the camp spread out between the pasture and the valley. 'You'll be at home with us.'

Lebasi went to sleep thinking about meeting the general, dreamed about him, and woke up with a tight feeling in his chest. El-Kazzak had told him he was the youngest of four brothers. Whichever this one was, he was likely to be even more frightening than El-Kazzak. Would he have the same hold over Lebasi's mind? If so, how would Lebasi stop himself from blurting out *I killed your brother?*

The work kept his mind busy. Yanna woke him at first light and sent him to join a team of horseminders he had met at dinner. They were a cheerful group, more like Verb and his friends than Lebasi wanted to admit to himself. Their leader, Barran, asked if Lebasi knew anything about looking after horses.

'Sorry, I don't.'

Barran grinned. 'You'll learn, soon enough. Because if you don't, you get the worst jobs.' He handed Lebasi a spade. 'Dung. When it's dried in the sun, it burns. It's what we cook on. Leave the wetter stuff, pick up what's been there since yesterday.'

Lebasi patrolled the field with a wheelbarrow, prodding droppings to test them. When the barrow was full he tipped it onto a pile that men from the main camp were emptying from the other side. He watched the other minders about their tasks – pairs of them going from horse to horse, lifting up their hoofs, digging at the underside with small tools. Sometimes they led the horse across to a group of wagons arranged around what looked like the kind of clay oven that Lebasi would expect to see inside a refreshment house back in Trengam. He heard the sound of metal hammering on metal but couldn't tell what was going on. After a while the horse would trot back out into the pasture.

He was called to breakfast, then sent out again to collect more dung. There was plenty of it. He wondered how many horses the army had. It was hard to count them, as they kept moving, but he was sure there were several hundred. There was also plenty of demand for what they produced – the pile grew smaller rather than larger as he worked.

When the sun was nearly overhead, Yanna sought him out. He had just emptied the barrow for what he reckoned was the twenty-second time and was mopping his forehead with his sleeve. A stinging pain reminded him not to rub his scar.

'How's it going, Lebasi?' the man asked.

Lebasi smiled at him. He hated tricking someone so open and friendly, and hoped he would never guess that Lebasi was one of his enemies. 'It's all right. I like being around the horses.'

Yanna made a clicking noise with his tongue, and Lebasi turned to see a horse – *their* horse – trotting up. 'I can see that. They can tell, you know. A lot smarter than most humans.' He reached up and stroked the horse's nose. 'And a lot more human than most sergeants.'

Lebasi held out some grass for the horse to nuzzle out of his hand. 'You called him Mountain. Do they all have names? Can you tell them apart?'

Yanna laughed. 'I suppose they look the same to you. Maybe we look the same to them.' He shook his head. 'No, we don't. This one knows who you are, you can see that.' The horse nodded and trotted off. Yanna went on. 'I've been looking after the horses since I was a boy. The Thrarn give them names in their own language - they call them things like "Raging Death" and "Night Massacre". I give them my own names. Mountain, he's the biggest and best of the lot.'

They walked across to where lunch was set out on a wagon – hot tea, plates of stew and vegetables. Yanna sat on the grass by Lebasi with his food, eating silently. He put his empty plate aside and leaned close.

'I don't suppose you're that keen to talk to the general.'

Lebasi spluttered into his mug. 'No! But do I have a choice?'

'Well.' Yanna laughed, 'if you carry on working hard shovelling dung, with any luck he won't want to talk to you. I'll advise him against it, if he comes.'

'You're not afraid of him?'

Yanna blew out his cheeks. 'Afraid? Of course I am. Some people are frightened of the horses because they're big and strong, but most horses are good-natured and predictable. Thrarn are big and strong like a horse, nasty as a wasp and unpredictable as a snake you've just trodden on in the long grass.' He clapped Lebasi on the shoulder. 'But they love their horses. They aren't always kind to them, but they respect them. And they don't like doing the hard work, or the dirty work. They leave that to me, and as long as the horses are fit and healthy and ready for Thrarn to ride, I feel fairly safe.'

In the middle of the afternoon, Lebasi noticed a group of Thrarn coming from the town towards the horse-pasture. He pushed his barrow uphill to be as far away as possible, then kept an eye on them as he worked. One huge man followed by six others keeping a respectful distance – that had to be the general and his attendants. Yanna went to meet him, wiping his hands on his apron before saluting.

The general's clothes had something on them that glittered in the sunlight. He wore no helmet, his yellow hair like El-Kazzak's fastened in a plait down his back. Yanna pointed towards

Lebasi, who looked down and earnestly shovelled another heap of droppings into his barrow. When he dared to raise his eyes again, the general was standing next to Mountain, stroking his back. Lebasi ground his teeth. The horse backed away, the man followed, it skipped around and yanked the rope that one of the other Thrarn was holding. The general yelled at the man in their own language as Mountain trotted off to join the other horses. Lebasi grinned. Maybe Tik was right. Maybe he had changed sides.

He smiled even more broadly as he watched the Thrarn party march away again without sending for him. As soon as they were out of sight, he wheeled an over-full barrow down to the dumping-ground. Yanna came to meet him. His face was serious.

'You need to go and have a wash, lad. I tried to fob him off, but he wouldn't have it. Get cleaned up, eat your dinner quickly. They're sending someone to take you in to where he's staying in the town.'

23
LOWER CAMP

Tik slept a little, but not much. It was too hot with the blanket wrapped round her head, but the insects were too annoying if she left her face uncovered. In between dozing, she tried to think of a plan.

At least they weren't going to leave Lebasi behind, not for the moment. It wasn't possible. Marrak had explained that the invaders were holding some of the Xessans in the valley until they had gathered all the food that was ready to harvest. The young, the old and most of the women had crossed the bridge two days ago or more and were on their way south; most of those who were left were men.

He had known who she was as soon as she told him she was Xela's niece. Afterwards, Sammas said she shouldn't be surprised. 'Marrak knows everything. Him and Xela, both,' he said. The agent had asked her for news of Lebasi, and she had told him the truth: 'He's in the camp up there, pretending to be one of them, because the Thrarn branded him before the battle.' Marrak had sucked in his cheeks, clicked his tongue, then said no more about him. Instead he told them how the camp was organised.

'Down that way, use the trenches as latrines. Go as far as you can. You will know when you are in the right place, your nose will tell you if nothing else does. On the way back, go to the main channel and wash. Washing is very important. We take water for cooking and drinking upstream, and we wash downstream. To avoid sickness. Understood?'

He pointed out a group of soldiers near the bridge. They were standing round a metal drum in which a fire was burning. Tik shivered. It reminded her of the Space at Marstor.

'Stay clear of them,' Marrak was saying. 'Their commander Niram is a decent man, but he sleeps in the camp, not here.' He sniffed. 'The ones he sets here to guard us, they are not good people. Do not give them a chance, an excuse, to do you harm.'

Sammas stared across at them. He muttered, 'There's only a handful of them. Why don't we –'

Marrak made a chopping motion with his hand. 'Do not think of it. Yes, they are few. They have swords and we do not, but we could overpower them, at a cost of a few lives. But what then? The Thrarn will come on horses, before we are even all across the river. How can we reach Enola before them? They have told us that we may follow the others when the harvest is complete. They are making ready to march south and have no interest in stopping us. They just need to complete their provisions before they start. We hope that they will take long enough in preparation for our people to be far ahead before they take to the road.'

Marrak told them that some people from Trengam were camped a few hundred paces to the east, not far from the water-channel, but Tik said she wanted to stay near the road. To her surprise, Sammas agreed straight away, without making a suggestion of his own. They found a clear space and put their packs down. As the sun sank the insects were even more numerous. Ruffur collected grass to make a smoky fire, which gave them a little respite.

'We'll keep watch, like before,' said Sammas. 'Turn and turn about. He probably won't come tonight, but he might. Let's start as we'll carry on.'

* * * * *

At the sound of wagon wheels close to her head, Tik pulled off the blanket and sat up. In the grey light before dawn an ox-cart trundled by her, heading towards the bridge. Another followed, and another, a long line stretching across the valley.

'You're the new arrivals, are you?'

She turned to find a man she didn't recognise looking down at the three of them. Tik nodded.

'Where are you from?' the man asked.

'I'm from near the Westwall, and these boys are from Trengam,' she replied.

'Well, we're all mixed together now. Funny, isn't it?' He held up his right hand, showing the red triangle tattoo that marked him as a Marstor man. 'All these years when we couldn't step across from one town's land to the next, and now everyone's the same.' He laughed bitterly. 'All in the same mess.'

He told them to go and do whatever they needed to do first thing in the morning, then come back for something to eat. Then they would have to work.

They followed a line of men down the road. On the way they passed another bridge over the channel with another group of soldiers gathered round a fire. Tik wondered if she would need to find somewhere separate at the latrine trenches to keep up her pretence, but the smell and the flies were so bad that no one was paying any attention to anyone else.

On the way back they walked beside the raised wall of earth that separated the channel from the fields. Ruffur stood on tip-toe but he couldn't see over it. He offered to lift Tik up, but Sammas pointed out some steps ahead. There was a shorter jump down on the other side onto a paved path, then a smooth slope to the water two manheights below. A little further upstream, someone had dug out a ledge by the water where a few people at a time could kneel and wash. They took their turn climbing down to it, holding onto each other to avoid taking a bath.

'Not far, is it?' said Sammas, nodding across to the other bank.

'Thirty paces? How deep d'you think it gets?' muttered Ruffur.

'Don't even think about it, boys,' came a voice from above them. They looked up to see a young man shaking his head. 'It's deeper than you're tall, and the bottom's the sort of mud that'll suck you down. Couple of people have tried it.'

'What happened?' Tik asked, secretly relieved that she wouldn't have to find an excuse for not being able to swim.

'One drowned, one didn't. But the soldiers heard the splashing and they were there to meet him on the other side.' He made a throat-cutting gesture. 'Better wait till they let us go. That's what Marrak says, and he's right.'

They walked back along the path. The channel ran completely straight, so they had a good view of the main bridge as they approached it. It was all made of wood, a lattice-work of trestles holding it up, with railings along the side.

Ruffur glanced around to check that he wasn't being overheard this time. 'Could climb over underneath, reckon.'

Sammas nodded. Then he glanced at Tik. He murmured, 'But we're not going to, for now. We're waiting for Basi. Until Tik gives us the word. Then we'll go.'

'Course,' Ruffur agreed.

Tik followed, realising that they were going to expect her to take the decision to leave Lebasi behind. She had to go south. But she couldn't abandon him, not yet. And trying to cross the bridge would be risky – if they were spotted, and if they were caught, that would be the end of everything. A few days might bring Lebasi back to them, and then they could cross over safely. Or face the hard choice, if he had not reappeared and the Xessans were still being held in the valley.

Just short of the bridge they scrambled back over the wall and jumped down onto the road. The last of the wagons was turning the corner to go up the valley. Tik guessed that was where the harvesting was going on. They would have to fill all those wagons, so the Thrarn would be able to get to Egator. She glanced back at the framework of the bridge. She would rather climb that than try to swim across.

She shook herself. Lebasi would come. He wouldn't let her down.

The Marstor man found them again and led them to where some tables had been set up beside a cooking fire. 'It's not much of a refreshment house,' he said, 'but it's a bit better than everyone

for themselves.' Tik was reminded of the Westwall Guard's cook-wagons, and then she thought of Tassie, and had to wipe her sleeve across her eyes.

After a small plate of rice and vegetables that plainly wasn't enough for Ruffur, they followed a crowd of men to the bridge and joined a line filing past the last few wagons, which had parked at the crossroads. They were loaded with farming tools. There were more soldiers now, men who had not stayed overnight. They were handing out a piece of equipment to each man, sometimes in silence, sometimes with an insult, sometimes with a cuff round the head. The Xessans shuffled by without reacting and marched off up the road with their spade or fork over their shoulder.

Ruffur was mumbling something, getting louder as he neared the front of the line. Tik heard Sammas mutter, 'Steady, Ruffie. Just take it, for now. Please.' Ruffur grunted, snatched his shovel and stepped smartly away so the soldier clipped empty air. Sammas took a sickle and a curse without lifting his head. Tik held out her hand.

'Not you, shorty,' the soldier said. 'You can go over there.'

Tik followed his finger to see a group of young boys gathered by the bridge. 'I can work,' she protested.

The man leaned down and snarled at her, 'Did I ask you a question? Now move.'

She shrugged and stepped out of line. As she did so, she realised that Sammas and Ruffur wouldn't know what was going on. 'Boys, I've been told to go with that lot over there. I'll see you later.'

They both turned and stopped. The soldier roared at them in Xessan and Tik waved them away, not wanting to draw attention to herself. She didn't think the man had realised she was a girl. She had her hat pulled down over her forehead, and his eyes had shifted when he saw the purple mark on her face.

There were eleven boys gathered by the bridge, all looking puzzled, muttering to each other. She whispered to the one standing nearest to her, 'I'm new here. What's going on?'

He hissed back, 'Don't know. Yesterday we all went to the fields together.'

'Sergeant, what is happening here?' They all turned to see Marrak marching up, his bald head shiny with sweat. He made the sign of respect to one of the soldiers. 'Why have these children been separated out?'

The man waved his hand dismissively. 'New orders, old man. Your people aren't working hard enough. We need them to hurry up'

'The wagons are full by the end of the day. We cannot fill more wagons than you bring down.'

The soldier wagged a finger in Marrak's face. 'Not fast enough. We want it done quicker, so we can get out of this stinking valley sooner.'

Marrak's voice stayed calm and quiet. 'We want the same thing, but in order to make it happen, I must talk to Niram. Where is he?'

The sergeant shoved him in the chest. 'No, dirtrag, you must dig.' He shouted to the men on the wagon, 'Give this weasel a spade, and something to remember me by.'

Marrak stood very straight, narrowed his eyes, nodded to the man, and went to collect his shovel. As he set off after the rest of the workers, he turned and called out, 'Do as you are told, children, and I trust they will not hurt you.'

The soldier turned to speak to them. 'Right. Some of you understand me. You can tell the others. Rest day for you. No digging.' He mimed the action, then shook his head. 'Just standing.'

The soldiers herded them onto the bridge. There was a rope lying across the deck, tied in loops like a chain. The soldiers made each child step into a loop and lift it up to their waists. They tightened the slip knots so they were all joined together.

'Now then, up you go.'

A soldier picked Tik up and lifted her onto the railing. It was solid, a good handspan across, but not as wide as her foot was long. She wobbled as he let go and moved to the next child. When they were all standing, the sergeant walked along the line, looking up into each one's eyes.

'When your families and friends have filled the wagons, you can come down.' Tik could hear someone whimpering. The sergeant scowled at him. 'Don't fall off. If you go backwards, you'll take everyone with you.' He reached up and put his finger on the boy's chest. 'And if you fall forwards, we'll throw you over.'

* * * * *

Tik was glad of her hat. The sun was pitiless. The insects buzzed around them, and they could do nothing about them for fear of overbalancing. From the smell, at least one of the boys had wet himself. The sergeant had gone in the direction of the harvest, while the soldiers he left behind rigged up a piece of canvas to give them some shade, and kept a fire going in their drum to keep the flies at bay.

An ox-cart came into view on the road. Tik wasn't sure whether it was blurry because of heat-haze or because her head was being baked. It came closer, slowly solidifying into a familiar vehicle. The grandmother was riding now, the son who had tied Tik up was leading the ox, the other man and his wife walked beside the cart, the children were following in a straggling line, the other mother bringing up the rear. Tik looked for the sheep, but they were missing.

One of the soldiers held up a hand. The ox stopped. The soldier asked, 'Do you understand me?'

The son nodded. The other man walked up to stand beside him. The children gathered by the wheels of the wagon,

'Right. The women and children, you can go. But the men stay.'

Both men started to protest. All five of the soldiers drew their swords and spread out in a line. The grandmother put out her hands for calm. She climbed slowly down and approached the soldiers. 'We were told that we would be allowed to leave. We have given our land to you. We surrendered our livestock to the people on the hill to pay for our passage.'

The soldier made an exaggerated bow, and spoke in a wheedling tone 'Why, thank you kindly for that. And leave you may, old woman, with the mothers and the children.' Then he stood up straight and snarled. 'But those that can dig, must dig. They can catch you up later, when the harvest is in.' He waved a hand at one of the other soldiers, who darted forward and grabbed one of the girls. Her mother screamed as he pulled her back with him. The sons squared up as if to fight, but the soldiers held out their sword points against the men's chests and throats.

'We'll give her back the moment you decide to take our offer. And be grateful. The terms might not be so generous tomorrow.'

The grandmother called out, 'All right, all right, we will do as you say.' The sons backed away, the soldier let the girl run back to her mother and bury her head in her skirts. They said hasty goodbyes as the soldiers told them to hurry up. One of the women took up the leading rope and started the ox onto the bridge. Tik stared down at them as they walked by, feeling the vibration of the wheels in her feet. One of the children glanced up at her. She saw his eyes and mouth open with recognition. He lifted his hand as if he was about to point her out to his ma. Tik shook her head, and he lowered it again.

The sons were given tools and directed to head up the valley until they found people working. The wagon crossed the short flat area on the south side of the channel and started on the first of the zig-zags up the side of the valley. Tik watched it trundling back and forth, wondering what would have happened if the horse hadn't rescued her. She could have been on that wagon, heading for Enola.

Instead of standing on this railing, longing for something to drink.

24
THE GENERAL

Lebasi joined the other horseminders who were washing in a pond upstream of where the animals went to drink. He put on a spare tunic that Yanna found for him, but he still reckoned he reeked of horse, with more than a hint of what he had been collecting all day. Maybe it was just what fear smelled like.

The sun was setting when they came for him. He was relieved that his escorts were two exile scouts rather than Thrarn. His relief disappeared when one of them spoke.

'Are you the turd shoveller we've been told to bring?'

There was no mistaking the whiny, wheedling voice that he had last heard denouncing him as a spy on the other side of the Westwall. He cast his eyes down and nodded to the man, not trusting himself to speak. *Muscot.*

Yanna clapped him on the back as he stood up. He called out as Lebasi walked away, 'Just tell him that you like looking after horses and you'll be fine.'

Muscot and his colleague walked ahead, talking to each other and ignoring Lebasi. The man showed no sign of remembering him. Lebasi wanted to ask him a hundred questions, but he was worried that his voice might trigger a memory. Or that his voice might crack. He was finding it difficult to breathe. As he walked across the field towards the town, his mind filled with images of El-Kazzak, overpoweringly huge, sitting in his tent, casting his spell over Lebasi's mind, raging at the commanders of his army as he gave them orders for the battle, addressing his troops before the attack.

Ordering the soldier to brand him.

Drawing his sword to kill Riadsala, after the battle, as Lebasi lay pinned to the ground.

Looking straight at him, pointing the sword, laughing – taunting him, 'You are my slave, little man.'

'I said, what's the general want to see you for, horsey? You got dung between your ears as well as smelling of it?'

Lebasi returned to the present. Muscot's friend was walking backwards, staring at him. He mumbled, 'Sorry. I don't know.'

Muscot laughed. 'We've been told to take you back afterwards. Maybe we'll need a bucket to carry the pieces.'

They passed the first buildings, rough shacks made of wooden planks. There was nothing like them in Trengam. Lebasi wondered that the largest town in Xessus was so badly built, particularly on what must be the main approach route. After a hundred paces he realised that his first impression from the other end of the town had been wrong: it had once had a wall and gates. The bottom of both were visible, standing waist-high. The gateway was as deep as the tunnels through the walls of Trengam and Marstor, so the town must once have been built in the same way. Lebasi guessed that this was something to do with Riadsala's Mercy. Xela had told him about Rednaxela's army laying siege to Awato. They must have destroyed the walls after Riadsala had defeated Dennara.

On the inside, the buildings were the solid stone and brick structures he recognised from home, but here built on flat ground. They loomed two and three storeys high on either side of the street, showing no lights. The sun had disappeared, and the thin sliver of a two-day old moon cast little light.

'Who goes?' Two man-shapes, normal-sized, stepped out of the shadows. One of them held up a lantern that dazzled Lebasi.

Muscot replied, 'Muscot and Orlan, taking this menker to El-Arnor.'

'All right. Know where you're going?'

'Course.'

There were more lights ahead. On the left, the houses were set back from the street, and lanterns showed in several of the windows. Lebasi could hear Thrarn voices talking. He guessed that he had walked past their gardens the previous afternoon with the horse.

On the other side of the road, most of the houses were in darkness, but there was one with a large lamp hung by the front door. Two exiles were standing to attention in the pool of light it cast. As they drew near, Muscot called out, 'Stand easy, lads, it's only us.'

The two men ignored his greeting and carried on staring straight ahead. Muscot paused beside them and one muttered, 'Thrarn inside questioning the prisoner. Keep your voice down.'

Muscot nodded, and they carried on. Lebasi had no time to wonder who would be held prisoner by the Thrarn and questioned, because they arrived at the largest and best-lit house in the street. Muscot and Orlan were now marching smartly, their arms swinging in time, and Lebasi tried to do the same. They turned in at the garden gate, led him to the front door and rapped at the knocker.

The door swung back. It was tall enough for the Thrarn who opened it to stand straight in the doorway.

Muscot saluted. 'We've brought the horseminder the general wants to talk to, sir.'

The Thrarn nodded and beckoned Lebasi inside. 'Wait here.' he growled at the others.

Lebasi followed the man through a broad hallway that reminded him of Alfas's house at Marstor, only bigger. They crossed an open courtyard with a fountain playing and entered a room on the far side. Lanterns hanging on the walls revealed a meeting in progress: eight Thrarn sitting round a table, all eyes turned to the man at the far end, who was a head taller than anyone else. Lebasi could tell immediately that this was nothing like El-Kazzak's conference with his commanders: there were wine bottles on the table, and laughter, and men leaning back in relaxation. El-Kazzak had worn a plain tunic that was probably what he put on under his armour when he fought. His brother was dressed in something much more colourful, with metallic strips woven into the material which glinted in the lamplight.

The man leading Lebasi cleared his throat and everyone turned to look. The general said something in Thrarn, and all the others stood up and left through a door on the far side of the room, taking cups and bottles with them. Lebasi's escort saluted and left Lebasi alone. El-Arnor beckoned him forward. He tried to march confidently, but he had to hold his arms stiffly by his side to stop them shaking. He made the sign of deep respect, putting his hand on his heart and bowing from the waist.

'What is your name?' The deep voice was not as harsh as some of the Thrarn. But Lebasi remembered how El-Kazzak had pretended to be friendly when he was first brought into his tent. And he remembered what Caldar had said – this man had beheaded some of El-Kazzak's commanders for their failure. It suddenly struck him that those might have included Thrarn as well as exiles. He gulped.

'Lebasi, sir.' As soon as he said it, he regretted that he had not come up with a lie. He had to hope that no one would remember his real name, which he was sure that El-Kazzak had used when he was talking to his commanders in his tent. Niram and a couple of other exiles had been there, and one or two Thrarn as well.

'Do you know why you are here?'

Lebasi had been asking himself that all the way from the grooms' camp. He tried, 'Because I brought back your brother's horse?'

El-Arnor leaned forward. 'Do you think I want to say thank you for that?'

Lebasi quickly shook his head. 'No, sir.'

'Why, then?'

Lebasi remembered El-Kazzak asking him questions, after he had blown a mysterious powder in his face. But El-Kazzak had been trying to find out about the defence of the Westwall. Lebasi didn't want to suggest what he suspected El-Arnor wanted to know from him.

'I don't know, sir.'

The man's eyes sparkled in the lamplight. Even without the powder, there was something compelling about the tone of his voice. 'Tell me, did you see my brother die?'

Lebasi's worst expectation was confirmed. This was not what he wanted to be interrogated about. He was glad he could at least answer this first question truthfully, in case the general was good at detecting the tremor of a falsehood. 'No, sir. I was hit on the head in the battle. When I woke up, everyone had gone, and the general was dead.'

El-Arnor leaned back in his chair and tapped his fingertips together. 'But you saw his body.'

Lebasi stared at the floor. Of course he must have done, if his story was true. But he had not been conscious of his surroundings while Tik helped him onto the horse. 'Yes, sir.'

'So, how did he die?'

'I don't know what you mean, sir.'

The general grunted and rolled his eyes up towards the ceiling, shaking his head. 'Make a wild guess from what you saw.'

Lebasi opened his mouth, then closed it. He shut his eyes, as if trying to remember, then opened them. 'Oh. There was a spear – ' He hoped he could make it seem that he didn't want to call the details to mind. He could only guess that the crossbow bolt had stuck into El-Kazzak. Surely it couldn't have gone straight through him.

El-Arnor nodded. 'A spear. Let us call it that.' He leaned forward again. 'Tell me, what did you think of my brother?'

Lebasi was finding it hard to breathe. What could he say that would not make the man angry? 'He was... he was... frightening, sir.'

The man laughed. 'Yes, I expect he was, to such as you.' He rubbed his chin and stared past Lebasi. 'You probably cannot imagine that he was once a child, that his older brothers would have been fond of him.'

Lebasi decided not to reply.

'Where were you, in the attack? Where did you receive your blow to the head, where were you when you woke up?'

Lebasi wondered what a soldier would say. He thought of Caldar. He could stick to something close to the truth. 'I was in the centre, sir. Niram's division. I went in through the gate. I was on the field somewhere below the tower. When I woke up everyone had gone. The horse was up on the skyline, near the general's body. I didn't know what to do. The horse – I just thought I should follow the horse.'

El-Arnor nodded. 'And it was a good thing to do. I am glad to have my brother's mount returned. My father gave him to El-Kazzak, and my father always treated El-Kazzak as his particular favourite.' He bared his teeth in a fierce grin. 'He is a better horse than mine.'

Lebasi kept his face blank. He hated the idea of giving Mountain back to the Thrarn, but there was nothing he could do about it.

El-Arnor tapped the table. 'A spear, you call it. Who might have thrown it?'

The question caught Lebasi unawares. He hoped that he did not blush. 'Er - I suppose the enemy, sir?'

The general shook his head. 'The enemy were beaten. There were none of them left. Only their captain, who was badly injured, remained on the field.'

Lebasi tried to look puzzled, but he couldn't think how to arrange his face. He felt that the truth must be written on his features. *I killed your little brother.* 'Then who?'

El-Arnor slowly rose to his feet. 'I had hoped that you could give me more of a clue. It was not a spear, you see. It was a bolt from one of our battle-crossbows. Only a machine could have cast it with such force. El-Kazzak's armour would have deflected a spear thrown by a Thrarn, let alone by one of your race.'

Lebasi gasped. 'So - it was someone on our side?'

The man nodded. 'It would appear so. I am calling in those who were in that part of the field to ask them what they saw. I will find out.' He gave Lebasi a humourless smile. 'And when I do, that man will be sorry.'

Lebasi kept his expression blank, his eyes fixed on the general's.

'Now go. I will see you tomorrow when I come to ride the horse.'

Lebasi saluted. 'Yes, sir.'

El-Arnor clapped his hands. The Thrarn who had met him at the door returned and led him out. Muscot and Orlan sounded disappointed that they would not be carrying pieces of him back in a bucket. He was determined not to show them how frightened he still was, but he felt that they could have poured him into one.

The guards along the road were relaxing now, lounging against the wall. Muscot stopped to talk to them. He asked, 'All done for the night?'

One of the guards replied, 'Ay, we've put him to bed.'

Orlan nodded towards the closed door. 'You don't sit in there with him?'

The other said, 'No need. He's chained up.' He showed them a bottle. 'We're just having a little drink of something we found inside, out in the fresh air.'

Muscot asked, 'Is he still complaining about the food?'

They both laughed. 'Doesn't get him anywhere. He may be used to giving orders, but he's going to get the same as everyone else now and eat it like a good boy, or he's going to go hungry.'

Lebasi tried not to react. He thought they might hear his heart. Instead of the lamplit street in Awato, he was in bright sunshine by the road from Nampetch to the Westwall. Riadsala was sitting beside him, holding a plate, explaining what he called the curse of Rednaxela: that men of his family could not eat food made of wheat or of cow's milk without getting ill. 'The cooks have to carry special rations for me,' he said, 'and half the men just think that I'm a fussy eater.'

25
PERRA

From early afternoon, loaded wagons appeared in the corner of Tik's eye, coming from upstream and turning to head across the valley. The soldiers sat under their awning. The children stood in silence. Even the whimpering had stopped. No one else came from Xessus to cross the bridge. Tik narrowed her eyes against the glare of the sun as it descended the sky in front of her, but she dared not close them for fear of losing her balance. Several times she had to steady herself as she nearly fell asleep.

At last, the sergeant strolled across from the soldier's post and walked along the line. Tik had seen the officers of the Guard inspecting the troops – it was the same. When he reached her, she stood very straight and stared fixedly over his head.

'That'll do.' he said, 'you can get down now.'

The boy at the far end fell forwards. The rope pulled the next boy down, and in a moment they were all lying on the bridge, examining scrapes and likely bruises. The sergeant laughed at them.

'Go on, untie yourselves and get back to your camp. We'll see you again in the morning.'

Tik walked stiffly back to where she had left her pack. Her tongue felt like a lump of wood. She found her water-skin and squirted some tepid liquid into her mouth, then lay on her back with her hat covering her face.

She heard running footsteps but was too tired to move.

'Are you all right, Tik?' Ruffur's deep voice came in between gasps for breath.

She pulled the hat aside and squinted up at him. He was very red in the face, leaning on his knees. She glanced past him, but Sammas was not in sight.

'I came back quick as I could,' Ruffur panted. 'If they've hurt you, I'll –' He slapped a fly that was biting his neck and muttered something unintelligible.

'I'm fine,' she replied. 'Tired. They made us stand on the railing all day.' As she said it, she thought, *that doesn't sound like much. Just standing there. But it was tough.* 'Didn't let us get down for anything.'

'All day?' Ruffur made a noise like an angry dog. 'The menkers. They've no call to do that. We were working hard as we could anyway.' He punched a fist into the other palm. 'If they didn't have swords –'

Tik stood up and put her hand on his arm. She had never had anyone stand up for her before, besides Lebasi. She knew Ruffur couldn't do anything to help – he would make everything worse if he tried – but she was surprised and pleased that he cared.

Sammas jogged up. 'Blood and bone, Ruffie, I've never seen you run so fast.'

Ruffur rubbed the back of his head and looked away. 'Just wanted to make sure Tik's all right.' Had he turned even redder?

Sammas grinned at Tik. 'He's only mentioned that a couple of times while we've been digging up turnips.' Ruffur swatted at him. Sammas winked. 'A couple of hundred times.'

Ruffur told Sammas about the bridge, and Sammas turned the same colour. He clenched his fists and growled in the direction of the soldiers. Tik was glad that they understood how bad it had been without her having to explain.

Once she had reassured them that she was all right now, they sat down and told each other about their day. Because she had hardly anything else to say, Tik described the family being stopped at the bridge.

Sammas interrupted her. 'You knew them? How?'

She realised that she had never told them – or Lebasi – what had happened outside Trengam. 'Sorry,' she said, when she had explained. 'I was in a bad mood that day. It didn't seem important.'

She was aware of Ruffur grinding his teeth as she explained. When she had finished, he asked, 'So the men are here now, in the camp?'

Sammas gave his shoulder a shove. 'Leave it, Ruffie. We're all on the same side now. Which is the wrong side of the bridge, for the moment.' He stood up. 'Come on. They're brewing up some tea over there. And I think I spotted someone we ought to go and meet.'

Tik drained the first cup, scalding her throat, and wanted to wait for a refill, but Sammas beckoned her on. 'Up here somewhere. I'm sure I saw him.'

They walked along the road that ran parallel with the channel, the setting sun casting long shadows in front of them. Sammas suddenly pointed. 'There! I knew it.'

Ruffur followed his arm. A slow smile spread over his face. 'That's all right. I wonder what Marrak thinks of him being here?'

Tik followed, guessing that they wanted her to ask who it was, but not playing their game. They picked their way between groups of men sitting and lying on the ground, stepping over packs and bedding rolls, and approached a young man who was on his own. He was staring at nothing. He didn't look up even when they stopped in front of him.

'Hi, Perra,' said Sammas. 'It's good to see you.'

Perra. Tik's pulse quickened. This was the man Lebasi had rescued from the town prison and kept hidden from his father, the one he had saved from Riadsala's sword when his ambush failed.

He lifted his eyes slowly and shaded them with his hand. He didn't smile. His voice was just as empty of expression. 'Sammas, Ruffur. I haven't seen you around.'

Sammas put his hand on Tik's shoulder. 'We only got here yesterday. Perra, this is Tik. She's come all the way from the Westwall. She's travelling with us now.'

Perra focused on Tik. 'From the Westwall? Are you –'

'Gortan's granddaughter,' she said. 'I heard that the Westwall Guard took you prisoner. What happened?'

Perra lowered his eyes again and examined the backs of his hands. Sammas sat cross-legged in front of him, leaning forward as if waiting for a story. Ruffur glanced at Tik and pointed to a flat stone, as if he was finding her a seat at table, but she preferred to squat with her arms round her knees. He sat down beside her.

Perra sighed. He rubbed the back of his neck. 'Not much to tell. Prince Riadsala and most of the soldiers marched off to stop the exiles returning. We were left at Nampetch with a few men to guard us. There's an old army post outside the town, they used that. It had rooms they could lock us in, ten to a cell. They weren't bad, for all that – they gave us food, they let us out for exercise one roomful at a time.'

Sammas asked, 'How did you escape?'

Perra shook his head. He stared into the evening sky over Ruffur's shoulder. 'We didn't. We were there about an eightnight. Then one morning the guards didn't come to get us. We hadn't heard anything in the night, but we guessed they'd gone. It took us half the day to break open the doors with only our hands.' He held up his fingers, which were covered in cuts. 'Makes it hard to hold a spade, even an eightnight later.'

Ruffur grunted, 'But you were out. What did you do?'

'We needed to know what was going on before we made a move. So we sent runners to Nampetch and Trengam, as well as to farms round about, to find out who was in charge.' He fell silent.

Tik prompted him. 'The Thrarn horsemen.'

He nodded. 'They captured some of my scouts and got them to tell where they'd come from. So they rode up to our prison and told us to leave. I said we were the Xessans who were on the exiles' side, and they just laughed at us. Told us to go south to the king, or stay and die.'

Tik remembered sitting with Gortan at the farm, the day Mallam died. She said, 'My grandda said that what he'd dreamed of all his life turned out to be a nightmare.'

Perra lowered his eyes and met hers. 'I've never met Gortan, of course, but we sent messages to each other. Yes, we had the same dream, and we were both wrong.'

Sammas leaned forward. 'So, what's the plan now?'

Perra looked at him blankly. 'Plan?'

'You're the man. Marrak's talking to the enemy, but people will want you to take charge.'

Perra stared at him for a long moment. Then he looked down. 'I don't think so. They believed me once. They believed in me. Why would they make the same mistake again?'

Sammas sat back again. 'I would. I mean, I believe in you. I don't think it's a mistake.'

Perra chuckled, a laugh without humour. He made a show of shading his eyes to survey the camp. 'I don't see anyone joining you, Sammas. The ones here who know me – well, some of them I led into an ambush and nearly got them killed, and the rest saw me march off to fight the Westwall Guard and turn up here as helpless as everyone else. They're better off with Marrak.'

Sammas protested, 'But –'

'But nothing. Anyway, I haven't got a plan. Beyond finishing this harvest and following everyone else south. I wouldn't have minded dying if we were setting Xessus free. There doesn't seem much point now, in living or in dying.'

26
TACK

The thought that Riadsala had survived, and was a prisoner in a house in Awato, kept Lebasi awake late into the night. He hardly seemed to have fallen asleep when Yanna was shaking his shoulder again.

'Morning, Basi.'

He yawned, stretched, and pulled off his blankets. He turned his boots upside down and shook them, as he had noticed the soldiers doing when they were camped in the countryside. As he started tying the laces, he realised that Yanna was staring at him, his arms folded across his chest, one finger tapping his lips.

'What?'

The man shook his head and smiled. 'Nothing important. The good news is that you get a turn doing something else today.'

Lebasi stood up and followed him towards the breakfast wagon. Yanna had been thinking about something – what was he looking at?

My boots.

Ruffur and Sammas had made fun of him for having proper boots on the road to the border, on that apprentice day back in the spring. He stole a glance at what Yanna was wearing on his feet. Shorter boots. Boots that looked older and more worn out than Lebasi's. His had been a long way since the spring, but they hadn't crossed a wilderness.

He thought about making up a story about finding them on

his travels, but he decided against it. It sounded false in his head, and it would be worse if he said it. He could wait for Yanna to ask, and hope that he wouldn't.

'What's my job today, Yanna?'

'Well, if you're going to be with us for a while, we might as well teach you to tack up a horse.'

With us for a while. That showed no sign of suspicion that Lebasi didn't belong.

'Tack up? What does that mean?'

'Prepare him for the rider. Put the harness and the saddle on, all of that.'

Lebasi looked around the field. 'The general said he was going to ride Mountain again today. Am I supposed to get him ready?'

Yanna turned and grinned at him. 'Not today. I'm too fond of having a head on my shoulders. I'll see if you get the hang of it before I let you near a horse the general's going to ride.' He clapped Lebasi on the shoulder. 'Or any Thrarn, for that matter. You can start off with Barran showing you how, just putting it all on and taking it all off again.'

✳ ✳ ✳ ✳ ✳

'First things first,' Barran said, leading the way towards a row of wagons at the top of the field. 'You've got used to one horse, and that one likes you. Don't assume they'll all be as well-behaved. Or as thoughtful. They're heavy and they're strong, and they can hurt you.'

Lebasi nodded. 'I know. I'll keep on my toes.'

They stopped beside the first wagon. There were rows of pegs on the side on which a variety of leather straps were hanging. 'Next thing,' Barran went on. 'We keep everything tidy, we keep everything clean. Yanna's all smiles today, but you wouldn't want to see him if anything's out of place.'

Lebasi nodded, thinking *I'm out of place*. He was sure Yanna knew it.

He had no time to worry. Barran chose a nearby horse and told Lebasi to bring it over to the wagon. He wondered if this might be a joke to play on newcomers, but Barran seemed to mean it. He walked towards the animal.

'Let him see you, don't give him a surprise.' Barran called out.

Lebasi stopped and looked back. 'What do you mean?'

Barran pointed at his own head. 'He's not like us. His eyes are on the side. If you come at him from straight in front, he might not notice you until the last moment. He might get jumpy.'

Lebasi nodded and took two steps to the left. The horse raised his head from the grass and regarded him coolly. He was already wearing a leather headcollar – much smarter and more complicated than the ones the donkeys at Trengam wore, but Lebasi recognised it as the same kind of thing. He found he was talking to the horse, softly, in the king's language. He hoped Barran hadn't heard. He reached up and gently took hold of the rope, stroked the animal's shoulder, then started to walk back towards the wagon. The horse bit one last mouthful of grass and followed.

Barran smiled and nodded at him. 'You'll do. Most lads we take on start by being frightened of them. They move too quickly, grab things, fidget. It makes the animals nervous. Much more dangerous that way. Just stay nice and relaxed.'

Lebasi spent the morning learning about bridles and bits, saddles and girths, reins and stirrups. He put everything on the first horse, then took it all off again. He collected another horse, tacked it up and untacked it. He learned to lift a horse's legs and inspect the hoofs. Barran explained the signs that the shoes needed replacing, or the hoofs needed trimming.

'Big part of what we're doing here.' he explained. 'Give the horses a rest, get them all in the best condition for a long march.' He pointed across to another group of wagons. 'Those are the farriers. They work on hoofs. They make shoes, they do the trimming. But we're their eyes. If we let a horse go lame, it's only good for meat.'

Lebasi thought it was reasonable to ask, 'Do you know when we'll be moving on?'

Barran turned to gaze over the valley. 'I hear they've nearly got in all the food that's worth harvesting. Then they're being sent on, and we'll probably follow a couple of days after that, maybe three.' He turned the other way and pointed to a group of riders trotting into the camp. 'There are still raiding parties going out making sure all the farmers have left. Encouraging anyone that's foolish enough to think they can stay put when the Thrarn have told them to go. We'll wait for all the locals to pass by. We don't want to share the road with them, any more than they want to share it with us.'

After lunch Lebasi had to scrub down and comb some horses that had been ridden in the morning. He remembered to talk to them in Xessan as he worked, in case anyone overheard him. He enjoyed being with the animals, their smell, their little noises, the expressions on their faces. If he kept busy, he didn't have to think about trying to find out if it really was Riadsala under guard, or how to escape and rejoin Tik.

The sun was halfway to the horizon when Barran pointed downhill. 'Here comes your man the general. Mountain's been saddled up waiting for him since breakfast.'

They watched as they worked. Lebasi wondered if Mountain had grown to like not having to carry anybody. He didn't make it easy for El-Arnor to climb on his back, and once he was in the saddle, the general seemed to find it difficult to tell Mountain where to go. His attendants stood to attention, gazing into the distance. Shouted words in Thrarn drifted up to Lebasi's ears. He guessed that they were making sure their faces showed no sign of disrespect.

At last, the general swung his leg over Mountain's back and stepped down to the ground. The horse moved sideways as he did so, and the man nearly fell over. Lebasi grinned, sure that his face couldn't be seen at this distance. His grin faded as he saw the general pointing in his direction as he shouted something at Yanna. Yanna saluted; the general turned and marched away, his men in a line jogging to keep up. Lebasi could see Yanna wiping his forehead with a cloth.

He waited until the evening meal to find out what the general had said. Yanna sat beside him on the grass with a plate of beans and said, 'I hope you've learned a lot today.'

Lebasi nodded. 'I think so. You'll have to ask Barran.'

Yanna's face was unusually serious. 'No. I really mean I hope you've learned a lot. The general wants you to tack up Mountain tomorrow, and to be there when he rides him.'

Lebasi sat with his mouth open. Yanna answered the silent question in his eyes.

'Why? These Thrarn, they're brutes around people, but they treat horses better than humans. They think of them as we think of our friends. He reckons you can make Mountain behave for him.'

Lebasi managed to gasp, 'But - I can't - I don't -'

Yanna rubbed his chin. 'It's not really up to you. It's up to the horse. Let's hope he's feeling a bit more cooperative tomorrow. Or both of you might regret it.'

The next morning, Lebasi followed Yanna to collect Mountain from the field. They combed him and dressed him, and talked to him constantly, cajoling him to let the general ride. Once again, it was afternoon before the Thrarn appeared, marching up the hill in a tunic that was bright blue with gold and silver patterns woven into it. Lebasi held Mountain's reins, sensing that the horse was

as unhappy as he was to see the general. He and Yanna stood to attention as El-Arnor arrived.

'So,' he said, 'you have told this horse what is required?'

Lebasi couldn't think of a good answer. He simply made the sign of respect and looked beseechingly into Mountain's eye. The general put his foot in the stirrup and pulled himself up effortlessly. Lebasi handed him the reins.

'Better,' El-Arnor said. 'Let us see if he will do what I tell him today.' Lebasi watched how he pressed the back of his calf into the horse's flank. Mountain walked forward, broke into trot, followed by a canter, then turned sharply left and right. He weaved in and out of the other horses as they grazed. Lebasi could always see the general, even when the horse was hidden.

He heard Yanna letting out a long breath. The attendants did the same. They started muttering to each other in Thrarn. Yanna put a hand on his shoulder. 'He might be right, you know. Maybe that horse listens to you.'

Mountain came trotting back. El-Arnor was red in the face from the exertion, but he was grinning. He dismounted just as gracefully as he had mounted and handed the reins back to Lebasi. He gave Lebasi a playful punch in the shoulder that nearly knocked him over.

'Now I will say thank you for bringing back my brother's horse.' He leaned forward and whispered loud enough for everyone to hear, 'As I told you, he is better than the one I have now.'

He turned to Yanna. 'I have other matters to attend to tomorrow, so I will not ride him. No one is to ride him but me.'

As he turned to leave, one of the attendants saluted and nervously pointed to the general's chest. He said something in Thrarn. El-Arnor looked down, then patted his clothing all over, muttering.

Yanna asked, 'What is it, sir?'

The general turned to him, just as red-faced as before, but now with a snarl instead of a grin. 'A medal. It has fallen from my tunic, somewhere in the field.'

Yanna saluted. 'We cover every pace of this field all day, sir. We'll find it and bring it to you.'

The man growled, 'See that you do. It is a precious thing, made of gold and diamonds, given to me by my father the king. If anyone finds it and thinks it is his to keep, he is wrong.'

27
ON THE BRIDGE

In the morning they lined up for tools again. Ruffur signalled to Tik to follow close behind him, and when they reached the wagon he grabbed two spades and put one in her hands. A watching soldier shook his head.

'Not the little one.' He pointed at Tik. 'You, over here.' The same line of boys was forming up ready for a day on the railing.

Ruffur stopped and drew in a deep breath. He seemed to make a low rumbling sound before any words came out. He got as far as, 'You'd better not hurt h–' when Sammas had a coughing fit and collided with him. The soldier squared up to them both, but Sammas held up one hand while pulling Ruffur back with the other. 'Sorry, he's just a bit protective of his brother, all right?'

Tik saw the realisation cross Ruffur's face that he had been about to say 'her'. She couldn't help grinning. Sammas did the thinking, all right. But the soldier wouldn't have understood anyway, neither the mistake nor the apology in the king's language.

'I'll be all right, my brothers,' she called out to them as they walked away. 'I did it yesterday and I can do it today.'

Some of the others didn't seem to be so sure. She heard some whimpering ahead of her. The soldiers tied them to the rope one by one and watched them climb onto their perch, then slouched back to their makeshift shelter from the sun.

Tik was at the end of the line today. She had tried to strike a balance at breakfast between drinking enough and drinking too much. For the moment, the sun was behind them and there was even a slight breeze. She glanced to her left to see how the others were shaping up. They were one behind another, of course, but she could see some bowed a little forward, some with their knees sagging already.

'How about a story?' she called out. 'Here's one about Xessus and his soldiers and how they stood on a bridge.' She heard laughter. She started to make something up, a mixture of half a dozen Xessus legends woven together to fit. She worked in 'a cradle holds no courage' but avoided mentioning graves. They would know the story, anyway. She didn't have to say all the words. She just wanted to remind them to be brave.

After a while she felt her throat drying up. 'I'll tell you how it ends tomorrow,' she said. 'I need to keep my mouth shut for a bit. The bugs keep flying in it.'

The boy next to her said, 'That's what my ma says to me when I talk too much.' He pushed a shaggy blond fringe out of his eyes and grinned at her. 'What happened to your hair?'

Before Tik could reply, another voice from further down offered to tell another story. 'I can't make it up like that, though. I haven't the brains.' So he told the story of Xessus and Artay and Shasho, and one of the other boys joked that Artay seemed to have settled on the bridge and they could do with a visit from Shasho.

The sun was nearly overhead when Tik spotted movement out on the plain. Two wagons were approaching, not empty like the carts the exiles sent for the harvest but loaded with luggage. 'Here come some more farmers,' she called to the others. Heads appeared one by one, leaning forward to take a look. 'Steady,' someone said. 'No wobbles.'

For the first time since they had put the children on the railing, the soldiers left their shelter and lined up across the road. Tik squinted against the sunlight. She realised that they were not the same men that had stood guard the day before. The one who stood in front – he must be the sergeant – was a taller man. The others were still swatting at the flies. Yesterday's squad had given up.

There was also something different about today's travellers. As they drew nearer, Tik realised that there were no younger men. Women were leading the oxen and shepherding a gaggle of children. There was an older couple on each driving seat, grandda and grandma. Behind them, sheets of material tied on with rope, holding down – and hiding – the baggage.

The sergeant held up his hand as the first wagon reached him. 'Hold up.' He pointed with his sword. 'Take your cart over there and find a space to camp.'

The woman holding the leading-rein stared at him blankly. The old man on the seat said, 'She doesn't understand. Talk to me.'

The soldier waved his blade again. 'Not much to understand, old man. Go over there.'

'We were told we could pass. We paid six sheep to be allowed to go.'

'You were told wrong. Your sheep got you this far, no further.'

Tik frowned. What did this mean? Something had changed since yesterday. The soldiers, their orders – what else?

The grandfather said something to his wife, then twisted round and spoke to the people behind. He turned back to the sergeant.

'We'll only be in the way. Women who can't dig, children. Two old men. Why keep us here? Have a heart, let us through.'

The sergeant took a pace forward and reached out a finger to lift up the head of the woman who held the leading animal. Tik shivered. Everyone told her that soldiers did terrible things to women. He held her chin and studied her face for a long moment. Without moving his gaze, he said, 'How about we have a look in your wagons, old man? How about we stick our swords in, just to find out if there's anything soft in there?'

The old man stared at him. He dropped his eyes. 'My dear, we need to turn and go where he was pointing.'

The soldier let go. The woman stumbled backwards. She stammered, 'What? Why? You said they would let us through.'

The old man kept his voice even. 'Do it now. We are in danger here.'

She pulled on the rope and the ox started to move. There was hardly room for them to turn the corner without backing up. The older people climbed down and pushed on the sides of the cart to force the front wheels over. The younger women and children joined them. The soldiers stood in their line across the road, watching.

Tik turned towards the boy next to her. He smiled. 'Maybe we can get some other sparrows to perch up here tomorrow, eh?'

She frowned at him. It was tough standing on this parapet, but she wouldn't wish it on anyone else. She said, 'Then you won't hear the end of my story.'

✶ ✶ ✶ ✶ ✶

The wagons loaded with the day's harvest trundled past.

During the day, Tik had worked out how they could get down without pulling each other over and giving the soldiers something to laugh at. She whispered to the boy next to her, 'When they say we're done, I walk towards you first, then there's enough rope between us. When I'm on the deck we both walk along and then you jump.' He nodded and passed the message on. It was tricky moving and balancing on stiff legs after standing so long, but they all managed it.

As they walked back towards the camp, rubbing sore muscles and stretching, the boy appeared beside her. 'Hello,' he said. 'I'm Callie.'

'I'm Tik.'

'Where are you from?'

'Marstor land. Up by the Westwall.'

Callie whistled. 'You must have seen them first, then.'

Tik nodded. She was still annoyed that he thought she might think the same as him about putting other children on the bridge in their place, so she wasn't keen to tell her story. Instead, she asked, 'What about you? Where are you from?'

'Same as you, Marstor land. But south, on the coast.'

'Farmers?'

'A bit of that, but mainly fishers. We had a boat, we took our catch to market in Anessam.' He smiled. 'Why do all that digging, if you can pull food out of the sea and swap it with someone who works harder than you?'

Tik decided she didn't like Callie. She was about to suggest that he would be digging tomorrow if he found someone else to stand on the bridge for him, when Ruffur jogged up. She smiled at him.

'Hello, big brother,' she said.

He grinned back. 'Hello, little brother. You all right?'

She nodded. 'Nothing to it. Just standing in the sun. How about you?'

Ruffur tugged at the shoulders of his tunic where they were stuck to his skin. 'Need a wash. Got to go downstream for it. Don't want to put this anywhere near where the drinking water comes from.'

She laughed and pinched her nose. 'This is –' she started, but when she turned to look, Callie had gone.

✶ ✶ ✶ ✶ ✶

The next day passed in the same way, but the whimpering had stopped. The children on the bridge told stories and sang songs. When the sergeant walked up and down the line they stood straight and stared over his head, then pulled faces when he had gone past. Tik smiled to herself. *The invaders may be stronger in some ways but that's not everything. We will fight them until they are beaten.*

Callie wasn't next to her. She listened for his voice from further along the line, but she didn't hear him. When they were allowed down at the end of the day, she checked the faces of the others as they passed, and recognised one of the boys from the previous day's wagons. The thought that Callie might have done something to put another child on the railing made her angry. She was about to go looking for him when Ruffur arrived, hot and out of breath, as he had each day so far, and distracted her.

She only remembered Callie later when she was on her way back from the latrine trenches, guided by the flickering from the soldiers' fire-drum in the gloom of dusk. Too late to go looking for him now. She would have to see if she could find him in the morning. She half-heartedly slapped at something biting her arm. She wondered that there was anything left for them to suck on.

'Where is Niram?' She heard Marrak's voice up ahead and quickened her step so she would hear what he was saying to the sergeant.

'Who wants to know?'

'My name is Marrak. I am in charge here.'

The man laughed. 'Hey, lads, this peasant thinks he's in charge. What d'you say we toss him in the river?'

Tik heard Marrak clicking his tongue. 'All right, have your little joke. Niram and I have an agreement. I make sure that the harvest is gathered quickly, and Niram helps us keep sickness out of the camp.'

Tik was close enough to see them now. She crouched down in the shadows.

'So what?'

Marrak pointed behind him. 'In spite of my efforts, we have some people who are ill. They need rest and they need care, not to be made to work in the hot sun.'

The sergeant drew himself up straight. He was a little taller than the agent, and he was making the most of that. 'Too bad. We need the food in quickly. Everyone works.'

Marrak spread his hands. 'Surely you can see that you do not want sick people gathering food that your men will eat. If you will not let them rest, then let us send them on ahead on wagons, so that the sickness does not spread.'

The man shook his head. 'Road's closed. Orders.'

Marrak knocked his knuckles together. 'Again I say, where is Niram? He talks sense.'

The soldier reached out and gripped Marrak by the throat. 'Oh, and I don't, is that it?'

Tik held her breath. Marrak did nothing to resist or protest. The soldier let go. He wiped his hand on his tunic as if it needed cleaning. He sneered, 'Anyway, who put you in charge?'

Marrak spoke quietly. Tik sensed the anger he was holding down. 'I am the agent for the magistrate of the Westwall District. These people do not know how to set up a camp. I learned it, long ago. I have stayed here to make sure that they stay healthy, as I agreed with Niram, so that your food is collected as quickly and safely as possible, and the people can leave.'

The sergeant clicked his fingers. Two of the other men walked over from the fire. 'Magistrate's agent, eh? Bind him, lads.' Once again, Marrak made no protest as the soldiers tied his hands behind his back. 'The general's collecting people we might use for bargaining. Reckon you fit that description.' He tapped one of the men on the shoulder. 'Fancy a walk, sonny?'

The man objected, 'Come off it, sarge, in the dark?'

The sergeant slapped his neck. 'Think of it as a holiday from these threbbing bloodsuckers.'

As the man set off with Marrak stumbling at the end of a leading-rope, the sergeant called after him, 'Maybe you'll see your pal Niram up there. He's been reassigned. Thrarn reckoned he was too soft on your lot. Now he's in charge of guarding the prisoners.'

28
THE PRISONER

After breakfast Yanna addressed the whole of his team together. 'Normal duties today, lads, we've got too much on for us to spare people to search for the general's gewgaw. But keep your eyes open for something shiny on the ground.'

Lebasi had spent the night convincing himself that Riadsala was the prisoner in town and had come up with a plan to give himself a chance of finding out for certain. He volunteered for dung patrol. Yanna studied him shrewdly.

'Two days of tack-work, and you want to get back to your shovel?'

Lebasi hesitated. He didn't have a credible explanation except for the truth.

Yanna checked that no one was close by and spoke quietly. 'Listen to me, Basi. I know that there's something different about you, right?' He held up his hand as Lebasi started to speak. 'But don't worry about me. Or the other grooms. We look after the horses. We don't care much for the bleggers who ride them.' He winked. 'Mountain likes you, and that's enough of a recommendation for me.'

Lebasi collected a barrow and spade and set off out into the field. He had to go where the droppings were, of course, but he did his best to remember where the general had ridden Mountain the day before. He tried to recall the size and shape of the general's medal, but he had avoided looking at him directly. He only thought it must be sparkly, from its description, and it ought to be easy to spot in the bright sunlight. He trudged backwards and forwards, through the morning and on into the afternoon, but found nothing in the grass except droppings. He took to breaking them up with the shovel after putting them in the barrow, in case somehow a horse had swallowed the thing.

He sat by the pool where the grooms washed at the end of day, worn out and disappointed. He would have to think of something else, but what other reason could he have for going into Awato?

As he waited for the evening sun to dry him, enjoying the cool breeze on his skin, he became aware of a group of the other grooms huddled together a little distance away. They were gathered around one man who had something in his hands – they were all staring at it, talking in low voices – it could only be –

'What are you looking at?' A tall lad on the edge of the group broke away and took two steps towards Lebasi, folding his arms across his chest.

Lebasi knew some things weren't done, not in Trengam and surely not on the other side of the wilderness either. He couldn't tell Yanna, he certainly couldn't tell the Thrarn. He couldn't even suggest that it would be dangerous to keep the medal – he had seen how angry El-Arnor was at simply losing it, and he didn't want to imagine what he would do if he thought someone had stolen it from him.

He shook his head and held up his hands. 'Nothing.'

Some of the other lads joined the first, hands on hips, jaws jutting. That was the same in both places, certainly – a bunch of young men trying to look intimidating. Lebasi stood up and squeezed some water out of the tunic he had rinsed in the pond.

One of them pointed a finger at him. 'If you tell –'

Lebasi jabbed straight back. 'Never. Don't even think it. If Yanna finds out, it won't be from me. But you'd better think about Yanna finding out. I'm new here, but I can see he doesn't miss much.'

He turned and walked away, slinging his damp tunic over his shoulder. He wondered if they would follow him, but he didn't want to look round. He went straight to his bedding roll and lay on it, waiting for the call to dinner. He wanted to make sure they could all see he talked to no one.

The cook rattled a spoon against a pan to summon everyone to the food wagon. Lebasi fell in line behind the lad who had been at the centre of the group. Neither of them spoke. Lebasi took his plate and sat near him, to make sure he couldn't be accused of anything.

Yanna whistled for silence. He called out, 'Has anyone found anything interesting out in the field today?'

Lebasi kept his eyes forward, but out of the corner of his eye he could see the groom fidgeting.

Yanna scanned their faces slowly. 'Don't play games with me, boys. A thing like that doesn't just disappear. Between you, you must've covered every blade of grass since breakfast.'

He pointed at Lebasi. 'Dung patrol. Anything?'

Lebasi shook his head, wishing he could transmit a message with his eyes that only Yanna would be able to read.

Yanna asked another groom, then another. On the fourth question, the boy with the medal stood up. 'I found it. Here it is.' He reached inside his tunic and pulled it out.

Yanna walked across and snatched it out of his hand. It glittered in the sunlight, a gold circle the size of a man's palm, with white jewels set in it.

'What in the name of Dennara did you think you were going to do with that? Blood and bone, Larko. It wouldn't just be your neck, it would be mine and half your friends.'

The lad studied the ground and mumbled something. Yanna grabbed his chin and forced him to look up. 'How about you take it down to give back to the general, eh?'

The lad struggled against Yanna's grip. His words were slurred. 'Don' make me do tha', please, Yanna. I'm sorry.'

'I'll take it.' Lebasi stood up.

Yanna let go of the other lad and turned. He raised his eyebrows. 'Why would you offer to do that?'

Lebasi shrugged. 'I've been there before.' He looked around at the faces of the horseminders, all staring at him. 'All right, he's frightening, but I'd be taking it back, wouldn't I? I was there when he realised he'd lost it. I'd just be doing what he said.'

Yanna stepped towards him. Lebasi held out his hand. Yanna put the medal in his palm, closing his fingers over Lebasi's and holding him there. 'All right. But show it to nobody on the way, tell nobody what you've got, and put it in the general's hand yourself.' He glanced round at the other grooms and said in a voice loud enough for them all to hear, 'It seems to muddle some people's heads. I wouldn't want you to give it to someone who forgot to return it to the general, when everyone saw you leaving here holding it.'

✳ ✳ ✳ ✳ ✳

Lebasi kept his hand on the medal in his pocket all the way down to the edge of town. The sun had set, but there was enough light from a moon just past the quarter to find a path between the horses. He smiled to himself. He was glad he had worked so hard all day – there was less muck to tread in.

'Who goes?' came the challenge from the shadows of the first house. The sentry stepped out with a lantern and held it up to inspect Lebasi.

'I've got a message for the general from Yanna.' Lebasi answered.

'Oh, it's you.' He recognised Muscot's voice. From his tone, Lebasi guessed that he had also found something to drink among the storerooms of Awato. He called out to someone still in the building, 'It's that dung-beetle again.' He cleared his throat and spat on the ground. 'What's your message, then?'

Lebasi closed his fingers around the medal. 'My message is for the general. If you want to delay me taking it to him, you'd better be ready to tell him why.'

Muscot whistled softly. 'My, my. Dung-beetle's a bit full of himself this evening.'

He lunged forward as if to swing a punch. As Lebasi staggered backwards to avoid it, the man flicked the door on the lantern shut, leaving Lebasi momentarily blinded. He heard the guard's footsteps and his low chuckle as he walked away.

Lebasi walked in the middle of the street, trying not to look suspicious. After all, he had a reason to be there. It was the way back that was occupying his mind. He watched out for the lanterns on the wall and men standing to attention that marked the house in which he was sure Riadsala was being held. He couldn't stop and look, but he was able to note that there was a turning just before it and the side of the building was dark. There was only one guard outside. Lebasi called out, 'All right there?' as he approached.

The man said nothing but continued to stand stiffly with his sword drawn and held out in front of him. Lebasi guessed the reason just as the door opened and a Thrarn stepped out. In the light from the lantern, he recognised El-Arnor himself. Surely only Riadsala would be important enough for the general to visit.

Two more Thrarn came out. The three men took no notice of Lebasi and started to march away towards the brightly lit windows of the house he had visited before.

'General, sir, excuse me!' Lebasi called after them.

'Not a good idea,' hissed the man by the door.

The three Thrarn stopped and turned. Lebasi couldn't see their faces clearly. He touched his forehead, bowed, and took the medal out of his pocket. 'Yanna sends his respects, sir, and one of his men found your medal.'

El-Arnor clapped his hands together, making a noise that reminded Lebasi of being hit with the stick in the Trengam courtroom. But the roar he let out sounded happy rather than angry.

'You have it? Bring it here, let me see it.'

Lebasi jogged forward, his hand held out. The general took the medal from him with surprising gentleness, holding it up so that it glinted in the lamplight from his house. He laughed, he punched his two companions on the arm one after the other. He moved his feet in what Lebasi suddenly realised was a little dance on the spot. At last he reached forward and ruffled Lebasi's hair.

'Did you find it, boy?'

Lebasi shook his head. 'No, sir. One of the others. But I knew where to bring it, so Yanna sent me.'

El-Arnor was hardly paying attention. 'Very good, very good. Tell Yanna to give the boy who found it double rations of food, or let him off duty tomorrow, or something.' He took one of the other men by the arm as he turned. 'Let's see if we can find a few more bottles of that half-decent wine.'

The second guard emerged from the house as the Thrarn walked away. Lebasi could just see his grin in the light of the lanterns hanging on the wall. 'Should've claimed credit, boy. They'd have taken you in to join the party.'

Lebasi shuddered, and the other soldier laughed. He said, 'Still, I reckon we won't be bothered again tonight, so thanks for that.'

Lebasi decided it was safe to try to find something out from them. After all, they had started the conversation. 'Do you have to stand out here all night?'

'No, we're about to be relieved.'

Lebasi decided that answered the main question – someone

would be there, even if not them – and anything more would sound overly curious. He glanced behind him to see the general going into the garden of his house, touched his forehead to the guards and wished them a good night, and sauntered off down the street.

At the second crossroads, he glanced back. He was sure the soldiers could no longer see him. He turned left and scurried one block to the north, then left again to come back to the street on which the prison-house stood. He crossed over and crept along close to the wall of a garden until he reached a gateway.

He stopped to get his bearings. The moonlight was tricky, but he reckoned that this was the back of the right house. He tried the handle. The gate opened. He stepped through, closed it silently behind him, and stood still, listening. Silence. He followed a path beside the wall until he reached the back of the house.

Croo CROO croo

He stopped, his pulse racing. Then he shook his head. It had to be a real pigeon. He felt his way along the brickwork until he found a wooden shutter. He put his ear against it and heard gentle snoring. The prisoner, or a guard? Did Riadsala snore? He had no idea. He tried the shutter with his fingertips, but it wouldn't move. It must be fastened from the inside. He edged along to look for another way in. The house hid the moon, so he had to do everything by feel. He stubbed his toe on something heavy on the ground and clamped his mouth shut to stop himself crying out. Another pace, another, another, hand over hand against the stonework – he felt the different texture of wood. Another shutter? He tested the edges with his fingers. This one swung gently towards him. He found the windowsill, sat on it and swung his legs over, moving as slowly as he could.

The inside of this room was completely black. Behind him, the shape of the window was a different shade of darkness, but it cast no light. Once again he edged around, looking for a door that would take him back towards the sleeper, one hand on the wall, the other held out blindly in front to avoid bumping his head. The darkness didn't bother him – he had spent a lot of time in the tunnels under Trengam – but the uncertainty made him hesitate. In the tunnels he had learned to walk confidently, knowing the shape of the space.

He felt a door frame, and beyond it a gap. He stepped through and listened again. Now there was a clue: to his right, he could see a thin line of yellow light, how far off it was hard to say. He guessed that must be the edge of the front door, lit up by the lantern outside. He was probably in a hallway. The room with the sleeper would be two paces in front of him. He put his hands out and stepped across. Yes, there was a door. He found the handle, opened it silently and sidled through. He heard the snoring again, slow and steady. He pushed the door closed again. The gentle thud of it touching the frame seemed to echo in the darkness.

The snoring stopped.

Lebasi stood very still, wondering whether to risk speaking. He ran over his escape route in his mind, if the sleeper – now perhaps awake – turned out to be a guard.

'Captain Riadsala, is that you?' he whispered.

The reply came, also a whisper – not a guard – 'Who is there?'

Not a voice he recognised. But Tik said Riadsala had been injured, had breathed the poison smoke. Maybe his voice had changed. And he spoke the king's language, not Xessan.

'Lebasi.'

'Who are you and what are you doing here?'

Lebasi moved towards the voice. 'It's Lebasi, the magistrate's son.'

'Xela's boy? What in the name of Xessus –' the voice rose, then returned to a whisper. 'Are you friend or foe?'

Lebasi's leg struck the edge of a bed. 'Friend, if you're being held prisoner.' He was sure now it wasn't Riadsala. He was risking his life to speak to someone he didn't know. But he was here now, and the man must be important to the Thrarn in some way – he should at least find out.

'Who are you?'

'Romesh, the mayor of Nampetch,' came the reply. 'Sit on the bed. I'm chained to it.'

Lebasi perched awkwardly, not daring to come within reach of the unseen man's hands. He remembered Marrak telling him that Romesh and Xela had argued, and he thought that Nampetch had maybe supported the revolution – he wasn't sure he trusted the man. But that was all before the invasion.

'What are you doing here?' Romesh hissed.

'I was looking for someone else. The captain of the Guard. I thought he might be a prisoner here.' Lebasi considered. 'Do you know if there are any others being held?'

'No. The only people I see are those brutes the Thrarn, asking me questions, and the menking guards who bring my food and escort me to the toilet. There may be others, I can't say.'

Lebasi wondered how he could leave the man, tied up and helpless, without offering to do anything for him, but what choice was there? While he was thinking, Romesh settled the question for him. 'You need to get out of here. You don't know how much good you've done me – if you're real, and not a dream – just by showing that there's something in the world that these people haven't beaten yet. Go, now.'

Lebasi stood up.

The voice came again. 'Wait. Come closer.' Lebasi edged towards the head of the bed. 'I put my badge on when I went out to talk to them, expecting them to show my office some respect.' He sniffed. 'Small chance of that. They didn't ask to see it, and they haven't even bothered to search me. It's still hanging round my neck. Take it. That'll do me good, as well, knowing they won't have it. Xela's son, you're a good person to give it to.'

Lebasi reached out in the darkness and found the man's head. He ran his fingers down past his ears and found the chain tucked under his tunic. It caught on Romesh's ears for a moment, then he felt the disc in his hand, and slipped it into his pocket to join the ones Alfas and Xela had given him.

'Keep it safe, if you can. Go well, Lebasi.'

He edged back towards the door. He pulled it open and felt a change in the air, as if he was outside. A thought occurred to him. 'Romesh, are you fussy about the food?'

The voice in the darkness said, 'Me? That's a laugh. They never give me enough.'

'Who's there?' A voice from the hallway. Lebasi turned and strode straight across into the room he had first entered, not turning his head, ignoring the brighter light that he knew would reflect in his eyes if he looked.

'Hey!' Rapid footsteps.

The shape of the window helped him now. He hoped there was nothing in the way that he couldn't see. *Four quick paces, on the sill, swing over, push the shutter closed. Scuttle round the edge of the garden again. Take no notice of lantern-light in the corner of his eye.*

He heard Romesh calling for a drink, speaking Xessan – doing his best to distract the guards – maybe hoping to persuade them that their eyes and ears were playing tricks.

Lebasi took a deep breath and opened the gate, hoping the other man wouldn't be waiting there. He stepped out and glanced back up the street. It was empty. He ran as silently as he could to the next crossroads and round the corner. Only when he had covered the next block and turned back towards the main street did he allow himself to stop and catch his breath.

He had done it. They hadn't caught him. And there must be another prisoner, one who complained about the food. Maybe he had used up the only chance he would get to break into the prison, but he was sure that other captive was Riadsala.

The main street was deserted. He jogged back towards the edge of town, passed through the dismantled gateway, and slowed to a walk.

'It's turd-boy again.' Muscot's voice was even more slurred than it had been earlier. He opened the shutter of his lantern, revealing that he was sitting on a chair outside one of the shacks by the roadside. There were three other men round a table, several bottles on the table.

Lebasi kept walking. 'I've delivered my message. I'm going back to camp now.'

Muscot stood up, propping himself with an arm on his chair. 'You've been a long time.'

'The general wanted to talk. I've only just got away.'

One of the other figures stood up, then a third. Lebasi recognised the voice of the guard who said he was waiting for his relief. 'That's not true. You were done in a moment. Where've you been?'

Lebasi considered running, but running would be an admission of guilt. In his moment of hesitation, the four guards surrounded him. Muscot's whine reminded him of the last time he had been caught out by the man.

'I think we'd better take you to see Niram.'

29
IN THE FIELDS

Tik counted in her head. She reckoned it had been Moonsday when they were caught on the seashore; Earthsday, Mindsday, Kingsday had passed. It would be Sunday in the morning. How many days could they delay before trying to move south? Should they wait for the harvest to be finished and go with the others? She sat by the roadside under the stars, listening for bird calls, hearing nothing but crickets. Lights twinkled along the top of the dark band that marked the far side of the valley. Some must be campfires; she reckoned others, faint and evenly spaced, were probably lanterns glowing in the windows of buildings in the town. She wondered what Lebasi was doing at that moment. Would she be able to tell if he had been found out? He might be dead, for all she knew. Sammas had been right. She needed to take her message south. She should take the decision, they should try to climb across under the bridge.

She shook her head. That was the night talking. He was lucky, he was clever – everyone said so. Tassie, Verb, Sammas, Ruffur – they all reckoned Lebasi was a survivor. And he had come back from the other side of the Westwall, when that had been impossible. She had waited outside Trengam when he had told her not to. He must come back. They could wait another day before taking that risk.

Still, there were only crickets. She guessed by the setting moon that it was time to wake Ruffur. She could only make out the rough shapes of the sleeping boys in the starlight, but it was easy to tell which was which. She knelt beside the larger lump and tapped him gently on the shoulder. He sat up straight away, nodded to her, and shifted to face north – not that there was anything to see.

'All quiet?' he whispered.

'So far,' she replied, as she wrapped herself in her blanket and tried to find a patch of ground with fewer lumps in it.

In the morning she followed the usual line to the wagons, expecting to be called aside, but she was handed a basket and told to go with the others. As they marched through the camp on the way to the harvest fields, she spotted Callie sitting on his own, just watching them pass by. Surely he would have to dig, whether he wanted to or not – there was no fishing to be done.

Sammas noticed him too. 'What's he up to?'

Ruffur shrugged. 'Reckon the soldiers will chivvy him along in a moment.'

Tik glanced back several times, but Callie stayed where he was.

It was a long walk. They left the camp behind and passed another bridge with another group of soldiers gathered round a fire. Ruffur pointed out where they had already harvested over the previous three days.

'There were people here at least three days before that, clearing the fields downstream of the camp. There's still a lot left, though.'

They reached the line of wagons parked on the road, waiting for the Xessans to fill them with food. A branded man directed them to a field covered with pumpkins and other squashes.

Tik filled her basket and carried it back to the wagon with Sammas. She frowned. 'I don't understand. We grow these on the farm, but they're never ready to harvest just after Midsummer.'

She studied the other produce on other wagons. 'All of this. It's too early in the year. But it's all ready. They're not just picking it when it's half grown.'

Sammas lifted the heavy basket up and tipped it onto the flat bed of the wagon. 'Someone from Awato explained it to me yesterday. It's to do with the land here being below the level of the sea, and sheltered by the sides of the valley, and the soil's really good. They harvest most things twice a year, some crops three times. He said it's the wonder of Xessus, this valley. Could feed three times the people who live here, even if we didn't farm the rest of the countryside at all.'

'But we do.'

Sammas balanced the empty basket on his head for the walk back. 'That's right. We don't get to eat anything that's grown here. It all goes south, to the king, every bean, every grain.' He chuckled. 'King's going to have to beat the Thrarn, isn't he, or he's going to go hungry.'

They worked all morning. A few exile soldiers patrolled the fields. They heard occasional orders angrily shouted in the middle distance, but the man who passed by them from time to time seemed happy with what they were doing and left them to get on with it. At midday he told them they could have a break.

'Go get yourselves a drink. There's some food for you over by the river. But don't take too long - you have to fill that wagon before you go back to camp.'

Tik translated for Ruffur and Sammas and followed them to collect their lunch. Some of the Xessans had been assigned to cooking duties rather than harvesting. Ruffur sat down heavily and stared at a small plate of vegetable stew with a glum expression.

'Not much to keep you going all afternoon,' he grumbled. 'Good thing we've still got some of my da's stuff back at the camp.'

They climbed up the low bank to look down on the water channel. Tik marvelled at how evenly it had been made – stretching in a straight line in both directions as far as she could see, the sides formed of smooth brown earth and gravel, the path along the top of the bank paved with flat stones. She shaded her eyes and tried to see where it went at the head of the valley, but she couldn't make it out.

'Why's it so empty?' Sammas wondered. 'D'you think Basi's already done what his da said, and turned off the water?'

Tik shook her head. 'It was like this when we arrived, remember?'

Ruffur scrambled back up the bank with filled water-skins for all three of them. 'It's funny,' he said, 'because the channels up in the fields are full, and they're higher up than the main one. It's like the sea being higher than the valley. Water's supposed to be all the same level, isn't it? In the town we say there's nothing flatter than a pond.'

Tik thought that was an unusually detailed observation for Ruffur, but she didn't say so. As they walked back to the pumpkin field, she thought of a possible explanation. 'Maybe there's something up at the top of the valley that sends most of the water into the fields, and it's only the extra that comes down the main channel. All this growing must take a lot of water. Even if it's a big river further up, there'd only be a little bit left over.'

They were distracted by more shouting, away to their right. They stopped to look. Tik checked that their exile supervisor was nowhere near, then took out the farsight. She crouched down between Ruffur and Sammas to hide what she was doing.

A group of Xessans had gathered round something on the ground, some standing, some crouching. Two of them were arguing with a soldier. Another soldier, then another and another came running up, swords drawn. One of the group stood up and shook his head. Tik directed the farsight back to the centre of attention.

'I think someone's collapsed,' she said. 'Yes, someone's taking his pulse. I can see – oh.' She lowered the instrument.

'What?' Sammas asked.

Tik folded up the instrument and put it away. 'I think he's dead. They folded his arms across his chest and made the sign of respect.'

Ruffur ground his teeth. 'You said Marrak told them people were ill. Menkers.' He hefted the spade in his hands and looked round as if to find someone to take revenge on.

'Steady, Ruffie,' Sammas said, taking hold of his elbow. 'If we were on our own, we could get stuck in. But Tik can't be involved in any trouble. She's got to get across that river and take her message south, remember?'

Tik stared at him. She had been ready to join Ruffur. But Sammas was right.

There were enough soldiers with enough weapons to make sure the Xessans did no more than argue. But the arguing went on for some time, more Xessans coming across the fields to brandish their tools at the line of soldiers. It was clear that no more food would be harvested for the moment. Tik spotted their own supervisor jogging down the road in the direction of the bridge. She pointed to a tree in the corner of their field. 'Let's find some shade and see what happens.'

The soldier returned with five more. Tik wondered if they had left the bridge unguarded, but dismissed the idea of trying to sneak across in daylight. They would be in clear view for too long on the other side.

The new group joined the others. One of them stepped out in front of the line and held up his hands. 'That'll be the sergeant,' Tik said. 'I hope he's got more sense than the one at our bridge.'

She took out the farsight again, sure that she was a long way from anyone's attention. She watched for a while, then passed it to Sammas, who passed it on to Ruffur.

'I can see Perra,' he said. 'There at the back. Surprised he's not doing the talking.'

'He's given up,' Tik said. They both turned to look at her. She blushed. 'I'm sorry. I know I did too. I needed you to tell me off.'

In the end the soldiers retreated slowly to the wagons, keeping their faces forward. The Xessans followed them and dumped their tools on carts that should have been filled with food. They carried the body from the field and laid him on a wagon as well, following behind it as it slowly bore him back towards the camp.

When they were nearly back to the main road and their own patch of ground, Tik spotted Callie again, walking towards them from the middle of the valley. She left Ruffur and Sammas rummaging in their packs for some of the dried meat they still had left, and went to intercept him.

'Hello, Tik,' he said, grinning broadly. 'How was digging?'

She put her hands on her hips and narrowed her eyes. 'What have you been doing all day? Why haven't the soldiers made you work?'

He studied her curiously. 'Your face, Tik.'

'What?'

He frowned. 'That mark you had. I thought it must be one of those ugly birth things, you know. But it's nearly gone.'

She disliked him even more. But it was a warning, even so – maybe the soldiers would look at her more closely. She growled at him. 'Don't change the subject. Why weren't you –'

'Oh, I've been working,' he interrupted, smirking again. 'I just don't like farm stuff. I told you.'

She pointed across the fields. 'Someone died out there today.'

His smile vanished, but Callie only shrugged. 'Not my fault. I wouldn't have stopped that happening, would I?'

Tik refused to admit that he had a point. 'So what have you been doing?'

'Ha! Wouldn't you like to know?'

Tik jumped forward and flung herself at him, wrapping her arms round his shoulders and knocking him over with her momentum. He was bigger than her, but she had years of practice with even bigger cousins who were more likely to expect an attack. She perched on top of him, one knee on his chest and the other poised to add more pain, her hands pinning his arms.

'Yes,' she said, 'I would.'

Callie spluttered, 'Gerroff, you're hurting me.' When she didn't move, he grunted, 'I told the sergeant I'd run messages over the valley for him if I didn't have to dig.'

Tik lowered her knee. Callie howled. 'You're working for them? For him, that – that –'

'Yes, but it means I know what's going on, doesn't it?'

That thought took Tik by surprise, and she loosened her grip enough for Callie to wriggle and overbalance her. She rolled off him and jumped to her feet, putting her fists up. But Callie didn't want to fight. He walked backwards away from her, smirking. 'I would have told you, but now I'm not going to. Pity. Like you said, you really would like to know.'

He turned and jogged away.

30
NIRAM

'Lost your tongue, have you?' Muscot sneered as he bound Lebasi's hands.

Lebasi said nothing. He remembered that his first plan, as he'd walked along the valley rim with the soldiers, had been to say as little as possible and pretend to be stupid. It was too late to try that now. He had spoken too much and proved that he really was stupid. Why had he risked everything, without even finding Riadsala?

Muscot tugged the rope and made him stagger. The others laughed and fell in beside him as they walked back through the ruined gate. To Lebasi's relief, they turned right into the street just inside the old wall. There was the smallest chance that Niram wouldn't have received a report of a possible intruder in the prison.

There was the smallest chance that there were two officers with the same name.

There was the smallest chance that Niram, the one he knew, wouldn't recognise him. It was dark, maybe his face wouldn't show in the lamplight.

But it would make no difference. He had been caught out in a lie, without the flimsiest excuse.

They stopped outside a modest house with lights showing through the ground floor windows. Muscot swaggered up to the door and knocked.

'Captain, are you there?' he called out. Lebasi guessed that he

was trying not to slur his words. He and his friends had probably carried on drinking all the time Lebasi had been with Romesh.

Lebasi wasn't sure he heard a reply, but Muscot pushed the door open and yanked the rope again. He stumbled over the threshold into a dim hallway. The soldiers behind hustled him forward and through a door into a large room at the back of the house. Lebasi blinked in the flickering light from a dozen candles and lanterns. In the centre of the room, a man was leaning over a table on which something was spread out – Lebasi could see pictures drawn on material, and guessed they were maps. The man raised his head. The smallest chances that he had hoped for disappeared: Lebasi recognised the man he had last seen the other side of the Westwall.

Muscot saluted with an exaggerated flourish and pulled Lebasi forward. He said, 'We caught this dirt-shoveller sneaking about.'

Niram stared straight into Lebasi's eyes. The light was strongest on the table where the maps were, but Lebasi was sure his face must be clearly visible even where he was standing.

The officer straightened up, his expression not changing. He snapped, 'What do you mean, sneaking about? A proper report, please, Muscot.'

Muscot cleared his throat and stood to attention. 'He's one of Yanna's horseminders, we've seen him before. He came into town earlier this evening with some story about having a message to give the general. Dremmen and Oster here saw him hand something to the general in the street and set off back. That was a long time ago. But he's only just come out of the gate now. What's he been doing in the meantime, I'd like to know?'

Niram's mouth twitched. Lebasi wondered if he might even be suppressing a laugh. He put his hand to his chin. 'Have you asked him?'

Muscot shook his head. 'No sir, brought him for questioning straight away, sir.'

Niram stepped out from behind the table. Lebasi was once again reminded of Narus, the old sergeant of the Westwall Guard. Niram wasn't as tall, but he shared the old soldier's short white hair and straight back. He stood in front of Lebasi, staring into his face. Without looking away, he said, 'Thank you. Muscot. I'll take care of this.'

'Sir?'

Niram's tone hardened. 'I think you had better get back to your post before any of the Thrarn come by and wonder why we have no one on lookout. Now!'

Lebasi sensed rather than saw the hurried salutes as the men turned and filed out of the room. He heard them muttering to each other in the hallway. The front door banged shut. Their footsteps faded into silence. Still Niram stared at him. Still Lebasi couldn't think of anything to say.

At last, the captain shook his head and sighed. 'What were you thinking of, poking about in the town after dark? If one of the Thrarn had caught you, you'd be dead already.'

Lebasi opened and closed his mouth. Niram didn't seem to expect a reply.

'And now - well, if I don't order a public flogging, then that drunken nogood will be wondering why I don't take any notice the one time he bothers to do his duty. And if I do order a public flogging, the Thrarn will want to know why, and if I tell them ...' He drew a finger across his throat to indicate what would happen.

Niram rubbed his eyes and peered more closely at Lebasi. 'What's your name, boy? I feel as if I recognise you, but I can't place you. One of the new lot who arrived with El-Arnor?'

Lebasi shook his head.

'You must be. I know every man who came across with El-Kazzak.' He scowled. 'Don't make me angrier than I am already. I will find out, of course I will. All I have to do is ask Yanna.'

Lebasi's throat was dry. His voice sounded strange in his own ears. 'I didn't cross the wilderness. You recognise me because you gave me charro when they were about to brand me.'

Niram staggered backwards, his eyes wide. He edged behind the table, not blinking, his mouth working on words without sound. Lebasi stood very still. A draught from somewhere made the candles flicker, sending shadows scurrying in the corners of the room.

The captain's voice was no more than a whisper. 'You cannot be him. What is your name?'

'Lebasi.'

Niram sank into his chair, still staring at Lebasi's face.

Lebasi was surprised to find that he wasn't frightened of the man any more, even if he was likely to order him to be beaten, or worse. The shock in his eyes made Lebasi feel sorry for him. After all, he had shown Lebasi kindness. 'You wanted to spare me the pain of the hot iron. Thank you for that.'

Something else stirred in Lebasi's memory. 'You said you hoped Dennara's ghost wasn't watching the cruelty that was done in his name. What happened at Anessam?'

The captain turned his face to the side as if he had been slapped. 'I wasn't there. If I had been...' He shook his head. 'How do you know about that?'

'I met a deserter who told me. His name was Caldar. The Thrarn caught him.'

Tears glistened in the man's eyes. He blinked them away and stared down at his hands. His voice became flat. 'Do you remember the story of Xessus and the dragon? How he heard of the beast and thought he could use him to win a battle? And then found that he was riding a monster that he could not control, that would kill him the moment he let go of it?' He spread out his palms and looked up at

Lebasi. 'We should have listened to our legends. The Thrarn are the dragon, and we are holding on for our lives. I am not sure that we could do anything else, if I am honest, but it is clear now that the battle we wanted our pet dragon to win is over, and we are powerless to control it.'

He stood up and walked round the table. 'Here, let me untie you.' To Lebasi's surprise, he smiled. 'You won't attack me, will you?' Lebasi shook his head.

Niram worked quickly and removed the rope. He held out a hand towards a second chair. Lebasi sat down, rubbing his wrists. Niram sat opposite him. He put his palms together and leaned his chin on them. He asked in a low voice, 'How in the world did you survive the battle? How do you come to be here?'

Lebasi briefly explained how he had been rescued when the dragon reached the top of the track up to the Westgate. He repeated the story he had told El-Arnor about being knocked out and waking up to find everyone dead or gone, and the horse setting off into Xessus.

Niram listened in silence, sitting perfectly still. When Lebasi had recounted the part about being captured on the sea wall and brought to the camp where he had joined Yanna's horseminders, he waited for a response. At last Niram narrowed his eyes and asked a question that he had not expected.

'In your travels with the horse, did you visit your father the magistrate?'

'How did you know...'

Niram waved a hand. 'El-Kazzak told us you were the magistrate's son. You have been wandering across Xessus for what, two eightnights? You told El-Arnor that you were simply following the horse, but then you told him that you were one of my soldiers. He thinks you were a stranger, but I know your home is here.'

Lebasi gulped. Niram began to remind him more of Xela than Narus. There seemed to be little point in lying to him. 'Yes, I saw my father.' The memory ignited Lebasi's anger. 'He was sick, probably dying of the disease that you people sent Rodera to give him.'

Niram nodded solemnly. 'Not my decision, I assure you. I am sorry.' He paused again, tapping his fingertips together.

Lebasi leaned forward. He couldn't bear the uncertainty. 'What are you going to do with me?'

Niram rubbed the back of his head and studied the ceiling. He folded his arms and leaned back in his chair. 'I suppose I had better get you back to Yanna by a different road. It wouldn't do to walk you past Muscot, would it? I'll have to think of something to tell him to keep him quiet.'

Lebasi gaped at him. 'You're not... you're just going to let me go?'

Niram ran his hand through his hair. 'I suppose our great-great-grandfathers would have called it a sign from the gods. I am not so sure. But call it what you want, you survived the battle when you should not have done. I am not going to fight against that.'

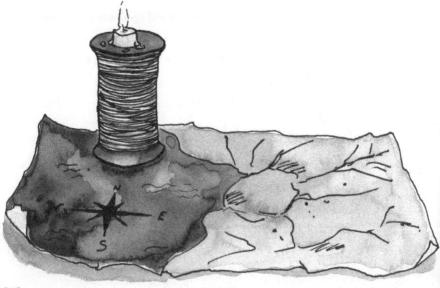

'But I'm...' Lebasi remembered what he had said to Niram just before he received his brand. He didn't finish the thought.

'Not on the same side? Is that what you are thinking, that you and I are enemies?' Niram must have remembered the same thing.

Lebasi nodded.

Niram sighed and stood up. 'I am not so sure of that, any more. You appearing here, like a ghost, has made me see more clearly. I have been trying to control the dragon, but it is futile. Too much cruelty has already been done. I cannot think of a way to stop it, but I will try.'

Niram led Lebasi out into the street and set off north, away from Muscot's guard-post. He took a turning on the right and passed out through the wall. They met two soldiers who stepped out of the shadows to challenge them, then saluted smartly and withdrew when they heard Niram's voice.

'Better men,' he murmured.

As they reached the open field and saw the shapes of horses in the moonlight, Lebasi dared to believe that Niram really was letting him go. He hesitated to take the risk, but he guessed he could ask the question. 'Who are you holding prisoner?'

Niram replied, 'We have three men who El-Arnor thinks might in some way be useful. There is the mayor of one of the towns, there is the magistrate's agent, and there is the captain of the guard.'

Lebasi opened his mouth with a question about Riadsala, but the realisation of what Niram had said stopped him. He stared at Niram. 'You have Marrak?'

Niram put a hand on his shoulder and started him walking again. 'Of course, you know him well. Yes, he was in charge of the camp in the valley until the day before yesterday, when one of the soldiers down there decided to send him up here.' He grunted. 'Idiot. Marrak was much more valuable making sure that the harvest was brought in. But El-Arnor doesn't see it that way, and it is dangerous to disagree with the general.'

They had reached the edge of the horseminders' camp. Niram's expression was hidden in the darkness. 'I will make up a story for Muscot. But if you see him, do not let him see you. He is a vindictive man, and he will not be happy to find that I have chosen simply to return you to Yanna.' He made the sign of respect. 'Do not draw attention to yourself. Even if the gods do not seem to want you yet, you should not give anyone a reason to betray you to the Thrarn. I will think about a way to reunite you with your friends in the valley.'

As he watched the man walking away, Lebasi realised that he had missed his chance. He knew that Riadsala was alive, but he had not found out if he had recovered from his injuries. Still, Niram had almost promised to see him again. He could ask him then.

The general came to ride again late in the morning. He was in a very good mood, grinning and laughing with his attendants who – the moment he turned away – looked just as frightened as they had on the other days. Lebasi and Yanna had tacked up Mountain, and Lebasi had talked to the animal all the time, trying to persuade him to behave.

Yanna clapped him on the shoulder. 'I think we must be related, somehow,' he said. 'We both speak horse.'

Lebasi noticed that the general was not wearing his medal today. He had on a different tunic, without the flashing metal strips, but with bright blue and red patches on the sleeves, back and chest. It was easy to spot him as he made Mountain trot, canter and gallop around the field.

Yanna told Lebasi that they might as well have lunch, because the general would not be back for a while, but Lebasi wanted to know what was happening to the horse. He grabbed a hunk of bread, dipped it in some gravy and took it back to a point from which he could watch.

El-Arnor was at the far end of the field when a group of riders appeared on the road that came in from the north. They were kicking up clouds of dust that hung in the still air. The general went to meet them. Lebasi wished he had the farsight to get a better idea of what was happening. They didn't look like one of the patrols returning after checking for farmers who hadn't left. Lebasi didn't think that any raiding-parties had ridden out for two days, and he had heard Barran say that all their horses were in the pasture. That meant that they had to be part of yet another army arriving from the wilderness. The horsemen spoke with El-Arnor, then all of them together cantered down towards the entrance to the town. A little while later, one of them reappeared, leading a string of horses. Yanna sent some lads to collect them, and Lebasi helped to clean and brush them down. They had been ridden hard – they were covered in sweat and dust. The lads grumbled about making work for them to do, while Lebasi wondered what message had been so urgent that it had to be brought that quickly.

After dinner, Lebasi strolled out into the field to talk to Mountain. The horse nodded to him and carried on eating. Lebasi made sure that no one was near enough to hear, and then started a one-sided discussion with Mountain about what he should do. He missed having Tik to talk and listen to. This was his fifth night in the camp, and he was no nearer a plan for rejoining the others. At least they were still down in the valley, but everyone said that the harvest was nearly complete, and he would have to make a move soon. Or they would have to go without him.

'Lebasi!'

He turned round at Yanna's voice and clenched his fists in shock. Niram was with him, marching quickly up the field. His first thought was that the captain had changed his mind about turning him in. Nonsense, he told himself. He would have come with soldiers, or maybe sent the soldiers and not come himself. In any case, there was nothing to do but wait. Where could he run to?

Niram was out of breath. While he recovered, Yanna said in a low voice, 'I'm not sure how you know the captain here, Lebasi, but he's got something for you to do. Tells me the less I know about it, the better. I'm just here to let you know that he's talked to me, and whatever Niram wants, you go with my blessing. All right?'

Lebasi nodded. Yanna turned and jogged away.

Niram waited until he was out of earshot. He put his hands on Lebasi's shoulders. Lebasi realised that his eyes were wide, as if he had taken charro. 'What is it, Niram?'

Niram took his arm and started walking downhill. 'I will explain on the way. I need you to take a message to your friends in the valley. I have spoken with Marrak, I can tell you where to find them.' He muttered something underneath his breath.

Lebasi asked, 'What did you say?'

Niram's voice was flat, but Lebasi could hear the words. 'We are losing our grip on the dragon, my boy. It is about to devour us all.'

31
THE PLAN CHANGES

Sammas agreed with Tik that they ought to find out what Callie was up to. Ruffur knew what he looked like, but he was too big for spying, so Tik and Sammas went for a walk to see if they could spot him without being noticed. They found a place on the bank of the channel near where Tik thought Callie's camp was. She lay down and scanned for him through the farsight while Sammas kept watch.

'It doesn't work so well in this light. It's hard to see – no, there he is.' She carefully laid the instrument down so that it was pointing in the right direction and changed places with Sammas.

'Which one is he?'

'Sitting down facing this way. Fair hair, a bit taller than me. He's looking at something in his hands.'

'A whistle?'

'Could be.' She crouched down and checked through the farsight. 'Yes, that's him.'

Sammas spent some time studying the boy and the people near him. At last he handed the instrument back to Tik. 'You'd better put it away,' he said. 'I don't understand how you make it shorter. I really don't want to break it.'

As they walked back to find Ruffur, Sammas said, 'I can try to follow him at first light and see what he does, maybe overhear what he says if he talks to the soldiers. What do you think?'

Tik started to answer, then stopped. All the way from Trengam, Sammas had made plans without asking her opinion. She smiled. 'I think that's a good idea.' Then she groaned and shook her head. 'They'll talk in Xessan. I don't think any of the soldiers speak the king's language.'

Sammas shrugged. 'So you're the one who's got to do any listening, but he'll spot you.' He punched one fist into the other palm. 'Still, it's the best we can do. I might find out something.'

✻ ✻ ✻ ✻ ✻

Tik had the first watch, and gratefully fell asleep as soon as she had handed over to Ruffur. When she next opened her eyes, the moon had set and the stars were fading. Even in the dim light, she could tell that Sammas's blanket was empty. She sat up and looked around. Ruffur was rubbing his hands against his upper arms for warmth.

'Have you been awake all night?'

Ruffur turned towards her. The glimmer in the eastern sky was just enough for her to see his smile. 'No, Sammie took his watch. He woke me up when it was time for him to go a-scouting.'

Tik stood up and swung her arms in circles to ease the stiffness from lying on the hard ground. 'I don't think Basi's coming now,' she said. 'We might as well go and wash.'

When they came back they found Sammas waiting for them. He grinned. 'That Callie is a cheeky little menker, I'll give him that.' He explained that he had pretended to be asleep next to the track near the bridge, waiting to see if the boy would report to the sergeant. 'He comes along at first light, whistling to himself, paying no attention to me. I follow him up to the bridge and watch him talking to the sergeant, no sign of respect or anything.'

Ruffur frowned. 'But you can't understand what they're saying.'

Sammas shook his head. 'Not a word. But there are some things you can see as well as hear. They both do a lot of pointing. Sergeant's pointing at the camp, Callie points across the valley. I'm guessing that sergeant wants to talk to someone who'll take charge of us, and clear as anything Callie's telling him that Marrak's the man and he's in Awato. Sergeant gets cross, tries to swat him, Callie dodges and dances out of the way. But in the end he goes off and finds someone. They were having a big talk when I spotted you. Something different's going to happen today.'

Tik crouched down again and took out the farsight. Ruffur sat beside her so she could use his bulk as cover. She quickly picked out Callie, the sergeant, some other soldiers and a Xessan she didn't recognise. He raised his hands in a gesture of resignation, and she spotted his tattoo.

'He's from Marstor land. I don't think Callie's got any family with him, so that must be someone he knows from home, or he's got to know on the way here.' She handed the farsight to Sammas.

He peered through it, then gave it back with a scowl. 'He doesn't look up to much.' He turned to stare across the fields. 'It ought to be Perra.'

Tik didn't say anything. She understood how Ruffur must have felt about her when she said things were hopeless, that day they arrived in the valley. She had heard so much about Perra – not all good, but she had expected him to be more than she had seen. She didn't think it was likely that Perra would take charge.

A whistle sounded from the direction of the bridge, the signal for the start of work. People stood up and started moving, muttering that they hadn't had time to eat breakfast yet, complaining that things were getting worse every day, but falling in line and shambling towards the soldiers regardless. A change was immediately obvious: no one was handing out tools. The whistle had summoned them to hear something, not to go to work.

Callie's man was standing on a wagon, waiting for everyone to assemble. Callie himself was perched on the driver's seat, looking pleased with himself. Tik glanced around and shivered. The Xessans were silent, their heads down. Perra wasn't the only one who had given up. They reminded her of the exiles' army on the Westwall Field after the battle – every man feeling the despair left behind when a triple dose of charro wore off.

'Can you hear me, everyone?' The man's voice barely carried halfway across the crowd, but no one replied. 'The sergeant says they've decided the sick shouldn't touch the army's food, like we've been telling them. So we're not going to harvest today.' That raised a murmur from the listeners. 'We're going to move anyone who's ill to the west of the road across the valley, and have some people look after them.' The murmuring grew louder. The man raised his hands to try to restore quiet so he could be heard. 'Listen! They're going to march south an eightnight from today, and they want all the food that's fit to harvest to be collected as quick as possible. They reckon it'll take another four days to bring it all in. But that's with everyone working hard who can. We want to be on the road a couple of days at least before they start. So, today we move the sick, four days we harvest, then we get going the morning after that. All right?'

Through the day, Tik lost count of the times she overheard people wishing that Marrak was there. Not just those with the red circle tattoo of Trengam – everyone, from all the towns and from the countryside, was sure that the magistrate's agent would have had a plan and known how to make it work. No one else did. The soldiers retreated to their shelter by the bridge and watched; groups of men argued about who should do what, how they should decide who was too ill to work, where they should put them, who would look after them. She waited patiently with the boys to see if there was anything they could do to help, but in the end they wandered a few hundred paces across the valley to keep out of the way.

'How many days is it?' Sammas wondered.

'Five,' Tik replied. She didn't have to ask what he meant. 'I was on the bridge three times, one day harvesting, and now this.'

'He's got to come soon,' said Ruffur, tossing a stone at a target they had set up. He missed and tried again. Sammas joined in, with no more success.

Tik didn't have the heart to beat them, as she knew she could.

✳ ✳ ✳ ✳ ✳

Towards evening they ambled back to their camp. A white-haired Marstor man was sitting on a rock fanning himself with his hat. Tik made the sign of respect to him.

'Hello father. We didn't think we'd be much help, so we've been staying out of the way. What's happened?'

The man ran his hand over his scalp and blew out his cheeks. 'A shambles, lad, is what it is. But I think we have just about sorted it out, taking four times as long as if that fox Marrak had been here.' He pointed across the road. 'There are about fifty people over there judged too sick to work, and another ten or so to look after them. The women and the old men who weren't allowed to cross the bridge volunteered.' He waved a hand behind him. 'The rest of us have spent the day arguing this and that, but I suppose we'll be fresher to get on with the gathering tomorrow.'

Sammas and Ruffur lay down straight after supper, while the sun was still setting, to be ready to take their watches in the middle of the night. Tik put her blanket over her head, hot though it was, and tried to ignore the insects. She rested her chin on her knees and

wrapped her arms round her shins as she stared along the empty
road into the gathering dusk. The zigzag line up to the exiles' camp
merged into the grey blur of the hillside, then the hillside became
the same colour as the sky. The stars faded as a ground mist rose
up to cover the valley floor. When the moon rose, a little less than
half full, the milky glow obscured everything more than twenty
paces away. The insects buzzed.

'Tik!' She started at a gentle hand on her shoulder. The
whiteness, the buzzing were the same but she knew she had fallen
asleep, and felt her face turn red.

'Sorry, I –'

'Never mind that,' Ruffur whispered. 'Listen!'

Croooo croooo

Tik's eyes watered. The sound was faint, but it was different
from the rest of the night noises. It was also different from a pigeon.
She put her hands to her mouth.

Croo croo, croo croo

Crooooooo

She heard the crunch of footsteps on the road. Ruffur was rousing Sammas. There was a figure in the mist. She stood up, her legs unsteady. The shape solidified, came towards her, held out its arms and wrapped them tightly round her. She pressed her head against Lebasi's chest and listened to his heart beating.

'You took your sweet time,' Sammas said from behind her.

Lebasi laughed. Tik let go of him and looked up into his face. 'Are you all right? They haven't guessed who you are?'

Lebasi put a finger to his lips and beckoned to them to follow him a little distance up the road where they wouldn't be overheard. To Tik's surprise, Ruffur gave Lebasi an awkward hug. They sat together in a close huddle.

'I'm fine,' he started. 'I've been working with the horses, and no one bothers me. But I've found something out.' He banged his knuckles together.

'What?' asked Sammas.

'Not easy to make it gentle. El–Kazzak's brother is in charge up there, and he's as mad as his brother was. But he was going ahead with the plan of driving the Xessans in front like the livestock in the story. Today some horsemen arrived in a hurry. I've found out that they were sent by the Thrarn king himself. He's three days away with the rest of the Thrarn and the rest of the exiles, and he's changed the orders.' Lebasi rubbed his hand over his face.

'Spit it out,' said Sammas.

'The new order is to kill everyone, bar a very few who will be sent south to tell the tale. The livestock plan was to confuse the defenders, but this is meant to terrify them. All the people here, when they've finished the harvest – all the people on the road south, they'll be caught by the horsemen.'

Tik dug her fingernails into her palms. Sammas whistled softly. Ruffur growled, 'What can we do to stop them?'

Lebasi leaned forward, his voice urgent. 'I had a message from Marrak – no time to explain how. You have to get everyone across the bridges, two nights from now. You can overpower the few guards they have down here and go over before they can send reinforcements from the camp. Then you have to burn the bridges behind you.'

Tik started to protest. 'But even if we manage to do that, they'll repair the bridges, and –' Then she realised what Lebasi had said. 'We can do that? What about you?'

'I have to go back. It'll take you two days to get people ready to move, and I'll be missed if I'm not there. We don't want them to pay any attention to what's happening down here in the valley. They'd come looking for me, and they'd find me straight away with this mark on my forehead. I can only hide up there, among them, not here.'

Tears sprang up in Tik's eyes. She didn't try to wipe them away. 'But you can't just go back – if we're burning the bridges – how will you...' Her voice trailed away.

He put his arm round her shoulders. 'I'll find a way. I'm here, aren't I? You've got to get moving, take your message. If I don't see you before, I'll meet you in Egator.'

Tik felt a pain in her chest unlike anything she had experienced before. She wondered if it was what they meant when they said in a story that someone's heart broke. All she could think was *I can't do this without you.*

Sammas was tapping his knuckles together. 'Two days to get this lot ready to take on the soldiers and move everyone across the river in the dark? I don't know. Took them all day to sort out something simpler today, with the guards' blessing.'

Lebasi nodded. 'Marrak said that Perra's here. If anyone can make it happen, Perra can.'

Tik's pain sharpened. It was all hopeless. They were going to be caught in a disaster in the valley, and Lebasi was relying on a man who had given up. The only thing that would make it bearable would be if they were together. An idea jumped into her mind. *Give him a reason to stay.* 'Sammas, you've got something to say to Lebasi.'

'What?' said Lebasi and Sammas at the same time.

'Faya,' hissed Tik.

'Oh.' Sammas cleared his throat. 'Basi, I'm sorry, when I said that Faya didn't leave a message for you, that wasn't exactly true.'

Lebasi sounded as if he expected another tease. 'And?'

Sammas rubbed the back of his neck with his hand. He spoke to the ground. 'She said she'd be looking out for you on the road south. Told us to tell you, if we saw you, that – well, she was hoping to see you again soon.'

Lebasi was silent for a long moment, then he chuckled. 'You really are a heartless menker, Sammas. But thanks for telling me now.'

Tik held on to his arm. *So you can't go back. You have to cross the bridges with us, find Faya.* She thought it so hard that she was sure Lebasi would hear her.

He stood up. 'I've got to go. I've got passwords to get by the guards on the road, but they may be no good after the guards change.' He hugged them one by one, Tik last, holding her tightly for what seemed like a long time. 'I'll see you in Egator,' he whispered in her ear. 'Promise.'

32
THIEF

Too many secrets.

Lebasi glanced over his shoulder as he ran, but the mist had swallowed up his friends. Should he have told Tik what he had in mind? The trouble was, saying it would commit him, and he didn't know yet that he could carry it through. Maybe he could just try to stay hidden in the grooms' camp, follow the army south, see what turned up. That was what Tik thought he intended.

Not good enough. The Thrarn king was coming. The orders had changed. He had to do something to draw El-Kazzak's attention away from the valley, something spectacular to give his friends time to organise the escape.

He slowed to a walk to catch his breath, but the insects were worse. Thoughts buzzing inside his head, flies outside.

Could they get everyone across the bridges? Perra was the man to do it. And if they didn't – well, the king was coming anyway, whether they were sitting in the valley or trying to cross the bridges. A small chance was better than no chance at all.

And he had to try to give them time.

'Who goes?' The challenge came out of the mist ahead.

'Friend.' Lebasi replied.

'What's the password?'

'Eagle.' Lebasi hoped he had run fast enough. Niram had told him the guards changed not long after midnight, and the passwords changed with them.

A shadow formed in the mist and hardened into the shape of a man. He growled, 'What've you been doing down in the valley, this time of night?'

Lebasi breathed out. If the word had been wrong, the question would have been different. Or there would have been no question at all. 'Running a message for Niram,' he said. It was even true.

'All right then. Lucky you, going back up top away from these bloodsuckers.' The man clapped him on the shoulder as he trotted past.

By the time he had climbed the road and crossed the upper camp, giving the password five more times, Lebasi would have given a great deal to be able to go to sleep. He didn't dare. He might not wake up in time. As he picked his way quietly between the horses standing in the field, he suddenly wondered if anyone nearby had some charro. That would keep him going.

He dismissed the idea. He needed his mind to be clear to do what he planned.

He almost laughed. He needed charro to believe it might work.

'Hello, Mountain,' he murmured, stroking the horse's shoulder. 'Will you come with me?'

Lebasi hadn't tacked up a horse on his own before, but he had done every part of it with Barran over and over, and Mountain was used to him doing it. Everything was laid out neatly on the wagons, and he was able to lift the saddle into place by standing on the top of the cart. Mountain stood perfectly still as he worked, making no noise. Lebasi kept glancing across towards where the grooms were sleeping, but no one was moving.

'Stay here, all right?' he whispered, wondering if the animal understood anything he said. He padded across to where his backpack and his bedding roll lay on the end of the line of sleepers.

He crouched beside it, listening and watching. There was nothing but gentle snores. He rolled up his blanket and tucked it under one arm, carrying the pack in the other.

There was a water-skin in his pack – empty, but he could easily put that right at the first stream he came to – but he would need food. He hoped the cooks were sleeping as soundly as the grooms, because he knew the price of stolen rations would be a beating at best. Questions he couldn't answer, at worst.

I'm stealing the general's horse. He tried not to laugh. The memory of his night-time walk across the Westwall Field came back, the dreamlike sense that he was watching someone else doing this. He shook himself. That had been charro. This was probably lack of sleep.

The problem was that the cook-wagons were too tidy. The food had all been put away, and he couldn't risk the time or the noise of searching for it. He knew there was still some of Ruffur's dried meat at the bottom of his pack. It would have to do. As he turned away, disappointed, something caught his eye. Lying on the counter where the cooks prepared the food was a meat-cleaver, something between a large knife and a small axe. He might need a weapon.

He picked it up and hefted it in his hand. His mind's eye took him back to the Westwall Field again, Rovert giving him the short spare sword and asking him if he could bring himself to stick it in a man. *I don't know*, he had said, and Rovert had told him that was the right answer. But he might have to. He set off back to find Mountain.

The horse greeted him with a flick of his tail. Lebasi put the cleaver in his pack and tied the rolled-up blanket on top. He swung it onto his shoulders –

Someone grabbed his arm, someone who had made no noise

as he approached. 'What are you doing?' hissed a voice.

Lebasi turned, his heart hammering. The moon had set, and in the starlight alone it was hard to be sure, but he thought he recognised –

'Larko?'

The groom had a strong grip. Lebasi said the first thing that came into his head. 'General's orders.'

Larko didn't let go. 'What orders?'

'When I took the medal you found and gave it to him. He said he wanted to ride this horse, first light today. I'm on my way to meet him. Top of the field.'

It didn't sound likely even in his own ears. But it was all he had. He tried to sound confident, carefree, when he felt the opposite.

'Yanna knows all about it. You can go and wake him up and ask him, if you like.'

Larko hesitated. Lebasi tried again. He managed a chuckle that sounded horribly false. 'Seriously, what else do you think I would be doing? This is the general's favourite horse. He's terrifying. I'm a bit early, but the last thing I want to do is be late.' Larko was relaxing his grip. 'Because it would be the last thing I would do, believe me.'

Larko let go. 'All right,' he said. 'Rather you than me.'

Lebasi tried not to let the relief sound in his voice. 'Go back to sleep. I'll see you later, as long as the general doesn't find a reason to cut my head off.'

Lebasi led Mountain up the gentle slope towards the wall that bounded the edge of the pasture, trying not to hurry. He listened hard for any sign of Larko rousing Yanna, but there was none. He found a gate that led out to a rough track running from west to east and felt safer with the stonework between him and the camp. He glanced up at Mountain's head and shook his own. He himself couldn't be seen, but the animal was taller than the wall. A horse outside the pasture would raise an immediate alarm. He hoped that any guard who spotted them would be afraid of the horse, like the men who had caught them on the seawall. Maybe they would send for Yanna rather than trying to stop him themselves. That would give him a little time.

Lebasi was sorry about Yanna. He was stealing El-Arnor's horse, but he was also stealing Yanna's horse.

Would El-Arnor take out his anger on Yanna? 'It wouldn't just be your neck, it would be mine and half your friends.' That's what Yanna had said to Larko. Lebasi imagined El-Arnor's fury, and shivered. But there were all the Xessans in the valley, and all the Xessans on the road south, who depended on him giving them time.

Among them, Faya.

✳ ✳ ✳ ✳ ✳

The sky ahead was growing pale when Lebasi heard a distant whistle. It was answered by another, then another. Mountain turned his head to look back down the track. Lebasi stroked the horse's nose and said, 'It's time, my friend. Will you carry me again?'

In the half-light, he worked to adjust the stirrup-straps to the shortest setting the buckles would allow, then scrambled up on the wall to reach the saddle. They were well beyond the end of the camp now, the green pasture on the other side sloping gently and emptily down to the rim of the valley. Lebasi slid his feet into the metal rings, took hold of the reins, and clicked his tongue, as he had heard the Thrarn riders do. Mountain made a noise that sounded like laughter, but he started to trot. Lebasi realised that this could be uncomfortable. His legs were spread too wide by the breadth of the horse's back, and the saddle bumped him in the backside with every stride. But he was going away from the camp faster than he could walk, and that was something.

At least he couldn't lose his way. There was only one track, and it was going in the right direction. It was better kept than the road they had followed on the crest of the hill coming south, so it was probably still in regular use. Or had been, before the Thrarn arrived. He didn't expect to meet anyone coming the other way. He reckoned everyone who had been allowed to go was already gone.

The rising sun cast long shadows into the valley to his right. Looking back over his shoulder, he guessed that he was ten thousand paces or more from the Xessans' camp. He wondered if Tik and the boys had found Perra yet, and if Perra had forgiven him for saving his life at the ambush by the bridge. Would he have realised by now that his rebellion would have achieved nothing, with the Thrarn at the Westgate? Lebasi smiled grimly. Releasing Perra from the jail, hiding him in the tunnels, helping him plan the revolution – those had been mistakes, but honest ones, as Xela saw them. Stopping Riadsala from killing Perra – which would have ended the Mercy, and most likely would have led to a massacre of the Xessans – was one thing he had been sure was right at the time, and he was still sure. But Perra hadn't seen it that way at the time.

A horn sounded somewhere behind him, interrupting his thoughts. He tried to control his breathing, but he could feel his heart thumping. There was only one road, and if the pursuers had guessed which way he had gone, it was only a matter of time before they caught up with him. Unless he could find a place to turn off, or at least to make them guess which way he had gone. Maybe they would have to split up, then split up again. He tried to remember how El-Arnor had held himself while Mountain was cantering. He squeezed with his calves and clicked his tongue and tried to keep his balance as the horse lengthened his stride.

He was concentrating so hard on staying in the saddle that he was only half aware of the scenery changing. The broad valley on his right ended abruptly and the road entered a gorge. The slope down to the river was covered with scrub and trees, too steep for any possibility of descent. He caught glimpses of the water far below, glinting in the sunlight as it wound between huge boulders. Even if he could make it to the bottom – with or without Mountain – he didn't think it could be crossed.

On his left, the wall of the gorge closed him in, sometimes rocky and bare, sometimes covered in undergrowth, up to the skyline. The road was the only level ground he could see. With the sun in his eyes, it was difficult to make out the land ahead in detail, but he had an impression of the line of the road as a scar through the trees, hugging the hillside into the distance, rising and falling.

The horn sounded again. It was a single, long, clear note, the only thing to hear beside the clatter of Mountain's hoofs and his own breathing. He told himself that it was meant to carry a long way, they were still far behind. But they were surely on his trail.

The road turned sharply left. Mountain rounded the corner without slowing down, and Lebasi had to grab the post on the saddle to avoid sliding off. They were heading up a side valley, a smaller copy of the main gorge. The other side was only fifty or sixty paces away, getting closer. He could see the road coming back again, and guessed that there must be a bridge at a narrow point. He wondered how many of these turnings there would be, and how far they went – he had had to make a rough guess of time and distance when he told Tik to cross the valley bridges on the next night, and with these diversions it might take him too long to get to where he needed to be. As long as he had guessed right, and the dam that Xela had described was the source of the river in the valley.

This detour seemed to go on a long time. At last he turned a corner and saw the crossing ahead – a stone arch between two rocky outcrops. Mountain slowed down to a trot and then a walk as he approached it. He tossed his head and nickered. Lebasi could see why: the bridge was broad enough – five paces at least – but there was no parapet. The drop on each side… Lebasi didn't want to think about it.

'Come on, Mountain, you can do this,' he said, trying to sound more certain than he felt.

The note of the horn sounded again, echoing from the sides of the narrow valley. It was impossible to tell from how far away it came, but it was definitely closer than before. Mountain walked forward. Lebasi kept his eyes on the hillside straight ahead. The sound of the horseshoes changed from clip-clop to click-clack as they struck stone. Even Mountain wobbled as he had to contend with the slope of the arch. The angle changed as he went down the other side. Then the regular sound of the hoofs on dirt resumed, turning right, speeding up. Lebasi breathed out and patted the horse's shoulder.

The main gorge was in sight ahead when he heard a shout. Then another, and another, followed by a long blast on the horn. He gripped the reins tightly and glanced across the side-valley. Horses and riders – five, six, seven – pointing, gesturing. Two of them urged their mounts to go faster up the track. Two turned round and headed the other way, faster still. Lebasi guessed they would be taken the message: *we've found him*. That would bring more of them.

Lebasi told himself it was a good thing. *Let them come.* Let them not pay attention to what's happening in the valley. Give Perra a chance to organise the Xessans, before the king arrives.

He didn't convince himself.

Mountain seemed to understand the need for speed. Lebasi told himself that this was the best horse, he surely could go further and faster than any that were following. But their riders knew what they were doing – how much difference did that make? And even Mountain would need a rest, would need to eat something and have a drink. When they stopped, they could be caught.

The road turned another corner into another side valley. This one was different. After only a short distance, the ground opened out into a flat area with a stone shelter built against the rock wall and a waterfall filling a drinking pool. The road carried on beyond the clearing, but there was something about the encroaching plants that told Lebasi it wasn't the main route. As Mountain walked forward into the centre of the space, he saw it – a turning down the hillside, towards –

'Fire and ice,' he breathed.

There was a bridge. It was nearer the stream in the bottom of the valley than the stone arch, where the span didn't have to be so great, but this close to the main gorge it was still thirty paces or more. It was not made of stone. There were ropes stretching across, secured to tall posts on each side, more ropes hanging from them, a lattice-work of rope, and suspended from it, planks of wood.

Thoughts tumbled through Lebasi's brain. Will it take a horse? Will Mountain cross it? Will the chasers cross it?

He realised that there was no choice at all. It had to bear Mountain's weight, because if he took the long way up the side valley to the stone bridge he expected to find, by the time he returned the Thrarn would be waiting – on foot or on horseback – and there would be no escape.

He twitched the reins to direct Mountain down the track. The horse tossed his head again, but he obeyed. He walked down to where the solid ground ended and stopped.

'Hold still, I'm getting off,' Lebasi said. He slipped his feet out of the stirrups and jumped down. His legs were so stiff from riding that he could hardly stand up straight, but he stumbled across

to examine the bridge. The first thing he noticed was the gaps between the planks – not wider than a finger or two, but if he looked down as he was walking across, he would see the drop. The second thing he noticed was hoof-prints in the dusty earth round the end of the walkway – big ones, quite fresh. He clapped his hands together and reached up for the bridle.

'It's all right, Mountain. It's strong enough to hold an ox, so it's strong enough to hold you.' He hoped it was true. 'Come on, we'll walk across it together.'

The horse wasn't willing. Lebasi pulled, but Mountain shook his head. Lebasi pleaded. He knew that there was nothing he could do to force the animal to follow him, so he would have to persuade him. He walked out onto the first few planks, trying not to react when the bridge wobbled under his weight.

He heard the horn again. Mountain pricked up his ears. Lebasi walked back and rested his forehead against the horse's face. 'Come on, Mountain, I need you. We can do this together.'

The horse took a pace forward. Lebasi took a step backward, holding on to the bridle. 'Just look at me. Don't worry about anything.' He was on the bridge. Another step. Mountain put a hoof on the first plank. The bridge shook. Lebasi kept walking backwards, kept murmuring encouragement. Mountain fixed one eye on him and followed, swishing his tail from side to side. The bridge swayed every time the horse lifted and placed a hoof. Lebasi sensed that they were at the lowest point, he was going up again, he had a foot on earth, two feet, he stepped to the side to let Mountain spring past him.

The horn blasted again, very close, echoing backwards and forwards from the rocks. There were voices. They must be at the clearing. In a moment they would see…

Lebasi took off his backpack and pulled it open. He grabbed the handle of the cleaver and jumped across to the first plank. Which rope? There were several that might be crucial. Some of them were out of his reach, stretched over tall posts above him. But the ropes that served as handrails – he could cut those. He started by hacking, but then realised that the cooks kept their blades as sharp as their wagons were tidy. Sawing worked better. The left-hand rope twanged apart. He turned and started working on the other side.

There was a bellow from across the valley. He looked up and took a step backwards. Five Thrarn, on foot, crowded around the far end of the bridge. Their height made them seem nearer – they wouldn't have a problem reaching the top ropes. The nearest man was the tallest, wearing a bright purple jacket with metal strips sparkling in the sunlight – El-Arnor himself. He was shouting – not at Lebasi, but at a soldier who was holding a crossbow. The man stepped backwards, his head and weapon lowered. Lebasi glanced behind him. He guessed that the general was worried that the man might hurt the horse.

The general turned and jabbed a finger across the short distance between them. His face was very red. He roared the single word, 'You!'

Lebasi hoped that Mountain's presence would protect him from arrows, but he couldn't help jumping back from the force of El-Arnor's anger. The right-hand rope was still connected by a thread. He was disappointed that the planks stayed where they were. He had to hope that he had weakened it enough.

'How dare you? How dare you steal my horse? Do you have any idea what I will do to you, how slowly I can make a man die?'

Lebasi backed towards Mountain, wondering how quickly he could climb onto the saddle. If they could still cross the bridge, it would all be over very soon. If he had done enough damage to it, maybe he needed to get El-Arnor to take a step.

'He's not your horse. Your father gave him to your brother, remember?'

El-Arnor let out another roar. 'You shall not speak of my brother. You are a worm, you defile his memory by stealing his horse.'

Lebasi stopped thinking about what El-Arnor might do. 'Your brother was mad and cruel. He thought he could control me, but I tricked him.'

'You are not capable of tricking El-Kazzak,' El-Arnor shouted back. 'He was a god beside a wretch like you.'

Lebasi brandished the cleaver. There was the answer to Rovert's question. 'He was no god. I tricked him. And then I shot him.'

33
REFUSAL

'He was along here somewhere,' Sammas whispered. Tik could only just make out her friend's shape in the dim starlight, even with his voice telling her where to look.

'Perra? Perra, are you there?' Ruffur's low growl broke through the chirping of crickets.

'Shut up, we're trying to sleep,' was the mildest of several replies. They moved on twenty paces and tried again. The protests were louder. Up ahead, Tik could see the glow of the soldiers' fire near the eastern bridge. She tried to remember where they had spoken to Perra before – had it been this far from their own camp? It was hard to judge distances in the dark.

At the fifth attempt someone replied, 'What d'you want Perra for?'

They moved towards the voice, trying not to tread on sleepers. 'Is he here?' Sammas asked.

There were groans and shushes and complaints, but at last a voice Tik recognised said, 'Who wants me?' She picked her way between the sleeping bodies and crouched down beside someone she could see was sitting up. His face showed as a pale patch in the darkness.

'It's Tik and Ruffur and Sammas,' she whispered. 'We've got an important message for you.'

The man grumbled, 'Give it up. Nothing you can tell me will change anything.'

Tik grunted in frustration. 'Come with us where we can talk, and you'll see it differently.'

'Talk to me here, and then I can go back to sleep.'

Sammas and Ruffur knelt beside her. Sammas said, 'Can't tell you here. But we're not going to let you sleep until you've heard it. So you might as well get it over with.'

Perra sighed, but he rolled back his blanket and stood up. 'Where?' he muttered.

Tik led the way back to the road and on to the river embankment. They climbed over and sat on the path. The water below made no noise. Ruffur sat on the wall above them to keep watch.

Tik repeated what Lebasi had told them. 'So we've got to get everyone across the river, not the coming night but the one after, and burn the bridges.'

Perra was silent. At last he said, 'Why are you telling me?'

Tik banged her knuckles together. 'Because you're the only person here who can make it happen. Lebasi said so. Marrak said so.'

'Marrak? I thought he's been taken prisoner.'

'He has, but the man who told Lebasi about the Thrarn's plan is holding him, and he doesn't want it to happen, so he passed on a message from him to Lebasi. To you.'

For a moment he did not reply, but Tik could make out the movement of his head shaking. 'You're wrong. They're wrong. I can't do that. No one would listen to me. Two days – less – to get everyone ready to move under cover of darkness? Impossible.'

Sammas said, 'We've got to try, though. Otherwise we all just get killed.'

Perra was quiet again. Tik thought of something. 'Basi told me you've got a sister.'

'Yes,' he replied. 'She had already gone south when I arrived here.'

'What about her, then? Are you going to let the horsemen

chase her down, along with all the others? The women and children and old people?'

Perra put his head in his hands. From the stifled noises, the sniffs and gasps, Tik guessed that he was crying. She knew that a few days ago she would only have been angry with him, but now she understood the hopelessness he must be feeling. She put her hand on his shoulder.

'Basi believes you can do it. So do Sammas and Ruffur. And Marrak. Riadsala beat you at the bridge because he knew the story, he saw your ambush. This time they won't be expecting us to do anything.' She paused, searching for something else to try. 'Xela reminded Basi of the Xessus story – you know, a cradle holds no courage, we choose what lies in our grave. If we can't find the courage to do something now, then we're all done for. We have to try.'

Perra stood up, silhouetted against the paler darkness of the sky. He swung his arm around, sweeping it across to take in the Xessans' camp. 'Were you here today, or were you somewhere else? Did you see them trying to sort out something as simple as where to put the sick? Arguing, taking short cuts that didn't work, doing things twice that didn't need to be done at all. When they come for me I'll go down fighting, but don't ask me to herd this pack of squirrels across the river.'

Tik sighed. Marrak had no reason to suggest Perra, the man who had tried to imprison and overthrow him and Xela, unless he really was the only man in the camp who could manage it. They had no way of finding anyone else, no time to look. She wished she could lose her temper with him – it would be simpler. She picked herself up, trying to think of something, and glanced over her shoulder towards the bridge where she had stood on the parapet. If he wouldn't –

'All right,' she said quietly. 'Go back to bed. Don't tell anyone. If people start to find out what's coming, and no one has a plan to escape, it'll be ten times worse than today.'

Sammas started to say something, but Tik cut him off. 'Tomorrow night, I'll go and burn that bridge.' She pointed. 'I hate it enough, and the soldiers. I reckon I can get by them, and maybe I can take some tinder and kindling. It's pretty dry. Perhaps I can get it burning before they notice.'

Perra protested, 'What good will that do?'

Tik shrugged. 'Not much. The people on this side of the river are done for anyway, if you reckon we can't get them to cross over. But I'm choosing what lies in my grave. If it slows the Thrarn down, maybe the women and children already on the road south will get a bit further away, maybe some of them will get far enough ahead to escape. Maybe your sister will live.'

Ruffur slid down from the wall and stood beside her. He grunted, 'Reckon I could have a go at that bridge over there.'

Sammas sighed. 'That leaves me with the one down by the latrines. Typical of you to leave me with the smelly job.'

Tik didn't look at them. She felt something fluttery in her stomach, as she had when she had rescued Lebasi from the branded man and he had told her she was the bravest person he'd ever met. It was a hopeless plan, but she was grinning in the dark. Grinning, and crying at the same time, and trying not to let anyone see.

34
UP COUNTRY

For a moment, Lebasi's words seemed to hang in the air between them. Lebasi was aware of the sound of the water splashing in the bottom of the ravine below, the croak of a crow flapping past, the swish of Mountain's tail behind him. The group of Thrarn on the far side of the bridge all stared at him. He wondered how many of them understood Xessan.

Then, with a bellow that was not in any language, El-Arnor sprang forward, drawing his sword as he came. Lebasi flinched backwards, but he knew he could not escape.

Out of the corner of his eye, he saw the right-hand rope spring apart where he had nearly cut it through. The bridge on its own had stayed suspended, but the weight of the man crashing across the first few boards pulled the web of ropes to pieces. The handrail-lines that he had cut were the link between the higher support ropes and the wooden planks – the rope whipped through loop after loop, and the lattice tore like a piece of worn-out cloth.

El-Arnor either didn't notice, or couldn't stop. He charged into the middle of the bridge, and then it broke beneath him. One moment he was running, the next he was flailing his arms as if he was trying to fly, and then he was gone.

Lebasi edged forward and peeked over the edge. The remains of the nearer half of the bridge hung down in a ragged ladder of planks. The slope was steep and covered in scrubby bushes, and there was no sign of the general. His sword had stuck in the ground where he had thrown it as he fell.

Lebasi glanced up at the other Thrarn. They were all staring downwards. He knew that in a moment one of them would think of his crossbow. He turned to lead Mountain out of range.

'Raa-aaa-aaa-arg!' Another roar from below dragged him back to the rim. He jumped back sharply, grabbed at Mountain's reins and started running up the path. El-Arnor had reappeared, pulling himself up on the bushes, just below his sword. His eyes were fixed on Lebasi, and the fury in his face was more terrifying than anything Lebasi had ever seen.

He spotted a boulder beside the track and skidded to a halt. Mountain stopped as well while he scrambled onto it and climbed into the saddle. He barely had time to slip his feet into the stirrups before there was another shout from behind – he twisted round – El-Arnor was clambering onto the track –

'Go! Go, Mountain, now!'

The horse understood the tone if not the words, and set off so fast that Lebasi had to grab hold of the saddle-post. The track ran uphill to join another coming down the side-valley. Mountain turned right, rounded the next corner and rejoined the main gorge. Fifty paces on, there was only the sound of water, birds, the horse's hoofbeats.

And Lebasi's heart, thumping in his ears.

Mountain slowed to a trot. Lebasi reckoned the horse knew what to do, and he wouldn't be able to give orders. They must be too far ahead for El-Arnor to chase them on foot. The horsemen would have to go all the way up the side-valley in the hope of finding another bridge. With luck, it would be at least as long a detour as the previous one. He turned in the saddle and stared back, wishing he had the farsight. How could he rest – how could he give Mountain a rest – when he wouldn't know how far the pursuers were behind him?

✳ ✳ ✳ ✳ ✳

Lebasi and Mountain emerged from of a wood where the trees grew close together and found themselves on a hillside that was bare for several hundred paces. It was strange to feel so exposed, but Lebasi was sure by now that all his enemies were behind, not ahead. At the far end of the open section a group of buildings clung to the slope, more than a single household, not enough to call a village. As they drew nearer, Lebasi took in the holes in the roofs, the bushes growing out of the walls. No one had lived here for a long time.

Even so, there was still water flowing down a stone channel into a trough by the roadside. Mountain stopped for a drink. Lebasi tried to guess who had lived here, so far away from flat ground which could be farmed. When they started again, he spotted a clue – a branch in the road, slanting down towards the river. There was a bridge down there, with a flat deck built on piers set into the river bed, like the ones outside Trengam. He could see the road cutting through the trees as it climbed the far side of the valley. That road went somewhere. Maybe this was a place where traders met, like the white stones halfway between Trengam and Nampetch. Before Dennara's rebellion, they could have stayed in the buildings and eaten together, instead of passing their goods across the line.

'Not that way, Mountain,' he said, nudging the horse's flank with his knee to take the upper track. He needed to follow the gorge. He was certain of it.

They came to another side-valley, where another bridge hung from ropes. Mountain stood at the top of the path leading down to it and turned his head to give Lebasi a quizzical look. Lebasi swung his leg over the saddle and jumped down. 'Come on,' he said. 'We did it before, we can do it again. And if we cut the ropes on this one too, I think we can take a rest.'

Mountain waited patiently while Lebasi walked across and back. There were no ox tracks here, so he took a close look at the ropes before he risked Mountain's weight on the bridge. Everything seemed sound, so once again he led the horse across, talking to him all the way. It held. He felt a stab of guilt as he sawed away at the ropes – the people who had made this road had built it to last. If they had made it before Dennara's time, that meant it had stood for a hundred and forty years or more. He was destroying it in an afternoon. But he had no choice.

Not much further on, he heard voices ahead. Mountain must have heard them too, because he slowed to a walk. Lebasi told himself that the Thrarn couldn't possibly have got ahead of him, this had to be –

'Xessan farmers,' he breathed, as he rounded a corner and saw an ox-cart almost completely blocking the track a hundred paces ahead. It wasn't moving. There were people standing in front of it, hands on hips, looking down at the poor beast that had drawn the cart to this spot. It had collapsed, and it didn't seem likely that it would get up again.

Someone screamed. The figures all turned towards him, then they scrambled to get behind their wagon. Mountain walked slowly forward. Lebasi held up his palm. He hoped they didn't have any weapons, particularly bows. He stopped twenty paces away. The ox was lying on its side, its breath coming in shallow gasps.

'Friend!' he shouted. Then, as they were country-dwellers who might understand Xessan, 'Friend! I'm not one of the invaders.'

A head, covered in a floppy straw hat, bobbed up above the back of the cart, disappeared, then reappeared. The man spoke to someone who stayed out of sight.

'He doesn't look like one of them. Doesn't sound like them, either. Looks like one of us, not even come of age.'

'I'm Lebasi, Xela's son from Trengam,' he called out.

The man stood up, and was joined by others – two more men, three women. Lebasi guessed there must be children somewhere – they were all of an age to have families.

'What're you doing riding one of their beasts?' the man asked.

'I've stolen it from them.' The thought of *them* made him turn to look back. Surely they were a long way away, but they would be coming.

'You've got to get away from here.' he said. 'Some of the invaders are following me, and they're really angry. If they catch you on the road - don't let them catch you on the road.'

The man walked round the side of the cart and pointed to the ox. 'What can we do? Our beast's dying here.'

Lebasi glanced up the slope. 'Is there a way out of the valley? Where have you come from?'

The man waved a hand behind him. 'We live up country. These big fellers came and told us to clear out or they'd come back and kill us all. Told us to go to Awato and south. This is the best road.'

Lebasi shook his head. 'Not now, it isn't. You've got to clear off it before they get here. I don't know how far behind they are.'

He listened to them arguing among themselves for a moment, then realised that he was wasting time. 'I've got to keep going.' he said. 'I'm telling you, take what you can carry and get off this road. If you hear them coming, hide.' Mountain picked his way past the wagon. The men stepped back to keep their distance from the horse. Lebasi looked down – he had been right. There were six young children huddled in front of one of the women. She had her arms around them – but that would be no protection against the Thrarn.

Lebasi put as much urgency into his voice as he could. 'In the name of Xessus, move - now!' An idea came to him. 'If you can, block the road with the wagon. Knock the wheels off, make it hard for them to shift. Anything to slow them down.'

The man stared at him, not seeming to understand. Lebasi shook his head and turned away. He had done what he could. He rode on.

※ ※ ※ ※ ※

It was Mountain who decided that they should stop for the night. They had just passed a narrow point in the gorge where the

rocks fell sheer from the skyline to the river, forcing the track up and out into the open for a few hundred paces. Lebasi scanned the view, realising that here he could take a different route and throw off the pursuers. There were lesser tracks leading off that must go somewhere, but that would be no good – he had to follow the river to its source. Some deer watched him cautiously before skipping away, but there was no sign of human life. He followed the road back into the gorge.

Shortly afterwards they reached a gentle side-valley with shallow sides and a grassy meadow at the bottom. The horse stopped and shook himself, then started to graze. Lebasi jumped

down and stretched. He was sore in places he expected – his backside in particular – but also in places he didn't. His legs were tired, his neck was stiff, his hands and wrists were cramped from holding the reins too tightly. The sun had set below the skyline, although there was still some daylight left. Surely they must be far enough ahead to rest by now. The Thrarn would have had to negotiate two detours up side-valleys, and if the farmers had blocked the road, that would have held them up as well. He didn't expect to sleep comfortably or long, as he didn't know how far they still had to go the next day, but he and Mountain had to stop somewhere. He couldn't ride in the dark. He hoped the Thrarn couldn't either.

He dug in the bottom of his pack for the remainder of Ruffur's father's dried meat and ate half of it. 'Some for the morning,' he told himself. 'And after that – who knows?' He wished that he could forage for mushrooms as Ruffur did, but he didn't trust himself not to pick poisonous ones. He tried to make his chewy meal last as long as possible, envying the horse the fact that there was as much grass as he could possibly want.

He found a sheltered place under some trees and wrapped himself in his blanket. He hoped that he would hear the chasers before they saw him. He tried to put out of his mind all thoughts of what he planned to do the next day. Even the thought of El-Arnor climbing up the broken bridge couldn't keep him awake.

✳ ✳ ✳ ✳ ✳

He woke suddenly, completely alert in a moment. Had he heard something? The valley seemed peaceful enough in the half-light of dawn. He sat and listened, straining his ears. There was nothing but the breeze in the branches and the horse still munching grass. He rolled up his blanket and tied it to the pack, took a drink, filled the water-skin again, and climbed into the saddle.

He patted the horse's shoulder. 'Come on, Mountain. Let's go and find this dam.'

35
SECRETS

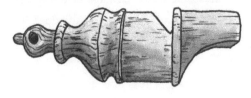

By lunchtime, Tik was not so sure that she could do what she had determined to carry out in the middle of the previous night. She sat with the boys on the riverside path and studied what they were now calling 'Ruffur's one'. It would be possible to sneak past the soldiers and climb out onto the timbers supporting the deck, but would it burn?

Sammas had the same thought. 'It's made of wood, after all. Even though it's standing in water, the rest of it's going to be very dry in this heat.'

Ruffur rubbed his chin. 'Some people have lamps with them. If we could get a bit of the oil, and some flint and tinder, maybe we could get it alight before anyone noticed, and if it's properly burning, it'll be hard for them to put out.'

Objections tumbled though Tik's mind. *If this, if that. We.* It would be one of them on each bridge, and unless they burned them all, it was hardly worth trying. She closed her eyes and told herself that the boys had supported her in the night-time. They were breathing the sky. She had to go through with it.

'We've got today and tomorrow to work out a plan,' she said. 'There'll be a half moon, but it'll rise long after dark. Between sunset and moonrise, that'll be the time to move.'

Sammas nodded. He swallowed the last of the piece of bread

he was eating and wiped his forearm across his mouth, staring downriver towards 'Tik's one'.

'I've been thinking,' he said slowly, then stopped.

'What?' Tik asked, wondering if he was seeing the hopelessness of the idea as well.

Sammas scratched his head. 'You're the important one, Tik. You've got to get your message to the king so he can get his army ready to meet what's coming. Ruffie and me, we don't matter so much. I reckon when we split up, even though you'll be going to the nearest bridge, you should wait until we've set the fire. You'll see it clear enough, up and down the river. The soldiers'll come running from yours to ours. Then you get to work, and make sure you're the other side of the fire. Don't wait around to see how well it burns. Once you've started it, you go.'

Tik stared at him. 'But –'

She was surprised by Ruffur's low growl from the other side of her. 'We'll catch up with you on the road, is what Sammie's saying. No one'll be able to follow us.'

She wondered if he believed it.

* * * * *

There were more soldiers in the fields today, and fewer workers without the sick people. Tik wondered if the bridge guards would be reinforced, but at the end of the day the extra troops headed back with the food wagons, shouting jokes to the ones who would have to spend the night being bitten by flies. There were only five men sitting round the firepit by the entrance to her bridge. They didn't seem worried about anyone trying anything – they were facing each other across the fire, talking among themselves, hardly watching at all as the Xessans filed past them to and from the latrines.

A young man waved at her from the line of people heading back to camp. She stood up, wondering who knew her. He said something to the people he was walking with and trotted along the road towards her. She nudged Sammas, who was laying out his blanket.

'Do you know who this is?'

He glanced up, then stood. 'Dalin. Friend of Perra's, from Trengam.'

The man grinned at them all, and said loudly, 'Ruffur, Sammas, you rogues. I didn't know you'd made it. How in Xessus's name are you? And who's this?' Then he dropped his voice to a whisper. 'Message from Perra. Act like we're just catching up on the news, all right?' He reached out and gripped Ruffur's shoulder as if he was greeting an old friend.

Tik felt her heart speed up. 'I'm Tik,' she said, wondering who was close enough to hear. 'I'm travelling with these two.'

Dalin threw back his head and laughed as if Tik had made the best joke he had ever heard. He clapped his hands, then pointed upstream as if he was explaining something. He dropped his voice again.

'I know you are. We don't trust everyone, so we're keeping it close, putting on an act. Perra sends an apology – he didn't say what for, but he said you'd understand – and he says it's going to happen tomorrow night, what you talked about. He's spent the day getting people together and we're passing the word. But we're telling people to be ready for the night after. So if anyone tells tales, we've still got a day's worth of surprise in hand. Might be enough.'

Tik opened and closed her mouth. She murmured, 'He's changed his mind?'

Dalin laughed again, and carried on his pretence, gesturing as if he was telling a story. 'I don't know about that, but he's woken up, that's the truth. He's not been his old self since he got here.' He glanced behind him towards the soldiers round their fire. 'Keep it to yourselves. If you hear anyone talking about it, shut them up. And if they say two days' time, don't correct them.' He raised his voice again. 'Well, I'll be seeing you. Wish your da was here, Ruffur. I could do with something more than all these vegetables.'

They watched him walk away. Both boys turned to beam at Tik. 'That's you, that is,' said Sammas. 'Woken him up.'

Ruffur sniffed. 'I suppose I won't have to go fire the bridge on my own. I was just starting to look forward to it.'

Sammas punched him on the arm. 'You'd have dropped the tinder in the river. Probably fallen in yourself. It'll be better this way.'

Tik scanned the people camping nearby – rolling out their bedding, slapping at flies, stretching out on the ground. How many of them had Perra and his friends told?

Who didn't they trust?

✳ ✳ ✳ ✳ ✳

In the morning, Tik woke once again to find Sammas missing. Ruffur said, 'He's gone to see if Callie's running any messages. See if anything's different today, if anyone's noticed anything.'

Sammas joined them as they washed in the river. He didn't have a chance to talk to them without being overheard until they were out in the fields picking maize.

'I'm starting to understand some Xessan,' he said. 'Not everything, but enough to guess what was going on, if I fill in the gaps. One of the older men – not one of Perra's friends, no one I recognise – went to see the sergeant and said we could speed up the harvest if we didn't have to wait for the wagons to arrive in the morning. Suggested that when the first wagons we load get across to the camp and are emptied, they bring them back down here again. Said that if we could get the crops in a bit quicker, we'd maybe save half a day and be ready to leave at first light on the fourth day from now. Made a point of counting it out on his fingers – I thought that was overdoing it a bit.'

Ruffur said, 'But we're going tonight.'

Sammas tapped him on the head with an ear of corn. 'Exactly. So he wants to put that idea as far from the sergeant's mind as possible. He's making it plain that we're going to be here for days.'

Tik asked, 'What did the sergeant say?'

'That was all a bit fast for me to follow, but he sent Callie off with a message. I reckon he must be asking them over in the camp if that's a good idea.'

Ruffur slapped his own forehead. 'Wagons! Perra's thinking big.'

Sammas grinned. 'He always did, before.'

They worked as hard as ever all day, constantly watching the soldiers for any sign that they were suspicious. There was none: they were the same as ever, some bullying, some reasonable. As the sun sank towards the horizon, they trailed back to camp, wondering if Perra could really make an escape happen that night.

'Looks like they fell for it,' said Sammas, pointing at a line of empty ox-carts coming back across the valley.

Ruffur put his basket and spade on one of the carts that held the farm tools. He muttered to Tik, 'Lot of things missing. But the guards don't count them.'

The evening meal seemed no different from other days. Tik thought that perhaps the servers were in more of a hurry, or the helpings were more generous, but no one said anything. She wondered if she had dreamed what Dalin said, or misunderstood. Could they really be moving out tonight?

It was only after dinner, as dusk settled on the camp, that she started to see signs of Perra's plan. A gaggle of men gathered round the empty wagons lined up on the road, as if they were meeting for a casual conversation. Some people were rolling up their bedding rather than laying it out, glancing across towards the soldiers by the bridge to check that they were taking no notice, putting possessions into packs. Tik and the boys had just finished fastening the straps on theirs when someone appeared in the gloom beside them.

'All ready?' came Dalin's low voice. 'Good. Moonrise is the signal. Ruffur, we could use you when we go for the soldiers. Come with me.'

Sammas murmured, 'What can Tik and I do?'

Dalin pointed towards the road. 'You can help keep watch over there, and run messages if anything happens. We're not expecting anyone coming across the valley, but if they do, we have to keep them quiet. You know how sound travels here, especially at night. We need to get everyone over the bridges before the army up there has any idea. We're going to take the sick people over on the wagons.'

Ruffur hugged Sammas and then Tik. 'See you later,' he muttered, and followed Dalin into the darkness.

Sammas propped the three backpacks against each other. 'Hard to see them at the moment, but when the moon's up they should be clear enough. We can grab Ruffie's between us if he's busy at the bridge.'

Tik found it difficult to walk in the opposite direction, to where the men were watching the road. She wanted to do something, to run, to fight. Her legs were itchy, her scalp tingled. Once again she pictured Verb and his friends sitting round the fire making ready for the battle at the Westwall. Had they felt the same, waiting for it to start? She felt a tightness in her chest. By the end of the next day, they were all dead, food for the crows and vultures on the Westwall Field. This night must finish differently.

Sammas murmured something to one of the men, who patted him on the shoulder. In the starlight, the figures merged into the

wagons – it was hard to tell how many of them there were. Tik guessed that might have been their intention. She strained her eyes to see if there was anything on the road, which showed as a faint pale line in between the dark of the fields, stretching towards the blank mass of the far hillside. There were lights up there – what must be campfires on the right, and the smaller, paler glow of lanterns in windows in the town on the left. She wondered where Lebasi was, and whether he would be able to escape with them that night. After all, he had made it across the valley once – why not again? He had to go back there in order that he wouldn't be missed and cause an alarm, but that reason would be over the moment they set fire to the bridges. She rested her hand on the farsight, tucked away under her tunic. It was no use in the dark, and she wouldn't know where to point it.

'What's going on?' Her thoughts were interrupted by a voice she recognised.

'Callie?' She turned round, searching for the pale patch in the darkness that would be his fair hair.

'That you, Tik?' A shadow detached itself from one of the wagons and approached her. 'Do you know what's happening? People are moving around the camp in the dark, and no one's telling me anything.'

Tik tried to think of something cutting to say – after all, Callie had taunted her with his secret knowledge. Before she found the words, one of the men growled, 'Nothing that you need to worry about, messenger-boy. Run along and get some sleep.'

Tik could hear a grunt from the darkness, then the sound of light footsteps on the road as the boy walked away. She touched Sammas's elbow. 'I'm going to follow him, all right?'

Sammas murmured, 'Good idea.'

When she passed the last wagon, she peered into the gloom

to see where Callie had gone. Straight ahead of her, a dark shape crossed in front of the light from the soldiers' fire. She broke into a run, glancing towards the eastern horizon. There was no sign of the moon.

Callie reached the soldiers before she could catch up with him. Two were stretched out on the ground, resting or sleeping. Three had their backs to her, sitting cross-legged. One leaned forward and poked the fire, which flared up, making the surrounding darkness even blacker. Tik skidded to a stop twenty paces away. She glanced down at her tunic – they would be able to see her. But she could always run.

'Sergeant!' Callie hissed, also standing far enough away to have a head start if the men were in a bad mood.

One of the lying figures sat up and looked round. In the flickering light, Tik saw that it was the same man that had sent Marrak away and had made her stand on the bridge. There hadn't been a change of the guard.

'What d'you want, little bug?'

Tik flinched. That was what her uncles had nicknamed her on the farm.

'There's something strange going on in the camp.'

She gasped. What was he doing? Helping run messages was one thing, but betraying them to the enemy?

She looked for help, but couldn't see anyone in the complete blackness. She bent down and felt for stones – there were plenty of them on the surface of the road – and edged forward, shuffling them between her hands so that the best one was ready if she needed it.

'What d'you mean, something strange?' The other soldiers stood up and moved into a rough circle round the fire, facing outwards.

One of them pointed at Tik. 'What're you doing, boy?'

Tik said nothing.

Callie half-turned, nodded at her, then spoke again to the sergeant. 'There are people moving about. Men on the road, as if they're on lookout -'

'That's enough, Callie.' Perra's voice came from somewhere to Tik's right. She couldn't see him in the darkness. Maybe he wasn't wearing a light tunic.

The sergeant stepped forward and peered. 'Who's there?'

Perra sounded a little closer. 'We're relieving you of duty, man. If you five just lie down on the ground, we won't hurt you.'

For a moment, the sergeant stood still, staring into the night. Then he grabbed something that hung from a cord at his neck – *the sergeants of the Westwall Guard all carried a whistle – sound travels* – Tik whipped back her hand antd threw.

There was a shout of pain, but no piercing blast. Men appeared on all sides, rising out of the ground, armed with pitchforks and spades, and rushed towards the fire. The soldiers hardly had time to draw their swords before they were overwhelmed. Tik turned away from the sound of thumps and crunches, the groans and cries of pain, and then a moment's silence, before a burst of laughter and low murmurs of relief and congratulation.

Perra's voice came again from somewhere by the fire. 'Quiet! Where's that menker Callie gone?'

36
DRALOR

The sun was hot on the back of Lebasi's neck. He guessed it was the middle of the afternoon. He had ridden all day and had seen no one. The track rose gradually, the gorge narrowed, the vegetation changed. The scrub and bushes from yesterday had been replaced by fir trees, covering the slope above and below him. Whenever he stopped to let Mountain drink and take a bite, he stared and strained his ears to catch any sign of pursuit, but there was none.

At last, there was a sign he was reaching the end. He crossed a side valley, so small that the track simply descended to a ford, and as Mountain climbed up the far side Lebasi realised that there was no more water in the main river – at least not enough to show up among the rocks. The stream he had just crossed was the last source for the channel in the valley far behind and below him.

Ahead, the gorge ended in a wall. He could see a notch in the skyline that must once have been a waterfall, but it was as empty as the river below. The track carried on, zig-zagging back and forth up the steeper ground. Lebasi had to turn his head to avoid looking down, trusting the sureness of Mountain's hoofs to find the way. He was relieved that the last section was a narrow defile cut into the rock, with no drop to worry about. It reminded him of the path from the Westgate up onto the Westwall Field. He recalled the Thrarn cavalry streaming out of that path after Nareb unlocked the gate. He shook himself. He had made his mistakes, but he had to carry on. It was what he did next that mattered.

The passage opened out onto flat ground. Lebasi stared all around him. After so long in the confines of the gorge, he felt exposed and defenceless. Straight ahead, he could see what had to be the dam. Xela had described it as the place in the legend where the hero had imprisoned Artay and Shasho, and it looked like something from a legend: narrow at the bottom, broad at the top, impossibly high and steep, filling the end of a much larger gorge than the one he had just left. It was on the far side of a broad, sandy plain, a thousand paces away. As he took in the scene, he guessed that there had once been a lake here. That must have been a long time ago – there were trees scattered across the dry bed, and some of them were older than those in the wood behind Lone Pine Farm.

'Come on, Mountain, nearly there,' he whispered, trying to press his calves into the horse's flanks. His legs were so sore that he could hardly move them. The animal snorted as if he was laughing, but he stretched into a canter. As the track took them between the trees, Lebasi searched the land ahead for any sign of the keeper's house, but he quickly realised that it wasn't there. There was another set of zig-zags climbing the slope to the left of the dam, higher and steeper than the end of the gorge. He leaned back in the saddle at the end of the flat ground and Mountain stopped, turning his head as if to ask what Lebasi wanted to do.

He didn't want to have to ride up another narrow path with a dizzy drop beside it. He slipped his feet out of the stirrups and tried to jump down without falling over. To begin with, it was a relief to be out of the saddle. Lebasi wondered how every part of him could ache so much when surely the horse had been doing most of the work. He walked stiffly, longing to rest but not daring to waste time. The horse ambled behind him, the leading rein slack between them.

The track ran backwards and forwards across the hillside. It kept an even and shallow gradient, but it was narrow, and even on foot Lebasi kept his eyes straight ahead. On the first stretch Lebasi was worried about how the horse would turn a sharp corner at the end, but when they reached it there was a broad flat platform cut into the slope. He guessed it had been built for donkeymen to manage their beasts. The horse stepped out onto it, shuffled his feet gracefully, and set off in the new direction almost before Lebasi was ready.

The dam loomed above them on the right, a mass of grey stone in the shadow of the cliffs above. Each time they came close to it, he tried to work out the significance of a series of round black marks in its face, about a third of the way up. Now that he was closer, he could see that they were holes, ten of them. He stared at them from below, from the same level, then from above, and could make out no detail in the black depths. They were each about two manheights across and perfectly round. They clearly didn't go the whole way through, because no water came out of any of them.

Lebasi found he was counting steps. He was too tired to think of anything else, to wonder what he might find at the top, to get ready for what he had to do. Three hundred and ninety-eight, three hundred and ninety-nine, platform, turn, one, two… They were halfway up the dam, they were two-thirds, three-quarters.

As they approached the end of the tenth zigzag, Lebasi realised that the line in the slope above was the edge of something. He tried to quicken his pace. Three hundred and ninety-eight, three hundred and ninety-nine, there… he stepped up onto the rim of a broad shelf about the size of the Space back in his home town, flat and open, with sheer rocky cliffs behind it. Nestled against those cliffs, a small house built of the same stone. Goats grazing. To his surprise, a small orchard of fruit trees. Walls that probably marked out a garden – and kept the goats out of it. A short distance ahead there was a river running from right to left – no, not a river, a water channel. He remembered seeing something similar – something the same – where the mountains started above Trengam, the day he ran away to try to warn Xela about the rebellion. His eyes followed the stream to the right, to where the top few manheights of the dam still rose above him. Water was flowing in a smooth cascade down a gully from the very edge of the barrier, filling the channel. He turned and followed it the other way, across the plateau and onto the hillside beyond, disappearing round the curve of the mountain. Flowing, he guessed, all the way to that spot above Trengam where he had quenched his thirst.

'Who're you?'

He snapped his head back to find a stocky man standing very still three paces away. He must have been in sight before, but his grey cloak was the same colour as the cliffs, and his beard and long hair were the same colour as the cloak. Dark eyes peered out of a mass of wrinkles. The man's soft voice was the first human sound Lebasi had heard all day. He stammered, 'Lebasi. I – Xela sent me. My father. Are you Dralor?'

Of course he was Dralor. He realised he had had a picture in his head of the keeper of the dam, and this short, grizzled old man wasn't what he had expected.

Dralor raised his eyes without moving his head. 'And what's that?' His tone didn't change.

'It's a horse.' Lebasi hesitated. If the man wanted an explanation, it would take too long. He had to –

'And who're they?' Dralor pointed across the dry lakebed. Lebasi turned, his heart beating faster. They were coming out of the defile by the dry waterfall – three, four, five, more and more. A whole company of riders, just like the cavalry on the Westwall

Field. Most of them bunched together, one ahead by several horse-lengths. Would that be El-Arnor?

'Enemies.' Lebasi took a step towards the man. 'My father sent me here with an order for you. We have to hurry, before they get here.'

Dralor didn't move. He tilted his head back and studied Lebasi coolly. 'An order, you say. Why would I take an order from you?'

Lebasi pulled the three metal discs out of his pocket. He spread them out in his palms. 'The badges –'

'Ay, I've eyes in my head, I see them.' Dralor nodded. 'What is the order, then?'

Lebasi glanced over his shoulder. They were already a quarter of the way across, coming at a gallop. They would still take a while to climb the hillside. But maybe they could ride up the path – that would be quicker. He had to give the order now. He had been thinking about it all day, all of two days, ever since he left Tik on the road in the valley. How could he be sure it was the right thing? It could be another mistake, maybe the biggest of all. He could do the simple thing, just pass on Xela's message – how could anyone blame him for that? But he knew that would not help. He was certain that would be the wrong thing.

Dralor stood silently, waiting for him to say something.

If Xela's instruction was the wrong thing, what was left? He had to do what he believed to be right, and he would have to live with the consequences if it turned out badly. He took a deep breath.

'Shasho. You're to set Shasho free.'

Dralor tapped his knuckle against his lips, took a long look at the badges, then nodded. 'Shasho, then. And I'm guessing she's needed quickly.'

'Yes.'

'Follow me. You'll have to help.'

The man turned and ran, surprising Lebasi with his speed. He had guessed that Dralor must be sixty or more and had assumed that he would be slow, but he covered the ground to the side of the dam so fast that Lebasi could not keep up.

There was yet another zigzag path cut into the cliff-face beside the top section of the dam. It was steeper still than the others and had a stone wall on the outside that made it an awkward fit for Mountain. The corners were tighter, too, and by the time they had turned one Lebasi realised it would be impossible for him to go back. He made the same noises he had used to show his unhappiness crossing the rope bridges, but he followed.

Dralor was waiting for them at the top, where the rocks of the mountainside joined the flat stonework of the top of the dam. 'You'll have to leave your horse here. It can't come where we're going.'

Lebasi didn't answer. He was staring. The smooth surface curved across to the other side of the gorge, maybe three hundred paces away. To the left, water lapped gently at the stones, no more than an arm's length below the rim. Water that went on, and on, and on – the lake stretched into the distance, steep rocky slopes on each side. The cliffs on the left cut out the sun, so the surface of the lake was dark and cold. It was hard to say if the point where it disappeared was the end, or possibly a corner with more beyond.

'How…' He started a question, but his voice trailed away. His brain was overwhelmed by the scale of the view.

'How big is it?' Dralor nodded at a small boat tethered to a post. 'I've been a way down in my time, but I've never gone to where it ends, or even seen where it ends.' He stood on the edge of the drop and looked down. 'No time for that. They're at the bottom of the track.'

There was a large pile of sticks and branches stacked against the cliff. Dralor picked some out and handed them to Lebasi. 'We'll need these.' He paused, staring at the wood, then at Lebasi. 'And

if anything happens to me, and Shasho's loose, you must set fire to this. You hear me?'

Lebasi examined it again and realised that it was not a woodstore – it was arranged for burning, kindling at the bottom, sticks criss-crossed to allow air to flow. A signal. *The goddess of flood and destruction is coming, unstoppable. Lights in the north-east, run for the hills.* Would there be anyone left in this part of Xessus to see it? There was no time to argue or explain. 'Yes.'

Dralor knelt beside the boat and reached into it, returning with a length of rope. He made a noose at each end and pulled each one taut around the sticks. 'Here, you'll need your hands. Put your arms through – and I'll tighten it a bit – there.' The sticks were held horizontally across Lebasi's back. Dralor produced a lantern from the boat, tied another piece of cord to attach it to his own back, then nodded again at the horse. 'You'd better hitch him to something. Don't want him following us. Don't want him falling off or falling in.'

Lebasi reached up and rested his arm against Mountain's shoulder. *If something happens to me* – he had brought the animal up here, but how could he get down?

'I'm going to leave you here, all right? If I don't come back, your own people will look after you. Thank you for carrying me.'

The horse twitched his head and pushed against him, as if telling him to get on with what he had to do. Lebasi tied the leading rein loosely to the boat's mooring-post, and turned to find Dralor staring at him.

'Talking horse, is he, like in the legends?'

Lebasi shrugged. 'He doesn't say anything. But he's cleverer than any animal I've ever seen before. Maybe he understands.'

Dralor led the way across the dam. It was wider than the Westwall, but there was no parapet – Lebasi kept his eyes on the old man's back, trying not to think of the drop on the right. The mass of dark water on the left was almost as intimidating. The fall wouldn't be fatal, but it must be as deep as the dam was tall, and there was nothing to hold onto to help a swimmer climb out. Lebasi shivered.

In the centre of the dam, Dralor stopped by a square opening in the roadway three paces across. He peered down. 'That's where we're going. We won't take the quick way, though.'

Lebasi stared into the black hole. His mind jumped to a conclusion and his stomach cramped. 'We have to climb –'

'Down the front, yes.' Dralor leaned his face close to Lebasi's. 'Xela wouldn't order for Shasho unless Shasho was needed. And Shasho's keys are down in the middle of the dam. Artay is easy – Artay I can release from up here. Come.'

He walked to the edge. Lebasi followed, his heart pounding, wondering if he could change the order, explain that he had made a mistake, had got the names confused, that Xela had said Artay. It was even true. But Artay would be no use. It had to be Shasho.

To Lebasi's relief, Dralor lay on the stones to look for the way down. Maybe he felt the same. Lebasi crawled the last two paces and peered over the rim. It was even worse than he feared. The face seemed vertical from here, a sheer drop to the lakebed. No, it couldn't be quite straight – Lebasi could see one of those holes, most of the way down. The face must bend out a little.

Movement caught his eye. The chasers were two-thirds of the way up to the keeper's ledge. They were riding, a long line of Thrarn, twenty or more. Still one out in front. Lebasi shuddered at the memory of El-Arnor's anger. *Even if we manage to let Shasho out, what then? We can't fight them.*

He had no time to think. Dralor was getting up, pulling him to his feet, grasping his head between his hands, fixing him with those deep-set, glittering dark eyes. 'There are good holds for hands and feet. I go first. Take it steady. Only look down far enough to see where you are putting your feet.' He paused. 'I won't catch you if you fall.'

Lebasi nodded, unable to speak. Dralor knelt on the edge. Lebasi saw that there were handholds cut in the roadway. The man put one hand in each, then lowered his left foot into space. His right foot. His left hand moved to the wall. His right hand. His head dropped out of sight.

Lebasi clenched and unclenched his fists, breathing deeply. He glanced back the way they had come. Mountain tossed his head. The sound of his *nee-hee-hee-hee* carried clearly across the empty air between them. Maybe he does understand. *Maybe he is trying to say something. Get on with it.*

He took one last look towards the track up to Dralor's home – the riders had reached another corner, only one more to the top. He put his hands in the holds and shuffled his body around. The lake stretched out into the distance. So much water. He paused to make sure the sticks were centred on his back and weren't going to swing about, then he felt for whatever Dralor had put his foot in.

37

CALLIE

'Where's he gone?'

Tik was already running back along the road. She knew. Callie had betrayed them – he must realise that he wouldn't be safe anywhere in this valley. She reached the wagons and looked for the smallest of the shadowy shapes standing by them.

She called out, 'Have you seen Callie? Has he come by here?'

Sammas's voice answered, 'No one's come or gone. What happened? We heard some noise.'

'Perra's taken the bridge. Callie tried to warn the soldiers.'

'The little –'

'No time for that. He'll be trying to get across the valley. I'm going after him. Tell people to get moving.'

Sammas started to say something, but Tik didn't hear it. If Callie hadn't come along the road, he must be in the fields, and in the dark that would slow him down. But she couldn't risk him getting ahead of her. She ran, trying to go fast but quietly, straining her ears and eyes for any sign of the traitor on her left or right. The road lay ahead, a pale line with nobody on it. In the distance, the campfires of the army marked out the rim of the valley. At least there was no sound from there, no whistles or shouts.

The moon rose, flooding the fields with its tricky light. Tik stopped to catch her breath and turned all the way round, trying to tell the difference between a bush and a boy, a pile of earth and someone crouching.

She peered back the way she had come, realising that she was halfway across the valley. As she tried to make out any sign of action around the bridges, one of the shadows moved, straightened up, stepped onto the road and started moving towards her.

She stooped and scrabbled for stones. He was thirty paces away, twenty.

'Stop there,' she said, her quiet word sounding loud in her ears.

He stopped. 'Tik? What are you doing here?'

'Stopping you. You can't do this.'

'Do what?'

She clenched her fists around the stones. 'You're going to tell the army that we're escaping.'

He snorted. 'Escaping? Is that what you think you're doing?'

She tried to keep her voice low. She didn't think the army posted anyone along the road in the night, but any sound might carry to the wrong ears. 'How could you betray your own people? Even if you didn't know what was going on, you had to know you were telling the enemy –'

'Not my people,' he said. 'Not my enemy.'

'What do you mean? The people in the camp, they're from Marstor land, like you and me. Your people. Your family are on the road somewhere south. The Thrarn are planning to kill all of us, and you're helping them.'

Callie grunted. 'Hah! My family. My da used to hit me, and my ma never stopped him. I won't miss them. And everyone else – what are they to me?'

Tik was speechless. Callie took a pace forward, so she raised her hand. 'Stop, or this stone's for your face. You know I can, you saw me hit the sergeant.'

Callie held up his hand. She saw a blade glinting in the moonlight. 'If you throw anything at me, you'd better keep throwing, and you'd better knock me out, because if you don't, I'm going to cut you, all right? If you just stand aside and don't throw anything, I won't. You're all right, I don't want to hurt you.'

Tik hissed, 'But you'll hurt me and all the other Xessans if you tell the army what's happening.'

Callie laughed. 'You're fooling yourself. Even if they don't come tonight, it'll be obvious in the morning and they'll catch you soon enough. They'll kill everyone, no doubt about it. But not me, if I take them the news now.'

He took another step forward. Tik took a step back. Could she do it? She had hit Tharkon when he threatened her with a knife, but he was a powerful and terrifying man, and she knew that he would kill her. Callie was only a boy. Did he mean it?

'They won't catch us. We're going to burn the bridges.'

Callie stopped and whistled. 'That's clever. But they can repair them. You'll get another day, two maybe. How far can you get? It's a long way south, I've heard.'

'We can get to where the Westwall Guard is camped. The ones who weren't at the Westwall.'

'Lot of good that'll do. How many are they?'

Tik hardly heard him. She was scouring her brain for something to say that would change his mind. There was no point in trying to persuade him to come back – he had made an irreversible choice – but maybe he would agree to give them a little more time.

'Remember that story I told on the bridge?'

'What about it?'

'It's like Xessus the hero said. If you go to the army now, you're choosing to be a traitor. You don't have to do that. You can choose to –'

'I'm choosing to live, not to die,' he snapped. 'Can't you see? The invaders are too strong. They're going to win. Why not join them?'

Tik shook her head. 'They don't want us. My family helped them get through the Westwall. It didn't stop them stabbing my da and calling us all traitors and slaves.'

'Well,' Callie said, 'I'd rather take my chances with them. Now stand aside, or I'm going to have to use this knife.'

Tik took another step back, readying her arm, steadying her determination. The farsight tapped against her stomach under her tunic. She hesitated. What would happen if she fought him and he killed her? Or even injured her, so she couldn't make it across the bridges? Ruffur and Sammas – and maybe Lebasi – might take the message. But Riadsala had given her the farsight as a sign to make sure the king would listen to her. The boys had nothing to prove that they had been sent by the prince. Now she was risking everything.

Callie glanced behind him. 'If they're going to burn the bridges, you'd better get back there. You really don't want to be the only Xessan this side of the river in the morning.'

That decided it. She dropped the stones and ran, passing him on the other side of the road. Why had she come so far across the valley? How long would it take her to get back? Her chest was tight, her legs felt weak, and in the moonlight she seemed to be going nowhere at all.

38
IN THE DAM

The holds were deep steps cut into the stone, evenly spaced, with a notch at the back for fingers to grip on. The wall was steep but not vertical. Lebasi counted his way down as he had counted the way up, trying to clear his mind of what was below him. *Four hundred and twenty-nine, four hundred and thirty, four –*

'Steady now, you're nearly there.'

Lebasi was startled by the voice and a hand on his left foot. He had blanked everything from his mind, and had almost forgotten where he was or why. He rested for a moment, breathing deeply, then took three more steps. Dralor's head appeared round the edge of the hole. He reached out a strong arm and pulled Lebasi across and inside. Lebasi sat on the floor, staring out at the the distant view in the evening sunlight, suddenly taken back to the secret route from his own garden to the storm drain at Trengam. The thought calmed him. He had been here before. He was underground, with solid rock under his feet. The dark was less frightening than the drop.

Dralor was working with flint and steel to light the lantern. 'Oil', he said, adjusting the flame. 'Useful for lighting the beacon, when the time comes.' Lebasi wondered how he intended to climb back up the face of the dam with the Thrarn above him, but there was no time to ask questions. Dralor set off into the hole, carrying the lamp above his head.

It was like the storm drain, but twice as big. There was no danger of bumping heads or elbows on the ceiling or wall. Their footsteps and their breathing echoed about them. Lebasi glanced over his shoulder at the entrance, round and white like the moon in a starless sky.

'Here.' Dralor slowed, then stopped. Lebasi realised that the quality of the sound and the air had changed. He craned his neck and saw that they were standing at the bottom of the shaft they had looked down. The distant square of sky above them was deep blue. The rounded stone floor of the tunnel gave way to a flat platform that seemed to shift slightly under Lebasi's feet. He wondered if his mind was playing tricks on him.

'Let's have those sticks, now.' Dralor opened the cover of the lantern and held one inside, turning it until it caught. He handed it to Lebasi and put the lamp on the floor. 'Hold that so I can see what I'm doing.'

By the flickering light, Lebasi watched Dralor examine a row of wooden levers set in the wall at the back of the chamber. He touched one, then a second, tapped a third, before stepping back and rubbing his chin.

'How does it work?'

'That's what I'm trying to remember. You'll understand I don't come down here often. Long climb back.' He rested his hand on the first lever again. 'And I've never had to let Shasho out before. I don't want to get it wrong.'

A distant shout echoed down to them. Lebasi looked up and sensed movement. He threw out an arm and pushed Dralor back against the wall of the chamber.

THUNK

A spear landed beside them and stuck in the floor, its tail vibrating with the impact. Lebasi pressed himself further into the stones, wondering if he should put out his torch – too late –

THUNK THUNK THUNK THUNK

Lebasi screamed. The sound was like a crowd of madmen, echoing in the confined space. Dralor gripped his arm. 'Are you hurt?'

Lebasi whispered, 'No, but they might think I am. They might stop.'

Dralor laughed. 'All right. Let's wait a moment.'

Lebasi stared at the spears, all with their points buried in the floor by the force of the impact. He asked, 'What are we standing on? It's not stone.' He thought about the noise they had made: like someone hitting a big drum at the Midsummer festival. And the floor had definitely trembled.

Dralor knelt down and felt it. 'Feels like wood. I've never looked that closely.'

Lebasi found he was counting again. Sixty, a hundred passed without any more spears. His first torch was burning out, so he lit the other stick from it and held it above Dralor's head. The man was pulling on the levers in turn, muttering to himself.

'Is it stuck?'

'Maybe. There's supposed to be an order to it, and if you do it in the wrong order, it doesn't work.' His voice dropped to a murmur. Lebasi caught odd words, 'left', 'halfway', 'back'. Then Dralor breathed out and said aloud, 'I never thought I'd need to remember it. The keepers of the water have been here since before the kingdom, passing the instructions down, but none has ever received the order.'

Lebasi gripped the torch tighter. How could the man not remember the one thing he had to do? He had been sure that bringing the message to the dam would be enough. That doubt brought another – would the machinery work, if it had never been tested? But the lockbox at the Westgate did – surely that had been built by the same people that made this dam. The magistrate tested that mechanism every year, on Midsummer, and it had always opened the door. Surely this would have been made just as well.

He stared down the tunnel. There was no longer a clear round light at the far end. He whispered, 'They're coming.'

Dralor muttered, 'All right.' He gripped the middle lever and pulled it halfway down. Lebasi could hear the echoes of footsteps now, growing louder. Dralor pulled the left-hand lever all the way down. He pushed the central lever back to its starting position, then the right-hand one halfway.

As he reached again for the middle lever, he shouted something and dropped to his knees, then fell forward on his chest. Lebasi saw a crossbow bolt sticking out of his shoulder. He crouched down, knowing it was over, wondering if he could help the old man. He had brought death here, too – something else to live with. If there was any time left for regrets.

Dralor groaned. 'Middle lever, all the way down. Then the right one, the rest of the way. Now.'

The footsteps were loud and continuous. Words were mixed in with them now, but Lebasi couldn't make anything out. He stood up and grabbed the middle handle. As he pulled it down, another bolt hit the wall where his head had been a moment before. He fixed the position of the last one in his mind and threw the torch away. Blindly, he groped for lever – there it was. He leaned on it and fell over on top of Dralor's legs as it shifted under his weight.

Something was moving, something mechanical, huge gears turning, distant, echoing, the sound coming from underneath them. The footsteps stopped. Uncertain voices, speaking in Thrarn, frighteningly close. The words were foreign but the meaning was obvious: 'What's that? What's happening?'

Lebasi felt for Dralor's body in the dark. He lay down beside him, hearing his laboured breathing.

'Can you hear me?'

'Yes.'

'Where does the water come out?' He realised that he knew the answer as he asked the question. He had always known the answer, from the moment he saw the holes in the face of the dam.

'Through here.'

Lebasi turned his head. The lantern was still burning, standing in the middle of the floor. It cast enough of a glow into the tunnel to light up the face and chest of a man holding a crossbow, edging forward, his forehead creased, his mouth a little open. The mechanical noises stopped with a final echoing CLUNK, immediately followed by the rush of liquid, fierce, unstoppable, all the water in the world surging towards them from the other side of the stones.

Shasho was free.

39
BURNING BRIDGES

Tik slowed to a walk, needing to catch her breath. She could not judge distance at all in the moonlight. A low mist covered the ground, and she had to concentrate to keep on the road. The south side of the valley was a uniform grey wall rising ahead of her, and there was no sign yet of the bridge, or even the wagons on the road where she had last seen Sammas. She strained her ears to hear faint noises that might be people on the move, but it could be her imagination. How long would it take Perra and his men to guide everyone over the bridges?

There was no sign of fire, either. Which meant they weren't all across yet, and there was still time for her. Was there also time for the Thrarn to catch them?

Somewhere behind her, a whistle sounded. She glanced round, quickening her pace. Another whistle, another, another, then a noise like a cow bellowing. Was that a horse, or human sending a signal? Whatever it was, another answered, then a third. The view didn't change at all: still the same shadowy hillside, red and yellow campfires, distant white stars. She knew that Callie had delivered his message, and the enemy would be moving.

She started to run again. At that moment, a small yellow glow appeared ahead and to her left. In moments, the light became flames, spreading and rising. The last Xessans must have crossed the upstream bridge and set fire to it. That would have given them away – Callie's betrayal had hardly cost them anything. But the Thrarn would come to the central bridge first, and if that was still passable when they arrived – she didn't want to think about it.

The noises from the hillside stopped as suddenly as they had begun. At last, Tik could see something in the road ahead – the wagons, half-hidden by the mist. In the stillness, she could also hear something else behind her – running feet. Surely the enemy couldn't be here so quickly? On horses, maybe, but this was a man – just one man.

Lebasi.

Or an enemy.

She kept running.

'Tik!' The shout came from in front, not from whoever was following. 'Is that you?'

She didn't have enough breath to call back and run as well. Whoever it was would get their answer in a moment. She slowed down as she approached the first cart, knowing that she could not rest – she had to cross the bridge first – but wondering where she could find the strength to take another step.

A man stepped out from the shadows and caught her as she stumbled. She tried to struggle free, and he relaxed his grip.

'It's me, Perra,' he said. 'What were you thinking, running off across the valley? Sammas told me.'

She leaned against the wagon wheel, panting. 'Trying to stop Callie. But I couldn't.'

Perra opened his mouth to say something, then simply nodded.

'There's someone coming,' she whispered. 'Just one, I think. It might be Lebasi.'

Perra shepherded her behind the wagon and picked up a pitchfork. The sound of footsteps was very near.

'Who's there?' he called out. 'Friend or enemy?'

The footsteps slowed to a walk. A figure appeared, ghostly in the pale light.

'Friend, I hope. Although we have not always been friends, you and I.'

'Marrak?' Perra lowered the pitchfork.

Tik felt a stab of disappointment. The agent stopped a few paces away, resting with his hands on his hips, gasping for breath as she had done.

'How did you escape?' Perra asked.

'Do you know where Lebasi is?' Tik demanded at the same time.

Marrak rubbed his hands over his face. 'There has been some confusion in the camp since yesterday morning. Caused by Lebasi, I think. No, Tik, I do not know where he is. But nor do they. I heard that he stole the general's horse, and the general is trying to find him.'

Tik gaped. Lebasi said he was going back to stay inconspicuous, but he had caused a diversion instead. He had lied to her.

Marrak turned to Perra. 'Niram came to see me this afternoon. He let slip that my guards this evening were fond of drink, and he had arranged for there to be several bottles handy for them. They were just sober enough to take me for my evening wash, but not enough to stop me breaking free. Or to catch me.'

The bellowing sound came again. All three of them stared out into the mist.

'Horns,' said Marrak. 'They are coming.'

Perra turned to peer past the wagons. 'They must have got everyone over the river by now. Why haven't –' He stopped abruptly and put a hand on Tik's shoulder. 'Tik, you need to get back there now. Tell them to set the fire, then get yourself across the bridge.'

'What about you?'

They all turned again to face across the valley. They could hear a new sound now, in between the blasts of the horns – hoofbeats.

'I need to slow them down. They'll get to the bridges before enough damage has been done.'

'But –'

'Go, Tik. You've got a message to take. I'm going to make sure you get the chance to deliver it. That's the choice I make, all right? And thank you for reminding me of that story.'

Marrak picked up the pitchfork. 'It will take two to slow them down, Perra. They will not want to risk their horse's legs off the road in the mist and the moonlight. One of us to each side of the wagon. That will make it difficult for them.'

Perra started to protest, 'Marrak, you should –'

The agent made a chopping motion with his hand. 'You know I am right. We have not always been friends, but we will do this thing together, you and I, for the people.'

Perra nodded. The sound of the horses was louder. 'All right.' He gave Tik a push. 'Go! Run!'

She ran.

The mist was thicker now, and it felt as if she was wading through water. The dense air seemed to cling to her, holding her back, slowing her down. The frame of the bridge appeared above it, a hundred paces ahead. There was something in the middle – another wagon – not moving. Was it stuck? Were people still trying to get across? There was no time. She shouted, 'Start the fire! Perra says you have to go now!'

'What?' She picked out someone standing on the wagon. The noise of the horses was a constant drumming.

She stopped so she could shout louder, cupping her hands to her mouth. 'START – THE – FIRE – NOW.' She started running again.

Something down in the mist tripped her up. She fell forward into the mist and felt the breath knocked out of her body. She rolled over, groaning, kicking at something that seemed to be gripping her ankle.

Something *was* gripping her ankle. Pulling. She tried to twist herself free, but the hand was too strong. *Hand?*

Time slowed down, and Tik was aware of many different things happening at once. She could hear the neighing of horses and shouting in Thrarn from the direction she had come. She recognised the voice shouting from the bridge as Sammas. 'Tik! Is that you? Where are you? Come quick before the fire takes.'

Most clearly she saw the figure rising up out of the mist, one hand holding her right ankle. She scrabbled away with her hands, still trying to break loose. The man's face was in shadow, but a flash of red light showed her who it was. He stared down at her, balling his other hand into a fist.

'It's you - the skinny little bald menker who threw that stone at me. Well, now -'

Sammas's voice came again. 'Tik! Where did you go? Come on!'

Hoofbeats, nearer. Shouts in Thrarn. Had Perra and Marrak been overcome so quickly?

The sergeant was distracted, first by the light of the fire in front of him, then by the sound of the riders behind him, very loud. He looked up, his face turned red by the reflection of the flames. Tik saw him turn his head and raise his gaze, as if he was watching something much taller than a man approaching.

WHACK

The hand let go of Tik's ankle. She huddled in a ball as the horse's hoofs landed beside her, then they were gone. She crawled, keeping her head down, aiming away from the shouting and the fire, trying to stay below the level of the mist. Her head met something solid rising up in front of her. From the shape of it, she guessed it was the wall that ran beside the water channel. She risked poking her head up for a moment.

Two riders were close by the bridge, struggling to control their horses. The centre of the bridge was burning, underneath and around the wagon that was blocking the roadway. In the distance, she could see the downstream bridge was also alight. She was sure no one was looking in her direction, so she scrambled up on top of the wall and rolled over. Crouching down on the far side, she let her breathing and her pulse slow down.

Callie's words came back to her: *You really don't want to be the only Xessan this side of the river in the morning.* She studied the bridge. The deck was blazing fiercely, but only in that middle section. They must have poured oil on it. The rest of the wood might catch, but it wouldn't burn so fast. And the trestles underneath – she took a deep breath. Maybe she could climb across, when the fire had died down up above. As long as the Thrarn didn't watch all night.

As long as the Thrarn didn't manage to stop the fire. More of them were arriving now. She blinked away tears at the thought of what must have happened to Perra and Marrak. She didn't think they would have been taken prisoner. The Thrarn hadn't bothered to check which side the sergeant had been on, after all. *That's the kind of people they are. We must fight them until they are beaten.*

That was part of the message she had to take to the king – but the fleeing Xessans ahead of her would tell him that, if they got away. Maybe she could rest, maybe it no longer mattered.

She shook her head. The weapons Riadsala had described to her – poison smoke, the fire-breathing dragon, charro, black powder. The ability to give a man a disease and the determination to send him to pass it on to others. She had told Sammas and Ruffur about these things, but she had seen the prince blinded and broken by the smoke. She had walked across country with Rodera. She had heard the thunder of the black powder rolling through the woods above her home. Only she could tell the king so he would believe it, so he would think of a way to fight back.

Only she could show him the farsight to prove that his son had sent her.

Several of the Thrarn had dismounted and were trying to get close enough to the wagon to move it. She could see now that it had been left there to stop them galloping through the flames – maybe they would be able to make their horses do that. But if they could pull it back out of the way… The scene was lit up by the fire so she could see every detail: they had made loops of rope and were casting them over the posts at the back of the wagon – they were driven back by the heat – they were trying again – they had hooked one side – they had the other – they were lining up, four huge men on each rope – the wagon was beginning to move.

Its wheels fell off. Tik put her hand over her mouth, suppressing a laugh. Maybe the fire had damaged them, but for all the wheels to give way at once – the Xessans must have taken out the axle-pins to make that happen. The body of the cart crashed down on the burning deck and broke through it. Sparks and embers flew in all directions as the wagon smashed through the trestles into the dark water below. The Thrarn pulling on one of the ropes all collapsed as the line broke, while the foremost one on the other rope was flung through the air and into the river after the wagon.

Most of what had been burning had gone into the water, so Tik had to let her eyes adjust to the dimmer light from the moon. She could just make out the shapes of men looking down into the

channel. They were calling out, but there was no sign that they received an answer. Tik wondered if the man could swim, or if he was even tall enough to stand on the bottom. But if he had been wearing armour, he would have sunk, and she had been told that the mud in the river would suck a person down. She shivered. She felt no sorrow for the Thrarn, only the sick realisation that she would have to face the river herself.

As her night-vision returned, the moonlight was bright enough to show that the wagon had destroyed the supports of the bridge all the way down. It wouldn't be possible to climb, and the gap was too wide to jump.

40
INTO THE CLOUDS

Lebasi's head banged against the floor as if he had fallen. How could that be? He was already lying on his back. He was being pressed down by a huge weight – a cold wind was blowing in his eyes – the distant square of sky was growing larger, the walls of the shaft shrinking, opening out. The blow must have knocked him into a dream. He heard the rumbling and roaring of the water, but where was it? He should be drowning.

There was a loud thump, followed by a sloshing sound. Lebasi felt himself lifted off the floor for a moment before crashing back down. He rolled over onto his hands and knees and stared all around him. The tunnel was gone, the Thrarn with the crossbow was gone. He was in the open air, looking out at the surface of the lake in one direction, the hills of Xessus with the light of the setting sun streaming across them in the other. The platform was level with the stone roadway across the top the dam. As he shifted his weight, he felt it rock underneath him. His mind had frozen.

Dralor's hand on his arm startled him. The old man croaked, 'You have to light the beacon. Take the lamp.'

He tried to focus. Dralor was still lying on his chest, the arrow sticking out of his right shoulder. Lebasi stood up, then dropped to his knees again as the ground moved beneath him. He crouched beside the injured man.

'Let me help you get off this,' he said, wondering how to lift or drag him without making things worse.

'No, no,' Dralor protested. 'Leave me be. The beacon. Shasho's loose. You must light the fire.'

Lebasi became aware of a whooshing noise that had not been there when they had been on top of the dam earlier. He put a hand on the solid stone, then a foot, stood up, and took one pace towards the drop down which he had climbed. The noise grew. The shadows of dusk were deepening in the valley below the dam, but he could see what they had done. A long way below, jets of water – ten of them, one for each of the holes in the face – were spraying out into space.

The man with the crossbow must be out there, somewhere. Along with anyone else who had been in the tunnel.

'The beacon, boy.'

He checked along the dam. There was no one in sight. Mountain was still tethered at the far end, by the pile of wood.

He knelt down and pulled Dralor's feet onto the stones. He said, 'I'm not leaving you here. This thing might go back down again. Come on, I'll just get you onto the dam.'

Dralor objected, 'It'll take a long time before that happens. Water in the shaft is the same level as the water in the lake, stands to reason. And those little holes won't drain this lake quickly.'

Lebasi took no notice but moved to his shoulders. He tried to slide him across as gently as he could. It was hard to tell how serious the injury was, but Lebasi could see blood soaking through the man's tunic. He couldn't turn him over onto his back with the bolt sticking out of it.

What can I do for a man with an arrow in him? He needs a doctor.

'The lamp – get the lamp. Light the beacon.'

Lebasi glanced at the platform and shook his head. 'It's fallen over and gone out.'

'Take it anyway. The oil will help.' Dralor put his hand into his pocket and produced a small bag. 'Here, flint and steel. You know how –'

'Yes, of course,' Lebasi interrupted. He crawled onto the platform again to retrieve the lantern. He shook it to check that there was still something in its tank. He crouched beside Dralor and asked, 'Did you know that was going to happen? The platform would come up on the water?'

The man's voice was weaker. 'Something like that, yes. The old man told me it would.'

'The old man?'

'The one before me. I can't remember his name. I came here fifty winters ago. He told me, and the man before told him, all the way back to when the dam was built. No one has ever tested it, until now.' He waved a hand in the direction of the beacon. 'Go!'

Lebasi said, 'I'm going.' He ran, sticking to the edge by the water, searching in vain for any sign of movement in the still surface. There was no sign on this side that anything had changed.

Mountain greeted him with a nod. He hugged the horse's neck as he had before he left and untied the rein. 'Come on, now,' he said, leading him away from the woodpile out onto the dam. He stroked the horse's nose and murmured 'You wait here,' hoping that the animal would not be spooked by the fire, the water, the drop or the sound of the rushing jets.

Standing by the unlit beacon, he peered down at the ledge below and groaned. The Thrarn's horses were all down there, grazing – but some of the riders were as well. They were standing in a group on the edge, staring at the water. He wondered if the one he had seen leading them earlier had indeed been El-Arnor, or if he had gone back to meet his father. And if he had come to the dam, had he –

One of them was pointing up at him. They all started running across the ledge towards the upper path. He didn't wait to watch. He gathered some kindling from the base of the beacon, tipped the oil from the lantern on it, and started striking the flint against the steel.

He remembered Perra turning to speak to him on the platform in the Town Space at Trengam on the day of the revolution. *The spark is in the tinder, and it has to burn.* And now Shasho is loose – and she is unstoppable. As the small sticks caught, he poked them into the bottom of Dralor's bonfire. It was well-made and very dry, and immediately started to crackle and snap.

He ran to Mountain, who was shaking his head to and fro, his great eyes glittering red with the reflection. Lebasi made soothing noises in his ear and used the bridle to turn him round the other way. A loud popping noise from the fire made the horse take a couple of quick steps forward. Lebasi gripped the rope and started to walk, horribly aware of the narrowness of the path and the size of the horse.

He muttered, 'Come on, we've got to hope there's a road at the other end. We can't go back.' He wasn't sure if he was talking to the horse or to himself.

It was darker now. Lebasi tried to pick out where he had left Dralor. There was a movement – Dralor must have stood up – no, it was someone climbing up over the edge of the dam. There must have been at least one Thrarn who had not reached the tunnel and had not been washed away. He was caught. He took another step, uncertain. Forward, or back? Maybe Mountain could force a way through – but at what risk? The shape was pulling someone else up over the last step. Two of them.

Another shape rose up from the roadway, an indistinct smudge against the dark background. It merged with the other two figures. Any noise of their struggle was drowned by the roar of the water. For a moment, the group teetered on the edge of the drop, then they fell, separating into three again, disappearing into the spray below.

When he reached the platform, Lebasi took care to lead Mountain around it. He did not stop to check whether there was anyone else coming up the ladder. If there was, he didn't want to know. There would be nothing he could do about it.

I will remember it, the captain used to say. Dralor had sacrificed himself to give Lebasi a chance to escape. He would find someone to tell.

At the far side of the dam, he stopped to look back. The beacon was ablaze, and by its light he could see people moving. They were trying to lead a horse past the fire, and the horse was not cooperating. But they were coming. He turned to face the hillside ahead, fearing to find it as blank as the cliffs at the end of the Awato sea wall – no, the path on top of the dam continued onto a road, rising gently and following the hillside to the right, away from the lake. It was hard to see with only the stars to help, but the surface seemed to be solid and even and four paces wide. Could he ride? He wasn't sure, in the dark. The slopes below and above were too steep to risk a false step. They started to walk.

A fold of the hillside hid the dam. The noise of the jets diminished. Lebasi realised that the beacon had given him some light even at this distance, and now it was very dark. But there was something – out there in the night, far away in the empty blackness to his right, there was the glow of another fire. He smiled, shaking his head. There was someone else like Dralor, then. Someone who knew that the beacon had to be lit, even if it had never been lit in hundreds of years. Even if there was no one left to see.

But there would be people in Shasho's path. He thought of Tik and Sammas and Ruffur, down in the valley. Would they have managed to get the people across the bridges? How long would the water take to arrive? It had taken him a day and a half to come from Awato. How fast would the flood travel in the other direction? He could not guess. He could only hope that water ran downhill faster than a horse rode up, and that there would be enough of it to block the way for the army.

The road carried on, gently rising, with no possibility of a turning. At last the moon rose, showing him the shape of the land around him. He stared back the way he had come, and for a moment he felt hopeful that his pursuers had given up. Then a glint of moonshine on metal in the distance made him shiver. They were still there, and they would surely be quicker than him now the light was better. He led Mountain to a boulder so he could climb into the saddle. From his seat on top of the horse, the path seemed very thin and the slope below very steep. As Mountain trotted on, Lebasi twisted round to try to spot the tell-tale gleam again, but it had gone.

The track followed the contours of the hillside, fording small streams and crossing wider ones on stone bridges. Lebasi saw no further sign of pursuit, but he dared not stop. The moon was halfway across the sky when they turned a corner into a broad valley. Lebasi tried to make out the skyline at its head, but there was only a pale blur where he expected to see a sharp edge and stars beyond it. A chill breeze blew down the slope and the blur spread towards him.

'Clouds,' he whispered. 'We're so high up.'

In the centre of the valley there was a bridge, and just beyond it the first turning he had seen since he left the dam. A narrower track doubled back across the hillside, while the main one carried on as before. Lebasi couldn't see where it went, because curls of mist were rolling down around him. He leaned back to stop Mountain. The click and clack of hoofs on stone stopped, and in the silence that followed he heard a horse neigh in the distance. Looking back, he glimpsed two riders rounding the rim of the valley. Then the cloud surrounded him and hid them from view.

He nudged Mountain gently with his calves and leaned to the left. The horse turned and started to walk up the side turning. A bright white blanket surrounded him, lit up by the moon from above. He could hardly tell which direction was which. He had to grip the saddle-post for balance. Even Mountain seemed to be uncertain. He stopped and waited.

Lebasi strained his ears. *Click-clack, click-clack.* Low voices. Ahead and below – below – behind and below – fainter – gone. In the mist, they had not seen the turning. How long would it be before they realised they were following no one? Were there any more behind them?

Lebasi decided he couldn't ride in the mist, and he couldn't stay where he was in case it blew away. He dismounted as quietly as he could and started to lead Mountain on foot, making out the line of the track one pace at a time. They reached a turn and doubled back, as they had on the way up to Dralor's house. Another, another, another. In the cloud, there was no sound at all – even the horse's hoofs seemed to be muffled by it.

He was counting again, thinking of nothing but covering the ground, putting as much distance as possible between himself and the Thrarn. At the back of his mind lurked the thought that he had hardly any food, and this barren hillside didn't even have grass for Mountain to eat. For the moment, though, it was enough to be escaping. He would have to think about everything else in the morning.

The light changed as the slope eased. All at once the moon appeared behind him, now low in the sky, and the stars were above him. The skyline was sharp again and only fifty paces away, a col between rocky ridges to left and right. He drew in a deep breath. It was something like the border between Trengam and Nampetch where he had broken the Mercy in the spring: a road, a col, something to mark the boundary. Then, there had been tall white stones on either side of the track. Here, there was an empty arch several manheights tall. It was like a gateway, but there was no barrier on either side. As he approached it, Lebasi could see no sign that there ever had been a wall – this was not something that had been dismantled, like the defences of Awato. This was how it had been built, something to tell people they were crossing a line.

He stood in the opening and stared down the track. The setting moon made it hard to see, but he could make out the beginning of a descent into another valley. He guessed it ran north-east, not the right direction at all. But anywhere without Thrarn would be better than going back. There were no lights in the view, no fires, no lanterns. No sign of life. He was keenly aware of the emptiness in his stomach and in his pack. He crouched on the ground, wondering how he could find the strength to carry on.

The movement reminded him of something. Kneeling beside Rodera at the Westgate on the day after midsummer – the branded man had pointed at the wall and said, 'If an army cannot cross the wilderness, why do you think they built this? To pass the time?' The people who made this arch had not been worried about an army – that was plain. But they had not done it to pass the time. This road led somewhere. Somewhere important, so it was worth marking the boundary.

Lebasi took hold of the rope and started down the track. He hoped that somewhere wouldn't be too far away. He hoped it would still be there. It had to be. He had made a promise to Tik. Even if it was heading the wrong way for now, this was the beginning of the road to Egator.

41
WATER

Tik kept her head down behind the embankment, listening to the Thrarn shouting threats across the river. Some of them were no more than angry noises in their own language; some she could understand.

'We will return at first light and repair this bridge. You cannot run fast enough. We will kill you all.'

They didn't search the riverbank, and as far as she could see, they didn't leave anyone behind. They simply rode back the way they had come. Tik guessed that they didn't care to spend the night being bitten – their size intimidated ordinary humans, but they couldn't fight the tiny insects. She curled up on the riverside path to rest, out of sight of anyone on the road.

She was afraid she would doze off and not wake up when the Thrarn returned in the morning, but she needn't have worried. The flies that had until yesterday had hundreds of people to feed on now had only one. She rolled herself into a ball, covering her face. She stood up and swung her arms around. She rubbed her legs, squashing a few insects that were instantly replaced by more. The only sound was their buzzing. There was nowhere to hide from them. At least they stopped her falling asleep.

The night seemed endless. The moon was obscured by mist rising off the fields. She could see it as a bright shapeless glow above her. Since the flames had died down, she couldn't even see where the bridges were. The Thrarn said they would return at first light, but she hoped that maybe that would be when they would start from their camp. While they were crossing the valley, she might have enough time and enough light to see if there was anything left of one of the bridges – enough for one small person to tiptoe across. There had to be.

She woke with a start. The moonglow had gone from the sky, but it wasn't black. When there was a little more light she would go to the nearby bridge and check it. That was probably where the Thrarn would come first, so she would hurry away to one of the other bridges if it was no good.

tik

Her ears were playing tricks. Or there was a bird with a call like her name.

tik

She turned her head this way and that, straining to listen.

croo croo croooooo

She laughed out loud. No bird sounded like that. She made the call back, wondering if the boys might be fooled into thinking they were talking to a real pigeon.

'Are you there, Tik?' Clearer now.

She cupped her hands to her mouth, trying to direct the sound only across the river, hoping that there was no one to hear it behind her. 'Here!'

She could hear Sammas and Ruffur talking to each other. They must be almost opposite where she was standing.

She called again, somewhere between a whisper and a shout. 'I'm waiting for first light so I can see if I can get across one of the bridges.'

'That won't work. They're all gone.' Sammas's voice. She was so pleased to hear him that she hardly noticed what he was saying. Then it sank in.

'Are you sure?'

Ruffur's deeper tone carried more clearly. 'The wagons finished what the fire started. Made sure the enemy couldn't follow. All three.'

Tik sat down and banged her hands together. Thirty paces. She could run thirty paces without drawing breath. But the bottom was sucking mud, and she couldn't swim.

Sammas called to her again. 'We're coming for you.'

Tik looked up. 'What do you mean?'

They were talking to each other again – arguing. Ruffur said, 'It's got to be me.' Sammas grunted something. Slithering, scrabbling noises. A splash. A lot of splashing.

Now she could see him. He was flailing about in the middle of the river, twenty paces upstream. She slid down the bank, digging her heels in to try not to plunge straight in. Ruffur disappeared under the water, then he was up again, nearer. Gone. Up. Gone.

His hand appeared right by her. She grabbed it and leaned back. The big boy broke the surface, spluttering and swearing, and grovelled up so his chest was out of the water. He spread his arms out and hugged the bank.

'Is he all right?' called Sammas, a hoarse whisper carrying across the stream.

'Are you all right?' asked Tik, rubbing Ruffur's shoulder.

He blew out his cheeks and nodded. 'I don't want to have to do that again.'

Tik shook her head. *These boys!* 'But that's exactly what you have to do! What good is it to have both of us over here?'

He managed to heave his body further up and smiled at her. 'We're not that thick. We've got a plan, see?' He reached behind him and pulled something – a rope appeared, dripping, stretching across into the mist. Tik realised she could now just make out the other bank, and a shadowy figure holding the other end.

'Where did you get that?'

'Found it by the bridge. Picked it up. You never know when something like that'll be useful.'

Tik took in the loops tied into the line, loops for people to stand in. 'It must be the rope…' She shuddered, not finishing the thought.

Ruffur nodded. 'Reckon it'll do us a good turn, this time. Come on, we've got to find something to tie it to.'

They scrambled up the bank together and down the other side of the low wall. There were rocks all along the edge of the field where they had been cleared for ploughing. Ruffur wound the rope round a big one, then rolled another two on top of it. He grinned down at Tik. 'You'll only need one of those, but I'm not taking chances for me. I'll go first, make sure it'll hold, all right? If it doesn't, I'll have to swim back and put another rock on the pile.'

Tik hardly heard him. She was staring out into the mist, watching it swirl and break into tatters. Blue sky was beginning to show above them. The enemy would be coming.

Ruffur stood up and put his head on one side. 'Did you hear that?'

Tik nodded. Voices. An order. The whinny of a horse. In the mist, it was impossible to say how far away.

They climbed back over to the riverside path. Ruffur slid straight down to the water and gave the line a tug. It dipped to the surface in the middle of the stream, then rose again on the far side.

Tik crouched just below the top of the bank and scanned the mist. The bridge had appeared now, only a hundred paces away. She tensed as the fog parted to reveal Thrarn horsemen – two, four, six – then exile scouts, lines of them, all walking in step with something on their shoulders.

Planks. They were going to repair the bridge. It was all for nothing.

'Come on, Tik,' Ruffur shouted from below her.

The nearest rider turned his head. She didn't wait to find out if he had seen her. She slid down and gripped the line.

'Wait until I've got across,' Ruffur was saying. 'If we both go at the same time we'll probably be too heavy.'

'Hurry,' she whispered. 'They're here.'

Ruffur walked straight into the water, holding onto the line. In a moment he was up to his neck, pulling hand over hand, seeming hardly to be making any progress. He dipped under the water.

'Tik, pull the rope taut,' came Sammas's voice from the far bank. She glanced behind her. No one – yet. She grabbed the rope and tried to get some purchase with her feet in the soft ground.

Ruffur was halfway. Three-quarters. His chest appeared. His legs. He turned and waved at her. She could see him clearly now, and Sammas behind him. But Sammas wasn't looking at her.

She glanced up. Two manheights above her, a Thrarn soldier was staring down. She didn't wait, but plunged forwards as Ruffur had done, pulling the rope, sliding her hand along, gripping, pulling again. Her feet left the ground and she kicked against nothing, trying to keep her head above the water. She felt it fill her shoes, soak into her clothes, pull her down.

She heard the soldier shout and managed to turn her head enough to see him. He had drawn his sword – he was raising it – swinging it –

She started to turn the other way, to see what Ruffur and Sammas were doing, but halfway she stopped. Everything seemed to stand still in that moment. She was up to her chin in the river, her feet in space, facing upstream, the man-made watercourse straight in front of her for hundreds of paces, the water sparkling in the morning sunlight.

Water was flat. There was a saying about it. She was on the surface – just – in the middle of the stream, with the banks rising above her on each side. So how, in the distance, was the water filling the channel from the top of one bank to the other?

She gripped the rope and tried to gulp in air. Not in the distance, not now. Nearer.

She felt the tension go out of the line as the Thrarn cut it, and then the wave was on her. Fierce, fast, colder than the streams that came from the Eagle's Nest. She could do no more than hold on, but she felt she was flying forward like a fish, deep under the surface. Her hands were slipping. She had no air. The current was tugging at her, rolling her over. She would have to breathe –

She felt a hand grab her leg. She was so shocked she lost her hold on the rope, but a second hand was on her waist, pulling her, turning her –

She was lying on the ground, looking up at Ruffur's worried face. 'Are you –' he started, but Sammas shouted something Tik didn't catch, and the big boy scooped her up in his arms and started running. She was so surprised she didn't protest. She could see over his shoulder – Thrarn on the far bank, scouts with crossbows. The river, full to the brim, surging past in a brown flood.

'It's all right, the crossbows aren't reaching us, we can stop,' said Sammas.

Ruffur laid Tik down gently and crouched beside her, his chest heaving. He put a meaty hand under her head. 'Are you all right? When you disappeared I thought we'd lost you.'

Sammas laughed. 'That big one cut the rope just at the right time. We hung on and the river washed you to the side. We pulled you in like we were fishing.'

Tik started by spluttering out some of the water she had swallowed. Between coughs, she managed to say, 'Thanks for coming back for me. I couldn't have got across without you.'

Ruffur turned red. 'S'nothing,' he mumbled. 'We're sorry we didn't wait long enough for you last night.'

Sammas stared at the water. 'What's happened to the river?'

Tik stood up and felt under her tunic. The farsight was still there. She had to hope that it wouldn't be damaged by water. 'It's Basi,' she said, pointing towards the distant mountains. 'Shasho comes from the hills, right? Xela wanted Basi to turn the water off, but he's done the opposite.' Not just a diversion. A much bigger plan than that.

She forgave him for the lie. He would never let her down.

Ruffur nodded towards the bridge, where the marching men

were laying the first plank across the gap. The flood was barely a handspan below it. He said, 'We'd better get going.'

'Wait a moment,' Sammas answered. He waved his arms at the soldiers on the bank, who had started moving back towards the bridge. Some of them stopped and shook their fists at him. When he was sure they were watching, he turned round, bent over and lifted the back of his tunic. 'Someone ought to show them a pair of melons, I reckon,' he laughed.

Tik shook her head, but she couldn't help grinning. 'If they get over the bridge…'

They crossed a thin strip of flat ground and joined the track that led away from the bridge – the road to Enola. It struck up the hillside to the left. They hurried uphill, resisting the temptation to look back, hoping that if they didn't see the men mending the bridge, it wouldn't be happening. But at the first corner, where the road doubled back on itself, they had to pause and look down.

Tik groaned. The mist had cleared completely: the line of soldiers was all too plain to see, stretching from the bridge to the far side of the valley. At the head of the line, thirty or forty horsemen were waiting for the carpenters to finish their repair. They would catch up with the escaping Xessans in no time.

Sammas grabbed Tik's arm. 'Look!' The upstream bridge was coming to pieces in the flood. A section of the deck, complete with its railings, tore away and sailed down the river like a boat. The carpenters didn't see it coming: it crashed into their half-finished repair and threw several of them into the water. The others scrambled back onto the bank as more debris battered the remains of the bridge.

Tik took out the farsight and checked it over. It didn't seem to have come to any harm. She put it to her eye and swept the lens over the soldiers, patiently waiting in the sun. The line really did reach all the way to the far side – she could see men standing on the road where it descended from the camp on the hillside. She wondered if the whole army had marched down into the valley, or if there were still more of them waiting up on the hill.

She turned to look towards the north-east. She wouldn't see Lebasi, of course, but she wondered where in that view he was – the valley, the hills behind it, the mountains in the far distance. Something caught her eye. She lowered the lens, then raised it again.

'Oh my,' she whispered.

'What?' said Sammas.

'Look over there.' She passed him the farsight and pointed towards the head of the valley. She could see what was happening even without it.

The nearer ground still showed fields with irrigation ditches making a patchwork. Then there was an area where the lines seemed to be blurry, a net made of rope where it had previously been thread. Beyond, there was a lake. The blurry section turned into a lake, and the nearer ground was turning blurry in its turn.

'Shasho's coming,' murmured Ruffur, taking his turn with the farsight. He handed it back to Tik.

She turned to look towards the sea wall. 'There must be too much water for it all to come down the river. And all that water is beginning to fill up the valley at the bottom end, as well. It's going to meet in the middle.'

Tik could tell it wasn't deep – yet – because there were buildings and trees here and there, and they still stood about as tall on the water as they had previously stood on the land. But Shasho was coming, and Shasho was relentless. Unstoppable.

The fields closest to the road were disappearing. Tik shook her head. 'The soldiers don't know what's happening. They can't see.'

She wondered if the Thrarn captains had realised, if they would know how to fight the goddess of flood and destruction. The horsemen were conferring by the end of the bridge, but there was no sign of them coming to a decision about what to do.

'I think they've got it now,' Sammas said. The water covered the last field upstream of the road and carried on. Only the river-banks, the remains of the bridge and the road itself still showed above it. The rest of the land had disappeared under a thin film of water. The column had been as still as an army of statues, but now arms were pointing, people were stepping off the edges of the road, the sunlight rippled on thousands of helmets twisting and tilting as men tried to see.

The sound of whistles carried over the whoosh of the water in the river. Shouting. The column broke apart. Men were spreading out to left and right and running away all along the line.

Sammas muttered, 'Don't they realise the road's the best place for them? It's going to take a while before it's even knee-deep.'

Ruffur shook his head. 'If I was that far from higher ground, and I was standing in water that hadn't been there a moment ago, I wouldn't be stopping to think about it.'

Tik said, 'They won't be able to see the channels if everything's water.' She pointed as one man after another went sprawling, tripped up by putting his foot in a ditch. Most picked themselves up and carried on running. Some stayed down, maybe exhausted by falling for the third or fourth time, unable to lift their armour.

Several of the horsemen set off at speed, having to go even further away from the road to avoid the scattering soldiers. The carpenters abandoned their tools and their timber and made for the roadway, sprinting past the remaining cavalry. One was cut down by a Thrarn sword, but the others disappeared into the back of the retreating army.

Tik put the farsight away. She didn't want to look at the unfolding chaos any more. It was nearly as horrible as the aftermath of the battle on the Westwall Field. That had been worse because she had had to walk through it. This was a victory instead of a defeat, but both made her feel sick.

Ruffur stood on the rock and faced north-east. He stretched his arms above his head and shouted as loud as he could, 'Well done Basi!' He turned round, grinning. 'He tells a good story, and he knows how to make one happen, too.' The grin faded to his customary puzzled expression. 'What are we going to do now?'

Tik picked up her backpack and pointed up the road. 'Thanks to you, I can keep my promise to Riadsala. I'm going to Egator to warn the king about the Thrarn's weapons.'

Sammas nodded. 'All right. Lebasi's given us enough time to get a long way ahead, even from horses. When that valley's full of water, they won't be able to cross it at all.'

Ruffur's face crumpled into a deep frown. 'We're going out of Xessus. Places we don't know anything about.'

Tik reached up and put a hand on each boy's shoulder. She grinned at them. 'I didn't think I could do it alone, and then I didn't think I could do it without Lebasi. But I've got you two, and we'll find the way to Egator together.'

COMING SOON

XESSUS V
THE ROADS TO EGATOR

Tik and Lebasi have escaped from the invading army, but they are separated and travelling in unknown country beyond the borders of Xessus.

Tik, Ruffur and Sammas find that the people of the kingdom do not welcome a tide of Xessan refugees. They know that the capital city is somewhere far to the south, but the road is full of obstacles. Tik has Prince Riadsala's farsight as a token that she is his messenger, carrying his warning about the enemy's terrible weapons to the king – but the news she brings is full of danger: the king's youngest son is a hostage, and one or both of his other sons is plotting to overthrow him. She knows that Tharkon, the mysterious southerner, is somewhere on the road ahead of her, and running across him again may be fatal.

Lebasi knows that the star burned into his forehead carried a death sentence in the kingdom, but he can hardly make himself inconspicuous when he has the horse Mountain as his only company. The Thrarn are still on his trail, the strangers he meets are hostile and the road is uncertain, but his promise to meet Tik in Egator – and the knowledge that his mother is also there – drive him on.

ACKNOWLEDGMENTS

Thank you for all your help to all the people who have read drafts, given encouragement and made suggestions. My writers' group, Jeannie, Kathy and Catherine have as always been a great source of ideas and advice. Catherine and Jane both did a great job editing the later versions, and Neil, Ruth and Zoe checked that the story made sense. Johanna's illustrations help to form the world as well as show it – and, sometimes, I wonder how she has pictured so exactly what was in my head. She is also my horse wrangler, taking me to a local riding stable to give me the experience of tacking up and untacking a real live horse. I knew as little about them as Lebasi and Tik did at the start of the story, and she tells me if Mountain is behaving as he should. Thanks also to Luisa for putting the book together: seeing the four volumes in the series side by side on the shelf makes me very proud.

Thanks most of all, though, to Kathy and to Izi. This book was written during the lockdown of 2020, and their company made that weird and worrying time easy. Of course, I spent quite a lot of lockdown wandering around Xessus in my head, which may be why I did not mind staying indoors.

ABOUT THE AUTHOR

I have always loved listening to stories, reading stories, making up stories. For me, the best ones come with a map – a new world to get lost in. I grew up with illustrated books, and it is a joy and a privilege to see the world in my head appear in Johanna's pictures on the page.

I started writing Xessus when I couldn't find exactly the kind of book I wanted to read to my daughter Zoe – an extended tale set in an imaginary country and time, about people who have to deal with real world problems in a real world way. I've got nothing against magic in stories, but I wanted to see how my characters would manage without it. I gave the first few chapters of the first version to Zoe, who came downstairs half an hour later to ask, 'Is there any more of this?' And so it began...

Fire and Water is the fourth instalment of an extended story. Tik and Lebasi have started a long journey, and the maps that appear in this book will be extended in the next.

Other books by Mike Thexton

What happened to the hippy man? – a memoir about surviving the 1986 hijacking of flight PA 073 and the aftermath

The Magistrate's Son – Xessus I

The Warning – Xessus II

The Westwall Guard – Xessus III

For more information, see
www.hippyman.com and **www.xessus.com**.

About the Illustrator

I was born in 1995 in a little mountain village in the South of France. My passion for books and my love of drawing naturally influenced my decision to work in illustration. I graduated from Middlesex University London in June 2017. Winning the Lanista Partners Competition in 2015 and working with Mike on the first Xessus book 'The Magistrate's Son' has been a wonderful start to my career and a wonderful collaboration. Such a good collaboration in fact that 6 years later we're still at it! Hard to believe that this is now our fourth book together! Here's looking forward to many more to come! When I'm not working with Mike on bringing Xessus to life I create animations and other art projects for musicians. You can see more of my work on my website: https://www.johannagousset.com.